BROKEN FLOWER

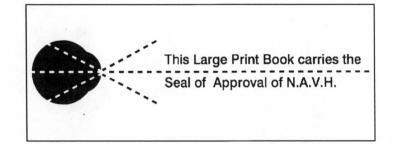

This Large Print Book carries the Seal of Approval of N.A.V.H.

EARLY SPRING #1

BROKEN FLOWER

V. C. ANDREWS®

THORNDIKE PRESS

An imprint of Thomson Gale, a part of The Thomson Corporation

Detroit • New York • San Francisco • New Haven, Conn. • Waterville, Maine • London

THOMSON
GALE
™

ALL RIGHTS RESERVED

Thorndike Press® Large Print Core.

The text of this Large Print edition is unabridged.

Other aspects of the book may vary from the original edition.

Set in 16 pt. Plantin.

LIBRARY OF CONGRESS CATALOGING-IN-PUBLICATION DATA

Andrews, V. C. (Virginia C.)
   Broken flower / by V.C. Andrews.
     p. cm. — (Early spring series)
     ISBN-13: 978-0-7862-9200-4 (lg. print : alk. paper)
     ISBN-10: 0-7862-9200-8 (lg. print : alk. paper)
     1. Teenage girls — Fiction. 2. Family secrets — Fiction. 3. Large type
books. I. Title.
   PS3551.N454B74 2007
   813'.54—dc22   2006034992

Published in 2007 by arrangement with Pocket Books,
a division of Simon & Schuster, Inc.

Printed in the United States of America on permanent paper
10 9 8 7 6 5 4 3 2 1

LETTER TO THE READER

It was not my idea to write all this down and tell this story. It was my brother Ian's.

Not long ago, when we saw each other after some time apart, he said, "When people reach our age, Jordan, they always try to make sense of themselves, their lives. They look back and they're really not sure anymore what was real and what was not. They are shocked to discover that the way they saw a major event in their life is not necessarily the way others who were there saw it, and they begin to wonder if their whole life has been a dream."

This is an attempt to discover if mine was.

Jordan March

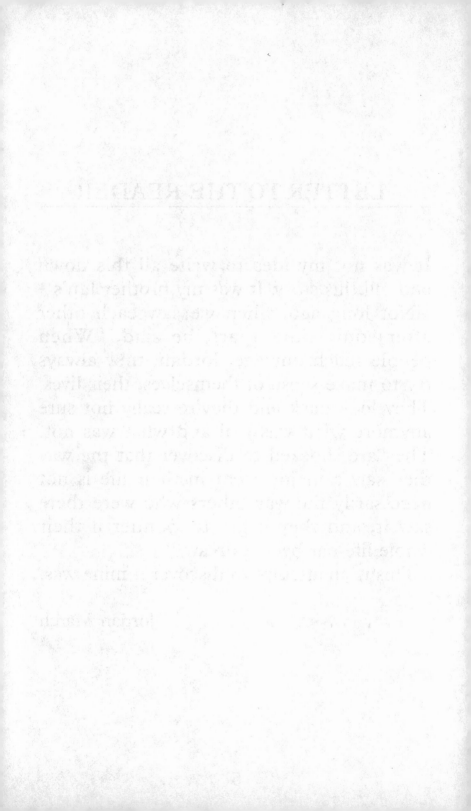

PROLOGUE

My mother didn't discover what was happening to me until just before my seventh birthday.

At the time I was in second grade and old enough by then to run my own bath and take care of my personal needs without her telling me when to do so or standing over me. I was proud of my independence and how I could successfully imitate my mother by putting just the right amount of bath oil into my tub, scrubbing my body with the same sort of soft brush she used, and laying out my clothing or pajamas neatly on the bathroom table, my fluffy pink slippers waiting eagerly below like two loyal servants.

Afterward, I brushed my hair exactly fifty strokes on both sides as she did hers, patted my face with some of her special skin cream, and went to bed. Most of the time she was there to kiss me good night, but I was always under my blanket by then, snuggling in anticipation of opening the doorway to dream magic, as I called it.

That fateful day, however, my mother stepped into my bathroom after I had prepared my bath and had just sat in the water.

"You're such a good girl, Jordan," she said as she came through the door.

She barely glanced at me in the tub before going to the medicine cabinet to search for something. However, when she closed the cabinet door, which was a mirror, she stood there staring into it as if she were looking at a television set and saw an incredible event taking place, like the events on one of those science or history channels my brilliant, thirteen-year-old brother, Ian, liked to watch. The cabinet mirror reflected me in my bath.

She spun around, blinked rapidly, and then very slowly approached the tub. The warm water was spiced with her wonderfully lilac-scented bath oil that I loved to suds up around me with the bubbles touching my chin. I felt dainty and feminine and anticipated her usual compliments about how grown-up I had become.

"Sit up, Jordan," she ordered instead.

Confused at her sudden harsh tone, I immediately sat straight, thinking she was criticizing my slouching. She always tried to correct my posture or my manners before my grandmother Emma had a chance to do it, because she believed that whenever Grandmother Emma criticized either me or my brother, Ian, she was really criticizing her for not bringing us up properly.

The bubbles popped and the foam fell away from my upper body.

She gaped and then slowly squatted beside the tub and reached over to touch my chest. "I don't believe this. You're . . . developing breasts!" she said. "You have buds!"

Her face contorted, her lips twisting, her eyes seeming to bulge. She shook her head to deny what she saw.

I looked down at myself. I had felt the development, but I hadn't thought anything of it. Somewhere in the back of my mind, I had stuffed a mental note to ask my mother about it one day, but I had forgotten. There was nothing painful or unpleasant about it.

"How could I have not noticed this? How long has this been going on?" she asked.

Lately, she had rarely been present when I dressed or undressed. My clothing for school was always decided the evening before and if Mama didn't set it out for me, Nancy, the maid, did.

I shrugged. I really hadn't marked the

calendar on the desk in my room and couldn't even take a good guess. One day I noticed it and the next day I didn't. I wasn't at all like Ian, who took notes about everything as if he were the secretary for human history.

"A while," I said.

As she continued to stare at me, I could see another thought tightening the corners of her eyes and stretching her lips. She looked even more fearful and brought her hand to the base of her throat.

"Stand up," she said. "Stand up, Jordan!" she shouted when I didn't move quickly enough.

I did so and her eyes, which were already wide and surprised, widened even more.

"You're getting . . . you have pubic hair!" she cried, as if I had been hiding something behind her back or had performed a magic act right before her eyes.

I looked down and once again shrugged. I didn't know what it was called, but I knew she had it, just more of it. Why shouldn't I be getting it, too? After all, she always told me girls were just little women.

"How could I have not noticed it? My God," she said, and I remember she actually flopped back on her rear and sat there on the tiled bathroom floor staring at me.

She grimaced in pain and reached out to clutch the side of the tub. She looked like she couldn't breathe.

"Mama?" I said. I could feel my throat tightening. Whatever frightened her was nothing compared to how she was frightening me.

She shook her head and put her hand up like a traffic cop, stopping all the crackling and buzzing going on around us.

"I've got to think. I've got to think," she chanted. Then she looked at me again, and again shook her head. "You're not even seven years old yet, Jordan. This can't be happening. It cannot!" she insisted.

She slapped her hands together as if she was really a magician and could make it all disappear. I looked down at myself almost with the expectation that I would see that it had, and then I looked at her again. From the way her face contorted and her lips quavered, I thought she was going to burst into tears, but she simply stared and bit down on her lower lip to stop the trembling.

"Can I sit in the water?" I asked, embracing myself. I was getting cold and beginning to tremble, too.

"What? Yes, yes. Sit, sit," she said. "Where has my head been? How could I miss this?

What if someone else had discovered it first?"

There was no question about whom she was thinking.

That put a new idea in her head.

Suddenly, she looked at the open bathroom door and rose to close it quickly. I'll never forget how she looked back at me. It was as if I had turned into something or someone other than her own daughter.

Perhaps I had.

I do remember thinking that I was no longer who she thought I was.

I had no idea how long it would take to find out who I would become.

1
TOO YOUNG

My mother grasped my shoulders and even shook me as she spoke. "Never, never let Grandmother Emma see you without any clothes on, Jordan," she warned in a loud whisper. "Don't tell Ian and don't even tell Daddy about this yet. He's likely to slip and say something. Your grandmother watches every little thing we do in this house as it is," my mother added, and let me go.

Why would all this anger my grandmother Emma? I wondered. If she did find out, would she tell us to leave her house? Would Daddy be just as angry?

Mama read my fears in my eyes. "I'm sorry, honey. I didn't mean to frighten you. It's not your fault. Everything that is happening to you is just happening to you too early," she said in a softer voice. "It's too much of a surprise. It's just better if no one else knows for now, okay?"

"Okay, Mama," I said. She looked relieved, but I was still trembling. She helped me into my pajamas and into bed.

Suddenly, something else occurred to her and she went to the dirty clothes hamper in my bathroom. I had no idea what she was doing, but she reached in and began pulling out my socks, panties, and shirts. She held up my panties and looked closely at them before tossing it all back into the hamper.

"What are you looking for, Mama?" I asked her.

She thought a moment and then she sat on my bed and took my hand into hers. "You're way too young for this conversation, Jordan. I don't even know how to begin it with you."

"What conversation?"

"The conversation my mother had with me when my body started to change, but you're not even seven and I was nearly thirteen before she decided I had to have the most important mother-daughter talk with her. Something very dramatic happened to me first."

"What?" I asked, my eyes wide with expectation.

"I menstruated."

"What?" I scrunched my nose. It didn't sound very good or like any fun.

She was quiet. I saw her eyes glisten. She

was holding back tears. Why?

"I'm not going to have this conversation with you," she suddenly decided firmly, and stood up. "This is just not happening. We don't need to talk about this yet. Remember my warning, however," she added, nodding at me. "Don't let anyone else see you naked. Especially Grandmother Emma," she emphasized.

My mother hated the idea of our moving in to live with Grandmother Emma. I think the saddest day in her life was the day we walked out of our home and came here. In the beginning she would often forget, make wrong turns and head toward our old home, not remembering it was no longer her house until she nearly pulled into the driveway. On a few occasions, I was the one who reminded her. She'd stop and look and say, "Oh," as if she had just woken from a dream.

I had lived there five and a half of my six years and eleven months. Ian was just a little more than eight when my parents bought the house. Before that they had been living in one of my grandfather's apartment buildings. In those days there was supposedly a great deal of hope and promise. After all, how could my father not succeed? He was the son of Blake and Emma March, and my grandfather Blake March had been a vice president of Bethlehem Steel during its heyday, what Grandmother Emma called the Golden Age, a time when Bethlehem Steel supplied armies, built cities, and had a fleet of twenty-six ships. If she had told me about it once, she had told me a hundred different times.

"You have to understand how important it was," she always said as an introduction. "Bethlehem Steel was the Panama Canal's second-best customer. Lunch each day for the upper management of which your grandfather was an essential part was held at the headquarters building along Third Street and was equivalent to a four-star dining experience. Each department had its own dining room on the fifth floor and each executive enjoyed a five-course meal."

Once Grandmother Emma permitted me to look at her albums and I saw pictures of their lawn parties during the summer months. Other executives from Bethlehem Steel and their wives and children would be invited, as well as many of the area's leading businessmen, politicians, lawyers, and judges. There was music and all sorts of wonderful things to eat. She told us that in those days the champagne flowed like water. She pointed out Daddy when he was Ian's

16

age, dressed in his suit and tie and looking like a perfect little gentleman, the heir to a kingdom of fortune and power.

My mother always said my father grew up spoiled. Whenever she accused him of it, he didn't deny it. In fact, he seemed proud of it, as proud as a prince. For most of his young life, he was attended by a nanny who was afraid of not pleasing him and losing her job. When he was school-age, he was enrolled in a private school and then a preparatory school before going to his first university. He flunked out of two colleges and never did get a degree. My grandfather eventually set him up in business by foreclosing on a supermarket, which was renamed March's Mart, in Bethlehem. It was expected that because the business now had the March name attached, it could be nothing but a success and the expectation was Daddy would eventually create a supermarket chain.

However, Daddy's supermarket business was always hanging by a thread, or as my grandmother Emma would often say, "Was always doing a tap dance on the edge of financial ruin." Our expenses grew and grew and our own home became too much to maintain. Since my seventy-two-year-old grandmother lived alone now in this grand house after my grandfather had died, she decided that it made no economic sense for us to live elsewhere. Economics reigned in our world the way religion might in other people's lives.

Mama always said, "For the Marches, the portfolio was the Bible, with the first commandment being 'Thou shalt not waste a penny.'"

Even so, my father never had much interest in being a businessman. He hired a general manager to run the market and was so uninvolved in the day-to-day activities that it came as a surprise to him to learn it was on the verge of bankruptcy. My grandfather invested twice in it to keep it alive and after his death, my grandmother gave my father some money, too, but in exchange, she forced us to sell our home and move in with her. Daddy was permitted to have assistant managers, but he had to become the general manager.

After that, Grandmother Emma took over our lives as if my parents were incapable of running their own personal financial affairs. "Practice efficiencies and tighten your belts" were the words we heard chanted around us those days. Once I heard Mama tell Daddy that Grandmother Emma had cash registers in every room in her house ringing up charges even for the air we breathed. I actually looked for them.

It didn't surprise me that my mother had complaints about Grandmother Emma. I don't think my mother and Grandmother Emma were ever fond of each other. According to what I overheard my mother say to my father, my grandmother actually tried to prevent their marriage. My mother came from what Grandmother Emma called "common people." My mother's father also had worked for Bethlehem Steel, but as a steelworker, a member of the union and not an executive. Both her parents had died, her father from a heart attack and her mother from a massive stroke. Mama always said it was stress that killed them both, whatever that meant.

My mother had an older brother, Uncle Orman, who was a carpenter and lived way off in Oregon where, according to what I was told, he scratched out a meager living, working only when he absolutely had to work. He was married to my aunt Ada, a girl he knew from high school, and they had three boys they named after the Beatles, Paul, my age, Ringo, a year younger, and John, two years younger, all of whom we had seen only once. They were invited to visit us but never came, which was something I think pleased Grandmother Emma.

"Your grandmother thinks your father went slumming when he dated me," Mama once told me. At the time, I didn't know what slumming meant exactly, but have since understood it to mean Grandmother thought he should have married someone as rich or at least nearly as rich as the Marches.

However, even though Grandmother Emma scrutinized us like an airport security officer when we entered a room, I didn't think it would be too difficult to keep my new secret from her. Since we had moved into her house, my grandmother had not once set foot in my room. She didn't even come over to our side of the house and said nothing about our living quarters except to warn my mother not to change a thing. She had set up imaginary boundaries so that Ian and I were discouraged from going into her side as well.

We were now living in what had once been the guest quarters in what everyone in our community called the March Mansion. It was a very large Queen Anne, an elaborate Victorian style house Grandmother Emma described as romantic even though it was, as she said, a product of the most unromantic era, the machine age. She often went into great detail about it and I was often called upon to parrot her descriptions for her friends.

The mansion had a free classic style with classical columns raised on stone piers, a Palladian window at the center of the second story, and dentil moldings. The house had nineteen rooms and nine bedrooms. Although a great deal had been added on and redone, the house was built in the early 1890s and was considered a historic Pennsylvania property, which was something my grandmother never wanted us to forget. Her lectures about it made me feel like I was living in a museum and could be sat down to take a spot quiz any moment of any day, which is what would happen if she asked me to recite about it to her friends.

Ian wouldn't mind being tested on the house. He could not only get a hundred every time, he could give my grandmother the quiz, not only about the house, but all the history surrounding it, even the history of her precious Bethlehem Steel Company.

Daddy's old bedroom was on my grandmother's side of the house, but we knew the door was kept locked. It was opened with what Ian called an old-fashioned skeleton key. Only Nancy, the maid, entered it once a month to dust and do the windows. I was always curious about it and longed to go into it and look at what had once belonged to him as a little boy. As far as I knew, Daddy didn't even go in there to relive a memory or find something he might have left from his younger days.

Mama told me this house was full of secrets locked in closets and drawers. She said we were all better off keeping them that way. Opening them would be like opening Pandora's box, only instead of disease and illness, scandals would flutter all around us. I didn't know what scandals were exactly, but it was enough to keep me from opening any drawer or any closet not my own.

Ian's bedroom was next to mine but closer to our parents' bedroom, which was across the hall and down toward the south end of the house and property. Although they were originally meant to be guest rooms, all of our bedrooms were bigger than the bedrooms we had in our own house. Even the hallways in the March Mansion were wider, with ceilings higher than those in any home I had ever entered.

Along the walls were paintings my grandparents had bought at auctions. There were pedestals with statuary they had acquired during their traveling and at estate sales.

My grandmother was supposedly an expert when it came to spotting something of value that was underpriced. When she was asked about that once, she said, "If someone is stupid enough to sell it for that price, you should be wise enough to grab it up or else you would be just as stupid."

So many things in my grandmother's house once belonged to either other wealthy people who had bequeathed their valuables to younger people who didn't appreciate them or know their value, or wealthy people who had simply gone bankrupt and needed money desperately.

"One man's misfortune is usually another's good luck," Grandmother Emma said. "Be alert. Opportunity is often like a camera's flash. Miss it and it's gone forever."

She tossed her statements at us as if we were chickens clucking at her heels, waiting to be fed her wisdom or facts about the house and its contents. The truth was there was so much about it that I, even so young, thought was breathtaking, and I couldn't help being proud when other people complimented me on where I lived. Even my teacher, Mrs. Montgomery, who had been at Grandmother Emma's house once, made flattering comments, comments that caused me to be more conscious of its richness.

Some of the grand chandeliers hanging over the stairway, the hallways below, and the dining room came from Europe, and one was said to have once belonged to the king of Spain.

"The light that rains down on us now once fell on royalty," Grandmother Emma was fond of saying.

Did that mean we were magically turned into royalty, too, when we stood within its glow? She certainly acted as if she thought so. She walked and talked and made decisions like someone who expected it all to be written down as history. After all, the mansion was historic, why wasn't she?

No two rooms had the same style furniture. Ian and I were often given sermons about it so that we would fully appreciate how lucky we were to be living in the shadows of such elegance and culture. Everything, even the knobs on doors, had some significance and value. She made the house sound like a living thing.

"Each room in a house like this should be like a new novel," Grandmother Emma said. "Every piece should contribute to some sort of history and tell its own story, whether it be the saga of a grand family or a grand time."

Some of the pieces of furniture in the

same room could have a different background and heritage, as well, whether it be a picture frame, a stool, or a bookcase.

The dining room had a table, chairs, and a buffet that was vintage nineteenth-century Italian and had once belonged to a cardinal. The sitting room, which was different from the living room, had a Victorian parlor settee, a Victorian gossip bench, and a Victorian swan fainting couch I loved to lie on when my grandmother was out and about and wouldn't see. The wood was mahogany and the material was a golden wheat brocade with a detached roll pillow.

All of her furniture, despite its age, looked brand new and there was always this terrible fear that either Ian or I would tear something or spill something on a piece and bring down the family fortune. Our own grand heritage and glory would be lost, for we were never to forget that this family once paraded through the Bethlehem community with great pomp and circumstance, our family crest flapping in the breeze.

There had often been overnight guests here and grand dinner parties during Grandmother Emma's Golden Age. She would describe them to us with an underlying bitter tone as if it was our fault she no longer had them. I knew she couldn't blame us for her not having guests anymore. There was still another guest bedroom downstairs and Daddy's old bedroom on her side, so there was plenty of room for someone to sleep here. She maintained a maid, Nancy, and a limousine driver named Felix, and a man named Macintire whom everyone called Mac, to oversee the grounds. He lived just down the street, so it wasn't a question of extra work for her either. Money was certainly no problem, although I often heard my father complain that his mother held such a tight grip on the money faucet, there was barely a drip, drip, drip.

I didn't doubt that. Grandmother Emma was always criticizing my mother for being extravagant. I thought that was at least part of the reason she stopped going regularly to the beauty parlor and stopped buying herself new clothes. Like someone living on a fixed income, Grandmother Emma would complain about the electric and the gas bills, too.

"If you would stay after your children and have them turn off lights when they are not necessary and close windows when we're heating the house, we wouldn't be throwing money out the window," she lectured. She threatened to fine us for every unnecessary expense.

"They're not wasteful," my mother said in our defense. "Especially not Ian."

Grandmother Emma would only grunt at that. She couldn't argue about Ian doing anything illogical or unnecessary. If anything, he was looking after wasteful practices on her side of the house. He would venture over at least as far as the switch on the wall and deliberately turn off a hall light. If she complained about having to navigate in the dark, he would say, "I didn't think it was necessary with so much natural light through the windows, Grandmother. Perhaps you should fine yourself."

Behind the hand she held over her mouth, my mother might smile at that. My grandmother would shoot a reprimanding look at Ian, who would stare back at her without so much as a twitch in his lips. He had two licorice black eyes with tiny white specks and when he looked at someone so intensely, he didn't even blink. Mama was always telling him not to stare at people.

"It makes you look like an insect and not a little boy," she told him. Other boys his age might have been upset about that, but Ian looked pleased. I knew that sometimes he did deliberately imitate creatures so he could better understand them.

"What would it be like to only be able to

crawl?" he asked me when I saw him doing it in his room. He'd walk about the house with his forearms pressed against himself so he resembled a praying mantis. Or he would wonder what it would be like to be a Venus flytrap and have to wait patiently for your meal to succumb to deception. He would sit with his mouth open for as long as he could stand it. He was studying carnivorous plants as well as insects. He was truly interested in everything.

Grandmother Emma was often disturbed about something he would do, especially when he stood very still and flicked out his tongue like a snake.

After trying to reprimand him for staring at people, my mother would only shake her head and walk away. Grandmother Emma would do the same. I envied the way Ian could make her shake her head and retreat.

When it came to Grandmother Emma's criticism of Daddy, however, she was relentless and unswerving. She never failed to tell him he was lazy and wasteful. She found ways to blame that on my mother, claiming she just didn't inspire him to be better or try harder.

"At times I think you are completely void of ambition and self-respect, Christopher."

She would say these horrible things to him

right in front of Ian or me and even in front of my mother sometimes. Her sharp, surgical comments were never dressed in euphemisms or subtleties. She refused to rationalize or make excuses for Daddy and especially not for my mother and us. On occasion, my mother would try to stand up to her.

"Is it wise to be so critical of Christopher in front of his children?" she once asked her.

"The sooner they learn to base respect upon reality and not false promises, the better off they'll be. As ye sow so shall ye reap," she added.

"So do you blame yourself for Christopher's failings?" my mother dared to follow up.

Grandmother Emma faced her firmly and replied, "No, I blame his father."

"That woman has an icicle for a spine," my mother muttered to me.

At the time I was young enough to believe that was literally true. I wondered how she kept it from melting.

There was so much tension and often so much static in our house, or I should say my grandmother's house, that sometimes, I'd look down the hallway toward the circular stairs and think of the inside of the mansion as having its own weather. I'd imagine clouds or storms no matter what was happening outside. Shadows in the house could widen or stretch so that I would feel as if I was walking under a great overcast sky. Even in the summer months, it could be chilly and not because of too much air-conditioning either. Fair weather days were happening less and less, not that there were all that many after we were forced to move in with Grandmother Emma, anyway. It was no wonder then that my mother was adamant, even terrified, about Grandmother Emma finding out about me.

I suppose anyone would wonder how someone so small could command such obedience and fear. She was just five feet tall with small features, especially small hands, but I never thought of her as being tiny or diminutive. Even in front of Daddy, who was six feet one and nearly two hundred pounds, she looked powerful and full of authority. She had ruler-perfect posture and a commanding tone in her voice. When she spoke to her servants, she whipped her words at them. She rarely raised her voice. She didn't have to shout or yell. Her words seemed loud anyway because after she said them in her manner of speaking, they boomed in your head. No one could ignore her, no one except Ian, but he could ignore a tornado if he was thinking or reading about something that interested him at the time.

My grandmother was always well put together, too. She never appeared out of her room without her bluish gray hair being brushed and pinned. She liked to keep it in a tight crown bun, but on rare occasions, she would have it twisted and tied in something called a French knot. That was when she looked the prettiest and youngest, I thought, although she was very careful not to dress in anything she believed was inappropriate for a woman of her age. Everything she wore was always coordinated, as well. She had shoes for every outfit and jewelry that seemed to have been purchased precisely for this dress or that sweater. There were butterfly pins full of emeralds and rubies, diamond brooches, earrings and bracelets that were heirlooms, handed down by her mother and her mother's mother, as well as my grandfather's mother.

I couldn't help but secretly admire her. In my mind she really was as important as a queen. When she criticized me for the way I stooped or ate with the wrong knife and fork, I didn't resent her as much as Ian did when she said similar things to him. I swallowed back my pride and tried to be more like her. I watched how she sat at the table, how she ate, how she walked and turned her head. I think she saw all this because once in a while, I caught her looking at me with the tiniest smile on her lips and I wondered, could it be that she likes me after all?

I was afraid that if she did, Mama would hate me and might even think I had betrayed her somehow.

But I was also afraid that if she didn't like me, Daddy would be disappointed.

Did she or didn't she?

In my heart of hearts I knew that finding out would be something I would do on the journey toward discovering who I was. And so with trembling feet, I stepped into my future.

2
OUR GREAT SECRET

It was spring. We had just ten days left to school. Grandmother Emma wanted Ian and me to go to summer camp, but Ian hated the idea because of all the boring things they made him do, and my mother refused to send me off at such a young age. Now, after she saw what was happening to me, she was going to be even more unyielding about refusing to send me to sleepaway camp.

"That's absolutely ridiculous," Grandmother Emma told her when my mother argued against it, using my age as an excuse. "I sent your husband away when he was just five and every summer thereafter."

"Maybe his failings aren't all because of his father's spoiling him then," my mother replied, and Grandmother Emma bristled like a porcupine. It was just as if my mother had reached out and slapped her cheek. Touch her anywhere and you would bleed.

"It was precisely my getting Christopher away from his father that gave him the few ounces of backbone he has," Grandmother Emma responded to my mother's sharp response. "At least at the camps he was made to bear some responsibility for his actions and himself. If he called here crying, I would hang up on him. Eventually, he matured. Somewhat," she added. She was always careful not to give Daddy a full compliment or say something nice about him without a qualification.

She looked at me sitting quietly on the medieval cross frame chair I was somehow permitted to use in the living room. I was quietly cutting out some paper dolls, but listening keenly to their conversation. As long as you didn't look at them when they spoke, adults thought you weren't listening.

"I might not start up the swimming pool this summer," Grandmother Emma threatened as an added reason to send us off to camp. "It's a costly luxury just to please two children who are bored silly."

"Do what you want. I'm not sending Jordan to a sleepaway camp," my mother told her, digging her heels into the ground.

"Ridiculous," Grandmother Emma said, and walked away.

Mama looked at me, her face flushed with

a crimson shade of rage and fear. She knew I understood why she was so determined not to send me off.

Despite the way my mother had reacted to the changes in my body, I was happy she and I shared a secret, a secret no one else in our family knew. It made me feel very special, even a little more grown-up. Everything else about Mama, Daddy, Ian, and me was pretty much out in the open, especially, as Mama had said, for Grandmother Emma to see or hear. There was little she didn't know about us, if she wanted to know it. She certainly knew all about our finances and whatever we bought. My mother couldn't do much in the house or even in the community without her finding out about it. She knew what we ate and if we ate. She knew all our clothes and shoes. She usually knew our daily schedules, too, even when we had our dental appointments. All the bills went through her hands at one time or another, it seemed. She especially knew if my father and my mother had an argument. How could they be mad at each other and not show it in front of her?

Lately, there were more and more arguments between them, too. Daddy always seemed to have a reason to go somewhere. He claimed there were endless food shows and conventions. Rarely, if ever, did he ask Mama to go with him. Grandmother Emma thought that was my mother's choice and was always critical of her not being more involved in his business.

"You could at least go down there and watch the cashiers and packers," Grandmother told her. "Didn't you used to work at a supermarket after high school?"

"I only worked there part-time to earn money for college, Emma. It hardly qualifies me to be a supermarket manager."

"Nevertheless, you know what to look for. I'm sure we're being robbed daily," Grandmother Emma told her. "You could watch for that. You know all the tricks."

"What do you mean, I know all the tricks? I didn't rob from anyone," my mother said, her light gray eyes sparking like shiny new dimes. "I worked hard for everything I had. We all did in my family, especially my father, who like his fellow workers, was exploited."

Grandmother Emma looked at her, raised her eyes a little as if my mother was living in a fantasy, and walked away. No matter how good or quick my mother's answers were, she never felt she had defeated my grandmother.

"Her skin is so thick. She doesn't bleed,"

my mother mumbled.

Could that be true? I wondered. I never had seen Grandmother Emma bleed or groan. I never saw her sick, in fact. If she didn't feel well, she wouldn't come out of her bedroom. Everything was brought to her until she was better. It was from her behavior and attitude about illness that I often felt guilty for having a cold or a sore throat, and when I had a minor case of the measles, I thought I surely had embarrassed the whole family.

I suppose this was why I had such a panic attack when I had cramps in my stomach and felt a warmth between my legs that turned out to be blood. It happened only a week after my mother had made her discoveries about me in the bathroom. I touched myself and then brought my hand into the glow of the small night lamp I had to have turned on beside my bed when I went to sleep. The sight of blood on my fingers took my breath away. Now I was certain something terrible was happening to me, something my mother had feared.

I cried out for her, which I knew immediately was stupid. My room was so far away from her and Daddy's bedroom neither could hear me. Ever since we had moved into Grandmother Emma's house, I was on my own when it came to nightmares. By the time I would get up, if I had the courage to do so, and walk out and down the hallway to my parents' bedroom, the nightmare had lost most of its terror.

Daddy was always wrapped too tightly in his cocoon anyway. I remembered going to their bed when I was only four and shaking him to get him to wake up and comfort me. He merely groaned and turned over without opening his eyes, and when I cried, he just waved his hand over his ears like someone chasing off flies.

"Carol, see what she wants," he would moan, and turn over so his back was to me. Sometimes Mama heard him; sometimes she was in too deep a sleep herself and I had to wake her. I hated the idea of waking her more than waking my father. Even at that age, I had the sense that 'she cherished every minute of sleep because it was so difficult for her to get to sleep. She was always worrying so much about everything.

Groggy, but full of comfort, she would put me back to bed and stay with me for a while. In the morning, she always looked the worse for it, worse than I did or felt, and I was ashamed of my fear and my nightmares. Ian said it was ridiculous to be afraid of a dream.

"Just blink your eyes and pop it out of your head," he told me. "Besides, bad dreams can be interesting. Wake me up if you want. I don't mind hearing about them even if they seem terrible to you."

This was different. I couldn't run to him. I knew instinctively that it was part of Mama's and my secret. Wake her or not, she had to be told. I started to get out of bed and then I worried that I would drip blood all over the rug and on the hallway floor. Nancy, the maid, would tell Grandmother Emma. Mama always said Nancy was an informer and a snoop, "an apple polisher who would sell out her own mother for one of your grandmother's compliments."

Ian agreed with Mama. He thought that the reason Nancy's ears were so close to her head was that she kept them against the walls so much.

For a while I just sat up in bed, wondering what I should do. I was tied up in indecision. Finally, I rose and, squeezing the blanket between my legs, hurried to my bathroom. I closed the door and put on the light. When I dropped the blanket, I nearly fainted. My pajama bottoms were soaked in blood.

I'm dying, I thought. It made me dizzy

and nauseated, and the cramps were still strong. I quickly took off my pajama bottoms and reached for a towel. For a few moments, I just stood there with it between my legs. My heart was pounding, but I didn't know what to do. If I went into the hallway like this, someone could see me, and even if I got to my parents' bedroom unnoticed, the commotion could wake up Daddy. Mother had been adamant about my not telling even him. What if Grandmother Emma was awakened? What was I to do?

I decided to curl up on the bathroom floor. At least if I dripped blood, it could easily be washed off the tiles, I thought, and hoped and prayed I hadn't dripped any on the rug when I came in here. It was cold on the floor and hard, but I was so sick and felt so tired, my eyes closed.

The morning light spilling through the window in my bathroom didn't wake me, but the shaking in my body did. I opened my eyes and saw my mother squatting beside me. She was in her robe and slippers. Her mouth was contorted as if she were the one in pain and not me.

"Jordan," she said. "Oh, Jordan. When did this happen?"

"Last night," I said, sitting up and grinding the sleep out of my eyes. I looked down at the towel, shocked myself at how dark and wide the stain was.

"I saw your bed," she told me. "We have a lot to do. We don't want anyone else to know about this. I can't believe this is happening. I'm running you a bath," she added, and started to do so. "Just sit there."

I heard her gathering up the blanket from my bed and then pulling off the sheet. She gasped so loudly, I had to rise and look out the door.

"What's wrong, Mama?" I asked.

"It went right through to the mattress. I'm going to have to turn it over so Nancy doesn't see it."

She struggled with it, but she didn't want me to help her. I was so involved in watching her work — turn the mattress, put on a new sheet, bundle up the old, and check the rug — that I didn't notice the water in the tub. It started to run over the top.

"Mama, the tub!"

"Oh, damn," she cried, and rushed in. She turned off the faucet, but water continued to spill over. "We've got to get this all up. If it seeped through and leaked down to the ceiling, your grandmother would have us executed."

She started to soak up the water with towels and I squatted beside her and helped, shaking and terrified at all the trouble I had caused.

"I'm sorry, Mama," I said, the tears chasing each other down my cheeks. Everyone was going to hate me, especially Daddy because Grandmother Emma would somehow blame him, too.

"It's all right. Don't cry. We'll be all right," she said. She repeated it under her breath like a prayer. "We'll be all right. Keep calm."

It took nearly six towels, but we were able to get the floor dry.

"Get into the tub," she told me.

I slipped into the water. My stomach grumbled so hard, I thought it would cause the tub to overflow. Mama looked at me with so much pity in her eyes, I was positive I was going to die. Would I be buried in the March section of the cemetery or far away from everyone, even Mama's parents, because I had been such an embarrassment?

"Just relax, honey," she said. "I'll be back soon."

I was afraid to move. Once, when I had cut my wrist on one of my toys, Ian told me I came close to cutting an artery and, "When you cut an artery," he said, "blood could shoot out so fast, you'd deflate like a balloon with a hole in it. Your body is about seventy-five percent liquid, which includes your blood."

Thanks to him I had one of my worst nightmares soon after that.

Mama returned with two large garbage bags. Through the bathroom doorway, I saw her force the blanket and the stained bed sheet into them along with my pajama bottoms and the towel I had used. She tied the bags and went out again. When she returned, she had something else. It looked like a white cigar. For a long moment, she stood there gazing at me in the tub. Then she raised her eyes to the ceiling and bit down on her lower lip.

"I can't believe this is happening," she said. "I can't."

I started to cry again.

"No, no," she said, kneeling at the tub. She brushed my hair back with her hand. "It's all right. It's not your fault, Jordan. We'll be fine." She retreated, closed the toilet seat, and sat on it.

"I'm going to have to show you how to use this," she said, holding up the white cigar. "It will seem messy and unpleasant to you, but it's very important because it will prevent what just happened from happening again. We're going to have to keep track of the day this started and the days afterward, too. We'll mark your calendar by your desk in a secret code that only you and I will know, okay?"

I nodded.

"Am I going to the hospital?" I asked.

"No, no. What happened to you happens to all girls, only usually much later. It's just starting early, very early," she added.

"Why does it happen?"

"Remember when I used that word 'menstruation'?"

"Yes." I also remembered how angry she became and how it had brought tears to her eyes.

"Well, that's what this bleeding is called when a woman has it. Woman," she repeated, and looked up at the ceiling while she took another deep breath. "She's only just becoming seven years old," she added, still looking up as if she were having a conversation with God. She took another deep breath and stared at me. I waited. What else would she tell me? I was holding my own breath in anticipation.

Then she shook her head. "You don't even know how babies are made and here I am starting this conversation." She sighed deeply and shook her head once again. "For now, Jordan, just get out and dry off. I'll show you how to use this. I'll help you every month."

"Every month?"

"Yes. That's why we have to mark the calendar, honey. We'll just make a small dot with a red pen so we both know what it means, okay?"

"But . . . won't I die if all this blood comes out of me every single month?"

"No," she said. "It's supposed to come out of you, only, as I said, not this early in your life. And we don't know. It might not happen again for a while. This," she said, holding up the white cigar, "will keep it from flowing out of you and I'll tell you what to look for in anticipation."

"What's that mean?"

"You'll know when it's going to happen. But as I said, it might not. This is so unusual. Let's hope," she said, and helped me out of the tub.

Then she showed me how to insert what she called a tampon. She told me I had to know because I had to change it for a fresh one every four to eight hours. The whole time she cried, especially when she made me do it myself. She hugged me to her and I cried without knowing exactly why I should. As long as I did it correctly, she told me, I wouldn't even know it was there. Having anything alien in my body, though, made me feel funny. How would you forget

45

it was there?

Afterward, she gathered up the wet towels and then she took the garbage bags out of my bedroom and quietly snuck down the hallway to the stairway to put them in the garbage bins. She got me a new blanket from the hallway closet, too.

I dressed and brushed my hair. My stomach felt a little better, but I was still tired and a little dizzy. She returned and sat on the toilet seat again, taking my hands into hers.

"You can't let anyone know about this either, of course. It's part of our great secret. Because what's happening to you is so unusual, I will speak with Dr. Dell'Acqua about it immediately. We might have to go see her, but I still don't want anyone else to know about it just yet, Jordan. You have a few days left to the school year. Be sure you don't tell any of your friends. Promise?"

"I promise, Mama," I said, even though she didn't need me to promise. Since she had emphasized how important it was for me to keep it a secret, I was fearful of anyone knowing about it, too. But I couldn't help but wonder if any of my school girlfriends had already had the same thing happen to them and if they had promised their mothers they would keep it a secret, too. All of us were walking around with our hearts locked.

"You'll take some to school with you in your purse, but don't let anyone see them, and you'll ask to go to the bathroom and change it. Okay?"

I nodded and she took deep breaths as if she couldn't get her breath. For a moment, it frightened me, but she stopped and quickly smiled. She kissed me.

"Let's just go down, have our breakfast, and pretend none of this happened," she said.

Pretend it didn't happen? Could I do that? What if I got stomach cramps in the middle of breakfast and groaned too loud or the tampon fell out? All sorts of horrors occurred to me.

"You'll be all right," Mama said once more.

We both heard Daddy walking in the hallway. Sometimes, he wore a pair of very expensive western boots and they clipped and clopped louder than shoes.

"Your father's up and dressed. I'd better get dressed myself," Mama said, and hurried out to do so. She took the folded wet towels with her.

After what had happened to me and what we had done, I was actually afraid to go down to breakfast without her. I was terrified that Grandmother Emma would take one look at me, point her finger, and say, "You had a menstruation! Get out of my house!"

Of course, she didn't. She barely gave me a passing glance at the table. She was too involved with Daddy and information she had about his supermarket. One of the employees had broken a bottle of mayonnaise and apparently not done anything about it quickly enough. A customer, an elderly lady, had slipped and fallen and broken her hip. Grandmother Emma's attorney, Mr. Ganz, had called to tell her he had received the summons for a lawsuit the woman was starting against March's Market.

"You can't imagine how embarrassed I was telling Chester Ganz I knew nothing about it. I could hear how dumbfounded he was in his silence. He knows how I run my business affairs."

Although Grandfather March had given the supermarket to Daddy, it was still part of a corporation that Grandmother Emma controlled. I didn't understand what all that meant, except I saw it meant Grandmother Emma could still tell Daddy what to do.

"Why didn't you tell me about all this,

Christopher?" she asked him. She leaned over the table toward him, clutching the papers in her hand.

Daddy continued to butter his toasted bagel with such concentration, it looked like he would not answer. Ian looked more interested than Daddy did and tried to read what was written on the papers Grandmother held. She snapped them out of his view with a flick of her wrist.

"Well?" she demanded.

Daddy paused and looked like he was trying to remember the reason himself. Grandmother Emma held herself so stiffly, she looked like she had been turned into a statue in anticipation of Daddy's reply.

He shrugged. "To tell you the truth, Mother, I forgot all about it," Daddy said.

"You forgot?" She looked at the rest of us to see if we were just as amazed. Mama looked down. Ian was full of curiosity and I was afraid to look back at Grandmother too long. Sometimes, she gave me the feeling she could read faces the way other people read books.

She slapped the papers on the table. "You forgot we were being sued for negligence? You're not ashamed to sit there and say such a thing?"

Daddy bit into his bagel and then

shrugged again. "I forgot," he said as casually as he had a moment ago.

Grandmother Emma turned to my mother and glared at her as if Daddy's forgetting was also my mother's fault. Mama put her fork down and fixed her eyes on her in preparation to do battle. My heart thumped so hard, it felt like it was going to pop through my ribs. Something terrible was about to happen.

Daddy caught the exchange of looks. "What's the difference anyway?" he asked. "The insurance company will take care of it."

"The difference, Christopher, is that in this family, we don't keep important things from each other.

"Especially," she added, her eyes moving toward me, "from me!"

I looked quickly at Mama, who shifted her eyes just as quickly away.

Grandmother Emma saw that. I knew she did. Her eyes were soaking in suspicion like little sponges as she glanced from Mama to me and back to Mama again.

And I was never as afraid of what would happen next in this house as I was at that moment.

3
TOO EARLY,
TOO QUICKLY

The moment I returned from school that day, my mother told me Dr. Dell'Acqua wanted to see me as soon as possible. That same afternoon in school I had a close call in the bathroom because Missy Littleton almost saw what my mother had given me. I didn't close the stall door fast enough. As it was, my girlfriends were curious about why I was so quiet all day and not interested in anything they said or did. I kept to myself as much as I could out of fear someone would finally notice the new things about me. I had never been as self-conscious about my body.

"I made your appointment for tomorrow. I'll pick you up at school."

One look at my face would tell her or anyone, for that matter, that I was petrified.

"Don't worry. No one will know why I'm coming for you. It doesn't mean you're sick and dying," she added quickly. "There are things we should do, however, to be sure everything is all right and will be all right."

I said nothing. I hadn't been to Dr. Dell'Acqua very much aside from our shots and an occasional sore throat or earache. Dr. Rene Dell'Acqua was the same doctor Grandmother Emma had. In fact, Grandmother had convinced Mama we should use her as our doctor, because she was "more sensitive to female problems," whatever that meant. Dr. Dell'Acqua was a tall, slim, dark-haired woman with soft dark brown eyes and a smile that put me at ease quickly whenever I did go to see her for anything. Because of Mama's tone of voice and obvious concern, I was more nervous about going to see the doctor this time, even more nervous than when I knew I was going to get a shot.

"It's time for us to tell Daddy about this, too," Mama told me.

With the school year ending, Daddy was talking about taking us all up to the family cabin on Lake Wallenpaupack in the Pocono Mountains of Pennsylvania, where we had a motorboat, too. It had been our week's summer vacation even before we had moved in with Grandmother Emma. She continually talked about selling the property since we rarely used it. My grandfather Blake had used it often because he was a fisherman and enjoyed bringing his business associates to the lake for what she said he called FFWWs, Freedom From Wives Weekends. From what I understood, Grandmother Emma didn't care. She wasn't fond of the cabin and rarely went up there. She told Ian and me it stank from cigar smoke.

"The stench is in the walls of the cabin and even leaving the windows open all winter won't get rid of it. Besides, how anyone can enjoy being at the mercy of mosquitoes and other bugs is a mystery I'll never solve."

Ian enjoyed going there for exactly that reason. He liked to explore nature and didn't get all that many opportunities for it at home. He, like Daddy, wasn't interested in fishing, except to capture a fish for a study. He'd rather examine the inlets and bushes, walking about with his magnifying glass and bringing specimens back for his microscope. He pressed them into a book and kept a library of creatures.

The cabin was a cozy three-bedroom, but it meant we would be more intimate and the chances of Ian and Daddy finally discovering what was happening to me were far greater. For that reason as well, it was time to share our secret with Daddy.

"I don't want to take you to Dr. Dell'Acqua without your father being aware of it anyway," Mama said, and decided to tell him about me right after dinner.

Although my father was very different from his mother, he was like her when it came to spending time with his children and being involved in their everyday lives. I understood from what I could garner from tidbits of my father's history that Grandmother Emma was always too busy with her charity events and social life to devote herself to motherly duties. Once, I heard Daddy tell Mama that he was sure he was an accident. At the time I had no idea what that meant. All I could think of were car crashes or falling off bikes.

For the most part, Daddy left our maintenance and needs up to Mama. Ian and I could count on the fingers of one hand how many times he had accompanied her to our school to listen to our teachers talk about us. He was always too busy for this or too busy for that. Even Grandmother Emma complained about how he neglected us.

"I don't see how you could possibly be busier than your father was, Christopher, and yet he had so much more time for you than you have for your children. You shouldn't leave so much to your wife," she added, which was her main reason for complaining. She wouldn't miss an opportunity to say, "Don't forget. As ye sow, so shall ye reap."

He always promised to do more and take more interest, yet when it came to disciplining us or following up on a complaint Grandmother Emma expressed about our behavior, Daddy would pass on the duty to Mama as if she had hatched us all on her own.

"Look after your kids and keep them from being so messy," he might say, which were words right out of Grandmother Emma's mouth.

"Your son was disrespectful to my mother again," he would tell her.

"My son? My daughter? My children, Christopher? Where were you when all this happened?" she would shoot back at him.

"Obviously out of my mind," he might say.

Once I heard my mother mutter to herself right after one of these arguments, "Some people are just too selfish to have children or even get married to anyone or anything but their own shadow."

She often talked to herself or if she spoke to me, she didn't expect me to understand or remember, but I usually did, and there was never any question Ian understood. I would go to him to explain and he always did.

That night after dinner, Mama came to my room to wait for Daddy. He was groaning and moaning that he had things to do and might even have to return to the supermarket office.

"I need you, Christopher. Just come to Jordan's room," Mama insisted.

Daddy came walking quickly into my room. He paused just inside the doorway, looked at the two of us sitting on the chairs by my student desk, and put his hands on his hips. "Okay, Caroline, what's going on now?" he asked. Whenever he was displeased, he called Mama "Caroline" rather than "Carol," which was what Grandmother Emma always called her.

He was in a white shirt opened at the collar and a pair of dark blue jeans with his light blue boat shoe loafers and no socks. Even though he was supposedly indoors most of the time, he had what Grandmother Emma called a Palm Beach tan. When she asked him about it, he confessed to going to a tanning salon regularly. On his right wrist, he wore a thick gold bracelet and on his left, his Rolex watch, a watch that had belonged to his father.

There was never a question in my mind

that Daddy was one of the handsomest men in the whole city. He had Ian's black eyes and wavy dark brown hair he wore a little too long in the back and sides for Grandmother Emma's liking, but unlike her or even Mama for that matter, he did not care to dress appropriately and look his age. He liked it when people told him that although he was forty-two, he could easily pass for a man in his late twenties.

"You'd better come in, close the door, and sit, Christopher," Mama told him, and nodded at the small settee across from us.

He smirked, closed the door, looked at the settee, and then with an expression of annoyance, glanced at Mama before sitting. He sat back, his right arm over the back of the settee, his left arm at his side. Both my parents sitting in my Tiny Tot children's furniture looked funny to me. It was rare to have them in my room simultaneously. I couldn't help but smile, which he thought was confusing.

"What is it, already?" he asked.

"Recently, I noticed some dramatic changes in Jordan," Mama began.

Daddy's eyebrows rose and closed toward each other. "Changes?"

"In her body. Changes that have come too soon."

"Like what?"

Mama leaned over and unbuttoned my blouse. Daddy gaped.

"As you can see, she's developing breasts."

He sat back, his mouth slightly open. "Is that bad?" he asked.

"My God, Christopher."

"Well, I don't know about female development, for God sakes."

"It's not only this," she said, closing my blouse. "She has pubic hair, and now," Mama said, swallowing back and holding in her tears, "she has had her first period."

"What? You're out of your mind. The kid's not even seven years old. I know that much at least."

"You're right. It's not normal. That's why I'm taking her to see Dr. Dell'Acqua tomorrow," Mama said.

Daddy was quiet. Then he brought his arm off the back of the settee and leaned forward.

"Does my mother know about any of this?" he asked in a loud whisper, as if Grandmother Emma kept her ears to the walls or Nancy had been sent up to do so.

"No, no one knows but us. I'd rather it be kept that way for as long as possible, Christopher."

"Of course," he said, and sat back again.

58

"That's very wise. Well, what does Dr. Dell'Acqua think about all this?" he asked, waving his hand at me as though I were a pile of trouble.

"She wasn't overly concerned about her beginning breast development and pubic hair growth, but when I told her she had experienced menarche —"

"Men what?"

"Her first period. When she heard that, she was convinced Jordan is experiencing what is known as precocious puberty."

"Which means what?"

Mama looked at me, obviously deciding how much more to say in my presence.

"She's becoming a woman too early, too quickly."

"You mean, a kid this young could have a baby!" he exclaimed, raising his voice.

My eyes nearly rolled out of my head. I turned to my mother, anxious to hear her answer.

"Let's not get into any of that just yet, Christopher. Physically, Dr. Dell'Acqua's afraid of her having an accelerated growth spurt that will cause her bones to stop growing and result in her being a stunted adult."

Daddy grimaced as if he had bit into a rotten apple. "You mean she'll become a dwarf?"

Mama looked at me again to see my reaction to Daddy's responses. "You're not helping the situation with this sort of reaction, Christopher."

"Well, what's she want to do?"

"Dr. Dell'Acqua wants to begin with blood tests. She also wants her to have a cerebral CAT scan. There are different types of precocious puberty and we have to determine which she has, what's causing it, and then treat it."

I'll never forget the expression on Daddy's face when he looked at me then. He made me feel as if he thought I was a freak. The distaste and disgust in his face brought tears to my eyes. I felt as if I couldn't breathe.

"Regardless," Mama continued, maintaining her firm demeanor and control, "she is going to have great psychological and emotional difficulty and we'll have to give her all the support and care we can. She might even need professional therapy."

"Therapy! A seven-year-old kid?"

"With divorces and other marital problems these days, that's not as unusual as you might think, Christopher. In any case, that's what Dr. Dell'Acqua told me even before she has looked at her. Jordan will have difficulty adjusting to the changes and the impact they have on her mentally. Besides," she said with a deep sigh, "her body is beyond a seven-year-old's so you have to stop thinking in terms of her age."

"Stop thinking in terms of her age? That's weird. This is horrible," Daddy said.

My lips trembled and I let out a small moan.

"You're scaring her, Christopher," Mama said, glancing at me and then putting her arm around my shoulders.

He looked away and then turned back quickly. "Anything like this ever happen to anyone else in your family?"

"Not that I know of, Christopher. Why does that matter now anyway?"

"Was it something that you might have done wrong when you were pregnant with her?" he followed without a blink.

Mama looked at me quickly and then back at him. "Don't be ridiculous, Christopher. I was under Dr. Dell'Acqua's care with her. Why are you trying to fix blame on me or my side of the family? Are you already worrying about what your mother's going to say or do?"

At the mention of Grandmother Emma, Daddy's eyes widened. "Look," he replied instead of answering her question, "I think you're right to keep this all secret. I agree.

61

No one has to know beside the doctor for as long as possible, especially my mother. Somehow, she'll find a way to blame it on me. I know her."

"Her appointment is at eleven tomorrow. I'm picking her up at school," Mama said, ignoring his self-pity.

"Eleven?" He thought a moment and shook his head. "I can't be there at eleven. I have an important meeting."

"It can't be more important than your own daughter's well-being and health, Christopher. Christopher!" she said sharply when he didn't reply.

"Okay, okay. I'll work it out," he said, and rose to his feet. He glared down at the two of us. "You should have done something when you first noticed, maybe. Maybe you could have nipped it in the bud."

"You're going to have to stop doing this, Christopher."

"Stop doing what?"

"You're going to have to stop shifting responsibility and blame onto me for everything that displeases you and your mother."

"Yeah, right," Daddy said. He turned and left the room so quickly, I felt a breeze in his wake.

I saw my mother fighting hard to keep her tears in check, but she couldn't win that battle. She wiped her eyes, took a deep breath, and then hugged me to her.

"You'll be all right, honey," she said. "Just be brave when we go to see the doctor."

I really did like Dr. Dell'Acqua. She was always very nice to me, but my mother warned me that one of the things she would do to me would be to stick a needle in my arm to take blood. I had a difficult time falling asleep that night thinking about it. She came into my room twice to reassure me.

All my friends were curious about why I was being taken out of school the next to last day of the school year. Why couldn't anything I needed to do have waited? My mother told me to say it was a dental appointment that couldn't be broken, if I were asked. I was never a good liar. My lips always trembled and I could never look anyone in the face. I had to look down or away, but my mother was so worried about strangers finding out about me, I had to do the best I could.

When we arrived at Dr. Dell'Acqua's office, Mama was immediately upset because Daddy wasn't there waiting, as he had promised. While we waited to go in to see Dr. Dell'Acqua, the receptionist received a phone call from Daddy, who told her to tell us he was just unavoidably delayed at the market. He would get to the doctor's office as soon as he could.

My mother said nothing. She didn't even thank the receptionist. She just stood there staring at her until the phone rang again and the receptionist had to take the call. Daddy didn't arrive before we were called to go into the examination room. Soon after, Dr. Dell'Acqua entered wearing her long lab robe and her stethoscope. Her nurse accompanied her.

"Now, what do we have here?" she asked. It was always what she said when she saw either me or Ian at her office. Once Ian replied, "That's what we're here to find out." After that, Dr. Dell'Acqua never said it to him again.

"How long has it been since I've seen her?" she asked my mother.

"About eight months, I think."

I was sitting on the examination table. She had me stand up, shook her head, and said, "She's sprouted."

"I didn't really take much note of it until this happened, but she's only an inch or so shorter than Ian already."

The doctor's face tightened with concern. "Very common with this condition, Carol. As I told you, bone maturity is hastened, but closure also occurs prematurely, creating a stunted stature."

"Oh, God," my mother muttered. Hearing it again in person was more overwhelming, both for her and for me. I fought back my own tears.

"Let's look her over and get going on this quickly," she said.

"You'll have to get undressed, honey," my mother told me, and began to help me take off my clothes.

Although my mother had continually reassured me that I was not sick and dying and did not have some horrible disease, Dr. Dell'Acqua's eyes betrayed a different opinion. She stopped smiling and looked very concerned and serious.

She then did something she had never done before. She looked between my legs. Both my mother and her nurse watched and waited. When she looked up, she shook her head.

"Her vagina is estrogenized," she said, and my mother smothered a cry.

"What do we do?" she asked.

"We'll check her blood and as I told you on the phone, Carol, do a cerebral CAT scan. We have to rule out a tumor," she said. I was sure she was unafraid about talking in front of me because she assumed I didn't understand any of it, but I knew what a tumor was.

Ian had once had a hamster that had developed a tumor. He didn't tell anyone because he was interested in how big it would eventually become and what it would do to his hamster. Whatever it was, it killed his hamster. Before Ian told anyone, he cut open the tumor and put it under his microscope. Then he buried his hamster, again without telling anyone it had died. It was weeks before Mama noticed it was gone.

Dr. Dell'Acqua wrote out an order for the CAT scan and then went to the phone to have her receptionist make an appointment for us at the clinic where it would be done. Mama sat with her hands clenched in her lap as if that was the only way she could hold herself together. Every once in a while, she looked at the wall clock and then at the door.

All the while we were there, Daddy had not appeared, and even when we left the examination room, he was still not there. I could see my mother was struggling to keep her tears locked up and her anger chained as well. She squeezed my hand hard as she led me out of the doctor's office and to our car, but I didn't complain. Dr. Dell'Acqua had somehow gotten us an immediate appointment so we were on our way there.

"Am I going to die, Mama?" I asked as we got into her car.

She took her hand off the ignition key and turned to me. "No, Jordan. It's not a fatal disease. It's just . . . just . . ."

"Just what, Mama?"

"Just damn unfair!" she cried, and hugged me to her.

Then she started the car and we were on our way, both staring ahead with tear streaks carved all over our cheeks and me wondering what terrible thing I had done during my short lifetime to deserve this fate.

4
A BROTHER YOU CAN TRUST

After we left Dr. Dell'Acqua's parking lot, Mama called Daddy on her cell phone. It took him so long to come on after his secretary answered, we were almost at the X-ray clinic.

"How could you not be there, Christopher? How could you leave this all on my shoulders?" she nearly screamed into the phone. Whatever Daddy told her didn't satisfy her. "We're almost at the X-ray clinic. That's right. I told you we would have to have the CAT scan. Too bad there isn't an X-ray machine to see if someone has a conscience," she said, and then she closed her phone and hung up on him without saying good-bye.

She had tears in her eyes again, but they were tears of anger, not of sadness.

"It's all right, honey," she said, reaching for my hand to squeeze. "We'll get all this done ourselves. As usual," she added.

Everyone was nice to me at the X-ray clinic. Nothing hurt but it was still scary to me. When it was all over, we went directly home. Daddy hadn't come to the clinic either, but Mama didn't call him again or even mention it to me. Grandmother Emma was out at one of her charity luncheons when we arrived, but Ian was home from school and in his room watching a documentary about spiders. I thought he hadn't heard us come home and didn't know anything about where we had gone, but not long after I was in my room, he came to my door. I thought he might be coming to show me one of his spiders and tease me, but he brought nothing.

"I know you went to see Dr. Dell'Acqua," he said.

I was just tinkering with my dollhouse, not really concentrating on it. I was still thinking about all that had been done to me. I didn't answer him and he came into my room and stood beside me.

"I overheard Mother call her and make your appointment. She didn't know I heard her, but I did. What's wrong with you?" he asked. "Is it catching?"

I shrugged. Was it? I wondered. Could one of the other girls in school have given me this?

"Well, what's wrong with you?"

What was I supposed to say? Mama didn't want me to tell anyone, but we had told Daddy. Did that prohibition still include Ian now? And even if it didn't, did I want to share a secret like this with him? I had no doubt that he could keep it secret even better than I could and I had no fear that he would tell Grandmother Emma.

With Mama off in her room probably lying down with a warm washcloth over her eyes, and Daddy not even coming to the doctor's office, I felt alone and frightened. Having a secret wasn't so wonderful, especially this one.

"Mama doesn't want me to tell anyone. She doesn't want Grandmother Emma to find out," I told him.

That was obviously the wrong thing to say. It only made him more interested, but I liked having him interested in me. I could count on my fingers how often he came into my room or how often he actually invited me into his. We spent many days without uttering a word to each other. He attended a different part of the school building, so sometimes after breakfast we wouldn't even see each other until dinner. Suzie Granger, a sixth-grader, had a crush on Ian and tried to get him to look at her, but even if she stood in his direct path, he acted as if she were invisible. One day in school, she grabbed me angrily and said, "Having Ian as a brother must be like being an only child."

I had no idea what she meant, but that was when I found out she wanted him to pay attention to her, and Lila McIntyre, a girl in my class, explained what it meant to have a crush on someone. Her sister had told her.

"Why do they call it a crush?" I asked.

"You love them so much you just want to squeeze them to bits," she said, which I thought wasn't that great anyway. It sounded painful.

"You're not talking to just anyone, Jordan," Ian said. "I'm your brother, and you should trust your brother more than any stranger."

"I don't trust any strangers. I don't talk to strangers."

"I didn't actually mean you talk to strangers," he said, a little frustrated. He put his hands on his hips. "Look, you're my sister. We're family, so what happens to you is important to me," he said.

What happens to me is important to him? I looked at him. He had never said anything like that to me before. I was never interesting to him and nothing I liked or did attracted him, but he did like to tell me about the things he did. It wasn't his fault that I was bored too much to listen or care. The truth was he talked to me more than he did Mama and especially Daddy. At least I listened, even if I didn't understand much of what he had to say.

"So? What's the big secret? Spit it out," he said.

It felt like something I would like to spit out, I thought.

He stood there looking down at me. He had lots of patience and never stamped his foot or shouted. Unlike some of my girlfriends at school who had older brothers, too, I never had mean fights with my brother and we never said mean things to each other. In fact, he didn't argue much with anyone. He would just say, "I'm not wasting my breath."

I looked up at him and then I looked at the open door. "Mama might get mad at me if I tell you," I said.

"So, I won't let her know you told me, okay?"

I knew when Ian said he would do something, he would do it, and when he said he wouldn't, he wouldn't, no matter what, but I didn't like betraying Mama. He knew what was bothering me. Ian was almost as good as Grandmother Emma when it came to reading faces.

"She won't get mad anyway, Jordan, and even if she does, I'll tell her it was my fault, okay?"

"Okay," I said, but I didn't say anything. I was trying to find the right words, words that made sense to me.

"Well?"

"I've got precocious," I said.

"What?" He squinted and twisted his nose. Then he smiled. Had I said it wrong?

"Precocious," I repeated.

"You're precocious? I doubt that," he said. "You're most likely an average student, not that there's anything wrong with it. Anyway, they don't take people who are precocious to see medical doctors, Jordan. Psychologists, maybe, but not MDs. You're not precocious."

"It's true, Ian. Dr. Dell'Acqua said so and she poked my arm and took blood out of me even though blood came out of me already," I blurted, and immediately regretted it. All that was still embarrassing to me.

"Blood came out of you? Where?"

I shook my head and turned away.

"Precocious," he repeated to himself. I thought he would turn and walk out of the room, but he surprised me by sitting on the floor beside me and folding his legs. He looked very excited and even more interested now. "Did they tell you why the blood came out of you?"

I shook my head. They hadn't really. There was just that long word Mama used. She had yet to explain it and for some reason didn't want to.

"Did they tell you that you had a period?"

"Yes," I said.

"Holy schmoly," Ian said, which was his favorite expression for something amazing to him. "You had a period. You menstruated," he said, and I widened my eyes. How did he know so much? In any case, from the expression on his face, I realized I was suddenly amazing to him, maybe as amazing as any of the creatures he studied or experiments he performed.

"Yes, that's it," I said.

"Of course. That's why they used precocious. You're just going on seven," he said, but more to himself than to me. "What else did the doctor do?" he asked, drawing himself closer. "Tell me everything."

I was embarrassed about the way Dr. Dell'Acqua had looked between my legs so I skipped that and told him about the special X-ray. I described the machinery and how nice everyone was to me.

"You had a CAT scan?"

"Yes," I said, now remembering what it was called.

"Holy schmoly." He thought a moment more and then he stood up quickly. "If they gave you a CAT scan, they were looking for an abnormality, probably cerebral. I'll research it all up on my computer," he declared with great excitement. I couldn't remember ever seeing him as happy about anything that involved me. "I'll know all about it in minutes. Hang in there."

Actually, I was glad Ian would do that. I knew he would eventually tell me more than either Mama or Dr. Dell'Acqua had told me. He walked out quickly, but a moment later, he walked back into my room to tell me he could hear Mama crying in her room.

"You'd better go see if she's crying about you," he said. "Maybe she heard something from the doctor already."

My heart started to pound so fast and hard, I couldn't get up. If Mama was crying because she heard something from the doctor about me, then it wasn't good.

"Go on," Ian ordered. "And then come to my room to tell me everything she says. I'll be on my computer. I know just where to look for information about all this." He marched out again.

I stood up slowly, sucked in my breath, and walked out cautiously. Even though Grandmother Emma hadn't been here when we had returned, I worried she was here now and spying on us or had Nancy doing so. Daddy was always so sure Grandmother Emma could find out anything she wanted about us. Ian once said he thought she had little microphones hidden in our rooms and listened in to our conversations. Mama told him not to be ridiculous, but it wasn't often Ian was ever ridiculous about anything.

I walked to her bedroom and listened carefully at the doorway. He was right. She was sobbing. I knocked on her door and she stopped.

"Who is it?"

"It's me," I said.

A moment later she opened the door. She had a handkerchief in her hand and was wiping her eyes. "What is it, Jordan? Do you have stomach cramps or something?"

"No. I heard you crying," I said.

"Oh. Well, sometimes I can't keep it all locked away. Your father's not coming home tonight."

Although she tried to make it sound like that was the only reason, I knew that wasn't enough to make her cry. There were many nights he didn't come home and she didn't cry or even seem to care.

"I told him about you and he still went off to do whatever it is he does," she added angrily.

Was I supposed to be angry at Daddy, too, for not being concerned about me? Should I cry?

"It's nothing," she added when she saw my face. "It's adult talk," which was what she usually said when she didn't want me to know why she and Daddy were fighting. "I'll be fine. Don't worry. Just wash up, brush your hair, and put on your pink and blue dress for dinner tonight," she said. "Make sure Ian's not late again for dinner, too, please."

I wondered if I should let her know that I had told Ian, but then I thought it might make her sadder still and she was crying enough as it was.

"Okay," I said, and left, relieved at least that she wasn't crying because of something terrible that Dr. Dell'Acqua had said about me.

I went to Ian's room. He was at his computer as he said he would be. He didn't have to turn around to know I had entered his room. He kept his eyes on his monitor screen and asked, "Why is she crying?"

"Adult talk," I said.

He turned and squinted. "Why?"

"Daddy's not coming home tonight. I think they had an argument."

"Was he with you and Mother at the doctor's office?"

"No."

He smiled and shook his head. "Why am I not surprised?" he asked himself. "Okay. Forget about all that now. I'm learning about your problem. I'll tell you about it later," he said. "Don't bother me right now." He waved at me to shoo me off.

"Mama wants me to get ready for dinner and she said to tell you not to be late again, Ian. Grandmother Emma will be upset."

He didn't answer.

"She said you can't be late."

"I won't," he said. I knew that I could talk and talk and even stand on my head and talk, but he wouldn't answer me anymore or turn away from his computer so I left to do what Mama had asked.

For my birthday last year, my parents had bought me a small vanity table and mirror. When Grandmother Emma saw it being delivered, she said it was the most ridiculous birthday present for a six-year-old she could imagine. At my birthday dinner, Daddy looked surprised about it, too, which made it seem like it was all Mama's doing and fault. I don't know why Grandmother Emma thought it was silly to buy it for me. I loved having it. I often watched my mother at her vanity table doing her makeup or brushing her hair, sometimes for hours when we lived in our own house. I used to ask her questions about her makeup, the creams and the shampoos she used. She did it here, too, during the first few months, and then she did it so infrequently or for so short a time, I rarely watched her anymore. But even though all I could do was brush my hair, I loved imitating her in front of my own vanity mirror.

A few times at our house, she let me put on lipstick and nail polish, too, but she would never let me do any of that here. She said Grandmother Emma would have a tantrum and only make us feel terrible. When I complained about it, Grandmother Emma told me her mother didn't permit her to wear lipstick or nail polish until she was sixteen. That seemed a long way off, and I did have girlfriends at school whose mothers let them wear nail polish at least.

I sat brushing my hair, which my mother liked long on me. Grandmother Emma wanted it to be cut and styled, but that was an argument Mama wouldn't lose.

"I'm not turning her into a proper little mannequin," she said.

Daddy tried to get Mama to have my hair cut, too, but she wouldn't budge on it.

"She pulls your strings, Christopher, not mine," she told him, which started another bad argument.

After I brushed my hair, I got undressed except for my panties and went into my bathroom to wash up well so Grandmother Emma would have nothing bad to say about me at dinner. While I was washing my face, Ian came to my bathroom door. He had reams of paper in his hands.

I had forgotten my promising Mama to never let anyone else see me undressed. I quickly raised my arms to cover my buds, as she had called them.

Ian looked at his papers. "Yes, you are suffering from something called precocious puberty, all right. Actually, it's becoming something more and more common. Nearly fifty percent of all black girls and at least fifteen percent of white girls have or would be diagnosed with the condition this year," he continued. "There are various theories about it. One idea is that all the growth hormones in meat and poultry are having an effect on humans."

Ian could sound just like Mr. Milner, the elementary school principal who also spoke through his nose when he was saying very important things.

Ian looked up from the papers. "I have noticed how tall you've gotten. In fact, I recall telling Mother not that long ago, but she didn't appear to hear me or care at the time. Since both she and Daddy are tall people, they would just assume it was natural for you to be tall. I'm not tall for my age," he added. "However, I could suddenly grow faster, taller. My shoe size would suggest it."

I looked at his feet and then at mine, which were not very big or long.

"The important thing is we'll have to keep track of your development on a nearly daily basis. From what you've told me, Dr. Dell'Acqua is following the correct protocol."

"What's that?"

"Medical procedure for diagnosing the problem. She'll soon come up with a treatment. I'm glad Mother found out about you quickly."

It wasn't that quickly, I thought, but didn't say.

He stared at me and then he walked up to me. "How developed are you?" he asked.

"You'd better go away, Ian," I said. "Mama will be mad."

"Don't be silly. I'm your older brother. Let me see," he said. "I'd like to compare you to this picture I brought up on my computer."

He showed it to me. It did look like my chest. I lowered my arms and he studied me.

"Holy schmoly," he muttered. "That's not baby fat. I assume you have pubic hair as well."

I nodded. That's what Mama had called it the night in the bathroom.

"Don't tell Mama I let you see my chest," I said.

"Of course I won't," he said, looking insulted that I would even suggest such a thing. "My research and observations are not something anyone else should know about, not even Father or Mother for that matter, much less Grandmother Emma. It will be something kept solely between you and me. Let's both swear to that. Put your right hand over your heart. Go on."

I did so and so did he.

"Do you swear never to reveal my research and involvement concerning your condition of precocious puberty?"

It sounded very official.

"Yes," I said.

"So do I and that's that," he said with his characteristic firmness.

He turned and left my bathroom.

How amazing, I thought. I had another special secret, this time with Ian, sealed with an official oath. I had never shared anything as important with him as this.

I didn't know if I should be sad or happy anymore.

I looked at myself in the mirror again. Ian had been very impressed with my buds. I slowly brought my right finger to my nipple. It wasn't the way Dr. Dell'Acqua had touched me, but it gave me a strange, new feeling, which both frightened and interested me. I had never thought to do that before and I had never felt like this before. My face even reddened.

I was staring at myself so long and so intently, I didn't hear my mother come into the bathroom and had no idea how long she was standing there.

"Oh, God," she said. She whimpered like a puppy and I immediately stopped touching myself, but it was too late because she began to cry again.

I started to cry, too.

She quickly embraced me. "It's all right, Jordan. It's not wrong for you to be curious about yourself. I was as well when I was growing up. I just can't fathom . . . can't get myself to accept it so quickly in relation to you. But don't worry. Dr. Dell'Acqua will help us."

"Okay," I said.

She didn't know it, but if Dr. Dell'Acqua was unable to help us, Ian surely would.

5
WHISPERS ON THE STAIRS

Mama rushed me along to get dressed. She seemed to have a need to be as busy as she could. Maybe it kept her from crying. Even though she had stopped at Ian's room to knock on his door and tell him to come down to dinner, he was late again. Grandmother Emma was furious, not only because of Ian, but because Daddy had not come home for dinner either and it was the third night this week.

"Why isn't he coming home this time?" she asked Mama.

"You'll have to ask him. I'm tired of making excuses for him."

"Excuses for him? When a man doesn't come home for dinner as often as Christopher doesn't," she told my mother, "something is sick in his marriage."

Mama stared at her. I could see something very explosive building in her face. Her cheeks had turned the shade of crimson like cheeks turn when someone is in a very hot room. Her eyes tightened and it looked like she had stopped breathing. I glanced at Grandmother Emma and saw that even she was a little frightened by my mother's reaction. She had no idea how much flammable tension and sorrow was swirling about in my mother's heart, otherwise she might not have been so quick to snap a spark in her face. Mama's shoulders rose slowly, as if her whole body was being pumped with air like a party balloon.

"Did it ever, ever occur to you, even for a moment, Emma, that Christopher might be finding something sick in this house and not in his marriage?" she began, speaking in a rather controlled, calm voice, which surprised me.

Suddenly, she brought her fist down on the table and the plates and glasses jumped like animations that had just been brought to life.

"Did it ever occur to you that your constant needling might be destroying all of us!" she screamed.

I had never seen Grandmother Emma back away from an argument with Mama as quickly, but this time she just calmly set down her napkin and rose.

"I will not take my dinner with such

insolence and primitive behavior," she said, turned, and started out.

Nancy had just entered with the platter of sliced filet mignon.

"Bring my dinner to my office. I have lost my appetite in here," Grandmother Emma told her, and continued to walk out of the dining room.

Nancy stood there gaping at us.

Mama looked stunned herself at what she had accomplished: driven Grandmother Emma out of her own dining room.

"I guess I'll never hear the end of this one," Mama muttered. She looked at Nancy. "Well, you can serve us here, Nancy. I haven't lost my appetite."

Just as Nancy brought the platter to the table, Ian entered, oblivious to everything as usual. However, he immediately noticed Grandmother Emma was not with us.

"What, she sick?" he asked, nodding at the empty chair and sitting.

Mama sucked in her breath and brought her hands to her head, resting her elbows on the table.

Ian looked at me for an answer. I didn't know what to say or how to begin to describe what had just happened.

"Just eat your dinner, Ian," Mama finally said, lifting her face away from her hands.

Ian shrugged and began to serve himself. Mama looked at me and I started to eat as well. We said little to each other. It was as though Grandmother Emma was still sitting there glaring at us. I saw that Ian suspected Grandmother Emma had found out about me. He gave me some quizzical looks and then waited patiently for his opportunity to talk to me after dinner.

Mama went right up to her room, first telling us not to make any noise or touch anything forbidden. "I don't want any more trouble with your grandmother tonight," she said.

After she started up the stairs, Ian suggested we go outside. "I want to talk to you," he told me. He looked around and added, "It's safer outside. C'mon, Jordan."

I followed him out. We continued down the steps. I gazed down the driveway at the street, anticipating the possibility of Daddy's arrival, but the street was quiet with barely any traffic.

All the time we had been living at Grandmother Emma's house, Ian and I rarely took walks together. Ian was too interested in making discoveries in nature and if I tagged along, it would be as if I were walking alone anyway. He wouldn't say much to me and I could stay interested just so long in his lectures about a stick of weed or a new species of bug. We were always warned about leaving any toys around the grounds or disturbing the flower beds, bushes, or lawn furniture. We never had any friends over to play with us here either. My mother had been considering having my seventh year birthday party outside by the pool, but it was only five days away now and she had done nothing about invitations or planning.

"With all that's happening," she told me, "I just can't concentrate on it. We'll have our own little birthday party for you, Jordan."

I hadn't had a birthday party with school friends or preschool friends since I was four anyway, but I had been invited to many parties — in fact, to Missy Littleton's just two weeks ago — and even at this young age, I felt a sense of obligation to return the invitation to those who had invited me. I was very disappointed. Grandmother Emma wasn't, I was sure.

"Did Mother tell Grandmother Emma about you?" he asked immediately. "Or did Father tell her?"

"No," I said. "They argued about Daddy's not coming home and then Mama banged the table and yelled at her and she wouldn't stay at the dinner table. She went to her office to eat."

"Banged the table and yelled at her? Holy schmoly. Sorry I missed it," he said. He wasn't even interested in the details of their argument. His mind was already traveling on another highway. "Anyway," he said, "I thought I should help you understand more about precocious puberty."

Ian had more of his computer-printer printouts with him in his back pocket when we walked out of the house. It was still light outside, the final minutes of twilight making it seem like the sun was hanging on for dear life before sinking below the horizon. Stars were just showing, popping out of the darkening blue like bubbles rising to the surface. This year spring was much warmer than it had been last year and I thought the birds especially were a lot happier about it. There seemed to be more of them and they were chatting louder and more frequently.

"How do the birds know when to return?" I asked Ian once, and it was like the best question I had ever asked him. I could see the respect and appreciation in his face for asking a question he didn't consider childish.

"Lower animals and birds have something called instinct," he told me. "It works better than clocks. It doesn't stop until they die."

"Can you see it?"

"No, no. Look, can you see your hearing, your tasting, your smelling? We know about the world around us from our five senses, but the animals and birds have a sixth sense, their instinct. It just clicks in their bodies and they know nature has told them it's time to return. When you're older, I'll help you understand it better," he promised.

Ian was always promising something like that, but not to get rid of me. I really believed he meant it and might even have made a note in his journal. I knew he kept one in which he made notations about things he observed and learned. No one was allowed to see it, not even Mama. He kept it locked up in his desk drawer.

"What exactly did the doctor or Mother tell you about your period?" he asked as we walked down the well-manicured lawn path that veered around the house and back toward the pool, the cabana, and the tennis court Daddy used with his friends from time to time.

"It will come every month," I recited, "but it won't kill me."

"Hardly. That's it? Nothing about female egg production in your body?"

"Eggs in my body? No," I said, grimacing.

"They are called eggs, but they don't look

like the eggs we eat for breakfast, Jordan."

He looked back and then he took out his papers and pulled one out to show me a picture.

"Sit here," he said, nodding at one of the decorative iron benches on Grandmother Emma's front lawn. I did and he sat beside me. "See, this is a female egg. It's really just a cell called an ovum. Once a month your brain sends a message to your reproductive organs to release an egg to receive the sperm."

"What's that?"

He showed me another picture.

"Looks like a . . ."

"Tadpole?"

"Yes," I said.

"It actually swims inside you, inside the female, trying to get to the egg. If it does and it's successful, conception or the creation of a baby starts inside the female. There are literally thousands of them at once."

"Babies?"

"No, Jordan. Sperm."

I looked at the two pictures and shook my head. I couldn't imagine how these two things could become a baby, but if Ian said they did, I was sure they did. And thousands of tadpoles? How did they all fit inside anyway? I was getting suspicious. Was this real or something Ian was creating like one of his science fiction stories?

"Where does this tadpole come from?" I asked.

"From the male, from out of his penis," he said. "He puts it into the female through her vagina," he added, and I popped up like toast in a toaster. What a horrible idea!

"You're lying to me, Ian. And you're being disgusting, too!"

He shook his head. "Why do you say that?"

"Who would let someone pee into her? I don't know why you're lying, but it's not funny," I said, and walked away quickly. I headed toward the rear of the house. I felt like throwing up our dinner. The very thought of what Ian told me made me shiver.

Ian caught up with me quickly and tugged my arm. "I understand why you're upset," he said. "You're way too young for this, but your body is forcing you to learn it and you'd better," he warned.

I spun on him. "Mama never said anything terrible like that."

He sighed and shook his head. "Believe me, Jordan, she will. She's just overwhelmed," he said.

"Why do you know everything?"

"There's no point in getting mad at me, Jordan. You can't get rid of the message by killing the messenger."

"What's that mean? I don't know what you say most of the time."

He produced the rest of his sheets. "There's a lot more to explain and I have the illustrations to show you."

"I don't want to see it!" I cried. I did start to burst into tears. "Stop it!"

I ran this time and went all the way to the pool before stopping. From this position, I could see Grandmother Emma's bedroom. Her lights were on, but her curtains were drawn closed. That didn't mean she wasn't peering out at us. There were many times I caught her doing that.

Who cares? Let her, I thought, and flopped onto a pool lounge. I folded my arms tightly across my chest and stared defiantly at the house. It suddenly looked more like a fortress, a castle with a dungeon and a torture chamber just waiting for me.

Ian walked slowly toward me. "Do you want me to help you understand all this or don't you?" he asked.

"I don't want you to lie and frighten me or make me sick with ugly ideas."

"I'm not going to lie about anything,

Jordan, and I don't need to frighten you. I don't need to play these childish games. You have a serious problem and the quicker you understand it all, the better it will be for you."

I looked up at him. I knew he wasn't lying about that. Everything that was happening to me was turning our world, or at least Mama's and my world, upside down.

"Well, then don't tell me silly things."

"It's not silly. You don't understand." He sat beside me on the lounge and we both looked at the house.

"No one would let someone pee in them."

"Of course they wouldn't," he said.

"You said they did."

"Something else comes out of a male person besides urine. When he does sexual things, he —"

"I know. His penis grows and grows."

"You know that?"

I shrugged. I didn't know what it meant. I had heard some girls laughing about a boy when they were in the bathroom and I was there, too. I heard what they said about his bulge.

"But you don't know why or what happens next, right?"

"I don't want to know," I said suddenly. I was getting frightened and I didn't know why I should. All I knew was I was shivering inside.

Ian looked at me without speaking for a long time. I could see his mind was turning thoughts over and studying each one carefully, as if each was a fine jewel too precious to display unless fully appreciated.

"Well, maybe you know enough for now," he decided. "The question is why what is happening to you is happening and whether or not Dr. Dell'Acqua can stop it until it's the right time for it. If she does that, I guess you're fine with what you know right now, but if you have any questions and you're too embarrassed to ask anyone else, ask me. Okay?"

"Okay," I said. It was easier for me to agree to putting it all off to some future date.

"Someday, I'm going to be a doctor myself," he told me. This was the first time he had told me his ambitions. I didn't think he had told Mama or Daddy yet. "I've just not decided on what kind, whether or not I want to deal directly with people or work in a research center."

I had no idea what kind of work he would do in a research center. I didn't even know what that was, but I was still very impressed.

"You'll be all right, I'm sure," he said, and

stood up. He looked around with his hands on his hips like Daddy when he was thinking or deciding something. "I overheard Father tell Grandmother Emma that we were definitely going up to the lake next week, and I'll let you in on a little secret," he said, turning back to me.

"What?"

"Grandmother Emma suggested we stay up there all summer."

"She did?"

"Yes, because Mother won't permit us to be sent to sleepaway summer camp. Father thought it would be a good idea, only he won't be there with us all the time. Just on weekends. Maybe," Ian added. "Did Mother say anything about it to you?" I shook my head. He smirked. "Wouldn't surprise me if she doesn't even know yet," he said, and started back to the house.

If she doesn't even know yet? We knew, but Mama didn't? This house was big, but it was filling up with secrets, I thought, secrets not only in shut-up rooms and closets, but also inside everyone's hearts. One day they all might just blow off the roof and everyone will see who and what we really were inside this grand house people treated more like a national treasure. Then maybe so many people wouldn't be so envious of us and want to be us.

When it grew darker, I also went back into the house and decided to watch some television. Ian had already gone up to his room and Mama had locked herself away. Daddy was still not home from wherever he had gone instead of coming to dinner. The house was so quiet, I could hear water running in a pipe to Nancy's bathroom. When the house was like this, and everyone was in his or her own place, I felt very small and wanted to curl up in a ball like one of the caterpillars Ian had in a tray. As soon as they were touched, they tightened into a circle. Ian said that was just being protective. He called it hope. Maybe that was what I was doing, too, hoping what frightened and bothered me would all just go away.

Grandmother Emma surprised me by looking in on me. I was alone in the study, where we had an entertainment center. Grandmother Emma was never very interested in watching television with us because her bedroom had an entirely separate area with settees and chairs and a big television set that my grandfather Blake had bought for himself two years before he had died.

Instantly, I lowered the volume on the television set because I anticipated her complaining. She looked at me, at the set, and shook her head.

"Now that school is over for you, I imagine you'll waste all your time in here watching nonsense," she said.

"I have lots of books to read, books my teacher told us to read," I said in my defense.

She looked skeptical. "Stand up," she ordered suddenly.

I did, my heart starting to race. I glanced back at the sofa. Did I do something to mess it up? She stepped farther into the room, and then with her eyes still fixed on me, started to circle me.

"You're growing quickly," she said. "Just as quickly as my sister did."

Grandmother Emma never, ever mentioned her sister, Francis Wilkins, to us. If her name came up in a conversation with Daddy, she quickly skated over it and went on to another topic. All I really knew about my great-aunt Francis was she lived alone on a failed farm my grandparents had bought a long, long time ago, primarily, it seemed, to give Francis a home. She had never married and had no children.

I once came across a picture of her when she was about twenty and I thought she was far prettier than Grandmother Emma. She had a wonderful, soft, childlike smile of delight. Her oval face with its high cheek-bones was framed in rich, wavy light brown hair snipped smartly just at the base of her neck and brushed so it fell an inch or so below her jawbone. She was wearing what looked like a riding outfit and I could see she had a firm, shapely figure. I imagined the picture had been taken on the farm, but what struck me most about it was she was alone and looked like she had been surprised by the photographer. How could someone so pretty be unmarried and alone her whole life?

It was on the tip of my tongue to ask questions about her.

"Growing quickly is not an advantage, believe me," Grandmother Emma said. "It simply hastens life's little problems and drops them on your doorstep before you're ready for them. Francis is living proof of that," she added, and I held my breath. Would she say more, tell me more? Did she know about my problem? Had Great-aunt Francis suffered the same problem?

When she was silent again, I dared ask, "Why doesn't she ever visit us, Grandmother, or why don't we ever visit her on her farm?"

"It's not her farm. Never mind her," she snapped. "Your mother has to buy you more appropriate dresses. The one you're wearing is ridiculously too short now. I swear, sometimes it seems I'm the only one who realizes anything around here," she added.

She looked at me even closer and I wondered if she had noticed the buds on my chest.

"It's simply stupid to not have you mixing with young people your age in a camp or summer school. Loitering about here is out of the question," she said.

I thought she was going to tell me that we were to go to the cabin for the summer, but she concluded, turned, and left me confused. She was upset with me, but yet she seemed truly to care about my looks and welfare. Was that the way her mother treated her? Or her grandmother? Did she care for my benefit or for her own, afraid I would somehow embarrass her in front of her important friends?

All of a sudden, I wanted to know much more about Grandmother Emma, but I was afraid to ask anyone, especially Mama, who might think I wasn't on her side. I made up my mind that one of these days I would sneak into Grandmother Emma's room and look at her picture albums and other family memorabilia that I knew she kept locked in closets, buried in boxes and drawers.

Would I, like Pandora, unleash more pain and suffering than I could imagine? When Mama had told me the story, I had read it myself. Pandora opened the box because she was curious, but also because she heard whispers coming from it. Didn't I hear whispers in this house, whispers on the stairs, whispers in the shadows, whispers from the empty rooms and from the closets? They were drawing me to them just the way they drew Pandora to the box.

After she had opened it and released all the pain and suffering, sadness and disease, her husband, Epimetheus, and Pandora, who had been stung by the brown moths of sadness and illness, heard another voice urging them to let it out. They opened the box again, and hope emerged. Evil had entered the world, but hope followed closely on its footsteps, to help us.

Couldn't I let hope out? Or would I just unleash the evil that crouched in the darkness, waiting to spring into our lives?

Like Pandora, I was destined to find out.

6
Not a Freak

Everything that had happened during the day made me tired much earlier than I had expected I would be. I turned off the set and went upstairs. I paused in the hallway and listened to see if Mama was crying again, but it was just very, very quiet. I closed my bedroom door and got undressed quickly.

Once again, I went into the bathroom and looked at myself in the mirror. I couldn't help but think of the things Ian had told me and tried to tell me. Little eggs were floating around inside me. If a boy put his tadpoles into me, I could have a baby grow in my stomach. The whole idea of it frightened me, but it also made me more curious about myself and what was happening now.

The feelings I had when I touched myself were so different from feelings I had before all this had begun. It made my head spin. My stomach bubbled and gurgled and even ached a bit. Was that because the eggs were bouncing around, waiting for the tadpoles? I did want to learn more and I was sorry now that I had been so angry and mean to Ian. After I got into my pajamas and brushed my teeth, I went out and knocked on his door.

"Who is it?" he called.

"Me. Can I come in?"

"Come in," he said. He was sitting at his desk, writing in his journal. "What is it?" he asked, looking annoyed at being interrupted.

"I don't want to wait to know about the tadpoles," I said, and he grimaced.

"Call it sperm, Jordan. I just said tadpoles because they look like that under a microscope. Males have reproductive organs, too, of course, and when they reach puberty, they can manufacture the sperm."

"Once a month, too?"

"No, all the time, instantly when aroused," he said.

"What's aroused?"

"Stimulated, excited. When they get hard and bigger like you heard. Blood rushes down there and makes it that way and then, at a certain point, the sperm shoots out. Okay? Now remember, don't go telling Mother I told you all this," he added. "She

104

might not like me doing it. If she tells you, pretend to be hearing it for the first time. Otherwise, she'll be angry at me and I'll never be able to tell you anything again."

"Does it shoot out of you yet?" I asked.

He stared at me for a long moment. "I think you know enough for right now," he said. Then he thought again and stood up. His eyes grew narrow and intense like Dr. Dell'Acqua's were and he stepped up to me. "This is interesting," he said. "I wonder if it's instinctive for you to have these thoughts now."

"You mean like the birds coming back?"

"Yes, something like that." He looked back at the door I had left open and then he went to it and closed it softly. "Did you just start thinking about boys?" he asked. "I mean after this thing started happening to you, this precocious puberty?"

I shook my head, but not with conviction. I wasn't sure what he meant. I certainly thought about boys in my class, how this one was cute or that one was ugly. Some were so childish and silly. None looked like they would become as intelligent as Ian.

He started to talk like a teacher again, making a speech as if there were many people in his room and not just me.

"Our reproductive urges are built into us.

105

It's not something we have to learn. I mean, we can learn more about it, understand what happens to us, but we don't have to be taught how to do it, just like we don't have to be taught how to go to the bathroom or eat or sleep. Our bodies need us to do it. The species needs us to do it."

"Needs us to do what?"

"Forget about that for a moment," he said with some irritation. Then he narrowed his eyes again. "Let's try one experiment," he said. "But don't ever tell anyone," he warned. "Remember," he reminded me, "how we swore in your bathroom to keep my research and investigation our secret, okay?"

"Yes."

He was spending so much time with me, I didn't want to upset him again. He reached out and carefully unbuttoned my pajama top. He opened it and looked at my buds. Had they grown bigger already? I stood there waiting to see what he had discovered when he surprised me by touching my nipple, only he didn't just touch it and pull away. He kept his finger there, moving it slightly.

"It doesn't just tickle, does it?" he asked.

It didn't. It was different, very different.

I shook my head and said, "No," but it

came out like a whisper.

"You're actually getting stiffer. Holy schmoly," he said, and then, as if he realized what he was doing was not right, jerked his finger away.

"What's that mean, stiffer?"

"Button up," he said without answering me, and returned to his desk.

I waited. His face was flushed. I thought he was upset at me again for some reason. He wrote something in his journal and then he looked up.

"Okay," he said. "That's enough for now. I'll teach you more and more, but let's go slowly so you don't get confused and frightened. You should never be frightened of knowledge anyway," he added. "Remember, don't tell anyone, especially Mother, or I'll never tell you anything again," he warned.

"I won't tell," I said.

"You'd better go to sleep," he said. "Go on," he nearly shouted.

I hurried out, looking back once at him before I closed his door. He looked different, still flushed. I knew he wasn't angry at me, but what was confusing was he looked like he was angry at himself.

I closed the door and went to my room. Not long after, Mama came to my room to see if I had gone to bed. She was in her nightgown already and I could see that she had been crying. Her eyes were still blood-shot.

"Grandmother Emma came to see me downstairs," I told her. "I was watching television and she came into the room and asked me to stand up."

"What? Why?"

"She said I was getting very tall, growing fast like her sister, Francis, and my clothes were inappropriate, my dress too short."

"Francis? That's interesting," she said. She thought a moment and then shook her head. "Did she ask you anything else? Did you tell her anything about going to the doctor?" she asked very quickly.

"No, Mama."

"Be sure you don't," she said. "We want to keep this from her as long as we can. I don't relish having her comment and complain or even offer advice." She fixed my blanket. "I intended to take you for new clothes. She's not wrong about that. We'll do it this weekend on your birthday. You need something nice for your birthday din-ner. Your father promised to take us all out to your favorite restaurant, the Japanese place where they cook the food right in front of you."

"And then we're going to the cabin?" I

asked before thinking.

"Yes," she said. "Maybe for longer this time."

I was happy she knew and it wasn't a secret kept from her.

"It will do us all good to get away from here," she told me. I knew she really meant to get away from Grandmother Emma. "Are you all right?"

I nodded and she leaned down to kiss me. "You're just a little girl," she said. "This is so unfair. Your youth is being stolen from you."

I didn't speak even though I wondered what she meant. Who was stealing it? How can youth be stolen anyway? It wasn't like anything you kept in drawers and boxes. Tears were coming from her eyes now as she stroked my hair. She sucked in her breath and flicked off her tears quickly.

"You'll be all right," she said.

"Why are you crying, Mama?"

"It's nothing. Don't mind me. I'm just not doing well tonight. I'll be better tomorrow. Good night," she said, and left me, closing the door softly.

I lay there with my eyes open and my hand on my stomach. Then slowly, I brought my fingers back to my nipple and touched it like Ian had done.

I saw from the expression on his face that what he learned about me had upset him. Did that mean something terrible was going to happen?

I curled up quickly like the caterpillar and filled my mind with hope.

It worked, not only because I fell asleep quickly, but because in the morning, after breakfast, Mama received a phone call from Dr. Dell'Acqua, who told her I had no tumor in my brain. My problem was a result of hormones, she said, and she was going to prescribe a medicine that she believed would stop the precocious puberty.

The news made Daddy happy, too. Suddenly, it was like a wind had come blowing through the grand house, pushing away the bad weather, the darkness and clouds. Grandmother Emma had obviously not complained to Daddy about Mama's yelling at her and banging the table either. They had no arguments about it.

In fact, Mama was smiling and she and Daddy were even laughing together. What's more, the school year ended and I left without any of my friends knowing anything about what was happening to me. I had been able to keep our secret locked up tightly. It all started to look perfect. Plans were definitely set for my birthday dinner.

Grandmother Emma was invited, but she hated the Japanese restaurant and the idea of cooking going on right in front of her nose.

She surprised me that morning, however, by having my birthday present at breakfast on my chair. All the other times, she waited until my actual birthday dinner.

"You may open it now," she said, and I quickly did. Everyone waited and watched.

I took out a coral shade silk dress with a hot pink slip. There was an embroidered flower garden on the hem.

"That should be perfect for evenings at the lake," Grandmother Emma said. "And it's the correct length," she added, glancing at Mama.

There was a shoe box, too, with a pair of light pink leather buckle sandals.

It was the cutest, most fashionable dress she had ever bought for me. I loved it, but when I looked at Mama's face, she looked upset, worried.

"You can go try it on," Grandmother Emma said. "I'd like to be sure it all fits you well."

"Let her do it after breakfast," Mama interjected.

Grandmother Emma didn't look pleased, but said nothing. Breakfast was served.

Daddy described some of the economic improvements he had made at the super-market. He was having the storage area renovated to make more efficient use of it. Grandmother Emma looked on him with approval in her eyes. She announced that in the fall she might hold one of her charity parties at the house just as she had during her Golden Age. It did sound exciting. Even Mama looked interested.

Were all our troubles really dissolving?

Afterward, I went upstairs to put on the silk dress and the sandals. Mama came into my room with me.

"Oh, God," she said. The bodice was snug so that my buds were clearly revealed, even prominent. She went to my closet.

"Put this undershirt on first," she told me, and handed the sleeveless undershirt to me. It at least subdued my nipples, but didn't flatten me entirely. "That will have to do," she said.

The sandals fit perfectly.

"I don't know how she picked out ones that fit you. I had no idea she knew your sizes. I guess she really doesn't miss much," Mama said. This time it sounded more like a compliment than a complaint about her. "Give the devil her due," she added.

We went downstairs to model it all for

Grandmother Emma, who was in the hallway, giving Nancy some orders about housecleaning. She was displeased with something so much that when she turned, she didn't look me over that carefully.

"Very nice," she said, concentrating on the hem most of all.

"I'm taking her for clothes this afternoon," Mama told her.

"Good idea," Grandmother Emma said, and returned to what she had been saying to Nancy.

"For once I'm happy she's absorbed in only what really interests her," Mama muttered, and hurried me away.

We spent the day shopping. Saleswomen were happy to see my mother in the department stores and all inquired after her health, as if they believed she had been away recuperating or something, because they hadn't seen her shopping that often.

"Look how big she's gotten," one of the more familiar salesladies said, looking at me.

Mama forced a smile to her face as if she was happy about it, but she tried to find clothes that de-emphasized my development — loose fitting blouses, athletic shirts. We bought new sneakers and sandals, but the most difficult thing to find was a new bathing suit. We finally discovered a rose petal two-piece skirted suit that had a bulky top and was very concealing. She bought me another in a blue color, too.

All in all, as we drove home, I could see Mama was happy about my new summer wardrobe. Once again, she told me she was actually looking forward to spending most of the summer up at the lake.

"I'll get a lot of reading done. We'll have picnics and go for boat rides and I'll take you and Ian to the fun park and we'll go horseback riding. They have that art show up there every summer and we'll eat in the nice little restaurants when Daddy comes up on the weekends. Ian needs to be out-doors more, too." She laughed, which was good to hear, and added, "I'd even go on one of his nature hunts with him."

"Me, too," I said.

I had forgotten how wonderful my mother's smile could be, but once she flashed it at me, it filled me with pleasure and cater-pillar hope.

We were both surprised to see Daddy's car in front of the house when we drove up. Usually, he spent all day at the supermarket office or meeting with people. He was never home this early. Maybe he was here because of my birthday, I thought. He was going to spend more time with me.

"I thought he had that meeting with the men renovating the storage area," she muttered when we parked. I could see the look of concern sinking into her face and darkening her eyes with worry.

The sunshine that had begun my birthday was being pushed away by bully clouds shoving the blue sky toward the horizon. I embraced some of my packages and bags and followed my mother into the house. The moment we entered, Daddy stepped out of the living room and glared at us, his face so red with irritation, he looked like he had broken out in a rash.

"My mother wants to speak to you," he told Mama.

"After I put Jordan's things away," she said.

"No, Caroline," he said. "Now. Just put all that on the bench there for the time being," he added, nodding at an antique bench in the entryway.

He was calling Mama "Caroline" instead of "Carol." No question about it, I thought, there was trouble.

No one seemed to take notice of me. I stood back while Mama did what Daddy had asked and walked to the living room. She didn't even tell me to go upstairs. She was that upset. I edged my way toward the living room and stood outside. Through the doorway I saw my mother standing and facing Grandmother Emma, who sat in her regal Victorian mahogany parlor chair, her arms on the chair arms, her back straight.

"What is it that couldn't possibly wait a few more minutes, Emma?" my mother demanded.

"I happened to have a conversation with Rene Dell'Acqua today," Grandmother Emma began.

I saw my mother's body stiffen, as if she had just been whipped across the back.

"A conversation that turned out to be more about Jordan than me."

"She has no right to discuss her patient's private medical information with anyone," my mother responded sharply, without having to hear another word.

"I'm not anyone, Caroline. I'm the girl's grandmother. I'm disappointed in both you and my son, keeping such a thing a secret from me."

"We live under your roof, but we do try to have our own lives, Emma," my mother said. She looked to Daddy to see if he would come to her aid, but he just stared at the floor, looking to me like a little boy who had been caught doing something naughty.

"Your lives, as you say, are not as separate from mine and from all this as you imagine or even would like, Caroline. Even though Bethlehem Steel is no more, I am still friends with the wives and families of former executives, not to mention many other influential people in this community. We are still on a stage, still looked up to, admired, the center of social attention. The March name follows you everywhere, and where you go, therefore, I go. Now," she said, waving her hand to chase away any further discussion about that, "who knows about this . . . this thing besides us?"

"No one, Emma. I don't go gossiping about my child's problems."

"That's unusual these days," Grandmother Emma said. "Most people can't wait to air their dirty laundry and others are glued to television sets watching them do it."

"I don't consider what's happening to Jordan to be dirty laundry. God, Christopher," she said, suddenly turning on Daddy, "can you speak up for once?"

"What do you want me to do? I told you we shouldn't keep it from Mother."

"What?" Mama literally cringed and pulled away from him as though he could infect her with a disease.

I stepped back from the door. I, too, knew that wasn't true and I didn't want Daddy to see I had overheard.

"Let's end this ridiculous bickering before it even begins," Grandmother Emma said. "None of that is important. What's important is the girl's condition. Rene will let me know if we need a specialist on the case. Thank goodness you're taking her to the cabin, where no one we know will be able to see her."

"I'm not afraid of anyone seeing her! She's not a freak," my mother practically shouted.

"It's no one's business what she is or what she isn't," Grandmother Emma said, this time not fleeing from Mama. She looked at Daddy and then at the floor as she shook her head. "I feel like such a fool, talking about how she's grown and buying that present without knowing the reason for all this. Such a fool. I won't have it," she said, slapping the arm of the chair. "Don't let me learn something about my own family from someone else again. I'm to be consulted about every decision and every action, do you understand?"

Mama stared at her and then she turned again to Daddy. "Christopher? Well?" Daddy didn't speak. "Did I marry you or you and your mother?"

Grandmother Emma grunted, but said nothing.

"There's nothing wrong with Mother being involved. She knows more doctors and even has connections at the university. Look, Mother," he said, "I'm sorry you were surprised by all this, but it all happened so quickly and —"

"That's all I want to hear or say about this," Grandmother Emma said abruptly. "The important thing is what has to be done will be done."

She rose and walked out of the living room, pausing when she saw me standing there. "Francis," she muttered to herself, but loudly enough for me to hear, and then she continued down the hallway.

Why did she call me Francis or think of her again when she looked at me? My heart was pounding, filling my chest with every thump.

And my curiosity about my great-aunt was too great to restrain. I'd open one of those locked closet doors yet, I thought. In fact, it was almost as if Grandmother Emma was urging me to do so.

7
THE BEST BIRTHDAY PARTY I EVER HAD

"How could you say that? How could you make me look like the bad one in front of her!" Mama shouted at Daddy.

Ian heard them and came midway down the stairs. They were standing in the hallway.

"Will you lower your voice, Caroline?"

"No, I will not lower my voice. I won't cower like some child in this house. How could you do that? Are you that afraid of your own mother?"

"I'm simply trying to make things easier," Daddy said, reducing his voice to a loud whisper. "It doesn't do us any good for her to feel we're conspiring to deliberately hide things from her, does it? It's better this way."

"You mean it's better that I'm the sole one at fault?"

"It's easier for me to make peace with her. Just calm down. It will pass," Daddy said.

"You're damn right it will pass," Mama told him. She marched to the stairway, remembered my things, and went back to the bench to get them. "C'mon upstairs, Jordan. We'll put your things away for now," she said, seizing my hand and practically dragging me to the stairway. "It is supposed to be a happy day, your birthday," she added, practically right into Daddy's face.

I looked at Daddy and then at Ian, who seemed disappointed it was only a spat between Mama and Daddy. He turned and went back upstairs to his room. I didn't know what it would take for him to become upset or troubled by something happening in our family. To me he always looked like he had expected it, anticipated it, or at times, even welcomed it, because it was something else to write in his journal, whereas I couldn't hide my fear and sadness.

"Don't worry, Jordan," Mama told me in my bedroom. "I won't let this ruin your birthday dinner."

I really wasn't worried about that. I was confused and troubled about Daddy's lying. It was the first time I caught him doing so. I never thought he was as perfect as Mama. I knew he had failed in his schoolwork and I knew he wasn't a very good businessman. Grandmother Emma never let us forget any of that, but I still thought of him as being a good person who loved us. He just couldn't love us as much as our mother loved us because he was too busy trying to succeed.

Whenever my mother complained about my father working too much or being away from us too long, he would throw up his hands and cry, "I'm just trying to get some independence for this family, Caroline. You don't want to be dependent on my mother forever, do you?"

"I don't ever want to be dependent on your mother," Mama would reply, and he would shrug.

"So? Let me work at it."

"Work at it forever for all I care," she muttered, and turned away from him.

Daddy would look at me if I were in the same room or nearby, and say, "Women."

I had no idea what that meant.

"Why didn't Daddy tell the truth?" I asked Mama after she put away my new clothes.

She looked at me as if she only then realized I knew he had agreed to keep my problems secret from Grandmother Emma and it wasn't just her idea. Had she forgotten I was right there when they discussed it or did she simply think I didn't understand?

"It's not easy to tell Grandmother Emma the truth," my mother said. "At least, it hasn't been for your father. He thinks it's easier to tell her what she wants to hear. People do that to each other all the time, Jordan. Don't be surprised. You might as well get used to it. Welcome to the adult world."

"How do you know when anyone's telling the truth then?" I asked, and she laughed. I was happy I made her do that.

She walked over to hug me. Then she squatted a little to look into my face.

"You're growing up so quickly, I feel like I've aged myself overnight. I know it's going to be extra difficult for you, Jordan, but try, try hard to hold on to being young for as long as you can. Live in a world of make-believe where lies and deceptions don't matter. Don't send Santa Claus to a retirement home just yet."

I was the one laughing now. "I don't believe in Santa anymore, Mama."

"I know, but sometimes, it's not bad to hope he'll come back."

I squinted at her. Come back? Come back from where? He didn't exist.

"Whenever you do that, you look just like your brother. When we first told him about Santa Claus, he squinted and asked how it was possible for one man to deliver toys to all the world's children in one night. I don't think he was three. You think he's happier being so smart?" she asked me.

"Yes," I said.

"Maybe," she said, standing. "Put on the new dress your grandmother gave you for tonight and the sandals. It is a very pretty dress and fashionably up to date, which surprised me. Showing her you want to wear it on your special night rather than anything I bought you today will help Daddy smoke his peace pipe with her."

"Daddy doesn't smoke, does he?"

"No. Well, he smokes cigars occasionally when he wants to look like a big shot. People say, 'Let's smoke a peace pipe,' when they want to make up or calm things down."

She started out and turned back to say, "Men."

I was just as confused as when Daddy said, "Women."

Did that mean she was no longer angry?

A little while later, she came in to help me fix my hair and then she went to dress. Despite the argument earlier, it did still feel like it was going to be a very special night. Ian put on his suit and tie, too, and then surprised me by giving me a birthday present that was just from him. I didn't know and neither did our parents that he had ridden his bike to the department store and bought it for me. Before we all went out to dinner, he came to my room to give it to me.

I started to unwrap it.

"I confirmed the reading level before I bought it for you, Jordan," he said, so I knew it was a book.

It was called *I Was a Girl and Now I'm a Woman.* I opened it slowly and saw there were pictures, too, and a page that had the tadpoles.

"It does a better job of explaining everything than I could do for you right now," he said. He glanced back from the doorway and then looked at the book. "Maybe for now you shouldn't let Mother or Father know you have it and especially that I gave it to you."

Another secret, I thought, another brown moth to keep locked up in my own Pandora's box.

I carefully folded up the gift paper and then put the book into my toy chest, the one that had my dolls and teacup set as well as some board games and other toys I never used anymore. No one ever bothered to look in it. If I left something out, Nancy might put it in there, so I had to be sure I was very neat about my things and didn't leave anything on the floor.

"Thank you, Ian," I said.

"You're welcome. You look very nice in your new dress," he added, which was the first time I could ever remember him giving me a compliment.

"Thank you."

"You're going to be a very pretty woman, Jordan," he predicted. It nearly took the breath out of me. "That really shouldn't come as any surprise to anyone. Father is very good-looking and Mother is beautiful. Even though I don't approve of how she uses it, Grandmother Emma is correct when it comes to the influences of genetics."

"What's that?"

"What you inherit, what's passed along. At one time people wanted to marry within their families to ensure they wouldn't lose their good genes. It was like breeding show dogs," he added with a smirk.

He paused and looked intently at me again, fixing those dark eyes on me like I was one of his specimens under his microscope.

"What's wrong?" I asked.

"Nothing's wrong. To the contrary, despite the many criticisms and complaints we all have about Grandmother Emma, we would have to admit she has good taste when it comes to clothes."

"Taste? How do you taste clothes?"

"That just means she knows what looks nice, what looks right. She knows quality, perspective. I've made a study of this house, its contents, and I can tell you that everything she has bought and placed in it complements something else," he said.

How could things complement each other? I didn't know what he meant, but acted as if I did. He knew so many words and even amazed Grandmother Emma when he did the *New York Times* crossword puzzle. Ian was smarter than my teachers, I thought.

We heard Mama and Daddy coming out of their room. Mama laughed at something Daddy had said.

"Looks like they made up," Ian said.

"Smoked the peace pipe," I added, and he actually laughed and not because I had done something he thought silly, but because I had said something he thought was clever.

"C'mon," he said, holding out his hand for mine.

When we stepped into the hallway, our parents stopped and looked at us both with an expression of amazement.

"You look very nice, Ian," Mama told him.

"Thank you."

"He's dressed as well as I am and ties a tie better than I do. That's for sure," Daddy said. "And look at the beautiful birthday girl. We've got to show you both to Grandmother Emma. Wait until she sees the dress actually on Jordan."

"She's already seen her in the dress, Christopher," Mama said. "Remember? She ordered it put on right away."

"Still, it's going to be good to show her all of us together," he emphasized.

Actually, I did think we all looked wonderful, especially Mama, who had put on one of her nicest dresses and fixed her hair so it looked pretty again. She wore makeup and earrings, a matching bracelet and necklace, too. It had been a while since she had dressed like this. I was happy it was because of my birthday, because of me. Instead of thinking about myself as the cause of new trouble, I could think of myself as the reason for good things.

I thought I understood what Ian meant by genetics, too. Our parents were attractive people. Ian was good-looking and I was going to be pretty. Maybe we were a family to be put on magazine covers after all and maybe the people who envied us weren't wrong to do so.

We marched down the hallway to the

stairs and then descended as if we were about to enter a grand ballroom as people did during Grandmother Emma's Golden Age. Ian continued to hold on to my hand, which surprised me. I was happy to see Mama keeping her hand on Daddy's arm. They did look like they had made up and loved each other again.

Grandmother Emma was in the living room sitting and waiting and looking like she had expected we would first come for her inspection. I think Mama thought Daddy had warned her because I heard Mama mutter, "How convenient she just happens to be waiting here and expecting us."

"Well, Mother," Daddy said, ignoring Mama, "how does the March family look?"

She ran her eyes over all of us like a general inspecting her troops on parade, pausing to look and nod approvingly at Ian before fixing her gaze solely on me. Her expression changed. She made me feel like she could see my whole future and what she saw filled her with concern. After another moment, she turned to Mama and Daddy.

"You had better gird up your loins," she said. "She will soon become a heartbreaker and keep you both on your toes."

Daddy smiled, but Mama glared back at her.

"There will be plenty of time before we have to concern ourselves with any of that," she said.

"Not the way children are brought up these days," Grandmother Emma insisted.

"You sure you won't join us, Mother?" Daddy asked her, obviously hoping to quickly change the topic.

"Thank you but no thank you. How anyone can enjoy smoke in his or her face before eating is a mystery to me."

"Let's go," Mama insisted, even tugging at Daddy's arm.

"Well then, we're off," he said, and we left the house and all got into his Mercedes sedan.

It had been so long since we had gone anywhere as a family. When we were together like this, I felt safe. I felt like Ian's caterpillar, protected, hopeful.

On the way to the restaurant, Daddy talked more about our impending trip to the cabin on the lake. We were going there in a few days. He said he would spend the first two or three days with us and then promised he would return on weekends whenever possible.

Mama said little. She listened and kept

her face forward. The only thing she said about our preparations for leaving was we had to be sure we had what we needed first from Dr. Dell'Acqua.

"I have to be sure we have enough," she said.

I looked at Ian. He wasn't supposed to know.

"What do we need from Dr. Dell'Acqua?" he asked, winking at me first.

Daddy and Mama looked at each other, and then Mama turned and said, "Something I need. Nothing to worry about, Ian."

"Good," Ian said. He smiled to himself and looked out the window all the way to the restaurant.

At the restaurant, my parents gave me my present. It was a gold locket on a gold chain. Inside there was a picture of two babies. At first I thought it was Ian and I, but my mother surprised me by telling me it was her baby picture and Daddy's.

"We thought that would be something you might cherish," she said.

Ian inspected it and nodded his approval like a jewelry expert. Then he helped me put it on, fastening the clasp. I ran my hand over it and smiled at how wonderful it made me feel to have both my parents close to my heart, always.

Our dinner was great fun. The chef tossed the food in the air and did wonders with his knives. He built a volcano out of onions and it puffed with a small explosion that brought cheers and applause. Afterward, the restaurant brought out a small birthday cake for me with seven candles, and everyone, including waiters and waitresses, sang "Happy Birthday" to me. Even Ian sang, and loudly, too. I thought it had been the best birthday party I had ever had. Maybe if Grandmother Emma had come, she would have been pleasantly surprised, I thought.

On the way home Daddy wanted to stop at his supermarket to check on the night floor manager. The market was open twenty-four hours and he had three floor managers now for three different shifts. We were going to wait in the car, but he took so long, Mama got out and went in to see what was happening. When she came out with him, she didn't look happy anymore.

They both got into the car without speaking.

"When did you hire her?" Mama asked as Daddy pulled away from the market.

"Just a few weeks ago," he said.

"What qualifies her to be the manager of a supermarket, Christopher?"

"She's had a great deal of experience in

the business world. After she left Bethlehem, she ran a department store in Philadelphia for nearly a year."

"And why did she leave Philadelphia? Was she fired?"

"No, no. She hated living in the city. Why are you so disturbed about it?"

Mama looked at him, looked straight ahead and then out the side window. I didn't think she would say anything else. Both Ian and I were fixed on each and every word.

"You have to be kidding," she finally said.

Daddy was quiet until we drew closer to Grandmother Emma's house. Then he turned to Mama and said, "It's just business, nothing else, Caroline. Don't read anything into it."

"I don't care," Mama said. "Do what you want." She turned away, but I could see she was wiping some tears before they could make much of an appearance.

What had happened to make her cry?

Grandmother Emma was up in her bedroom by the time we arrived. The house was very quiet and Mama didn't look like she cared to say another word to anyone. We all went upstairs. Shortly afterward, Mama came in to wish me a happy birthday one more time. I was already in my pajamas and crawling into my bed, still thinking about how sad she had become after we had stopped at the supermarket.

"Why were you crying in the car?" I asked her.

"Adult talk, honey. Don't worry about it," she said. "Happy birthday and many, many more." She kissed my cheek, fixed the blanket, and left, switching off my light.

I really wasn't tired. I thought I would be, but my mind wouldn't stop twirling and spinning, thinking about the events of the whole exhausting day. I remembered my present from Ian and got out of bed to take it out of the toy chest. Then I went back to bed, switched on my night lamp, and slowly turned the pages. The girl in the book was older than I was. She had just had her twelfth birthday and had all sorts of questions about herself. I skipped ahead.

I couldn't help looking at the tadpoles. I wondered if females felt them swimming around inside them. How long did they swim? Where did they go if and when they missed the egg? There was so much to know. Would the book tell me everything?

A whole new world had suddenly opened in front of me just because things had happened in my body that weren't supposed to happen for a while yet, maybe for years and years.

Why did Grandmother Emma say I would break hearts and what did she mean when she told my parents to gird their loins? Would that be in the book? Why was Mama angry about a new floor manager? How could that be adult talk? Did Ian know the answers? How was I supposed to fall asleep ever again with all this bouncing about in my head?

I finally did though. The words and pictures grew fuzzier and fuzzier until I couldn't keep my eyelids from shutting. I fell asleep with the book opened and sprawled over me, which was a big mistake because Mama was in my room before I woke up and found it. I felt her lift it off me and look at it.

"Where did you get this?" she asked as I opened my eyes and sat up. "Jordan?"

Now Ian was going to be angry at me, I thought. I ruined a secret and I had made him a promise, taken an oath. He would stop caring about me again. Could I lie?

"I found it," I said.

She smirked. "Jordan, I asked you a question. I know this book was nowhere in this house. I want an honest answer."

I started to cry. "I wasn't supposed to tell

135

you," I said.

She stared, her eyes brightening. "Ian," she said. "Did he give you this? Jordan?"

My answer was written on my face.

"Why did he give you this? How did he find out about you? Did you tell him?"

"He heard about me going to see Dr. Dell'Acqua and he wanted to know why." I was determined not to tell her anything more about his research and all his "Holy schmolies." "I promised I wouldn't tell you he knew. Now he's going to be mad at me."

She thought a moment. The fear left her face and her body relaxed. Then she smiled. "It's all right. I shouldn't have kept it from him anyway. If anyone in this house is mature enough to understand what's going on, it's Ian. I'll speak to him. He won't be angry at you for telling me. In fact," she said, turning the pages and looking at the pictures and information in the book, "this was a very smart thing for him to do for you."

"It's my birthday present from him," I said.

"Your birthday present?" She looked sad again. "Yes, it's a nice birthday present, only I wish it had been years from now," she muttered.

She looked around my room and pressed

her lips together. Then she said a strange thing, whispered it as if she wasn't sure she wanted me to hear it.

"It's this house. Everything changed once we moved here."

She realized I heard her and quickly smiled again. "It's all right, honey. Everything will be all right," she said, and kissed me. "Go on and get up and dressed. There's lots to do before we leave for the lake."

I couldn't help but think about what she had said about the house. Was it true?

She left me listening for the whispering I now thought she surely heard as well.

8
THE SISTER PROJECT

Mama did talk to Ian and complimented him on his intelligent birthday present. She explained why she didn't want anyone else to know just yet. However, he wasn't entirely pleased. When he came to my room I had just finished getting dressed. As soon as he came in, I could tell from the expression on his face that he was upset with me and surely thought I had violated our oath.

"I fell asleep with the book on me," I moaned before he could utter a complaint. "Mama came into my room and found it. I didn't show it to her. She made me tell her how I got it, Ian. I swear."

He grimaced. I had still disappointed him. "You can see how important it is to always think first and act second, Jordan. I know you didn't want to break our oath, but there will still be things we'll do that I'd rather we kept secret between us. I'm making you my special project, Jordan," he added to impress me. "I'll still do other things, but you will be the most important. I will call it my Sister Project, okay?"

"Yes," I said, even though I couldn't imagine now why we should keep anything secret from Mama.

She had gone to the drugstore to get the medicine Dr. Dell'Acqua had ordered for me. It was a nasal spray and I was to use it every morning. I had to spray twice into each nostril. Mama said she would be sure to remind me and help me do it. Later, Ian came in to see what it was. He copied down the name and quickly returned to his computer to find out everything he could. A little more than an hour later, he came back into my room to report to me.

"The doctor is obviously diagnosing your condition as central precocious puberty," he said. "It just means you're having what's normal too early in your life, so don't worry about getting cancer or a heart attack or anything like that," he told me.

I hadn't even thought of those things. Could that have happened to me?

"The medicine should work. However, it won't work overnight, Jordan. Don't expect everything to change right away. In fact, you might have some side effects first. I printed out the list so I'll watch for them with you.

Did Mother tell you about that?"

I shook my head.

"She probably just didn't want to worry you," he said, and I wondered, so why was he telling me? Now I would worry.

He read my thoughts on the page of my sad and troubled face. "Don't be upset. Knowledge is never a bad thing and you can never get too much of it, Jordan. It's better people know everything they have to know about themselves. Remember, don't go blabbing everything I tell you to Mother, okay?"

"Okay." Even though our first oath had been broken, Ian didn't ask for another promise.

Then he looked at me in a strange way and said, "It's interesting that this happened to you and not to me. Very interesting. The causes of this are not really nailed down yet. As I said, some think it has to do with all the growth hormones in meat and poultry today, but I just read that the problem is occurring even with people who don't consume meat and poultry heavily in their diets. Who knows? Maybe by doing my Sister Project and studying you and keeping track of it all, I'll come up with something the medical world will appreciate."

Ian was not quite fourteen and he was

already thinking he could solve medical problems adults couldn't. Maybe he could. Maybe I was lucky to have a brother who was such a genius, I thought. I vowed to myself to keep his secrets and be grown-up about it.

My own thoughts wound around and back to what had happened between Mama and Daddy in our car on the way home from the supermarket. Ian knew so much. Perhaps he knew why Mama was so upset and why she cried about a floor manager. That still troubled me because it almost ruined my birthday and she was so upset. I asked him.

"The woman father hired for that shift was one of his old girlfriends," he said.

I had never thought of Daddy having any other girlfriend besides Mama.

"When was she his girlfriend?"

"I'm not sure," Ian said. "I didn't overhear all that much, but I did hear that much after we got home last night. I think she was one of Mother's friends once, too. We have more important things to think about," he said, looking annoyed even talking about it. "I'm going to start arranging my things and deciding what I want to take with me to the cabin. You should do the same," he told me. He thought a moment. "Give me the book I gave you. I'll put it in one of my suitcases for you so it won't be forgotten or misplaced and you'll have it up at the lake. Also, we'll be sure Nancy doesn't tell Grandmother Emma about it. The more you read on your own, the easier it will be for me to conduct my research and investigation."

I wanted to talk more about Daddy's old girlfriend even if Ian didn't. Did I know her, too? Where was she his girlfriend? At one of his colleges? In high school? Why would Mama be upset about an old girlfriend? He didn't marry her.

I wondered if having precocious puberty would someday get me past the boundary of "adult talk." If it did, it might be worth having it, I thought.

I handed the book to Ian and he left to start his packing.

Ian always liked to be organized. His clothes in his closets were perfectly arranged, even by colors. Everything in his bathroom was neatly lined up. He hated when Nancy moved things and put things in drawers he had reserved for something else. Once he locked himself in his room on the day she was to clean it and when she came there, he wouldn't answer her knocking or open up. She complained to Grandmother Emma, who told him if he didn't let

Nancy in to do her work, he would have to do his own. Nothing could have sounded better to him. He agreed and to everyone's surprise did his own vacuuming, polishing, and window washing. He looked after his own clothes, folded and even ironed his own pants. Ironically, instead of making Nancy happier to have less to do, it made her angrier and sadder. She never stopped complaining about it to Grandmother Emma. Daddy finally told him he had to let her do her work.

"We're guests in this house and we live by the rules Grandmother Emma has laid down," he told Ian. "She wants her house kept by a professional housekeeper."

Reluctantly, Ian gave in and let Nancy take care of his room and his clothes again, but he never stopped finding fault with things she did. At least at the cabin, there would be no maid and he would be in control of his own things all the time.

At first I was worried about our being at the lake so long this year. Maybe because I was younger and couldn't do much on my own, I always grew bored there quickly. The things that interested Ian didn't interest me. Mama enjoyed just sitting around and reading. Daddy met some friends and went boating or went to the clubhouse to drink and talk. I was clearly told that the boat and the club would be no place for a little girl. The men would be worried about me, worried about using bad language in front of me. At least, that was what Ian said.

Our cabin was quite large in comparison to other cabins on the lake. It had two bedrooms upstairs and one master bedroom downstairs with a loft. We had a big television set, but we couldn't get all the channels, which meant Ian couldn't watch his science and nature shows. The cabin had a large fieldstone fireplace, which we had to use or wanted to use on what were surprisingly cool nights in the summer. One summer, it rained nearly the whole time we were there and everyone hated it so much, we left early.

I had to admit Grandmother Emma was right about the stench of cigar smoke. I could smell it in the walls, just as she claimed. One of the first things Mama did when we arrived was open all the windows. They had screens on them, but the mosquitoes and other bugs still managed to find ways to get inside and buzz around our heads, especially at night. Ian told Mama what to buy to keep them at bay. We had incense burning and sprays to use. Nothing worked completely and I usually had little bites on my legs and arms. The cabin wasn't my favorite place. Maybe I was more like Grandmother Emma than I cared to admit.

So it was with mixed emotions that I greeted the morning of our trip to the lake and the mountains. My mother was in my room before I got out of bed so she could help me start using the nasal spray. She said she would keep it all and take care of it with me every morning at the cabin. I hurried to wash and dress and check my things one more time before they were to be carried out to the car.

Ian, who seemed to have a knack for visualizing things better than anyone, helped Daddy pack the car so that everything fit neatly. We had risen earlier than usual, which meant Grandmother Emma would not be at breakfast, but she came down from her bedroom just before we were about to leave.

"Mr. Pitts has seen to the electricity, gas, and phone being turned on again," she told Daddy. "He had his wife clean the place as best she could, but you know the quality of that work," she added with a scowl. "According to what Mr. Pitts tells me, the grounds have been cleaned up as well and the boat is at the dock. He says the engine has been maintained well. You'll let me know. I pay him far too much for all this as it is and I never know what he does and doesn't do anymore."

I remembered Joe Pitts, the man who looked after the property. He and his wife lived nearby in a house that looked like it might just topple over one day. Mr. Pitts took care of a few of the cabins on the lake as well. As far as I knew, they had no children and lived there year-round because they couldn't afford to live anywhere else. Grandmother Emma once said he would starve on his Social Security. I thought he looked at least as old as she was, only his gray hair was still thick and curly. He had been a redhead once and still had freckles, which looked more brown than orange to me.

"I'll call you right away, Mother," Daddy said.

"I imagine you'll need to air out the bedding, Caroline," she told Mama, who said nothing. "Everything must be stale and stuffy and stink of cigars."

"Thanks for making it sound so inviting," Mama told her.

"It was never inviting for me, but you're different."

"Yes," Mama said. She smiled as if Grandmother Emma had given her a wonderful compliment.

"Actually, your getting away under these circumstances," Grandmother Emma said, looking at me, "is probably very wise. I'm glad I can provide such an escape at this particular time for you. Perhaps there'll be some improvement of the situation before you return."

"Oh, we can hope," Mama said, and looked at Daddy. "Can we get started, Christopher, or are there more instructions yet to earn our keep?"

"I'll call you," he told Grandmother Emma, and got into the car. "You're not helping the situation by being so contentious, Caroline," he told Mama before starting the engine.

"I'm being contentious? Me? How would you describe what she's being?"

"Mother is Mother," Daddy said, as if that explained it all. "It's so easy when you just nod or tell her what she wants to hear."

I raised my eyebrows. That sounded familiar.

"Easier for you. Not for me," Mama insisted. "I'm the one she'd like surgically removed from this family."

Daddy shook his head. "Did you ever think about what you're going to have someday, Caroline? All this," he said, waving his hand at the grounds and landscaping as we drove down the driveway. "You never sound appreciative."

"I'd leave tomorrow if we could," Mama said. "This isn't a home. It's a giant echo."

"What?" Daddy smiled with confusion. I looked at Ian. He was mesmerized by their conversation. "An echo? How is all this an echo?"

"Your mother is still living in the past. Her world is long gone. She hears voices no longer there. Did you ever look at her friends and her when they gather for one of their weekly teas at the mansion? I mean, really look at them and listen to them? What am I talking about? You're never there, so you don't see it and hear it. I don't know if there's a sentence uttered that begins without a 'Remember when.'

"And all those women in their seventies, even eighties, with their plastered hair and collagen-riddled lips. They're not comical; they're farcical. Some of them are so weighted down with jewelry, they stoop. It's a wonder their spines don't snap. They're self-anointed queens who have lost their kingdoms and have to settle for ruling over desperate salesgirls and salesmen in department stores who kowtow to put food on their tables."

"Oh, come on now, Caroline. All that just sounds like envy to me."

"Envy?" Mama laughed. Then she suddenly grew serious. "Actually, you're not all wrong. I'm not so different from them, I suppose. I live in a dream, too."

Daddy didn't say anything. He glared at her and then he turned on the radio.

My stomach gurgled and I felt cramps coming. Was I making eggs again? Or was I just nervous and upset listening to Mama and Daddy argue?

Where was all this heading? Where was it taking us? Was my problem going to bring us together or help tear us apart? I looked at Ian. As usual he stared ahead with his eyes locked on his own thoughts. He traveled on roads I couldn't see. Suddenly I wished he would take me along.

The radio music didn't seem to lift the heavy silence in our car. The tension and the static that hovered over and around us in the house stuck to us, I thought. We carried it off, wore it like our clothes. I hoped the farther we went, the less and less it would be and we would suddenly burst into sunshine and leave the dreary clouds of unhappiness behind us.

"There she blows," Daddy announced when the lake first came into view. "Everybody excited?"

"No," Mama said. "Your mother always makes me feel like we're a homeless family accepting charity whenever we come up here, Christopher. Before I have a chance to even think about enjoying myself, she sucks out all the possible pleasure by reminding me just how much in debt to her we are."

Daddy smiled at her as if she had said something wonderful and pleasant.

"I'm serious!" Mama exclaimed.

"I know you are. You're just too sensitive. Try to be more like me and ignore it. Yes her to death until we get up here and forget about what she said anyway."

"I don't forget and I'm not you," Mama told him.

"Oh, c'mon, Carol. Let's try to enjoy ourselves, okay? Lately, you see only the dark side to everything."

"Maybe that's because that's all there is," Mama muttered, folded her arms, and turned away from him.

Ian, who had been reading nearly the whole trip, looked up as though he just realized someone had spoken.

"Look at those boats out there," Daddy said. "The lake's crowding up quickly this year. Lucky for all these well-to-do people nature formed it, huh, Ian?"

"Lake Wallenpaupack is a man-made lake," Ian said dryly. "It was created by the Pennsylvania Power and Light Company for hydroelectric power in 1927."

"Really? You know, I don't remember hearing about that. It's big, nevertheless."

"It's fifty-seven hundred acres, thirteen and a half miles long with fifty-two miles of shoreline."

"How do you know all that, Ian?" Daddy asked him.

"I always read up on something before I do it or visit it," Ian said.

"Very wise," Daddy said. He turned to Mama. "I don't know where he gets it from."

Mama turned back to him. "I wasn't a bad student, Christopher. I had every intention of finishing college before you swept me off my feet with sky banners full of promises."

"And they're all going to come true some-day, too," Daddy said.

"Yes, but it wasn't supposed to be depen-dent upon inheritance and as I recall, we were going to build something on our own," Mama reminded him.

Daddy laughed. He wasn't insulted. It oc-curred to me that he was like his mother in one very important way — he was as thick-skinned. Neither Grandmother Emma's criticisms and complaints about him nor Mama's really seemed to bother him. Every reprimand, every accusation, was, as Grandmother Emma once put it, "like water off a duck's back," only she claimed that made him more like his father and less like her.

I realized that whenever she spoke about Grandfather March, she seemed bitter and critical. I wondered what sort of a life they really had together or even if they had been together. Had they been in love? Why was it they only had Daddy? Was he right saying he came into this world as a result of some accident? My grandfather had died before I was old enough to really know him. Ian remembered him far better, of course, but didn't have a lot to say about him, much good that is.

What, if any, of all these characteristics and ways did I inherit? Whom would I be more like, Mama or Daddy? Grandmother Emma or Grandfather Blake? Or, and this made me wonder and think even more, Great-aunt Francis? Everything about us seemed to come directly from Daddy's side of the family. Mama's side was nowhere as flamboyant and impressive. The only one who had any real interest for me was Uncle Ormand out in Oregon, who, according to

Mama, had a clock in his room without hands to make the point that time didn't matter for him. She said he would never punch a time clock at a job or live according to a schedule, and having a family to support didn't seem to make a difference either.

We made another turn and the lake came into view again. With the sunlight spread like butter over it, the water looked as smooth as ice peppered here and there with sailboats that glided with ease in what looked to be random courses taking carefree people into dreams. It was hard, at least at the start of a vacation here, not to be drawn to it and excited by it.

"What else can you tell us about the lake, Ian?" Daddy asked.

I sensed that Ian knew Daddy wasn't really interested in the information, but liked to tease him by drawing amazing information out of him. His teachers had already agreed he functioned on a level far above his peers. They believed he could be one of those children who get admitted to and attend college before they are old enough to graduate from high school. At thirteen, he was doing senior grade math and reading books the seniors struggled to read. Everyone thought he would be either a brain surgeon or a nuclear physicist. It was second nature to him to analyze and work to understand everything in his life. Mama said he was born with the question "Why?" on his lips.

I could see that Daddy was often confused about him and even alienated from him. I sometimes caught him looking at Ian as if he was wondering if Ian was really his son. They were so different from each other. Daddy rarely did anything with him that other fathers and sons did together.

That was partly Ian's own fault. He avoided sports and never wanted to go with Daddy to ball games or watch them on television, so Daddy stopped asking him. Ian was keen about keeping himself in good health and physically fit, but not because it would make him a better athlete. It was simply the intelligent thing to do. He thought of his body as just another machine. It had to be maintained, well-oiled, and serviced regularly. To do otherwise was merely stupid. He had disdain for people who were overweight or people who smoked. He never snuck alcoholic beverages except as an experiment.

"An original survey showed that it started with a twelve-thousand-one-hundred-fifty-acre parcel transferred from the estate of

William Penn to James Wilson, who was one of only four men who signed the Declaration of Independence in 1776 and the Constitution in 1787. George Washington appointed him to the first Supreme Court."

Daddy laughed again. "I've got my own walking encyclopedia. There's nothing I can't find out."

"Except how to handle your mother," Mama muttered.

Daddy ignored her.

"You want to try to do some waterskiing this year, Ian?" Daddy asked him.

Ian looked out the window. "Not really," he said.

It was as if his words shut off a television set. Daddy's smile faded quickly and he concentrated solely on the road, making the turn into our cabin's driveway. We could see Mr. Pitts trimming some bushes in the front yard.

"Probably rushing to finish what he was supposed to have done by now," Daddy said.

"Yes, Mrs. March," Mama told him.

Finally, he glared at her angrily. "At least she knows how to take care of what belongs to her," he said. "Being wealthy requires a great deal of responsibility."

Mama looked at him but she didn't reply.

We came to a stop and Mr. Pitts walked

toward the car. "Welcome back," he called.

He didn't look much older to me, but that was probably because he always looked old to me. He was heavier, though, with a bigger belly that challenged his shirt and pants, a paint-splattered pair of blue jeans. His curly white hair was just as thick, but his nose looked thicker, redder.

Daddy got out and shook his hand and then looked around and nodded at everything with approval. Our property was wide and long with old maple and hickory trees and a thick patch of front lawn that sprawled to the ditching at the road. Ian once told me the highway department had to keep those ditches as clear and clean as they could to carry off heavy rain before it washed out the macadam. The property along this particular street was owned by wealthy people like Grandmother Emma, and there was constant attention to their needs.

The air was fresher up here in the Poconos. Behind our cabin was a thick forest full of pine trees and I could almost smell the stickiness in the cones that fell. The redolent scent cleared my nose and swirled about in my head. Birds were chattering loudly, probably reporting our arrival. I saw a rabbit hop toward us, smell the air, and then hurry away. Ian nudged me and pointed at a baby garter snake sunning near a rock. I would never have noticed it and wasn't too happy about noticing it now.

"Let's get our stuff inside," Daddy called. Mama was already sorting things out in the trunk.

"I'll help you with all that," Mr. Pitts said. "Welcome, Mrs. March," he told Mama.

"Thank you. How is Helen?"

"Oh, the same. Complaining about this ache or that. Her arthritis spreads like tree roots through her body, if you believe what she says."

"Why shouldn't you?" Mama asked him a bit sharply. Even Daddy raised his eyebrows.

"Wouldn't help if I didn't," Mr. Pitts said.

"Was she able to clean up some?" Daddy asked him.

From the way Mr. Pitts looked at him, I was afraid he had forgotten to tell his wife to do that, but he smiled.

"Oh, more than some, Mr. March. I'm sure you'll be satisfied."

"Good," Daddy said.

Mr. Pitts looked at Ian and me and smiled. "Boy, are they growing fast. Let's see now. It's Ian and . . ."

"Jordan," I said, not waiting.

"Right. You're getting as pretty as your

mother," Mr. Pitts told me. "How old are you now?"

"I'm seven."

"And Ian's . . ."

"Thirteen," Ian said. "I'll be fourteen next January."

"I remember when you were just a little bigger than a squirrel."

"Squirrels range from as little as five ounces to about three pounds. I don't imagine I was ever that small," Ian said.

"Is that so?"

"Here," Mother said, handing me my little suitcase. "Christopher, get the cabin opened."

"Oh, I done that already," Mr. Pitts said. "Opened all the windows for you yesterday. Fireplace is cleaned out. I had the chimney done this year, too. Your mother knows, I suspect, Mr. March. I sent her all the bills."

"Then she knows," Mama quipped. "Christopher, are we getting our things inside or what?"

Daddy was standing there with his hands on his hips, still turning slowly and looking over the property as if he already had title to it.

"Yeah, sure. Looks like you're taking care of things fine," he told Mr. Pitts.

Mr. Pitts smiled at him. "Thank you. Appreciate it. It's the finest cabin on the lake as far as I'm concerned."

"That it is," Daddy said, looking up at the cabin. It had a small porch with a swing seat on it and two hickory wood rockers. He glanced at Mama, who was just staring at him now, and then hurried to the bags. Ian had his two out. Mr. Pitts dug out the others and we all headed for the short, wooden stairway.

Mama stood in the doorway for a moment looking over the living room. The wooden floor had a large red and black checker wool area rug. Grandmother Emma had at least been the one to decorate and furnish the cabin in rich, rustic furnishings, including quilts on the walls, cast-iron lamps, a split log mantel, and a stairway with the steps built out of split logs, too. She included rustic leather furnishings like the grizzly bear leather chair and ottoman. The small bar had western iron bar stools with tooled leather seats. Above the family room was a large chandelier made of elk antlers, which Daddy said cost as much as all the furnishings. Apparently, Grandmother Emma agreed to the cabin only if she could decorate it her way.

Ian and I both had queen-size beds in our rooms upstairs. We had warm bedding, reversible comforters, and pillow shams. His was in hunter green and mine was light khaki with maroon. There were nightstand lamps also made of antlers and both our bedrooms had centered chandeliers that were shaped like pinecones. My windows looked out on the rear of the property and Ian's more to the north side. From the porch we could see the lake.

Somehow, this time it all looked more promising to me. Maybe it would be good for us here. Maybe we would become the family I knew Mama wanted us to be.

Was it possible?

Or was it just another dream to lose in the morning?

9
AT THE CABIN

It took two trips to get everything we brought into the house. Mama checked the refrigerator and the kitchen pantry and told Daddy we had to go shopping for food immediately. He wanted to go after we had gone to dinner, but she thought we'd be tired and not very enthusiastic about going to a supermarket.

"You're right about that, Carol. The one thing I'm not looking forward to seeing is another supermarket," he said, and groaned.

"Then I'll just go myself," she said. I offered to go with her. Ian was already outside exploring. I imagined he was hoping to find a hive of wasps or bees. Last year he had and spent all his time studying their movement and activity, writing about it in his journal and even making little drawings. He won a science project award for it in school.

Daddy quickly agreed to Mama and me going alone. He decided he would go to the dock to check on the boat with Mr. Pitts. Minutes later, my mother and I were off to shop. When we returned, Daddy was still not back and Ian was nowhere in sight either.

"Figures, neither male would be here to carry in the groceries," Mama remarked. That took us two trips, too.

I helped her put things away and then she went up to unpack her and Daddy's things and put them in closets and drawers. She said she would help me with mine, but I should get some air and look for Ian to tell him to unpack his things. I went out front and called for him a few times and then I wandered around to the rear of the cabin. Finally, I saw him coming out of the woods. He looked very excited.

"Where were you?" I asked as he walked toward me.

"I was looking for a carnivorous pitcher plant. They live on insects. I read about *Sarracenia purpurea* being found up here and went looking for some bogs. I kept walking and walking until I was on the other side of the woods and found myself in the state park. They've opened up more of it for camping and I met this girl who knows more about plants than I do. She's sixteen."

He paused. "She thinks I'm sixteen, too, so don't tell her I'm only thirteen. Her name's Flora and that's no accident. Her parents have a nursery in Albany, New York. She's not very pretty," he added, "but she knows a lot about flowers. But here's the best thing," he added, "she and her brother Addison saw a black bear yesterday. We're going to go look for it tomorrow. Addison's fifteen, but he's already six feet two. Very skinny. Flora says he grew like a weed."

I stood there with my mouth slightly open. I had never heard Ian go on and on about anyone like this.

"They're here for another few weeks," he said. "Oh," he added, "I didn't find the *Sarracenia purpurea,* but Flora says she thinks she knows where to look. She also claims to have a great butterfly collection. I didn't see it yet, but she seems to know what she's talking about."

"Mama wanted me to find you and tell you to go unpack."

"What's the rush? We're here for a while, aren't we?"

Again, I was surprised. Ian was always so concerned about being organized and set up.

"Ah, it's too late to do much more today

anyway and Flora had to go with her parents to visit someone." He started for the cabin, stopped, and then turned back to me. "By the way, Jordan, plants can be precocious, too."

"They can?"

"And there's sweet corn that's known as precocious," he added, and continued toward the house.

I ran after him.

"How come you never told me that before?" I asked him. He kept walking. "Ian?"

He stopped and looked at me. "I told Flora about you and she told me about the plants," he said, and continued walking.

"You told someone about me?" I cried. "Mama will be very upset."

"Don't worry about it," he said, continuing to walk toward the stairway. "I don't think Flora's a gossip and silly like most girls her age. And besides," he said when he reached the front step, "more important, she's like you. She had the same thing happen to her when she was about your age, so you'll want to talk to her."

He continued into the house, leaving me standing in shock and amazement until I heard Daddy call to me from the bottom of the driveway.

"How was the supermarket?" he asked,

laughing. His face looked flushed and when he drew closer, I could smell the whiskey on his breath. He had stopped at the little restaurant and bar near the dock, I thought. Mama hated it when he drank during the day. This was going to upset her and she wasn't very happy as it was.

"All right," I said.

"Everything easy to find, properly labeled, aisles wide enough, clerks helpful, checkout efficient?" he rattled off. Then he laughed again. He swayed a little as he stood there looking at me. "You feel okay, Jordan?"

"Yes," I said.

"You started your medicine, right?"

"Yes, Daddy."

"Well . . ." He paused and looked back down the driveway as if he had forgotten something. "You'll be fine," he said, ran his hand softly over my head, and walked to the steps. "Let's get inside and hear all the complaints. The quicker we let her get it all out, the better off we'll all be," he muttered.

I followed. Both Mama and Ian were in their rooms getting things organized.

"Lucy, I'm home," Daddy called from the living room, and laughed at his own imitation of the *I Love Lucy* show. Although it was on reruns, it was practically the only television show, other than sports, that he watched.

Mama stepped out on the loft. She had a mop and a pail in her hands.

"What's going on?" Daddy asked. "Why are you playing maid already?"

"Our Mr. Pitts didn't check the toilets. One apparently froze and cracked this winter. Ian used it and it leaked all over the floor."

"Damn," Daddy said. "Mother is going to be fit to be tied."

"Mother? What about me, Christopher? I'm the one doing the mop-up or hadn't you noticed?"

"I'll call him right away and get him to install a new toilet immediately," Daddy promised. The news sobered him quickly.

"Good," Mama said.

"Where do you want to eat tonight? The Italian place or the Beehive or what?"

"I don't care at the moment. Whatever," Mama said. "Jordan, get up here and start putting your things away."

"Welcome to your summer," Daddy whispered in my direction, but the way his eyes rolled, I wasn't sure if he meant it for me or for himself.

Afterward, while we were having our dinner at the Beehive, Mr. Pitts installed a new toilet. He was waiting for us when we returned to tell us he couldn't imagine why the old one had cracked.

"I'm just surprised neither you nor Mrs. Pitts noticed," Mama said.

"It had to just happen recently." He looked at Daddy.

"Sure, that could happen," Daddy said. "It's no one's fault," he added

"I checked every other fixture, faucet, everything," he told Daddy. "Nothing else has a problem. Sorry about this mess, Mrs. March. If you want, I'll have Helen over here tomorrow to redo the bathroom."

"It's done," Mama said. "Forget about it."

"Sorry," he said again. He handed Daddy the bill for the new toilet and left.

"I'll just take care of this myself," Daddy said. "No need to bother my mother about it, now that I think of it."

"That's a good idea, Christopher," Mama said. "No need to bother your mother."

"Really, Caroline, she'll just take it out on Mr. Pitts. Why should we get him into trouble over something like this?"

She looked at him in the strangest way, I thought.

"Well, at least I'm happy you're protecting someone from your mother," she said.

Daddy just laughed and went into the living room to watch the end of a baseball game.

Ian came to my room and gave me my birthday present book. "After breakfast, we're going to hook up with Flora and Addison," he said. "Morning's the best time to catch sight of the black bear."

I wasn't too happy about surprising a bear in the woods, but Ian assured me that if we kept our distance, we'd be fine and it would be an experience I would not soon forget.

"It'll be interesting watching it for a while and then we'll go looking for some carnivorous plants. You can talk to Flora. She won't mind questions, but don't let her brother hear any of it," he advised. "He's a bit of a dork."

"What's a dork?"

"Goofy. You'll see," Ian said.

"How did you learn so much about them so fast?" I asked him.

"People reveal themselves very quickly to you if you're observant."

"What's that mean?"

"You listen to how they talk, carefully watch what they do, how they act, their facial expressions, everything," he explained, a little impatient with me. "Just don't be oblivious."

"I don't know what oblivious means, Ian."

"Jordan, for now, take my word for every-thing, will you? It will save time," he added, returning to his usual impatience when it came to talking to me. "I'm setting up my stuff."

He left to arrange his microscope and his computer equipment in his room. Mama came in soon afterward and placed my medicine on my dresser.

"I'll come in every morning as soon as I'm up and make sure you do it," she told me. She looked around the room. "Is every-thing okay in here?"

"Yes, Mama."

She smiled. "We'll have a good time here despite the rocky start," she promised. "Any problems, cramps, anything?"

I shook my head. Could the medicine have already begun to work?

"Okay." She glanced at the book Ian had given me. It was on the table by my bed. A wave of sadness washed over her face and then she sighed, shook her head, and forced a smile. "Don't forget to brush your teeth," she said, and left.

I guess I was more tired than I had thought because I fell asleep very quickly that first night in the cabin, and if I had any dreams, bad or otherwise, I didn't remem-ber them. As she promised, Mama was right there when I woke up to give me my medicine and make sure I took it correctly. At breakfast Daddy asked Ian to go with him to try out the boat, but Ian was determined to meet Flora and Addison.

"How can you not want to go in the boat, Ian? If you don't want to waterski, there must be interesting things to see on the lake, too, at least."

"Next time," Ian said. "I met some kids and we're going to look for carnivorous plants." Wisely, he said nothing about the bear.

"Carnivorous plants?" Daddy looked at me and Mama. "What about you two?"

"Sure," Mama said. "We'll go. Right, Jordan?"

"I wanted to go with Ian," I said.

It took Mama by surprise. She looked at Ian. She knew he wasn't fond of me tagging along on his nature expeditions. "What does Ian have to say about that?"

Ian shrugged. "She should meet some kids, too," he replied.

"I don't know if I want her wandering about just yet," Mama said.

"Oh, let them be, Carol. They're kids. Wandering about, meeting other kids, makes it fun for them to be here."

Mama looked worried, but Ian promised

not to wander ten feet from me and not to go terribly far from the property, whatever that meant.

"You're always saying he's more responsible than I am," Daddy told her. "So what are you worried about?"

"Being more responsible than you, Christopher, isn't very much," Mama told him. He laughed.

"Do you hear how your mother constantly tears me down, kids?"

"I have a good tutor," Mama said. Daddy shook his head at her, sipped some coffee, and then went up to dress for his boat ride.

"You two better promise you don't get into any trouble," Mama told us. "I'll be back for lunch." She followed Daddy upstairs.

"If we see the bear, don't mention it to them," Ian told me. "They wouldn't understand. Okay?"

"Okay," I said. Secrets were being wound around me like rope. Soon I wouldn't be able to move.

"Put on your oldest shoes. We might step through some mud and water."

Excited, I ran upstairs to finish dressing, too. We left before Mama and Daddy went to the boat. She called her warnings after us as we walked around the cabin and headed for the woods.

"If the weather changes, come right home," she added.

Ian said there was no chance of that. It was going to be a very sunny day with barely a ribbon of clouds in the distant horizon.

As we traipsed through the forest, Ian pointed out things, insects, plants, and a rabbit, which he called a herbivorous mammal. "There's a difference between rabbits and hares," he said.

"Hairs?"

"Hares, H-A-R-E-S. Hares are larger with longer ears and legs and their young are born furred and open-eyed. Rabbits are born blind. They are mainly nocturnal, which means they're out and about in the dark more. Both rabbits and hares excrete soft pellets."

"Excrete?"

He stopped. "Make, Jordan. Go to the bathroom."

"Oh."

"Then they eat it."

"Oh, poo," I said, grimacing.

"And then they drop it out of them again in a dry pellet. Both rabbits and hares are famous for how quicky they breed new rabbits. They do it in about thirty days. People take nine months. Rabbits usually drop

172

about five to eight in a litter."

"Babies?"

"That's right." He paused and looked at me. "I wonder if instances of precocious puberty occur in lower animals, like rabbits. I'll have to do some research on that."

We walked on with me trailing behind him and occasionally hearing him throw off some information. I was back to thinking about myself, however. I remembered Daddy asking Mama if I could have a baby. She wouldn't talk about it. Could I? Would I have one or many more like a rabbit? Did precocious puberty mean it could happen in less than nine months? Every day there seemed to be more and more questions to be answered about myself.

"Hurry up," Ian called. Because I was in such deep thought, I fell too far behind him.

A little while later, we stepped into a clear field and I saw the campers and recreational vehicles. A tall boy to the right of one vehicle was throwing rocks at birds.

"Addison," Ian called.

The boy stopped and looked our way. "Hey," he called back, but continued to throw rocks.

The door of the RV opened and a heavy girl not much taller than I was stepped out. Her light brown hair was chopped short in a crude pageboy. She wore a gray athletic shirt and jeans that hung loosely off her wide hips. As we drew closer, I saw she had acne over her chin and cheeks. Her eyes were a vague blue, but lost in her round face because her cheeks were so plump. She had thick lips, too.

"Hi, Flora," Ian said. He addressed her with as much excitement as I had ever heard him address anyone.

Why did he like this girl so much?

Her brother stood smiling at us. He had a long, beaklike nose, thinner lips, and a very sharp jawbone. His clothes, a pale gray T-shirt and jeans, seemed to just hang on his frame. He had long arms and very long fingers, and clutched another rock in his right hand.

"I nearly got one," he said.

Flora smirked at him. "Their eyesight is so much keener than ours, Addison. You'll never surprise them with a rock. Give it up."

"I nearly got one," he repeated.

Flora looked at me. "You're Jordan, then," she said.

"Yes, I'm Jordan."

She studied me a moment, just the way Ian did from time to time, and then she turned to him. "There's a creek about a hundred yards north. We follow that and it will bring us to that small patch of wild berries I was telling you about."

"Great."

She showed him her small camera. "It has a five-to-one zoom, so we could get some good shots without getting that close."

"Let's go," Ian said anxiously.

Flora looked at Addison. "If you come along, Addison, you have to be quiet. No whistling and singing stupid dirty songs to impress anyone, okay?"

"Whatever," he said, and tossed his rock at a pair of sparrows that lifted off the branch the moment he threw it. He looked at me. "I nearly got one before," he said.

Flora and Ian started away and I hurried to stay close to them. Addison trailed behind like someone not sure he was going to accompany us. Something attracted his attention and he went off to the right for a moment and then, when I looked back, I saw him resume following us.

Flora and Ian were already in a discussion about something called indigenous plant life.

I was beginning to wish I had gone with Mama and Daddy on the boat.

Then Flora fell back to walk alongside me. "I understand you had your first period already," she said.

Ian didn't turn back even though he must have heard what she had said. I glanced at Addison. He was five or so yards behind us, still tossing rocks.

"Yes," I said.

"You could have an orgasm, you know," she said. "Sometimes it just happens, even when you're sleeping, and sometimes, you can't help but bring it on yourself. It's better you know all about it so nothing frightens you. I don't imagine your mother will tell you about it. Mine didn't."

Despite what she said, it sounded frightening. "Does it hurt?" I asked her.

She shook her head. "On the contrary," she said. "You're going to like it. Some girls like it so much, they're like rabbits," she told me.

My eyes could have been on springs. That was how much I felt they had bulged.

She laughed. "Don't worry," she said. "I'll clue you in on it all. Hey," she called to Ian, "go to the left up here. The stream is just ahead." She ran to join up with him.

Addison drew alongside me and nudged me. "My sister thinks she knows everything," he said.

Oh no, I thought, he heard what we were talking about and Ian had warned me not to let him hear anything.

Then he leaned down to whisper in my ear. "But I'm sure I just hit one."

We walked on, my heart feeling like it was flapping as quickly as the birds that fled Addison's rocks.

10
A Flood of Hormones

We reached the wild berry patch about ten minutes later. I thought we had gone much farther from our cabin than Mama would have wanted us to go, but Ian seemed completely unconcerned. He and Flora decided on a place to hide behind a very big, old maple tree where there was a carpet of thick moss. We were to wait to see if the black bear would appear to feast on the berries. Addison stood behind us, obviously deciding if it was worth it to remain. He looked very bored. He held another rock in his hand and juggled it as he eyed some birds flitting from branch to branch.

Flora frightened him and me, too, for that matter, when she told him if he threw rocks or made too much noise or moved around too much, it might rile the bear.

"It could be right around here, Addison, and it will come after you. Bears, even though they are big and heavy, move very quickly. They can climb trees, too, so you can't escape that way."

Addison said nothing, but when I looked back a few moments later, he was gone.

Ian laughed. "Good work, Flora, although black bears are nowhere as dangerous as you made them sound. They're not like grizzly bears."

"I know," she said, "but I really wanted to get rid of him. He would just be annoying and," she added, looking at me, "Jordan and I couldn't talk in front of him."

"Right," Ian said, and turned to look at the berry patch.

Flora slid herself back to sit beside me. "Tell me how it all happened to you first," she said.

"I don't know how," I said. I wasn't sure what she meant. Ian turned around and looked annoyed at my answer.

"You noticed your breasts developing," she prompted. "You saw hair appear. What did you do about it?"

"Nothing."

"Did you tell your mother right away or what?"

I described how Mama found out. Flora was amused at Mama's reaction. I didn't think she should be laughing at her.

"She was very worried," I said.

179

"Sure she was and that was good. She should have been. When it began to happen to me, I told my mother right away," she said. "And you know what she said?"

I shook my head. How would I know?

"She said, 'So?' Then she went back to making her meat loaf. When I had stomach cramps and got my period, I was in school and my teacher rushed me to the school nurse. I told her what had been happening to me and she then called my mother.

"Who then," she added, raising her voice a bit, "was annoyed at me for not telling her first. I reminded her that I had told her, but she didn't remember. Addison is more like my mother than I am," she added.

Ian looked back at her and smiled. "I agree," he said.

"Ian's met my mother. The first thing she did was offer him a peanut butter sandwich. Sometimes, she has that for breakfast, along with a ton of other food. When you see her, you'll understand why I am not exactly Paris Hilton."

"Who?"

"Thin," she said. "I inherited a proclivity toward fat cells."

I stared at her. What was she talking about? Why did she think I knew that word? What was a fat cell? She was just like Ian, always assuming I lived in a dictionary, too.

He saw the confusion on my face. "She means a tendency toward gaining weight. She has a slow metabolism."

"It's so slow I'm still catching up with my baby food," Flora said, and she and Ian laughed, but quietly, always worried about the bear.

What did metabolism mean? It was like being in quicksand. The more they explained, the deeper I sank. Sitting between them, I felt like a foreigner who barely spoke English and wasn't sure what she should do or say next. I decided not to ask any questions.

"Actually, precocious puberty can lead to obesity."

Ian nodded.

"I think I heard something," he said.

They were both so quiet now, studying the woods and searching for signs of the bear I secretly hoped would never come. I thought that was the end of it, and that Flora had lost interest in me, but I was wrong.

"Anyway," she suddenly continued, "one of the older girls at our school, Toby Whitfield, worked in the nurse's office helping her secretary. It was part of a program for honor students who didn't need to sit quietly in study halls and who were thought mature enough to handle such duties."

"We have a similar program at our school," Ian said. "I'll probably join it next year."

I had no idea what he was talking about, and I was sure neither Mama nor Daddy knew either, but I didn't say anything.

"Toby Bitchfield," Flora continued, which brought a smile to Ian's face, "overheard the nurse's conversation with my mother and snuck a view of the nurse's notes about me. She told some of her friends who told some of their friends and before long, older girls were teasing me in the halls and in the bathroom whenever they found me there. They nicknamed me Miss Puberty. I tried to ignore them, but they started to tell boys as well."

Ian looked at her, nodded as if he had been there, and then looked out at the woods again.

"Soon, the parents of my classmates found out about me and then it was as if I had the plague. I wasn't invited to any parties and girls who used to pal around with me avoided me. It wasn't that they thought what I had was catching. They were afraid I would corrupt them with sex talk, which was ridiculous because I knew nothing more than they did. It got so I hated going to school."

She paused and shook her head. "I feel sorry for you. I'm sure when you get back to school in September, all your friends will have been told about you."

"No they won't," Ian said. "We haven't spoken to anyone about her."

"It doesn't matter. News gets out. Maybe there'll be someone in the nurse's office at her school who'll find out."

I looked at Ian. This was terrible. No one would want to be my friend? I wouldn't be invited to any parties?

"It won't happen," he insisted.

"Sure. Dream on."

"Don't tell her that," he said more sternly.

She shrugged. "Whatever. Anyway, I complained to my mother about what was happening to me at school and her response was, 'What can I do? Just ignore them and they'll go away eventually.' She wasn't all wrong. It's true they get bored teasing someone, but they never go away. I was taking medicine like you are, but it wasn't helping as much or as quickly as I had hoped. Everyone's different, so don't think that will be the way with you, too," she added quickly.

"Absolutely," Ian confirmed. "She already

knows there are different possible causes and that could make for a variety of prognoses."

"That's true," Flora said. "The latest article in the medical journal confirmed that. You take the medicine until you reach an age for normal puberty. It's like holding back a flood," she added, and laughed. "A flood of hormones."

They made me feel like I was sitting in Dr. Dell'Acqua's office again. I was beginning to wish I had gone off with Addison. They stopped talking and I thought finally, this is the end of it, but Flora nudged me so I would look at her.

"Unfortunately for me or fortunately, depending on how you look at it, I suppose, I eventually attracted the attention of an older girl, Qwen Edwards. I caught her watching me from time to time and finally, one day when I left school to walk home, she followed me and caught up with me after a few blocks. She stepped up beside me and bumped me with her hip so I stopped. 'I heard what happened to you,' she said. I wasn't sure if she meant my condition or what Toby had done. 'You have an orgasm yet?' she asked me, and like you, I didn't know if that was like having heart failure or what. I just shook my head and kept walking, but she stayed right beside me."

"What did she look like?" Ian asked. I didn't see how that mattered, but Flora smiled at him with understanding.

"Not what you're expecting. She was tall, slim, with an attractive figure and face. Let's just say her chances of becoming Miss New York were pretty good."

"Really?" Ian said, now looking more interested himself.

"You can't judge a book by its cover," Flora said. "Poison ivy is a good example."

Ian laughed.

"Anyway, Qwen continued to walk beside me and then told me if it happened to me without warning, I would be so frightened by it, I could drop dead. She claimed that almost happened to her. She was so much older than I was and as far as I knew, a big shot. I didn't run away from her and was actually a little flattered that she was taking any interest in me at all."

"Maybe you shouldn't be telling Jordan this story," Ian suddenly said, a look of concern washing over his face.

Flora smiled. "Hey, she's gotta learn about these things."

Why was Ian so worried for me? Why didn't I understand any of this? Why did it still seem like they were speaking in another language only the two of them understood? What did this story she was telling have to do with me anyway?

"Her house was just a block and a half off the route to mine. She invited me to come with her, promising to tell me more about this orgasm thing. An older girl was asking me to her house. That was very impressive and tempting. I knew I had to get home to do my chores at the nursery, but I went anyway.

"There was no one at home at her house. She was an only child and both her parents were at work. She took me to her room and started asking me more questions about my precocious puberty. Then she went to her closet and pulled a jewelry box out from under her shoe rack, unlocked it, and took out something she called a vibrator."

"Flora," Ian said, his voice full of warning. His face took on a crimson shade very quickly, too.

"Relax," Flora said, and turned back to me quickly. "When she described what she did with it, the whole idea was terrifying. She offered to demonstrate and did. A tow truck couldn't drag me out of that room after that."

"You don't have to go into the nitty-gritty

details about it," Ian said.

Flora smiled at him. "Sure. I know you boys just love hearing such things."

"Not me," he said firmly.

I was beginning to get very annoyed. This whole conversation seemed to be more for them than for me and I still didn't understand where it was going or why Flora was even telling me about it. I began to think seriously about getting up and running back to the cabin. I was a little unsure of the direction, so I hesitated.

"She talked me into trying it, coaxing and guiding me until I lay back on her bed and did what she instructed. At first I felt silly, of course, and still a little frightened, thinking I would hurt myself, but then —"

"Flora!" Ian practically shouted. She smiled at him and turned back to me as though she was going to leave him out of the rest of the story.

"I felt myself get wet and my pelvis tingled. There was a wave of excitement, a rippling between my legs that made me feel like my whole body had turned to jelly or something. I wanted to stop but I couldn't and she was doing more than urging me on. She had her hand on my hand. When I looked at her face, I saw she was enjoying it as much as I was or even more."

"That's enough," Ian said.

"Okay, okay. Relax. Afterward, I practically ran all the way home. My parents were so busy they didn't notice how late I was, and of course, I never told anyone about it. Matter of fact," she said, pausing and nodding, "I haven't told anyone until now."

"We're flattered," Ian said dryly, and she laughed.

"Qwen tried to get me to come back to her house with her a few more times, but I wouldn't do it. That, my dear Jordan, was my introduction to sex."

Sex? I thought. That's sex? How can babies come from something like that?

"That's not going to happen to my sister," Ian said. He looked angry about it, but it still gave me a good feeling to hear him sound protective.

Flora laughed. "You never know what's going to happen to anyone," she said. "You're not with her all the time."

"It's not going to happen to her that way," Ian insisted.

I thought they might get into a real argument about it, but Flora simply shrugged and looked out at the berry patch. I still didn't know what it was all about or understand what exactly had happened to her in that older girl's bedroom. Her body turned to jelly? She was frightened, but couldn't stop? Qwen was enjoying it more than she was? Enjoying what? What was strange about it all was that even though I didn't understand, my heart was pounding.

I saw Ian staring at me in a strange way. His eyes shifted back to Flora. He still looked angry and upset. Then he turned completely to stare at the berry patch. Flora adjusted her camera. We were all very quiet. My mind was in turmoil, my body a kaleidoscope of emotions and feelings. I really wanted to go back to the cabin and be near Mama. I thought I even whimpered, but neither of them looked at me. There was some rustling in a bush. Ian reached back to touch Flora and they both moved closer to the tree. I held my breath and then the black bear appeared.

When it paused and sniffed the air, both Flora and Ian suddenly froze and looked like they were holding their breath, too. The bear turned to the berries and squatted to pick and eat them. I was fascinated, but so frightened, I broke out in a cold sweat. The bear stopped and turned to look our way.

"He knows we're here," Flora whispered. She chanced clicking a picture and then another. "Don't move," she warned me.

The bear decided not to bother with us

and returned to its feast. It moved farther away in the berry patch.

"Beautiful," Ian said. "I've never been as close to one before except for the zoo, of course."

"I think we should get going," Flora suggested. "Don't look a gift bear in the mouth."

Ian laughed and then they crawled back and we all stood up and moved quickly toward the path we had followed. My heart was still pounding so hard I thought I would lose my breath as I did when I ran and ran. Ian reached for my hand to pull me along with them and we eventually did break out into a jog until we reached the field and saw the campers.

"You'd better be sure to keep this secret, Jordan," Ian warned me. "Mother finds out where I took you and I'm a goner."

"I won't tell," I said.

"C'mon to my camper," Flora said. "I'll make you a peanut butter sandwich."

"We have to go home for lunch," I reminded Ian.

"She's right," he said.

"I thought you wanted to see my butterfly collection."

"Yes, I did," Ian said.

"So. That won't take long. And," she said,

"I have something to give Jordan." She smiled at me and reached for my hand. She held it so tightly, I couldn't run off if I wanted.

I saw Addison had joined three other boys who looked much younger. They were off to our right in a parking lot hitting rocks with sticks toward the woods.

"It doesn't take much to amuse Addison," Flora said.

Before we reached her camper, the door opened and a heavy woman with dark brown hair chopped short around her ears stepped out. It looked like it had been hacked with a hatchet. She waved a tablecloth in the air to disperse crumbs or something. She was wearing a pair of jeans and the faded gray top of a sweat suit and looked like an older and larger version of Flora. Her heavy bosom rolled about like globs of putty beneath her top as she shook the tablecloth more vigorously. Finally, she saw us and stopped.

"Who do we have here?" she asked Flora while she looked at me.

It wasn't difficult to see the resemblances in their faces. They had the same smile, twisting their thick lips crookedly. She folded the tablecloth as we drew closer.

"This is Ian's sister," Flora replied. "Jordan."

"Hello, dear," Flora's mother said, still holding on to her smile. "Your father's gone fishing," she told Flora. "I'm going to meet him down at the pier restaurant for lunch. I have all sorts of cold cuts, potato salad, fresh rye bread, and a chocolate layer cake for you and Addison. You can invite your new friends, too," she said. "Just don't mess up the mess," she added, and laughed. She went inside.

"That's my mother," Flora said. "My father is six feet two and only one hundred and forty pounds. My mother says a brisk wind will blow through him. I call them Night and Day," she added.

"We'd better go home, Ian," I repeated. "Mama will be very angry."

He looked at his watch. "I would like to see the collection and we have at least an hour," he told me. "You want to go back, go."

I looked at the woods.

"The bear could have come around and might be in there," Flora said.

"That's possible," Ian said.

I knew they were just trying to frighten me, but even though I knew it, I was still afraid.

Flora's mother emerged again and went down the small stairway. She waved at us and continued to her right to walk out of the campground and down to the lake. Her hips were so big, she looked like she waddled instead of walked.

"C'mon," Flora said, and we went into the camper.

The first thing that I noticed was the odor. It smelled like burnt toast. There was a very small kitchen to our left and a table just to our right, now covered with the tablecloth Flora's mother had shaken out a few minutes ago. The dishes from breakfast and maybe from dinner the night before as well were still piled in the sink.

The camper had a small living room and down a hallway after that two bedrooms with the bigger one being at the very end. Flora explained that Addison slept on the pullout sofa and she had the other bedroom.

"My father keeps promising to get us a cabin up here one day, too, but I'm not holding my breath," Flora said.

She led us to her bedroom. It was really just a double bed with built-in dressers. The bed wasn't made neatly. The blanket had been folded back unevenly and the top sheet hung down on one side. There were magazines and books on the floor. She went to one of the dressers and opened the bottom drawer to take out what looked like a big album.

"This is it," she told Ian, and sat on the bed. She opened it on her lap and I saw butterflies in little plastic bags stuck to the pages. "I have five swallowtails on this page," she began, and pointed as she identified them: "A pipevine, zebra, black, eastern tiger, and a spicebush.

"On this page I have the fritillaries. Here I have the northern metalmark and here," she said, turning another page, "I have three checkerspots.

"When we were in Florida last year, I got three sulphurs and this great purple hairstreak."

"Fantastic," Ian said.

I thought they were pretty, but I felt sorry for them trapped in little bags. Did they die in the bags or before?

"I'm getting a danaid from Hong Kong. Should be here in a few weeks," she told Ian.

"Why are you collecting them?" I asked, and she looked up at me as if I was the dumbest person on earth.

"They're beautiful to look at, aren't they?"

"Yes."

She looked at Ian. "Do you know that

Japanese haiku about the butterfly?"

"Which one? There are a number of them," he said.

"What's a haiku?" I asked.

"A poem, a three-line poem," Flora said. "I'm in advanced English class," she bragged.

"You don't have to be in advanced English to know that," Ian said.

"The poem I'm thinking of goes, 'A butterfly died on the water. He thought he died on the moon.' "

"How could he die on the moon if he died on the water?" I asked.

"The moon's reflection on the water," Ian said.

"Do butterflies think?" I asked, looking at them in the plastic bags.

"Not like us, but butterflies are a wonder in nature, Jordan. They start as caterpillars, you know."

I looked at Ian. I had forgotten that and I remembered now how interested he was in caterpillars and what he had taught me about them.

"They live to consume, eat. They're always hungry. Finally, they die, in a way. They form a chrysalis, pupa. It looks like a tiny leather pouch under a leaf. Inside it, the caterpillar is changing, metamorphosing into a butterfly. They actually go through four stages of life, an egg, a caterpillar, pupa, and then finally, the beautiful butterfly."

"Egg?" I said.

"Yes. We begin as eggs, too."

"I know."

"Good. Then we're just like caterpillars, cute or ugly but just eating and sleeping until we hit puberty," she said, and my eyes widened. "Through puberty we mature. A little girl becomes a woman. Imagine when the butterfly comes to life and looks at itself. Its own body is probably the most fascinating thing in the world, just as ours becomes to us."

"We don't know that they look at themselves," Ian said. "Aside from *Homo sapiens,* I know that only capuchin monkeys have a self-image."

"Imagine that they do," Flora said, impatient with him. "It's how a teacher might explain it to her."

"Is that what you want to be, a teacher?" Ian asked her.

Flora shrugged. "I don't know what I'll be. I'm still metamorphosing," she said. Then she looked at me again. "You're coming out of the pupa, Jordan. Early, but nevertheless, you're coming out. They might be able to stop you for a while with the medicine, but you're getting a taste of what it will be nevertheless. I hope it's easier for you than it was for me. I might be able to help a little."

She paused and went to another drawer, took out some of her clothes, and then brought out a cloth bag tightly tied with a cord.

"What's that?" Ian asked nervously.

"Something she can have if you want her to," she said, and slowly opened the bag.

"Hell no!" Ian said when she took out what looked like a toy rocket.

Flora shrugged. "She gave it to me. I left that out of the story about Qwen and me. You sure?"

"Of course I'm sure."

She put it back into the bag and tightened the cord again. "Whatever," she said, and looked at me. "Whether your brother likes it or not, Jordan, one way or another you're going to be a butterfly. And the medicine you take won't stop you from knowing what it's like."

11

THE CATERPILLAR
AND THE BUTTERFLY

Ian was strangely quiet all the way home. In fact, he looked angry, angrier than I had ever seen him. At one point, he stopped walking but he didn't speak. He just stood there staring at the ground.

"What's wrong?" I asked. Mama was surely home by now and waiting for us.

"Forget about them," he said, waving in the direction of the campers.

"Who?"

"Flora and Addison. Forget about them. Promise never, never to talk about what she showed you in her room or what she told you in the woods. It would be worse than sneaking a peek at the bear," he said. "You hear me, Jordan?"

"Yes," I said. He was frightening me with his furious eyes firing up like hot coals.

"Okay, good."

"You're not going to be friends with her anymore?" I asked him as we continued.

"I wasn't friends with her before," he said. "She was a curiosity. That's all."

What did that mean? I was back in his dictionary, swimming aimlessly. "But you wanted her to talk to me, Ian. You told me."

"I know what I told you. I thought she was going to help you understand your condition, explain the physiological aspects, what things to expect emotionally and psychologically, and not tell some lurid story instead. Imagine her keeping that thing in her dresser drawer, bringing it along on their trip. She's probably done using it and she wanted to give it to you," he muttered, more to himself than to me.

He walked faster, so fast in fact, I had to run to keep up.

"Why did she say I would become a butterfly and the medicine wouldn't stop me from knowing it?"

He kept walking.

"What did she mean, Ian?"

"I told you to forget about her," he said, stopping. "I made a mistake about her. Forget about everything she said."

It was easy for him to forget, I thought, but not for me.

We walked on in silence.

Mama was home when we arrived. She was getting ready to make us toasted cheese sandwiches. "Where were you two?" she demanded as soon as we entered the cabin. "I went back there and called for you as soon as I returned from the lake. I nearly got hoarse shouting at the woods."

Ian glanced at me and then stepped forward quickly. "We must have been just out of hearing range, Mother. I discovered some *Sarracenia purpurea,*" he told her.

"What? Oh, never mind," she said, waving at us. "Just go wash up for lunch."

"Where's Daddy?" I asked.

"He's off with his boat buddies. I'm so glad he's come up here to spend some quality time with his family," she added dryly.

Ian nudged me to follow him to the bathroom. "She's in a pretty bad mood," he said. "Don't even suggest where we were or what we saw."

"Why is she in a bad mood? I thought she wanted to be here."

He wiped his hands on the towel and looked at me with an expression on his face similar to the one Mama often had while she was deciding whether or not to tell me anything. I started to wash my hands.

"Our parents aren't exactly the loving couple they were when they first met," he said.

"What does that mean, Ian?"

"They argue a lot. Haven't you noticed?"

Of course I had, but I didn't sit around thinking about it as much as Ian obviously did.

"Our mother sees it as a case of false advertising," he said. "Promises were made and never realized. There's a lot of shattered glass around her, around them both, so tiptoe when you walk near them."

"Where's shattered glass? Tiptoe? I don't understand you," I said. I was about to cry, too.

"Don't worry about it," he said quickly. "It's not important at the moment. Just keep your mouth shut about you know what," he said, and left the bathroom.

Mama had our sandwiches ready and made some chocolate milk, too. She put a bowl of fresh fruit on the table. Everything she did, she did fast and abruptly, nearly shattering the dishes and glasses when she placed them on the table, and nearly tearing off the faucets when she turned them on and off.

"Aren't you eating any lunch, Mama?" I asked.

She had her back to us and looked like she was mumbling to herself over the sink. She didn't answer. Ian shook his head at me and started to eat his sandwich. Mama paused and with her back to us, wiped her eyes. Then she turned around and smiled. It was like the sun coming out after a terrible dark rain.

"What do you say we all go to the Claws 'n' Paws Wild Animal Park this afternoon? I'm sure you'll find it interesting, Ian. They have tigers and panthers, as well as giraffes, as well as all sorts of exotic birds. You can see black bears, too," she added.

"That will be great," Ian said quickly. "I remember we were there once about five years ago. I'm sure Jordan doesn't remember any of it," he added, eyeing me.

I shook my head.

"Good. If the weather is nice, I thought we'd all go horseback riding tomorrow. I'll call and make a reservation for us. You'd like that, wouldn't you, Jordan?"

"Yes, Mama."

"Look at all the things we can do together," she added. She sounded happy, but she looked like she was going to cry when she placed the pamphlets on the table. Besides the riding academy, there were descriptions of art galleries, museums, wildlife sanctuaries, an Audubon festival, and the Carousel Water and Fun Park.

"Is Daddy going with us to the animal park?" I asked.

"I wouldn't hold my breath," she said, and turned to the counter to pour herself a cup of coffee.

She faced us while she sipped it, but she seemed to be looking through us. I looked at Ian. His eyes told me not to ask any more questions about Daddy.

"We're going to have a good time here," she suddenly said. "Damn it, we're going to enjoy ourselves."

She smiled at me again and then began to clean up the kitchen. Afterward, the three of us got into the car and headed for the animal park. Ian brought his camera. Daddy hadn't come back to the cabin. When I asked Mama if he would know where we had gone, she said, "He'll figure it out somehow." Ian poked me and that was all we said about Daddy.

There were wonderful exhibits at the animal park and we did enjoy ourselves. My favorites were the capuchin monkeys and the beautiful parrots. Ian was intrigued with the alligators and the snakes, especially the boa constrictor. He knew a lot about reptiles, even more than the guides, it seemed, and added information for us on our way home. I had the feeling he was talking continually to keep Mama from thinking about Daddy.

I truly expected him to be watching television and waiting for us when we arrived, but he was nowhere in sight. Mama began to prepare our dinner. I helped her by peeling the potatoes and cooking the string beans. She was doing some chicken cutlets for us. She liked to cook and missed doing it after we went to live with Grandmother Emma. I set the table for four. The whole time Ian was in his room writing in his journal. As the clock ticked on, I kept waiting for Daddy to appear. I was afraid to ask about him, afraid it might start Mama crying. Finally, the phone rang and I could hear from the conversation that it was Daddy.

"What do you expect me to do, Christopher, throw out all the food I've prepared? How was I supposed to read your mind from this distance when I can't when I'm right next to you?" she asked.

She listened and sighed and shook her head and turned to me with her eyes big. "Okay, Christopher. Okay," she said in a tired voice. "I'll feed the children first."

She hung up and returned to the kitchen. "Your father has made arrangements for me to join him and another couple for dinner at the Boat House," she said. "And from the way he sounds, he wouldn't be able to make it back here for dinner anyway. Ian!"

she shouted.

He came out and she told him, too.

"You two just stay in and around the cabin."

She served the chicken cutlets and then, while we were eating, went up to dress for dinner. I knew she hated rushing herself and wasn't happy about it. We were still eating when she came down.

"Clean up the best you can," she told us. "I don't expect us to be late, but just in case, be sure you get to bed by ten, Jordan. See that she does, Ian."

"No problem," he told her. "Have a good time."

She smirked, kissed us both, and left.

Ian continued to eat quietly. Why wasn't he as upset as I was? I wondered.

"I think Daddy drank too much again," I said.

"Very likely," he said, nodding.

"Mama was not happy."

He continued to nod and then he said, "Shattered glass."

We cleaned up the kitchen and put away our dishes. Afterward, Ian returned to his room and I watched television. I almost fell asleep on the sofa, but just before my eyes closed completely, I heard a tapping on the living room window. It took me a few moments to realize what it was. Flora was standing there and beckoning to me.

I looked toward Ian's room to see if he heard, too, but he didn't appear. Flora beckoned harder and made a face. What did she want? I rose and then hesitated. Shouldn't I tell Ian? I wondered. She tapped again on the window. I went to the door and unlocked it and stepped out on the porch. She came around and looked up at me.

"Where's Ian?" she asked.

"He's in his room working," I said.

"Working? What kind of work does he do?"

"He does writing and reading and projects."

"Your brother is a real character," she said. "I think he overreacted a bit in my room today."

"No, he didn't," I said in defense of him, even though I wasn't quite sure what she meant.

"Believe me, he did. But I understand why. Despite how smart he is, he's immature."

"Ian's not immature!" I said.

"Relax. It's not a crime to be immature. Does he have a girlfriend? Well?" she asked when I didn't reply.

"No."

"Did he ever have a girlfriend, go out on a date?"

I shook my head.

"See? He's sixteen and he hasn't been with a girl."

I was about to say he was only thirteen, but I remembered he had said he told her he was sixteen, too.

"What you and I have to talk about, he can't appreciate even though he's so brilliant, Jordan. He's a boy and we're girls and there are things boys just don't understand about girls and their problems and vice versa. I know you think you're too young for all that, but believe me, you have had a period. You're not too young."

"I gotta go back inside. My mother doesn't want me out here at night without Ian," I said.

"Look, I didn't mean to scare you or anything. If you want to talk to me about yourself, I don't mind. You can find your way back to my camper without Ian. I'll tell you the things you should know about yourself," she added in a whisper.

She looked behind me at the door.

"I have to go inside," I repeated.

"Go, but I'd advise you not to tell Ian what I just told you. Girls should have their privacy, you know, their own secrets. I don't tell my brother anything hardly. I never told him what I told you, for example, and I never will."

I didn't think her brother would care anyway. I started to turn away and she reached out and seized my wrist.

"All I'm saying, Jordan, is you need a girlfriend and I would be your girlfriend."

I looked back at her and then to get her to let go, said, "Okay."

She smiled and released my wrist. "I was just like you," she called to me as I stepped up to the porch. "Don't forget that. I can help you deal with your problems. You won't meet many girls like me. Your brother can read about precocious puberty and tell you stuff from books, but he didn't live it. I did and you are."

She waved, turned on her flashlight, and started away. I watched until she disappeared into the shadows and was gone. Then I went back inside and turned the door latch closed. I expected Ian to be out of his room asking me why I had gone outside. Maybe he had heard Flora talking, I thought, but he hadn't come out of his room. I went to his doorway and looked in to see what he was doing. He was lying on his bed, still dressed in his clothes, but asleep. I thought about waking him up and telling him what had just happened, but I didn't do it.

Instead, I went to my own room and thought about the things Flora had said. Maybe it was true about boys not understanding girl problems. Despite the way Ian had reacted to her story and what she had tried to give me, I couldn't help thinking about it all. And what about Ian? I never ever thought of him as immature, but it was true that he never had a girlfriend or from what I could tell, even a crush on a girl at school. He rarely if ever went to parties and if he did go, he always left early and claimed it was boring and stupid.

It would be nice not to have to ask him everything all the time. True, he was kinder and more patient with me these days, but he could be very short with me and even make me feel foolish and unimportant.

For now, at least, I decided not to tell him about Flora coming to see me. Besides, it would only make him angry that I talked to her and didn't go to him first. It could cause more trouble and, using his words, I thought we didn't need any more shattered glass.

I got undressed, into my pajamas, and into bed. A strange question came into my head. I wondered about Grandmother Emma. Despite how she was and how she treated us, did she miss us? Was she lonely in that big house with just the maid and the cook? She was taking all her meals alone now, sitting at that big table and looking at the wall. Had she forced Daddy and us to move in with her because it was economical or because she wanted some family around her, even if just to criticize?

I gazed out my window at the night sky. It looked like the moon was trying to outfox the clouds, but every time it got around one, another would slip in and block it again. It made me think of the poem Flora had told us about the butterfly who thought he died on the moon.

Was I really going through a change like the butterfly went through, a change she had described? What did she mean by "one way or another you're going to be a butterfly" even if the medicine worked? Ian was so angry, he wouldn't talk about it. Even now, I didn't think he would tell me anything. Maybe Flora was right. Maybe he didn't understand because he was a boy. Perhaps the only way I would ever know was to talk again to her.

I closed my eyes and started to drift into sleep when I heard a large bang and then Daddy's laughter.

"Get up, Christopher," Mama shouted.

I sat up and listened. Daddy was still laughing.

"You tripped me," he said.

Tripped him? I slipped out of bed and went to the door to peer out at them. Daddy was on the floor looking up at Mama just inside the front entrance. She had her hands on her hips and was glaring back at him.

Daddy reached up for her, but she didn't move.

"Get up yourself. You embarrassed us both at the restaurant. I'll never go back there."

"Have you no mercy, woman?" he cried as she started away.

Daddy fell back to the floor and moaned, but Mama continued walking toward the stairway. She glanced in my direction and saw me and I saw her look of anger change to a look of sadness and concern.

"Just go to sleep, Jordan," she said. "Go on. I'll see you first thing in the morning."

I closed the door and listened to her go up the stairs. I couldn't help but peek out again to see what Daddy was doing. It shocked me to see he was still lying there and had even turned on his side. He didn't look like he wanted to or could get up. Should Mama have left him like that? I wondered. Where was Ian? Hadn't he heard the commotion?

I closed my door again, but I didn't go right back to bed. I just stood there listening for his footsteps. When they didn't come, I opened the door and stepped out. Without realizing I was doing it until I nearly stood beside him, I tiptoed over to Daddy. I heard him moan.

"Daddy, are you all right?" I asked in a loud whisper. He moaned again. "Daddy?"

He stopped moaning and turned on his back to look up at me. Then he smiled. "Well, now," he said, "look who's come to my rescue. Our little precocious young lady." He laughed and then he reached up and I took his hand. "Pull," he cried, and I did with all my might.

He sat. I held his hand while he looked down for a moment and then took a deep breath and started to stand. He was very wobbly and nearly pulled me to the floor with his effort to rise.

"Up," he cried. "Up, up, and away."

He stood there, looking like he was going to totter over, but he smiled at me and put his hand on my head and then on my shoulder. He started toward the stairway with me walking slowly alongside.

"Good, good," he said. He paused to look at me and smile. "Now that you're on the verge of woman wood, I mean womanhood, Jordan, you had better learn what makes a man happy and what doesn't. Your mother has a knack for the doesn't. And women have it better than men do, Jordan," he said as we reached the first step and he took hold of the banister. "Let me tell you about the birds and the bees here. Women can have multiple orgasms, ten to a man's one. That's not fair, now is it? Huh?"

I stared at him.

"You damn fool!" I heard Mama cry.

Daddy turned and looked up at her, swaying as he stood there.

"She's only seven years old!"

"Huh?" He looked at me. "You're talking about the woman I love," he said, leaned down, and kissed the top of my head. Then he stumbled over the first step and fell on the stairway.

"Mama!" I cried.

Ian came to his door and looked out.

"Go to your room, Jordan. I told you to go to sleep," she said, coming down the stairs.

Ian rushed out and helped her get Daddy to his feet. He looked totally dazed and confused. They guided him up the stairway.

"Thanks, Ian. I'll take it from here. Go to sleep, dear," Mama told him. "Get Jordan back into her room."

"Okay, Mother," Ian said.

Daddy said nothing. Mama guided him to their bedroom and Ian came down the stairs, yawning.

"What happened?" he asked.

"Daddy fell on the floor when they came home. Mama left him there and I went to help him."

"You should have left him there," he said. "Go back to bed."

"Ian, did you hear what he said to me?"

"No, but I'm sure it was something very stupid, Jordan. Go to sleep."

"It was about that thing, that orgasm," I said, but he didn't hear me. He was already back into his bedroom and closing the door.

I looked up the stairway and then at Ian's closed door and I thought, Flora will know what Daddy meant. She'll tell me.

Ian just doesn't want me to know. He likes it when I have to ask him everything.

But that was when I was a caterpillar, and I was beginning to feel more like a butterfly.

12
SHOW ME

Mama was a deaf and dumb person the next morning. She came into my room and almost like an actress in a silent movie, she went through the motions of getting me to take my medicine. I was very sleepy. When I started to wake up, I asked her how Daddy was. She didn't answer. She acted as if she didn't hear me and left my room. It wasn't until Ian and I were at breakfast that she said anything.

"I forgot to tell you both. I couldn't get the horseback riding reservations for today. They're all booked. I made it for tomorrow."

"That's okay, Mother," Ian said. "I have some things I want to do today."

Mama nodded and then turned away quickly. I saw her shoulders tremble. She had seen Daddy drunk before, but never looked as sad about it as she did this morning. I glanced at Ian and saw his eyes were narrowed into those penetrating slits he made when he was in deep thought about something. He looked at me and I realized how concerned he was. He rarely looked this upset about anything that happened between Daddy and Mama. At times I had the feeling he saw their arguments as just part of some television comedy show. This week it was this; next week it would be that. He could turn it on or off, so it frightened me to see him this concerned.

"Is Daddy still sleeping, Mama?" I asked her.

Ian turned to see how she would answer.

"It's more like someone in a coma," she said without looking at us. She took another deep breath. "Finish your breakfast and go outside, Jordan. It's a beautiful day. Don't waste it waiting around for your father to return to the living."

I did as she asked. Afterward, I asked Ian what he was going to do. He said he was going to continue his exploring for carnivorous plants. He wanted to collect them for a study he was making in preparation for his next science project. He entered a science fair every year. Last year he came in second and thought he should have been first.

Left on my own, I took the book Ian had given me for my birthday and went out on our porch to sit and read. It did help me understand the development going on in my body, but at the same time, I grew more frightened of the possibility that the medicine wouldn't work and I would soon indeed look foolish with a bosom and monthly periods while I was only in the third grade. Contrary to what I had hoped, Ian's book only raised more questions in my mind, especially about the sex act between males and females. I wanted to ask Ian things, but he was in the woods already, and despite his clear and very factual manner of answering, I was still a little embarrassed about it. I had never told him the full extent of Dr. Dell'Acqua's examination. I couldn't remember the word she had used when she was finished, but I knew it meant things were far more serious than Mama had hoped and maybe Daddy's scary question when she had first told him was a real question. Could I have a baby grow in me?

Once again, I thought about Flora's offer to help me. Even though she was a stranger, she was still a girl, and a girl who had been through what I was experiencing. Ian really had been unfair to her. She was just trying to tell me about something so I would know what to expect.

Maybe she was right about Ian. Maybe he

was immature, at least when it came to sex. He certainly had a more dramatic reaction to the things she had told me than I had. He was the one who was embarrassed by it. I didn't understand enough and Flora wasn't embarrassed at all.

Listening to her was better than reading this book, I thought. I didn't even see the word *orgasm* in here. It was hard to imagine the tubes and tadpoles and eggs inside me. I wanted to know more about how those tadpoles got inside me or anyone. How long did it take? How did you know it was finished? Would any boy be able to do it or only a boy you loved?

Ian had told me he was going to make me his Sister Project, but that was so he would learn things about me or from me. I wanted to learn things from him. He was simply using me to do another science project. He even said he thought he might make a big contribution to medical science. What was more important, me or his becoming famous? This wasn't fair.

I closed the book. I thought I would just go inside and ask Mama more about it all. I would make her tell me things, but before I got up, she came rushing out of the house. She had a paper shopping bag in her hand,

and without even looking at me, started down the steps toward the car. She looked absolutely furious, pressing her lips together and striding away.

"Mama, where are you going?" I called.

She stopped and looked back at me. "Oh, Jordan. Just hang around. I'll be gone for most of the day. I made your and Ian's sandwiches for lunch. They're in the refrigerator. If your father ever gets up and asks you where I am, tell him I went on an errand I should have gone on years ago," she added, and got into the car.

I stood up and watched her back out of the driveway and then drive off very quickly. I stood there looking after her until the car disappeared around a turn.

An errand? She should have done it years ago? What kind of an errand could that be? Why didn't she ask me to go along with her?

I sat again, confused, and for reasons I didn't understand, feeling very frightened. Not long afterward, I heard Daddy come down the stairs and go into the kitchen. I went inside.

"Where's your mother?" he asked.

He stood there in his underwear. His hair looked like rats had been running through it all night and his face was gray, his eyes like two poached eggs.

"She went on an errand."

"An errand? Why didn't she make any coffee this morning, damn it?"

He started to grind some coffee beans. The noise made him grimace.

"Why didn't she take you along?" he asked, turning back and squinting at me as if he just realized I was there in the kitchen, too.

"I don't know. She went very quickly," I said.

He held the coffee pot and stared at me a moment. "What sort of errand?"

I shrugged and then remembered what she had said. "An errand she should have done years ago."

"What?"

"That's what she said, Daddy."

"What the hell's that supposed to mean? Damn it," he muttered, put water in the pot, and began to make himself some coffee. "Between your mother and your grandmother, I'm sure to end up in the loony bin," he said.

"I could make you breakfast, Daddy," I offered. I could make scrambled eggs and toast. Nancy had taught me and even let me make it twice. I was never sure if Grandmother Emma knew or not.

"Naw, I just want some coffee and some

peace and quiet," he said. "Just go play. Don't make any noise, and when your mother returns from her ancient errand, tell her thanks a lot for bringing me up a cup of coffee."

He flopped into a chair and waited for the coffee. His eyes closed and opened, closed and opened. He looked like he was going to fall asleep any minute. I knew what was the matter with him. I had heard the word *hangover* a few times before when Mama complained about his being drunk.

"Do you have a hangover from drinking whiskey, Daddy?" I asked.

He seemed to struggle to open his eyes. His forehead filled with creases and he brought his thumb and his other fingers up to squeeze his temples.

"I don't need whiskey to get a hangover from this family," he said. "Go on and play. I'll talk to you later," he said, and closed his eyes again.

I hesitated and then went back out to the porch. Where was Ian? I wondered. He should know about Mama leaving on this errand. I wandered around to the rear of the cabin. The sky looked like God had dipped a paintbrush into a pail of clouds and wildly drew long and short strokes across the blue, some of them thick and others so thin they looked like pieces of tissues. It didn't look like it would rain, however. I ventured closer to the woods and called for Ian. He didn't respond so I walked into the woods and shouted louder.

All I heard were the distant sounds of motorboats on the lake, cars on the roads, and then a commercial jet plane making its way west. Even though I had been in planes like that one when we went on trips and vacations, it was still almost impossible to imagine people up there eating and drinking and watching movies. I watched it until I could no longer see it and then I ventured deeper into the woods until I recognized the path Ian and I had taken to Flora's camper.

Maybe, I thought, he had decided to go back to see her and her butterfly collection after all. Maybe he just didn't want me tagging along, taking their attention away from their exploring. I thought I might just continue through the woods until I could see the campers and see if Ian was there. If he was, I could tell him about Mama's leaving.

I walked slowly, tentatively, nevertheless, thinking that any moment, I might just decide to turn around and run back to our cabin. The deeper in I went, though, the more courage I had and the more determined I became. Then I heard some branches cracking off to my right and I stopped to listen. I didn't hear them again.

"Ian?" I called.

The branches of bushes snapped. Was it the black bear?

"Ian, if that's you, you're not being nice trying to scare me like this! Ian?" I shouted, panicking more now.

The snapping and whipping branches seemed to be happening closer and closer. I listened, and then I started to run. I was closer at this point to the end of the woods and the beginning of the field where the campers were located. The branch of a bush caught onto my dress skirt, but I didn't stop, and the force of my lunging forward ripped my skirt, the branch just grazing my thigh enough to make it burn. I screamed and ran harder, bursting out of the woods and into the field. I didn't stop. I kept running until I reached Flora's camper. I hurried up the stairs and then knocked on the door.

I waited but heard nothing so I knocked again, this time harder and longer. Again, I heard nothing. Very disappointed, I turned and looked back at the woods. What would I do? I was afraid to go back.

I started down the stairs slowly and stood there, panting and thinking. My thigh still burned. The thorn of that bush did more damage than I had thought. When I lifted the skirt to look, I saw the scratch, deeper in the center, with blood streaking down my leg. It felt like someone had run a lit match across my skin. The pain brought tears to my eyes.

"What happened to you?" I heard, and looked up quickly to see Flora coming around the rear of the camper. She was carrying one of those little plastic bags and had a living butterfly in it. I knew it was living because it was trying desperately to get free.

"I got caught on a bush," I said. "Is Ian here?"

"Ian? No. Why, did he say he was coming back?" she asked.

I shook my head. "I thought he might be here."

"Well, maybe he'll come later. Come on inside and I'll get something to clean your scratch and a bandage for it."

She walked past me and up the stairs. The door was unlocked. She opened it and looked at me. "Are you coming or not?" she asked.

I looked back at the woods. Where was Ian? Why hadn't he answered me? Was he watching from the woods? Should I scream for him?

"I haven't got all day to wait," she said.

I started up the stairs and she went inside, leaving the door open for me.

"Where's your mother and your father and Addison?" I asked after I entered and closed the door.

"They went to the arts and crafts fair. It's the same thing every year with the same people and the same stuff to look at. Boring," she sang, and went to the bathroom.

I looked around. The kitchen was still a mess and in fact, their breakfast dishes were yet on the little kitchen table. There were empty or partially empty soda cans on the living room table, along with some paper plates with potato chips and what looked like ketchup.

When she came out of the bathroom, Flora saw me looking at it all. "My brother never cleans up after himself. I was supposed to clean up the kitchen, but what's the rush, right?" she asked, and sat on the small sofa. "They'll be gone all day. I have plenty of time. Come here and we'll clean off the scratch with this antiseptic." She held up a bottle and a cotton ball.

I went over and sat beside her. She lifted my skirt and looked at the scratch.

"This is why I don't wear skirts when I go into the woods," she said. She was wearing another pair of well-worn jeans that looked stretched out in the waist and rear, the same thick faded blue sweatshirt, and a Phillies baseball cap.

I looked down at the plastic bag and the weakening butterfly contained within it. She started to clean my scratch with the antiseptic. It burned and I jumped.

"Easy. It won't hurt for long," she said. "This bandage isn't going to be big enough. We'll need to put some gauze on it and some bandage tape." She rose and returned to the bathroom.

I looked at my scratch. The bleeding had stopped. I looked again at the butterfly. It had stopped struggling. I touched the bag to see if it had died and it started flapping its wings again.

"Don't mess with that," Flora said. "It's a perfect hoary elfin."

"It's not dead."

"Of course not. If it was dead, it wouldn't be in this good a condition. It'll die and I'll have it pressed perfectly."

"That's mean," I said.

"It's going to die soon anyway. Don't be a wuss."

"What's a wuss?"

"A sissy, weakling."

She started to fix the bandage so it would cover the entire scratch. "Lift your leg a little," she said, and ran the adhesive around my thigh, pushing up my skirt more to do so. She smiled at me. "Did you think about the things I was saying last night?" she asked.

I didn't know what to say. I just nodded.

"Good. I'm glad you came here," she said. She cut the bandage tape and pressed it neatly. "I was just as confused and afraid as you are when all this happened to me. One day I was playing with dolls and toy teacups and the next day, it seemed, I was worrying about getting pregnant. Danny Hopkins, one of the older boys in my school, tried to do it to me, you know."

I shook my head. "Do what?"

"Put his thing in there," she said, nodding at my still exposed panties. "My new best friend Qwen Edwards told him about me and he thought it would be funny, I suppose. He talked my brother Addison into bringing me over to his house to play Show Me."

"What's Show Me?"

"Show me yours and I'll show you mine. First, you flip a coin to see who goes first. I was a big curiosity to him, you see. Not much older than you are now, and growing boobs and stuff. He paid Addison off by giving him an electronic game, and Addison stayed in the other room playing it while Danny Hopkins got me to take off my panties. Don't trust any boys," she added quickly. "Not until you know a lot more and even then, don't believe any promises they make. You should learn about yourself with a girl like me and not take the chance of learning things from any boy, even your own brother. A boy's a boy's a boy," she sang, and smiled.

I stared at her. What she was saying frightened me a little but fascinated me, too.

"Look, a boy can talk you into letting him touch you here," she said, putting her fingers between my legs. "And it might seem harmless at first, but soon, you like how it feels and you let him do a little more and a little more and before you know it . . ."

"What?"

"He's trying to do what Danny tried to do to me and if he does, he could make you pregnant."

"You mean put tadpoles in there."

"Tadpoles? Oh, yes," she said, smiling. "Is that what Ian told you?"

I nodded.

"See, he's just like any other boy. That

sounds almost harmless. Tadpoles. It's not tadpoles, it's . . ."

"I know. Sperm," I said. I had just read it this morning in the book Ian had given me.

"So you know. Good. Let's see how far along you are," she said, and before I could stop her, she reached farther up to the elastic of my panties and brought them down enough for her to look. She nodded. "More than I had at your age," she said, as if I had done something better. "I don't know if your doctor can turn this around. I didn't get a period like you did."

Then she touched me. "How does that feel?"

I didn't speak and she touched me again, keeping her fingers there and moving them until I did feel a tingling and a warmth that traveled so quickly up my body, I thought I had been electrically shocked. I practically leaped off the sofa.

She laughed as I pulled up my panties. "Easy. That's nothing. If a boy did that to you, you would be in more trouble. Come on, sit down again," she said, patting the sofa where I had been.

"I gotta find Ian," I said. "My mother left the cabin and I have to tell him."

"Oh, Ian's out there somewhere looking for bugs or plants. You won't find him.

Come on. Let me tell you more stuff you have to know."

I shook my head. "I gotta find him." I started toward the door.

She stood up to block me. "You're not going to find him, Jordan."

"I gotta," I said.

She thought a moment and then smiled. "I'll tell you what. I'll go out with you in a while and help you look. Together, we'll find him. It will be too difficult for you by yourself."

I hesitated.

"You're not going to go running back through the woods by yourself again anyway, are you? If we don't find him, I'll walk you back to your cabin."

"You will?"

"Sure I will. I said I would." She grasped my wrist. "Sit on the sofa. I'll tell you more about what happened with Danny Hopkins. You want to hear about that, don't you? You want to learn about boys, right?"

"Yes," I said.

"Okay."

She guided me back to the sofa. "You ever see your brother naked?"

I shook my head.

"Any boy?"

"No."

"Pictures?"

I shook my head again.

"Where do you live, Never Never Land?"

"Bethlehem, Pennsylvania," I said, and she laughed.

"Okay, okay. I shouldn't laugh at you. I wasn't all that much more sophisticated than you are when it all happened to me. Let's get back to my story. So Danny loses the coin toss. He said heads and it was tails and he has to go first. He unzips his pants. I think he enjoyed it more than I did. I have to tell you I think I was in a little state of shock. I was like numb and I was all alone with him, too. He could deny everything and I couldn't prove it.

"That's why it's important you don't learn all this from a boy, Jordan. You get too surprised and you're off guard and they can take advantage of you. But how are you going to know what it's going to feel like? You can do it yourself, but you'll be afraid and you won't understand without someone older and experienced to tell you about it. That's why I can help you," she said, and put her hands under my skirt again.

As she manipulated my panties, I felt tears begin to well up in my eyes. Where was Ian? What was that noise in the woods? Was it the black bear? Would I get lost if I ran out

231

of here? Mama was going to be so angry and she was so furious already.

When she had my panties down again, I put my hand on hers to stop her from touching me.

"Relax. Don't be afraid. I'll take you home," Flora said. "Stop worrying about it. Think about what I'm trying to teach you, okay? Okay?"

I nodded and stopped pressing so hard on her hand.

"Close your eyes," she said. "Just lean back. Go on. I'm going to show you something and then we'll take you home."

Her fingers moved. My heart was pounding and the feelings I was getting in my chest moved like another hand, an invisible one, over my buds.

"See?" she said. "See how it makes you feel. See how you feel a little weak inside. Then the boy does this," she said, and this time, I screamed, jumped off the sofa so fast and hard, I bumped her head and she fell over and onto the coffee table. My panties weren't even pulled all the way up, but I charged for the door.

She screamed as I opened it.

"You idiot!" she shouted as she lifted herself off the table and held up the plastic bag. She had fallen over it and rolled over the table.

"You ruined my butterfly!"

13
FIGHTS

Black bear or no black bear, I ran headlong and wildly across the field and back into the woods. Charging down the path I remembered taking to the camper, I took the best care I could not to run into another thorn bush. I kept my eyes fixed ahead because I was too frightened to look left or right. If anything was near me, I wouldn't hear it either. My ears were thunderous with the rush of my blood roaring through my veins. My side ached with the effort to run as fast as I could.

I was doing well until I was nearly home. Excited by the prospect of being safe, I didn't watch my steps. I tripped and went flying headlong into a pool of muddy water. Trying to break the fall with my hands out, I skinned my palms on some rocks. The instant I hit the ground, I rushed to get up, splashing the dirty water over my shoes and socks and lower legs. My dress was soaked with mud. I knew I was crying, even though I couldn't hear my sobs. Finally, I reached our cabin's backyard. Only then did I stop to catch my breath. I gasped and gasped, pressing my hands into my sides to see if I could stop the pain.

"What do you think you're doing, Jordan?" I heard, and looked to my right to see Ian coming out of the toolshed. He closed the door and gaped at me. "Where were you? What happened to you?"

I couldn't speak. Instead, I ran around to the front of the cabin. Our car was not there. Mama had not returned from her errand. I was both happy and unhappy about that. I didn't want her to see me like this, but I needed her, too. I needed her arms around me and her shoulder to cry on.

As soon as I entered the cabin, I took off my muddied shoes and socks so I wouldn't track dirt all over the floors. I heard Ian coming up the stairs outside, so I ran into the bathroom, carrying my shoes and socks. I closed and locked the bathroom door.

I was just too ashamed to face him, especially since he had told me to forget about Flora and Addison. I knew he would be angry. When I looked at myself in the mirror, I couldn't believe how filthy I was. The mud was even in my hair and down my neck. Now I was very happy Mama wasn't here to see it. She would surely cry at the sight of me.

Ian knocked on the door. "Jordan? Jordan, where were you? What happened to you?"

He tried the door and rapped it harder. "Open the door, Jordan."

"Leave me alone, Ian. I have to get clean," I said.

"Not until you tell me where you were. Why did you come out of the woods? Did you go back to the campground? Did you see Flora? Jordan, you'd better answer me."

I couldn't help my crying now. I just stood there, holding my side and sobbing, my body shaking. He knocked again and again, urging me to open the door. Then I heard Daddy shout from the top of the stairway.

"What the hell are you kids doing down there? Quit that banging! I'm trying to get some sleep."

Ian stopped knocking, but he didn't walk away. He brought his lips close to the door and whispered through the crack. "Jordan, you'd better tell me where you were and why you were running like that. Come on. Come out. I'm not going away until you open this door, Jordan."

I knew he would stay there all day and all night if he had to. Ian was like that when he made his mind up about something. Daddy said he would make a great prisoner of war. He would never reveal a secret even if they pulled all his hair out strand by strand with a tweezer.

"I've got to take a bath first, Ian," I said.

He was quiet for a moment, and then he said, "I'll be right out here, waiting."

I had to gather my thoughts. Would I tell him what had happened exactly or could I lie and get away with a story? Maybe I could do it so he wouldn't know I had even seen Flora? But what if he saw this bandage on me? He'd want to know about that, wouldn't he? I'll have to take it off. It will fall off when I'm in the tub anyway, I thought.

I ran the water into the tub and began to remove my muddied dress. The dirty water had gone through and even stained my panties. I took them off and then waited for the tub to fill. Before I stepped into it, I heard Ian again. He was still right at the door.

"I want to know if you went back to that campground and saw her, Jordan. I'm not waiting here to find out. You'd better tell me."

My heart started to race again. I got into the tub without saying a word. It felt good just to soak and the warm water did calm me. I thought I could hear Ian's breathing through the door and imagined he was leaning against it, impatient and growing angrier and angrier.

"I went looking for you!" I shouted. "And I fell in the mud." It was much easier to lie with a door between us.

"I thought the bear was after me," I added. After all, that was the truth. "I wanted to tell you Mama had gone on an errand and it would take her all day, but I got frightened and ran and ran until I fell."

"All day? Where did she go?"

"I don't know."

I waited, holding my breath. Would he believe me?

"She'll blame what happened to you on me for sure," he said. "Let me in. I'll put your clothes in the washer and I'll clean up your shoes. Maybe we won't have to tell her."

"I'm in the tub, Ian. Wait until I finish."

"Why did you lock the door? You should never lock the door, Jordan."

"I'll be out soon," I said. I took off the bandage Flora had put on me. The scratch hurt again and brought tears back to my eyes. Mama was sure to see this, I thought.

I started to wash it with the washcloth and soap.

Then I heard what sounded like scratching at the door and realized Ian was doing something to unlock it. Before I could stop him, he succeeded and stepped into the bathroom. He closed the door and looked down at me in the tub. The bandage was on the side of it. His eyes went from it to my leg and then back to me.

"How did you get that?"

"A thorn bush scratched me when I ran. I told you. I thought the bear was after me or you were teasing me," I said.

"Where did you get the bandage?" He picked it up and studied it. "Well?"

"I put it on myself," I said.

He smirked. "Jordan, why would you put it on, get in the tub, and take it off?"

"I don't know," I said.

"Jordan, tell me the truth. Stop your lying." He narrowed his eyes into those slits of penetration. "Why are you lying anyway? What are you afraid to tell me?"

I looked down but it was too late. He knew where I had gone.

"You saw Flora," he said. He squatted beside the tub. "What else did she tell you? Well? Talk."

I shook my head.

He stood up. "I guess I'll have to tell Mother and Father what you did then," he said. "Mother won't like it that you went into the woods alone, and when she finds out about that girl . . ."

"Don't. Mama's very upset, Ian."

"Then talk. I have to know everything, Jordan, or I can't help you."

"She told me about a boy who tried to put his sperm in her," I blurted.

He simply stared at me for one of those famous Ian moments.

"She's disgusting," he muttered. "Did she do anything else to you besides putting on that bandage? Did she?" he followed quickly and loudly. "You'd better tell me, Jordan. She could hurt you."

"She wanted to show me what could happen," I said.

"What? Show you? How did she do that, Jordan?" He knelt beside the tub again, his face now inches from mine. "Tell me exactly what she did. Exactly," he emphasized.

I bit down on my lower lip. I didn't want to talk about it.

"You have to tell me," he said. "It's very, very important." He put his hand on my shoulder and fixed his eyes on me so intently, I started to cry again.

"Damn her," he said. "Tell me everything

right now or else."

I told him, blurting it all out as quickly as I could to get it over with.

Anger washed a crimson tint through his face that darkened his eyes and tightened his lips. He stood up slowly when I was finished.

"She's a sick person," he said. "I'm going to make sure she never bothers you again."

He turned and walked out of the bathroom, but suddenly returned to the doorway. "When you get out, put another bandage on that. There is some antiseptic in the cabinet. Put it on first. Dry around it and put the bandage on. Then take your dress, socks, and panties to the washing machine and put them in. I'll take care of it when I return. Leave your shoes by the washing machine. Do it all quickly before Mother returns. I don't think Father is coming downstairs for a while yet," he added.

Then he left.

I did what he told me and changed into a pair of jeans and a blue cotton blouse. I put on some sandals and socks and went out on the porch to see what he was doing, but he wasn't anywhere in sight and didn't answer when I called for him. It was almost lunchtime so I thought he would be back any moment. I went into the kitchen and took out the sandwiches and put them on plates on the table. I thought he might want lemonade so I took that out as well and set out some glasses and napkins. I wondered if Daddy was hungry yet and went to the stairway to listen to see if he had gotten up, but it was very quiet.

Returning to the kitchen, I sat and waited. Finally, I got too hungry to wait any longer and started to eat my sandwich. I was almost finished when I heard Daddy on the stairway. He came down and into the kitchen. He was in his bathrobe and barefoot, but he looked more together and more awake. He had brushed his hair.

"Hey, Jordan," he said. "Lunchtime, huh?"

"Yes, Daddy."

"Where's Ian?"

"I don't know. He went out again," I said.

Daddy went to the refrigerator and looked inside. "I'm actually starving," he said, and began to take out the ingredients to make himself a sandwich of turkey and cheese. "I vaguely remember your telling me something about your mother going on an errand, Jordan," he said as he prepared his sandwich. "Where'd she go?"

"I don't know, Daddy."

He looked at me and then brought his

sandwich to the table. "She didn't tell you anything?"

I shook my head. "She was carrying a paper bag," I said, remembering that.

"A paper bag?" He bit into his sandwich and thought. "Maybe she had to return something she bought."

"She said it would take most of the day," I reminded him. "She said she should have done it long ago."

"Yeah, you said that." He continued to eat. "Where is your brother? Did you call him and tell him to come in for lunch?"

I nodded. "I don't think he heard me," I said.

He shook his head and bit into his sandwich. "How that kid can amuse himself all day with that science stuff is beyond me." He gazed at Ian's uneaten sandwich.

"Looks like you and I have been deserted," he said, fumbling with a smile. He stretched his lips awkwardly. Every movement he made in his face seemed to bring him some pain. Why would anyone want to get so drunk he suffered like this? I wondered.

Suddenly, we heard the front door open. We both turned to see if it was Mama or Ian.

It was Ian.

His right eye was swollen and closed and

his lip was split and bleeding. Both Daddy and I sat there with our own mouths wide open.

"What happened to you?" Daddy finally asked him.

"I got into a fight," he said.

"I figured that. With who or what?" Daddy asked, smiling with ease this time.

Why was he so happy that Ian got into a fight?

"Some boy over at the park campground," Ian said, and looked at me.

Addison, I thought.

"Over what?" Daddy asked, still a half smile on his face.

"A butterfly," Ian replied.

"What? A butterfly?" Daddy's smile evaporated. "What kind of reason for a fight is that?"

Ian didn't answer.

"Go clean yourself up, Ian, before your mother gets home."

He started toward the bathroom.

"Wait a minute," Daddy called to him. "How did you do? What's the other guy look like?"

"An idiot," Ian said.

"Did you get in a few good shots, too, at least?"

"I kicked him in the shins."

"Kicked him in the shins?"

"He's a lot taller than I am."

"Go wash up," Daddy said, sounding obviously disappointed. He turned to me after Ian went into the bathroom. "My first real fight was with a bigger, taller boy, too, but I hit him in the breadbasket with a haymaker that bent him over and then I drove an uppercut into his jaw and broke his front tooth. My father never stopped bragging about me, even though he had to pay for the kid's dental work," he added proudly. "Of course, I was suspended from school and your grandmother wasn't pleased, but I made my place in the standings and didn't have to get into too many fights afterward. It's all just part of growing up. Normal, that is," he added, looking toward the bathroom. "Kicked him in the shins. That's something a girl would do."

He returned to his sandwich. Then the phone rang and he got up to answer it.

"Hi," he said, sounding happy. Maybe it's Mama, I thought. "When?" he followed, his happy face disappearing. "She did what? Came right into the store? No, I didn't tell her your schedule. Why would I do that?"

He listened and then looked at me.

"She said she found it here? But . . . did

you leave it here? Did you admit it was yours?"

He listened and squeezed his temples with his thumb and forefinger. Then he shook his head. "Initials don't prove things, Kimberly. That was really stupid. Right. Sure. It's my fault. Nothing could be your fault. Just don't say anything more to anyone, will you? I'll handle it. I said, I'll handle it. I'll call you. Really stupid," he added, and hung up. He just stood there staring down at the floor.

"Is Mama coming back now?" I asked. He continued to just stare. "Daddy?"

"What?"

"Is Mama coming back now?"

"Oh, she's coming back, all right," he said. "I'd better get dressed and put on my bulletproof vest," he added, and headed quickly for the stairway.

I started to clean up after Daddy and myself, but left Ian's sandwich and lemonade on the table. He came out of the bathroom and hurried to the refrigerator to get some ice cubes. I watched him wrap them in a cloth and then press them to his lip first. Then he turned and glared at me.

"I found her and she denied everything, but I told her she was lying. She put her brother on me like a guard dog. He punched me before I knew what he was going to do. Their mother came out and I shouted at them all. Of course, Flora continued to deny it all. She claimed you made it up."

"I didn't make it up, Ian."

"I know that. You wouldn't have known what to say, but I told you not to go there!" he screamed.

I started to cry. He sat at the table and shifted his ice pack to his right eye.

"I'd call the police but you would be in a mess," he said. "What did you tell Father?"

"Nothing," I said through my sobs. "He didn't ask why you had a fight about a butterfly."

"Good. Where is he?"

"Someone called him and he ran upstairs to get dressed. I think Mama's on her way back."

"Let me think of a story," he said. "Maybe I will stick to the butterfly story. I know she would be very, very upset if she knew what you let that girl do to you."

"I didn't let her, Ian."

"You should have run right out and not waited."

I started to cry again.

"Okay, okay," he said. "Stop crying. Just don't tell her anything about it. I'll handle it," he said. "Did you clean up that scratch and put a new bandage on it like I told you to do?"

"Yes."

"And you put your clothes in the washer?"

"Yes," I said, sucking in my tears.

"All right. I'll get right on that."

He tried to eat but moaned with pain when he chewed. Finally, he pushed the sandwich away, got up, and went to the washing machine. I finished cleaning up the kitchen for Mama and then went to my room. I had other books to read and games I had brought along, but nothing kept me interested. I kept going to my window and looking out for our car and Mama's return. I heard Daddy come down the stairs and go into the living room to turn on the television set and watch a ball game.

Mama would be upset when she saw Ian, but maybe he would make it good again with his explanation. She always believed whatever he said. Tomorrow we would go horseback riding and everything would return to the way it was. I wouldn't set foot in the woods again unless Ian asked me to go somewhere with him.

I lowered myself onto my bed and closed my eyes. I felt terrible about disappointing Ian. He was only trying to protect me and even got into a fight because of me. All of this was happening because of my precocious puberty. I couldn't wait for the medicine to work. I wanted to return to the girl I was and not have to think about tadpoles and eggs and new feelings. I was never very worried about boys. If anything, they were just annoying. Now I would be afraid to be in the same room alone with any boy.

My sadness made my fatigue deepen. I couldn't open my eyes. My legs were aching, too. Before I knew it, I fell asleep and I didn't wake up until I heard the sound of something smash against the living room wall.

I sat up and listened.

It was strangely quiet. Had I imagined it? I slipped off the bed and opened my door to peer out.

Mama was standing in the living room. She had that bag in her hands and suddenly turned it upside down. A gold cosmetic case fell out, along with a locket.

Daddy sat there looking at her.

"Don't bother to make up any stories, Christopher," she said. "Either you pack and leave or I will get the kids together and leave."

She turned and walked toward the stairway. Ian was standing in his bedroom doorway, too. She didn't look at either of us. If she had, she surely would have stopped to ask Ian what had happened to him. Instead, she went up the stairs, her feet pounding on the steps.

Daddy turned back to his ball game. He watched it for a few moments and then he slammed his fist down on the chair, stood up, turned off the set, and followed her.

He didn't look at us either.

We looked at each other.

And for the first time I could ever remember, Ian looked absolutely terrified.

14
THE CRAZY HOUSE

Daddy left, not us. Mama and he were shouting at each other upstairs, and then he packed his bag and rushed out of the cabin when a rental car company delivered another automobile. I watched out of my bedroom window. He didn't even stop to say good-bye to Ian or me. He got into the car quickly and drove off fast.

"Ian, Jordan," I heard Mama call as she descended the stairway. "Come out here."

I came out first and then, when Ian stepped out and she saw him, Mama brought her hand to her cheek and moaned as if all the pain had flown from his face to hers.

"What happened to you, Ian?"

"It's all right. I'll be all right," he said. "The swelling's gone down considerably."

"What happened?"

"I got into an argument and then a fight with a boy over at the campground in the

251

park," he said. "It's not important. Forget about it. I'm not going over there anymore."

"Did your father see you?"

"Yes."

She shook her head. "He didn't tell me a thing about it, which doesn't surprise me. What was the argument about, Ian?"

"It was stupid, Mother. I don't want to talk about it anymore."

He looked down at the floor, which was usually his way of letting someone know they could talk until they were blue in the face and he wouldn't answer or speak about the subject. Whenever he did that to Daddy, Daddy would shake him so hard it looked like he was trying to rearrange everything inside him, but that did nothing and Daddy would give up and walk away.

Mama sighed. She knew the conversation had ended.

"Okay, come into the living room, both of you," she said, looking at me now.

Ian glanced at me with eyes that said, *Keep your mouth shut,* and then we followed her. She stood by the window.

"Sit on the sofa," she told us without turning around. She sighed so deeply, I thought her heart had cracked. "Your father and I are going to separate," she said. "I'm getting a divorce. There are lots of reasons for it, but as they say, the straw that broke the camel's back was my discovering he's been seeing someone else on the sly, apparently for some time, too."

She turned around to face us. She looked pale, but the area around her mouth was crimson. It looked like it had been burned. Her eyes were certainly inflamed.

"It's not my intention to turn you two against him. You'll make your own judgments about him when you're older, although I suspect Ian's old enough to do so now," she said, looking at him.

"Are we going to live here?" he asked.

"No. I'll be finding us a place to live back in Bethlehem. For the time being, however, it's good we have this place. I've already made a phone call to a real estate agent who is lining up potential houses. I'll rent one first and then we'll see. We'll return to the mansion to get our things, too. I just don't want to do it immediately. I'm not in the mood to face your grandmother.

"There's never been a divorce in the March family and that will be her primary concern and complaint. There's no doubt in my mind that if she wasn't confused about what is and what isn't important, she would have divorced your grandfather rather than tolerate the way he treated her.

The March men are all apples that didn't or don't fall far from the tree," she added. "I'm no March woman. I'm not going to pretend nothing has happened or is happening and busy myself with distractions so I won't think about it.

"However, I am sorry that all this is happening to you two. It's no fun being part of a broken family. You're going to have more challenges, more problems. Just never blame yourselves for any of this. It has nothing to do with either of you. It's just between your father and me."

"Daddy's not coming back here?" I asked.

"Not while we're here, Jordan. You'll see him in about a week or so back in Bethlehem when I go look at some of the possible new homes."

"Did you call a lawyer already?" Ian asked her.

She smiled. "Yes, Ian. I called a lawyer before I returned to the cabin today and it's not one of the March lawyers. He's the son of the man who was my father's attorney, Peter Morris. Did you both have your lunch?"

"Yes," Ian said quickly. He glanced at me again. "Jordan went looking for plants with me and slipped and fell in mud. I have her dress washed and in the drier. I cleaned her shoes, too," he said.

She nodded. "I know you'll always take care of your sister," she said, and then shook her head. "Look at you. Why did you get into a fight, Ian? You've never gotten into a fight before, have you?"

"The boy was a jerk. He hit me first. That's the only way he knows how to settle an argument. Forget about it. I'll be fine," he told her.

"I know," she said. "We'll all be fine. We will," she said, but her face was beginning to fracture like a piece of fragile china. Her lips quivered. Her eyes grew glassy. "I'm going to take a rest now," she said. "Don't wander away from the cabin. We'll be going out to dinner. I don't feel like cooking tonight."

"Okay, Mother," Ian said.

She started out, stopped, and returned to hug us both. Then she hurried back to the stairs and up to her room. Ian looked at me because I was already crying, tears streaking down my face.

"If there's one thing she doesn't need now, Jordan, it's you being a baby. We have to be strong for her. Don't let her see you cry," he warned. He closed his eyes because he had a shot of pain in his lips.

"What did she mean about Daddy seeing

someone else?"

"Probably that old girlfriend he employed. Apparently, he was seeing her here. No wonder he was so nice to Mr. Pitts. He didn't want him blabbing about it."

"I don't understand what you mean."

"Forget about it for now." He grimaced from another shot of pain in his lip.

"I'm sorry you got into a fight because of me, Ian."

"I'm sorry, too. I'm sorry you went over there. I can see I have to take even more interest and responsibility for you, especially now. When you have questions about yourself, don't bother Mother and certainly don't go ask any strangers anything. Do you understand, Jordan?"

"Yes."

"Good. I have some things to do," he said, rose, and went to his room.

I stopped crying and went to my room, where I sat and stared out the windows. I wanted to keep crying. I knew enough about divorce to know it would turn our world topsy-turvy. Our parents were no longer going to be husband and wife. There were kids in my class whose parents had gotten divorces. The other kids called them ping-pong balls, bouncing back and forth from one house to another, one side of the family to the other side, each time pretending they liked the side they were with better. Some of the ping-pong balls took advantage and asked one parent for things the other one wouldn't give them or couldn't afford. I heard their stories. They tried to make it sound as if they were happier, but I knew in my heart that they weren't.

One of the ping-pong balls was a girl named Denise Potter. She lived with her father, not her mother, because her mother had run off with someone. I didn't know that. Ian told me because he knew her older sister, Janet. He said Janet was forced to grow up quickly and take on some of her mother's responsibilities in the house. She had to go home right after school and couldn't join any teams or activities. He told me she hated her mother now.

Would we hate Daddy? I wondered. Did this mean Mama hated him already? Would Grandmother Emma hate us and never talk to us again? If Daddy wasn't with us all the time anymore, would Ian have to become the daddy just like Janet Potter had to become the mother? There were so many new questions raining down upon me that I thought I would drown in a downpour of question marks.

I fell asleep on the rug, probably because

of all the aches in my body and in my heart. When I opened my eyes again, I could see that some clouds had come rolling in over each other, thickening and promising a thunderstorm. I sat up. The scratch on my leg thumped. I didn't do all that good a job of bandaging it. I realized Mama still didn't know about it either. She came into my room just as I removed the bandage to look at it.

"How did you do that?" she asked.

"When I fell," I said quickly.

She stared at me. "Why did you fall, Jordan? Were you running after Ian? Did he not want you to be with him?"

"I just wasn't watching where I was going," I said.

She knelt down and looked at it. "This is a bad scratch. You put something on it?"

I nodded. "Ian told me to."

"Good. Let me fix you a better bandage," she said, and we went into the bathroom.

I looked closely at her face as she worked on me. Her eyes were filled with such pain, it made my heart ache again.

"Are you going to marry someone else?" I asked.

"What?" She smiled. "At this point, Jordan, I wouldn't be the one to recommend marriage for anyone."

"Are we going to have enough money?"

"Sure we will. Don't worry so much," she said, running her hand through my hair. "We're going to do just fine, honey, just fine. Your grandmother doesn't think we can live without her, but she's in for a big surprise. Just let me worry about all that. Be a little girl," she said. "As hard as that is for you."

Her lips started to tremble again.

"With all this, he chooses to be so selfish," she said, sucked in her breath quickly, and rose. "Come on, we're going to have a fun dinner tonight. Brush your hair and meet me out in the living room. Ian's almost ready," she said.

She took us to a place called the Crazy House. It was a restaurant where the waiters and waitresses were dressed in funny outfits, shirts and pants that didn't match, two different shoes and socks, dresses that were too big or too small. The waitresses had their lipstick on too thick or off their mouths, too. Occasionally, they would do things wrong deliberately and there were silly songs playing. The menu had food described in a funny way, too. There was the Paranoid's Delight, which was really a hamburger but with an extra half of a bun, Neurotic Shakes, and Claustrophobia, which was meatballs and spaghetti that had to be served on two plates. Ian liked the restaurant very much. Mama said she thought considering all that had happened, we belonged there. Despite it all, we had a very good time. I never saw Ian laugh as much. His eyes looked a lot better and he was able to eat without pain.

In my secret heart of hearts, I was hoping Daddy would be there when we returned to the cabin. I was hoping he had regretted all the bad things he had done to Mama and he had returned to apologize and beg her to forgive him, but he wasn't there. When we drove in, the smiles and laughter seemed to evaporate. We didn't say much. Mama went upstairs to put some things together and Ian and I watched television.

"Are you mad at Daddy?" I asked him. I wasn't sure how I should feel toward him.

"Yes and no," he said.

"How can it be both?"

"I'm mad at him for what he did, but I'm not surprised. I doubt any of this will change him either. We just have to stick together and help each other, Jordan, especially Mother. You have a double whammy."

"What's that mean?"

"You have to grow up faster because of what's happened to your body and now this."

"You have to grow up faster, too," I said.

He looked at me and raised his eyebrows. "I grew up years ago," he said. He turned back to the television set.

Maybe he did, I thought, but did that make him happier? He didn't have many friends because he was so much smarter than everyone else his age. When Flora had asked me if he had a girlfriend or even if he once had one and I said no, I suddenly wondered why not. He wasn't ugly. There were girls who thought he was cute and handsome. Did I dare ask him? I was afraid to, afraid to get him angry at me again. Mama might hear and get even more upset.

Ian went to bed before I did. When I finally did, it was difficult to fall asleep. Maybe I had slept too much during the day, but every time I closed my eyes, I thought I heard the sound of a car coming into the driveway and then listened hard for Daddy's footsteps on the steps and porch. Before I had gone to bed, I had stood there by the window for the longest time waiting to see a car's headlights. I guess it was just wishful thinking. Finally, I fell asleep, but it seemed like I had drifted off just before morning because my eyes snapped open when the sunlight washed over my face. I had forgotten to close my shades.

Mama was in my room before I sat up. "Don't forget your medicine every morning," she said. "We can't let any of this interfere with your medical problems, Jordan."

I took my dosage and then I asked her if Daddy had come back. Perhaps he had while I had slept and I hadn't heard him.

"No, Jordan," she said. "This is not a children's story. It doesn't have a happy ending, I'm afraid. Come on. Get yourself up and dressed. There are things to be done."

I did as she said.

Ian was already in the kitchen having breakfast. "Are we still going horseback riding today?" he asked.

I had forgotten all about that. I looked quickly at Mama.

"Of course," she said. "We have reservations. Your father's leaving is not going to stop us from doing fun things together."

Ian didn't look happy or unhappy about it. He nodded thoughtfully.

"You know I read about this program for disabled children in which they use horses to help them. Somehow, riding energizes them. Some even stop being disabled for a while."

262

"Really?" Mama asked. "That is interesting, Ian."

"Maybe they'll cheer us up," he said, and I wondered if in his mind we were considered disabled now.

Mama did, too. I could see it in her face, in the way her eyes narrowed and looked like they were filling with pain.

"You must never, ever think of yourselves as anything less because of what's happened between your father and me," she said as firmly as I heard her say anything. "Do you hear me, Ian?"

"Of course I don't think that way," he replied. "I am what I make myself," he said.

It sounded like he needed no one, not Daddy, not Grandmother Emma, not me, and not Mama, but Mama still smiled.

"Good," she said. "Good. You listen to your brother, Jordan. He's very wise."

I looked at Ian. Whenever he was contented, he had a way of bringing the corners of his mouth in just a little. It wasn't a smile on the outside, but it told me he was smiling on the inside. Sometimes, I thought my brother had two bodies, one everyone saw, and one only he saw and knew existed.

"Jordan, put on your jeans. You can't go horseback riding in a skirt," Mama said.

I had gone horseback riding a few times.

Only once before had Ian and I gone to-gether and that was up here at the lake, too. When I recalled it, I realized Daddy hadn't been with us then either. Mama was a very good rider. She had a friend from high school who had a ranch and horses and they often rode on weekends before she married Daddy, she said. In fact, that was where she first met Daddy. When she told me that story, she sounded very happy.

"I knew who your father was, of course. I expected him to be more stuck up, but he was more a flirt than a snob. Snobs don't make good lovers, you know," she had told me, and laughed.

That was only last year.

How different our world was now.

Going to the horseback riding ranch in the mountains was a good idea. It took our minds off the family crisis. It was a beauti-ful day with a nice breeze, so it wasn't too hot for the ride. Mama made sure both Ian and I put on some sunscreen. She gave me one of her hats to wear. Ian had a cowboy hat that had been left at the cabin.

Even though we had gone horseback riding before, Mama insisted we take an-other lesson. Ian was annoyed about that. The young girl instructing us had no idea what she was in for when she began.

They had mounting blocks for us to stand on.

"You always mount on the left side," she began.

"You mean the near side," Ian corrected.

"Huh?" she said. The other children and adults in the lesson looked at Ian.

"It's called the near side. The right side is called the off side," he explained.

She just looked at him a moment and then returned to her memorized directions.

"Hold the reins tight so your horse doesn't wander while you're trying to mount it, but not too tight or it will start to back up. Keep the reins in your left hand and take hold of the pommel with the same hand. Then with your right hand, turn the stirrup clockwise so you can get your foot in it. Be careful not to kick the horse or it will think it should move. Place your right hand over the back of the saddle."

"The cantle," Ian said. Again, she paused and looked at him.

"That's what the back of the saddle is called," he told her.

She forced a smile. "Thanks, but for now, let's just get everyone mounted."

"It helps to know what it all is," he said.

She was obviously warned to always be pleasant because she kept her plastic smile and nodded. "Straighten your left leg as you spring up and swing your right leg over like this," she said, doing it. "Then turn the right stirrup clockwise for your foot and put the reins into your right hand. See?" she said, speaking quickly so that Ian couldn't interrupt with any corrections.

Everyone tried it. Some of the adults were very clumsy and had to be lifted up and over the saddle. Ian mounted perfectly and sat straight.

"Okay, everyone, be sure you're balanced on your saddle. Sit at the lowest point and make sure your heels are lined up with your hips. Just keep the ball of your foot in the stirrup firmly. Keep your lower arms bent like this so your arms are like extensions of the reins."

She trotted by each of us to be sure we were sitting correctly. She went past Ian quickly and instructed everyone else in how to hold the reins. She advised us all to try to keep straight and balanced as best we could. Many people were looking at Ian, who sat perfectly. It was as if they thought they should watch and listen to him more than the instructor.

"We'll start with the walk," she said from the front of our line. Ian was right behind me. "Move your arms with the horse's head so you keep your hold on it firm."

We went around in a circle and she gave each person some more instructions. Ian was obviously riding perfectly, as was Mama, who was behind him.

After that, she instructed us on how to turn our horses and then slow them down and stop them. For our first ride, she said she would avoid trotting. This was the beginner's ride, after all. Ian was immediately upset about that.

"If you feel you can go faster, go on," she told him. She made it sound like a challenge.

Mama stayed alongside me all the while. Ian did break out of the line and was so good at controlling his horse, the instructor finally pulled alongside him and complimented him. When she heard how little he had really ridden, she was even more impressed.

It was a beautiful ride and very scenic. It took us nearly an hour and a half and I was sore when we finally stopped and were instructed in the proper way to dismount. My scratch was hurting again as well, but I didn't utter a single complaint because the whole time, Mama seemed happy. What was happening between her and Daddy was forgotten.

Ian was right about horseback riding, I thought. We were disabled emotionally and it had, for the time being, stopped the bleeding of our tears inside or out.

But reality was waiting for us when we returned to the cabin.

It took the form of Grandmother Emma.

She had been brought up in a limousine and she was waiting in the living room. Her chauffeur sat in the car like a robot turned off and waiting.

"I half expected this," Mama muttered. "As soon as we get inside, say hello and then excuse yourselves and go wait in your rooms or together in Ian's room, Jordan."

I looked at Ian. As usual it was hard for me to tell what he was thinking, but he certainly didn't look as frightened as I felt. My heart was thumping.

We followed Mama in and saw Grandmother Emma sitting in the living room.

Even the rustic chairs looked like thrones when she sat in one.

"Hello, Grandmother," Ian said first.

"Hello, Grandmother," I followed.

She looked at us, but mostly at Ian, who still had some swelling around his eye. "What happened to you?"

"Nothing," Ian said.

"Nothing? Who struck you, and don't

make up any stories."

"I got into a fight with another boy. It's not important."

"I'm not surprised," she said, even though Ian had never ever been in any sort of trouble at school or otherwise like this.

"You can be sure it was not his fault," Mama said sharply. "Ian is a good boy."

"Yes," Grandmother Emma said. "I'm here to speak with your mother, children," she said.

Ian reached for my hand. "Call us when it's time to speak with us, too," he said, and pulled me gently to follow him to his room.

I felt guilty leaving Mama behind. When I looked back at her, however, she was smiling.

And it occurred to me that she really did love Ian very much and appreciated his brilliant mind far more than Daddy did or even I did. How lucky we were to have him, I thought, and followed him more quickly.

When we went into his room, he surprised me when he didn't close the door completely. He left it open enough for us to peer out and listen.

"Grandmother Emma will be angry if she sees us eavesdropping on her," I warned.

"Why? We'd be just like Nancy, her maid," he said. He put his finger to his lips so I would be quiet and we could listen and learn exactly what our fate would be.

15
GRANDMOTHER EMMA REARRANGES OUR LIVES

"Did Christopher send you up here to do his dirty work?" Mama asked Grandmother Emma.

"Please, sit down, Caroline," Grandmother Emma replied. "Unlike my husband, I didn't and don't cover up for my son's failings and errors, as you should readily know by now, having lived in my home this long. I have never seen the value in helping someone avoid responsibility for his or her actions. I don't do anyone's dirty work."

"Really?" Mama said. "Refusing to admit to those errors and sins or pretending they don't exist is just as bad, and from what I know, that was your way of life when it came to your own husband."

I could just see Grandmother Emma bristling. Ian glanced at me, a tight smile of satisfaction on his face.

"Making small sacrifices for the greater good is not a bad thing, Caroline. You don't know all there is to know about my marriage and what life was like for me, for Christopher. I do not say I am beyond reproach, or that I didn't make mistakes. Of course I did. I'm human, but I don't dwell on them and wallow in self-pity either.

"Look," she continued, her tone suddenly softer. "I know you and I have not hit it off, as they say, and some fault for that resides with me, but like it or not, we are in a sense in the same boat and it does neither of us any good, especially at this particular moment, to be adversaries. I'm here not to cover up or do my son's dirty work, as you say, but to ensure that you, your children, do not suffer needlessly as a result of Christopher's failings. That, indeed, none of us do," she added.

"It's too late for this conversation, Emma."

"Oh, of course it isn't," Grandmother Emma retorted instantly. "Believe me, I've seen many, many similar situations like this one. Probably ninety percent of the people I've known and socialized with have gone through identical crises. Some let it get the better of them and compounded all the misery for themselves and their families. Most took the sensible route and avoided unnecessary bloodletting."

"What is the sensible route in your eyes,

Emma? Bury my head in the sand as you did? Pretending to be deaf and dumb when it came to your husband's indiscretions?"

"You don't know me after all, Caroline," Grandmother Emma said. "What the public saw was one thing, but what went on behind our doors, within our walls, was quite different, believe me. Christopher's father paid a very high price for my deaf and dumb act, as you might call it. In the end it was he who came to me to plead for forgiveness and understanding. Yes, this powerful executive at one of the world's most successful companies groveled at my feet, not only because his future and his reputation were in grave danger, but because he couldn't sleep. Conscience is king after all.

"Oh, they put on their acts, their bravado performances, their macho faces, but in the dark, especially as they grow older and their own mortality comes into question more and more, they become little boys again, running home to Mother and seeking to be soothed, cuddled, and forgiven."

"I am not in the mood to soothe, cuddle, or forgive Christopher, Emma. In my heart I've always known how weak he is, how selfish and spoiled and . . ."

"Yes, yes, yes. We've both known that, but you married him, Caroline, and I can't believe you didn't know him for who and what he was then. What's more, you said, 'For better or for worse.' You took marriage vows."

"You didn't come here to hold me to that, Emma. I know what you think of religion, of sacraments and commandments. Of all things you are not, you are not a hypocrite. I'll give you that, Emma. What you believe in, you believe in strongly and consistently."

"Precisely," Grandmother Emma said. She was quiet a moment.

"Besides, you're not here because I violated my marriage vows. You're here because Christopher did."

"There are all sorts of violations, even violating yourself. Would it be possible to have something cold to drink?"

"I have juices, sodas, beer."

"Some plain soda water, if you have it."

"Fine," Mother said.

Ian closed the door a little as Mother walked past us to the kitchen. He left it open just a crack. I knelt down and looked out. We both saw Mama through the kitchen doorway. She paused after pouring Grandmother Emma a glass of soda and held her hand over her eyes. I thought her shoulders shuddered. Then she straightened up and returned to the living room.

"Thank you," Grandmother Emma told her.

"Listen, Emma, you're wasting your time here. I have already contacted my attorney. Papers are being prepared. Christopher has been cheating on me for years. I know only of one woman, but I have the sense there were many. You yourself have criticized him for being a poor father, for being self-centered. There is no point in prolonging anyone's agony."

"Very noble speech," Grandmother Emma said.

"I mean it, every word," Mama said sharply back at her.

"I'm sure you do. But that's the little girl in you, the bruised ego. I'm here to make sure you listen to the woman in you, the sensible and intelligent voice you bear as well. As it turns out, you and I are not so different after all, and it's not just that we both married March men. You have pride and you are stronger than your husband, just as I was stronger than mine. You've held your family together, just as I held mine. Now, unfortunately, you have reached a fork in the road, as I did, and you have to look down one side and ask yourself, Is this the road I want to take, a road that will satisfy the little girl in me, but not be as helpful to my children? Or should I take the other road, the road I'm willing to ensure brings great opportunities to my children?"

"Why aren't they your grandchildren as much as they are my children?"

"I wouldn't be here if they weren't," Grandmother Emma said, "but if you take them away from the March world, they will be less so."

"Is that a threat?"

"No, no, just a statement of fact, Caroline. I don't come here armed with threats. I come armed with promises. I simply want you to avoid tragic mistakes."

"My God, Emma, this is the twenty-first century. People survive divorces and their children do, too. You're still living in that Golden Age of yours. Those sorts of social mores, rules, and beliefs are gone. They're gone!"

"Not for me, they're not," Grandmother Emma said firmly.

"What do you want from me?" Mama cried.

"Call your attorney and tell him you've changed your mind. He's not the sort of attorney you would want involved in something like this anyway. He's an opportunist, an ambulance chaser, a low-class gutter fighter."

"Exactly the sort of attorney I would need to do battle with a March," Mama said.

"Don't be ridiculous. He's no match for what I can produce. It will be a long, drawn-out affair. You'll be in battle for every nickel and dime. We'll even fight you on custody of your children."

"Custody of my children? How could you even think . . ."

"Jordan's condition would be exposed and how poorly you've handled it."

"What? As soon as I found out —"

"You kept it secret. You were too embarrassed or whatever to take her immediately to the doctor. Never mind that you hid all this from me, another woman, you hid it from your own husband until she had an abnormal menstruation, and now you have her thirteen-year-old brother tutoring her about sex."

"Tutoring?"

"What did he give her for her birthday?"

The silence we heard thundered in both our hearts and minds.

"Christopher told you about that?"

"Of course," Grandmother Emma said. "And also that you approved and even complimented him on the gift."

"He was just trying to be helpful, to be a big brother."

"A thirteen-year-old boy is now an expert on female matters? What other advice has he given her? Do you even know?"

I looked at Ian. His face was bright red.

"Did you say anything to Daddy or to her about my Sister Project?" he whispered. I shook my head quickly.

"Just imagine," Grandmother continued, "what it would be like to have such information, such embarrassing information, revealed in a public courtroom.

"The child will have to be brought in to testify as well," she added.

"You would do that?"

"Once it's in the hands of attorneys . . ."

"You're more of a monster than I imagined," Mama said.

"Don't be melodramatic. All I'm saying is we should avoid all that. I am prepared," she continued, "to give you a confident sense of independence. I will tomorrow go into my attorney's office and set up a very sizable trust fund for the children. I will deposit a quarter of a million dollars in an account solely in your name with no conditions whatsoever."

"What about Christopher?"

"Christopher will pledge to end his sexual travels," she said.

We heard Mama laugh.

"Pledge? Promise? Even if he wrote it in his own blood, it would be no more valuable than the paper itself."

"I have already seen to it that the woman at the supermarket was fired. She is gone from the scene and will never return."

"You paid her off?"

"What I did is not of any importance. The dirty episode is over," Grandmother Emma said. "I am also taking a firmer control of Christopher's purse strings."

"He'll only resent me more," Mama said.

"Maybe . . . maybe he'll finally grow up. In the meantime coexistence is the order of things. Countries that have adversarial positions to each other can do it, why can't a man and a woman?"

"I don't know," Mama said, but she sounded like she was softening.

"He's truly a little boy. He came running to me just the way he did when he broke something or got into trouble as a teenager. I was the one he came to when he was asked to leave his first college. Once, you saw something of value in him, some reason to tie your own destiny to his," Grandmother Emma reminded Mama. "Think about that."

"As you said, I closed my eyes to what I knew he was. I was too young and impressionable to see the truth back then."

"Well, now you do, I hope. He wants to come back to apologize to you. Listen to me, Caroline. You have problems with your children. You don't want to be out there alone. Jordan needs the best of everything, medical, therapeutic, everything. She has new and heavy emotional issues. Why load on the horrors of a broken home, a mean divorce proceeding?

"I realize Ian is a brilliant young man, but he has issues as well that will require stability. As I said, you and I are in the same boat. Let's keep it afloat for the sake of the children," she concluded.

Once again, there was a heavy silence. I looked at Ian. He lowered his head slowly like a flag of defeat.

"When is he returning to perform this apology?"

"The moment I call him," Grandmother Emma said. "I have a suggestion in that regard."

"What?"

"A man and a woman sometimes need time alone, time to restore their relationship. Let me take the children back to Bethlehem. I'll have them brought back here in a few days. I did start up the pool. This cabin has possibilities as a romantic retreat," she said.

"You never used it for that."

"I never had the opportunity you have," Grandmother Emma responded quickly. "All the money issues I promised will be concluded by the end of the day tomorrow."

"You enjoy the power of arranging and rearranging people's lives, don't you? It's what you did with your own sister."

"As I said before, Caroline, you don't know all there is to know about me, my marriage, and my family. It's easy to jump to conclusions about people and make judgments."

"You did that to me."

"What's that saying, 'Do as I teach, not as I do?' So be a better person than I am."

"That might not be as difficult as you imagine."

Grandmother Emma laughed. "You're right. I have underestimated you. In an ironic way, this episode might just bring us closer. If you don't mind being closer, that is."

"Let's just concentrate on doing what's best for my children for now," Mama told her.

"Yes, let's. Well, let me look around the property and see just how miserably this caretaker has done his job while you get the children ready to leave with me. I'll stop on the way back and take them to dinner."

"It will be the first time you've ever done that, taken them anywhere alone."

"Yes. I realize I have my own new challenges and responsibilities to face, thanks to my errant son."

"Jordan has medicine she must take every morning."

"I'll see to it myself."

The silence told us they were finished talking. Ian closed the door softly.

"What's an errant son?" I asked him immediately.

"A screw-up," he said. He walked over to his bed and sat thinking.

"What's going to happen to us?"

He looked up to answer, but Mama stepped into the room before he could speak.

"Well, it looks like your father is going to return to apologize for his behavior," she began. She had no idea we had eavesdropped on the whole conversation. I was still unclear about some of it, what it meant. "When a husband and a wife have problems like this, it's better if they can spend time alone. It wouldn't be pleasant for the two of you. I'm not sure how it will end or how it will be and I'll only be worrying about you.

"So," she said, "for the time being, I'd like you to return to Bethlehem with Grandmother Emma. You don't have to pack much because you'll be coming back very soon. Jordan, you should take your new bathing suits, however, because she has opened the pool for you two. I'll call you every day. Jordan, you'll have to be sure you take your medicine in the morning. She knows about it and will see to it as well."

"You mean she'll come to my room?" I asked.

"Yes," Mama said, smiling. "She'll cross into no-man's-land. Ian, I'll be depending on you to see that all this occurs and you look after her, okay?"

"Yes," he said. "We'd better get started packing anything we want for those days," he said to me.

Mama smiled at him, at how efficient and businesslike he could be.

"I love you both very much and want only what's good for you," she said, hugging me and then him.

Ian fixed his eyes on her. "If it's not good for you, Mother, it won't be for us," he said.

She pressed her lips together and nodded. "I know, Ian, my little wise man. I know."

She kissed him again. He looked very

content. Then she told me to follow her into my room to get what I would need together. When we stepped into the room, however, she closed the door and took my hands into hers.

"Jordan, I know how unfair it is to you to ask you to be grown-up at a time when you should have nothing in your head but bubbles and lollipops. It's not the way I wanted it to be for you, but I have to ask you to be as mature and as grown-up as you can be until this storm we're in passes over us.

"But I'd be a liar to tell you life isn't full of little storms. You have to make the most of them, get stronger because of them, and never let them defeat you. Look at you," she added, and knelt to brush back my hair. "You look so much older to me already. Those eyes are still full of wonder, but I can see a young lady's wisdom beginning to show its first blossoming. You call me anytime if anything isn't right back in Bethlehem and I'll come get you immediately, okay?"

"Yes, Mama."

"Okay. Let's get the show on the road. This show anyway. The next one is coming soon after," she said, and started to sort out what she wanted me to take.

Grandmother Emma was waiting in the rear of her limousine for us and her chauffeur was standing by the open door as Ian, Mama, and I came out. Mama kissed us both again and we stepped into the limousine. Ian and I hadn't been in it that often, and never with just Grandmother Emma. The chauffeur put our bags into the trunk and then closed the door.

"Did you both go to the bathroom?" Grandmother Emma asked.

"Of course," Ian said.

"Yes," I said.

"Good. I'd like to get close to Bethlehem before stopping for dinner. What sort of food would you two like tonight?"

I waited for Ian to answer. He took a while. The chauffeur got behind the wheel and started the engine. Ian glanced at him and then at her.

"I think I'd like a hamburger."

"Very well. And you, Jordan?"

"Me, too," I said.

"Well, that will be easy, I'm sure. Felix," she called to the driver, "take us to a good hamburger joint outside of Bethlehem, please."

Joint? I never heard Grandmother Emma use such a word.

Ian looked like he was smiling. His eyes

said he was, but he kept his lips tight.

We both looked back at the cabin. Mama was standing on the porch with her arms folded watching us turn onto the road. She looked so small to me.

She looked like someone who was slowly disappearing.

It made my heart stop and start as though it had a mind of its own and knew things I did not.

16
FILTHY AND DISGUSTING

Grandmother Emma tried her best to make conversation with Ian and me. She asked us what we had done so far at the cabin and Ian went into a long lecture on carnivorous plants. He left out the black bear and the butterflies. Even so, he had so much to say. He looked like he was trying to teach her not to ask any questions or this is what would happen, a lengthy lecture full of hard to pronounce things.

Although Grandmother Emma sat and listened to him patiently, I could see her eyes moving constantly from him to me. It hadn't been that long since she had seen me, but I sensed that she was interested in any changes. Actually, her long, studied looking at me gave me a creepy feeling. I began to wonder about myself. Was my precocious puberty making me grow and mature even faster than any of us thought, even Dr. Dell'Acqua? Would I wake up one morning and look like a fully blossomed teenage girl even though I was only seven?

"That's very interesting, Ian," she finally interrupted. "I'm sure you have more to say on the subject, but I'd also like to hear what your sister has been doing."

"We went horseback riding today," I told her.

She looked absolutely shocked. "Today? Your mother took you two today?"

"Yes," Ian said. "We had reservations. When you make a reservation, you have an obligation to appear. The stable might not be able to replace us."

"Well, that sense of responsibility is very admirable, Ian, I'm sure, but you weren't exactly sailing on calm waters today," she said.

Ian smirked and then turned away to look out the window.

Grandmother Emma returned her attention to me. "How are you feeling, Jordan?"

"Okay," I said.

"No problems with appetite, nausea, bowel movements, anything like that?"

"It's not symptomatic of her condition," Ian muttered, without looking at her.

"I was referring to the possible side effects of her medication," Grandmother Emma said sternly.

Ian didn't speak or move. She was right, of course. He had given me the list of possible side effects.

"No, Grandmother," I said. "None of that has happened to me."

"Good. Let's hope it all goes smoothly and we put an end to this irregularity," she said. "I would hope you would have a normal spring, summer, fall, and winter in your life," she added.

That turned Ian around. Her comparison of the stages of human development to the four seasons interested him.

"Where would you place yourself now, Grandmother?" he asked her.

She actually laughed or really smiled and shook. "From the way things are going, I'd call it my winter of discontent, Ian, but I expect it will return to just winter soon."

I had no idea what she meant exactly, but Ian seemed to not only understand her, but appreciate her. He, too, nearly smiled.

"I must say," she went on, gazing at the scenery that flew by as we traveled, "it's very lush up here this year. There must have been lots of rain."

"The average rainfall for the Pocono Mountains is four inches for April and they had nearly ten," Ian said.

"Is that so?" She stared at him a moment

and then, to my surprise and I'm sure Ian's, she smiled. It was a warm, friendly smile, too, something we rarely saw printed on her otherwise firm face. "Your grandfather Blake was a weather fanatic, too. First thing out of his mouth in the morning was 'What's the weather today?' One would have thought he was a farmer. The weather had little or nothing to do with his work, but if we had an unusual amount of rain or snow or the temperatures went too far in one direction or another, he took it to be a betrayal, a broken promise, and ran on and on about it all morning. He absolutely hated it when weathermen got it wrong and he would not be beyond calling the stations to bawl them out. He thought everything in his world should do what it was expected or designed to do."

I didn't want to interrupt her. I had never heard so much about my grandfather from her before and had a hunger to learn more, but Ian was annoyed.

"I am not a weather fanatic, Grandmother," Ian said. "I'm merely aware of what goes on around me."

Her musing came to an abrupt end. The softness in her face dissipated like smoke. "No, you're not, I imagine," she said. "Actually, you're not at all like your grandfather, Ian."

I wasn't sure if that was a compliment or a complaint and neither was Ian. He turned back to the window and for the next half hour or so, no one spoke. Grandmother Emma closed her eyes and rested and while her eyes were closed, I was able to study her because I had rarely, if ever, come upon her sleeping in a chair. She always acted as if being tired was the same as having to go to the bathroom. You didn't sleep in public either. She would immediately excuse herself and go to her bedroom.

She did say once that she thought Grandfather Blake's falling asleep in a chair watching television and then snoring was the most vulgar and impolite thing imaginable, especially if there were other than family members present.

Despite the harshness in her voice and the almost mechanical perfection in her appearance and her manners, there was something soft and feminine just below the surface, I thought as I studied her face. She had to have been very pretty when she was younger or my grandfather, who we were often told had an eye for the ladies, wouldn't have wanted her to be his wife. From the few occasions I had looked at her photographs and seen pictures of her sister, my great-aunt Francis, I knew that they had both inherited nice features from their parents.

Even now, her skin was smooth and her complexion, relatively unchanged by makeup, made her appear younger than she was, especially when I saw her with some of her friends, women about her age, who even with their heavy makeup and surgical implants and corrections, still looked like degenerating mannequins. Their voices cracked and their posture was poor as well.

There was nothing feeble about Grandmother Emma, despite her tiny hands and diminutive features. She didn't tremble or warble. She had no problem raising her voice, which always had a firmness. According to Daddy, her grip on anything was steady and true enough to allow her to be a brain surgeon.

And yet, when I looked at her now, and thought about what she had and what were her challenges and problems, I didn't think of her as a happy person. I thought of her as someone trapped in her own fortress, concerned only with patching the walls and keeping the demons away. Laughter, music, friendship, and even love were more often on the outside of those walls as well.

Did she love Ian and me at all? Could she?

Or even more, did she even want to love us? Were we just a nuisance? Surely, she had these feelings about Ian, I thought, looking from her to him. He wouldn't let her love him anyway. He barely let Mama love him. I never ever saw him run to her and embrace her. It was always she who embraced or kissed him.

I wanted Grandmother Emma to love me, to care about me. I don't know why it was so important to me, but it was, and now, I had this illness, this precocious puberty that obviously disgusted her or at a minimum, annoyed her. Instead of growing closer to her, I had been dragged and pushed farther away by forces beyond my control.

Her eyes opened and she looked at me and the way I was looking at her. Unlike most other times, I didn't immediately shift my gaze. We stared at each other a long moment. She didn't smile, but she didn't look at me angrily either. She looked like she had seen something that, at least for this moment, frightened her.

"Felix," she called.

"Yes, Mrs. March?"

"I'm sure the children are hungry. How close are we to the restaurant?"

"Five more minutes and we'll be there," he said.

"Good." She straightened up in the seat. "I must say, I'm somewhat hungry myself, although I do hope they have something other than hamburgers, Felix."

"Oh, indeed they do, Mrs. March. It's a good menu. I'm sure you'll be pleased."

When we arrived at the restaurant, she, Ian, and I were led to a booth. Felix sat at the counter as if he had nothing whatsoever to do with us. Ian ordered a deluxe hamburger, but I saw Mama's favorite lunch on the menu and ordered a Chinese chicken salad. I saw my choice impressed Grandmother Emma. She ordered the same thing.

"Is my father on his way to the cabin now?" Ian asked after the waitress took our menus.

His question surprised me almost as much as it did her. I knew we were supposed to behave as if we knew nothing about what was happening between our parents.

"If he's not there now, he will be shortly," she said.

"I hope so. I wouldn't want Mother to be left there alone," Ian said sharply.

"I think your mother is capable of taking care of herself, Ian."

"So do I, but she's had a shock," he said. "Don't you think she's in great emotional pain?"

I know my mouth was opened when she glanced at me.

"I don't think this is a subject for discussion for young people your age."

"Adult talk?" Ian said, smiling at me.

"Precisely, adult talk," Grandmother Emma said.

She smoothed out her place mat on the table, and after a few moments of silence to let the tension weaken and fall away, she folded her hands and looked at Ian again.

"Tell me, Ian," she said in a friendlier tone of voice, "you are an excellent student, you read a great deal, you have a strong interest in nature and in science, what is it you would like to be, exactly?"

Her interest in him took us both by surprise.

"I'm still exploring my options," he said. "It will be something to do with medicine, however."

"You want to help people, ease their pain and suffering?"

Ian's eyes blinked and then narrowed. "I think I'd be better in research," he replied.

"Yes, so do I," Grandmother Emma said. "Research." The way she said it made it sound like something inferior.

"In the end I'll still be helping people," Ian said defensively. "I just won't have to deal with and be distracted by all the unnecessary bureaucratic business."

"Make no mistake in your brilliant thinking, Ian," Grandmother Emma told him, "even research scientists working in some laboratory are still affected and involved with politics. Money has to be raised. Contributors convinced. Don't neglect your people skills. Your grandfather was very bright and capable, too, but he was also very good at public relations. He was an expert when it came to diplomacy. You can't live in a vacuum."

Ian stiffened as if he had been scratched down his back. "I know that. Nothing can live in a vacuum," Ian told her. "It's like burying your head in the sand."

He could have reached out and stuck his fork in her and gotten the same reaction. She bristled, her eyes widened, and she pressed her lips so hard against each other, they resembled two nightcrawlers glistening in the rain. It was too much of a coincidence not to know that Ian, and perhaps I, had listened in on her conversation with Mama.

Fortunately, before anything else was said, our food was served. None of us spoke. We ate quietly. When we were nearly finished, she asked if either Ian or I wanted any dessert. I did, but Ian said no, so I shook my head. He looked anxious to leave. It was starting to rain anyway.

"Then let's get home," Grandmother Emma said, "before this rain gets worse." She signaled for the check.

We rode the rest of the way in silence. The sprinkles turned into a downpour.

"We're in for a night of thunderstorms," Felix said, and then we saw some hail. It pelted the car and made it sound as if a chorus of dancers were doing a tap dance on the roof. As we approached the house, Grandmother Emma asked me about what time I took my medicine every day.

"As soon as I wake up," I said. "That way I won't forget."

"I'll check on her," Ian told her.

She said nothing. When we arrived, it was still raining and hailing. Felix held an umbrella over Grandmother Emma and got her into the house. Then he brought in our bags and we carried them up to our rooms. I was worried about Mama and wished she would call to let us know she was all right. I was sure Ian was worried, too. After Grandmother Emma left us to go to her room, I asked him about it.

"I have the telephone number for the cabin," he revealed. "If we don't hear from her in the morning, we'll call her," he promised. "Go put your things away. I'll be in to see you before you go to sleep."

I was glad he said that. I felt so frightened and alone knowing Mama and Daddy were having a serious discussion that could get mean and angry while we were so far away. It had been a long roller-coaster day, mixed with sad moments, fun moments at the stables, and then unnerving moments at the cabin and afterward in the limousine and restaurant. I truly felt like I had been tossed and turned, bumped, shoved, and bounced, just like someone in a car crash, rolling over and over down some steep embankment.

Because I hadn't taken a shower or a bath today, I decided I would do that before I went to sleep. I started to run my bath and put my things away. Then I went into the bathroom, took off my clothes, and put the bath oils into the water. I got into the tub and closed my eyes. It was so soothing and warm, I nearly fell asleep and probably would have if Ian didn't come in.

"That's good," he said. "I meant to tell you that you should probably take a bath first."

"Did Mama call yet?"

"No," he said. He stood there, looking down at me. I saw he had something in his hand. It looked like a small soup bowl.

"How long have you been in there?"

"I don't know."

"Well, it's time you came out. I want to do something that I think will help us understand if the medicine is helping with your precocious puberty."

He reached for the bath towel and held it out. I rose and began to dry myself. He stood there watching and waiting. When I reached for my pajamas, he told me to wait. He picked them up and walked out to my bedroom.

"Come over here and lie down," he said. "You don't need the towel," he added, so I put it in the hamper.

He pulled back the blanket and told me to lie down on my back.

"What is that?" I asked him, nodding at the cup in his hand.

"Something I invented. It's a device for breast development measurement," he said. "I have it marked in centimeters so it will be more exact," he said. I didn't know what that was, but I could see the precision with which he created his invention.

I crawled onto my bed and lay down as he wanted.

"Just relax," he said.

He leaned over me and put the cup over my right bud. I saw him adjusting it so it would tighten and close until he was satisfied. Then he wrote something on a pad he had in his pocket and took the cup off. He then put it on my left bud and did the same thing.

"Okay," he said. "Sit up. I want to do this with you erect. This is a different measurement."

I sat up and he started to do the same thing. He had his back to the door, but I turned and saw Grandmother Emma standing there and looking in on us. I will probably never forget the look on her face. It was as if some terrible and horrible monster was about to pounce on her. She leaned back and even raised her arms to block out what she saw or keep the monster from her. In her grimace she brought the corners of her lips so deeply back and into her slim, thin cheeks, it looked like she had bitten on a sharp long knife. Even at this distance, her eyes resembled two bubbling volcano openings about to explode.

"IAN!" she finally managed to scream. The shout echoed around the room.

I felt my body freeze and my heart shrink in my chest. I knew I wasn't breathing.

Ian calmly and simply turned to look at her as if it was nothing to see her in my doorway, to see her on our side of the mansion, but mostly as if there was nothing wrong, no reason for her to scream or look the way she looked.

For a moment his coolness and steady composure did throw her. I saw the confusion ripple through her face. Where was his shame, his fear, his guilt? Was she crazy? Was she the person doing something wrong?

Ian still had his hand on his cup invention and it was still under my budding breast. He hadn't even winced when she had shouted. He remained calm, waiting.

Grandmother Emma's mouth seemed unable to find words. It opened and closed, opened and closed, and for a moment, she looked like a fish out of water, gasping. She lowered her arms and took a step forward. "What do you think you're doing?" she managed.

Ian looked at me and then back at her, still holding the cup against me. "I'm keeping track of Jordan's precocious development to determine the effectiveness of the medication," he said.

"This is disgusting. This is . . . filthy and disgusting. Get away from her this instant and go to your room. Go on!" she shouted.

Ian took the cup away, but paused to write in his pad. Then he walked slowly out of the room, halting in the doorway and turning back to her.

"Scientific investigation is never disgusting, never filthy, but only in the minds of people who think that way themselves," he said.

Grandmother Emma's already reddened cheeks looked so crimson, it seemed a fire was burning in her mouth. "Don't you ever, ever come near your sister when she is undressed again," she warned. "This is sinful and incestuous and I will not have it under my roof. Do you understand?"

"No," Ian said. "I've never understood ignorance," he added, and went to his room.

She stood there, literally shaking and looking after him for a few moments and then she burst forward and shut the door before turning to me.

"What else has he done to you or with you?" she asked. "I want you to tell me immediately, Jordan. You are not to lie to me, ever. What else?"

I shook my head. I was even too frightened to cry. My tears were stuck somewhere behind my eyes. "Nothing else, Grandmother," I said.

"He touched you. Did he touch you?" She stepped up to the bed. "Well? Show me. Where did he touch you? Show me!" she shouted.

Finally, my tears, like water dammed up, burst forward and streamed freely down my cheeks.

"I know he gave you that filthy book to read, that book about sex. What else did he give you?"

"Nothing," I said. "Nothing."

"Don't you know something terrible could happen between the two of you? No, of course you don't know," she answered for herself. "Where are your pajamas?"

"Right there," I said, nodding at them on the chair where Ian had put them.

"Get them on immediately," she ordered.

She watched me get dressed. I crawled back into bed and quickly pulled the blanket up and under my chin.

She stood there, still staring at me. "What else has he done with you?" she asked again. "Where else has he touched you?"

I was afraid to tell her about his touching my nipple so I shook my head, but she was as good as the X-ray machine that had taken pictures of the inside of my head. She read lies.

"I know you're not telling me everything, Jordan. I know you're frightened, but you must never, never let him touch your body like that again. Do you understand? Do you?"

"Yes, Grandmother."

"I will have a discussion about this with your mother and father as soon as possible, but until then, he's not to come into your room unless I or some other adult is present as well. Is that clear, too?"

I nodded.

"I should have suspected something like this. A boy that age having no friends, not going to any parties, not belonging to any teams, spending all that time alone doing who knows what with himself. I should have known. I did know. In my heart, I knew but refused to admit it to myself. Your mother isn't all wrong about me. I do bury my head in the sand too much sometimes, but I won't anymore. I promise you that," she said, nodding with clear and firm determination in her eyes.

She started for the door and then turned and looked back at me. "I'll be here in the morning," she said. "I'll be around here much more often, too. Don't disobey me."

"Okay, Grandmother," I said.

"Disgusting. Horrible. A disgrace piled on a disgrace," she muttered, and then opened the door, switched off my lights, and went out, closing the door behind her.

I lay there in the darkness, my heart still pounding.

Minutes later, the door was opened again. It was Ian.

He stood there looking in at me. I was about to tell him he should stay out. She might see him or hear him.

But he wasn't coming in. He just wanted to tell me something.

"I hate her guts," he said. "I hate her more than anything or anyone."

Then he backed up and closed the door, leaving me in the darkness with lightning flashing on my windows and crackling in every corner of my room.

17

THE WORLD IS FULL
OF "SHOULD HAVES"

Ian would blame Grandmother Emma for the rest of his life. Although I never thought him capable of great love for anyone, even great love for anything, including science, I realized quickly he was capable of great and deep hatred. It would fester and grow inside him and, despite the pride he took in his self-control, his command of himself, his emotions and thoughts, it eventually would overtake him and turn his pursuit of happiness into a vain dream. It was as if a filter tinted dark gray had fallen over his eyes and changed his view of the world. In the end I pitied him more than I pitied any of us, which was ironic because I always believed Ian would find success and contentment. He had such confidence and clear ambition. How could he ever get lost?

It would be years before the pieces would come together for me. Each moment, each action, even each word, would have to be placed correctly so the puzzle would make sense. At the time I was too young to understand, but gradually, small revelations would help me guide my hands so I could fit it all together to create the picture I would live with, the picture locked in my heart like the two pictures of Mama and Daddy sealed in my birthday locket.

It began almost immediately after Grandmother Emma had left my room that night she caught Ian examining me. I try, even now, to understand her. Ian, of course, refused to do that. Understanding is, after all, the first giant step toward forgiveness and that's a place he will never go.

"I can forgive the fox that eats the rabbit, the snake that eats the mouse, because I can understand them. They have a selfish purpose, yes, but it's the natural order of things. It's beyond their control," he told me once. "They're not mean about it. They're aggressive and determined so they can survive, but Grandmother Emma is like a fox that kills a rabbit and leaves it to rot. It's aggressive and determined just to satisfy some meanness."

It would take me a long time to decide if he was right or wrong.

Some of the pieces of the puzzle Ian brought to me. He was far more perceptive

307

and aware at the time, of course, and he could turn his microscopic eyes and probing mind on the events like a giant flashlight, washing away deception, confusion, half truths, and excuses. I was at an age when I would miss much that went on around me. Innuendos, subtle meanings, a look or expression, even a blank stare or words unspoken were within Ian's vision.

He was sullen and still, poised, but keenly listening and watching, recording every second, every gesture, every detail with a genius for detecting I'm sure every policeman, detective, law enforcement agent would love to possess. He fed everything to me, revealing what he learned and thought like some translator at a high level government meeting between dignitaries of two foreign countries.

And so to his best ability and mine, we first came to understand the chronology of the series of events that would change both our lives forever and ever.

After what she had seen going on between Ian and me, Grandmother Emma called the cabin.

Mama and Daddy had been talking, discussing their marriage and Daddy's bad behavior. Daddy answered the phone and Grandmother Emma described what she saw happening in my bedroom.

My parents put everything aside and rushed out of the cabin to come home.

The hail and rain thunderstorms were still swirling about, even growing stronger, when the inclement weather cell, as Ian called it, thickened.

Daddy was driving.

He took a sharp turn too quickly and the car lost traction. It hit the guardrail broadside and turned over the railing.

The car rolled and bounced nearly one hundred yards before it rested upside down. The lights fortunately remained on and a passing motorist saw it almost immediately after the accident had occurred.

Fire trucks, tow trucks, and an ambulance arrived with the police.

Both Mama and Daddy were alive and taken to the hospital.

It was nearly four in the morning before Grandmother Emma was woken by the phone call from the highway police.

She called for Felix, her driver, dressed, and left for the hospital in Honesdale, Pennsylvania.

She had left instructions for Nancy and at seven a.m., Nancy came to our bedrooms to tell us our parents had been in a car accident. Nancy had been told to be sure I took my medicine. She had also been instructed to stay close to me and be sure Ian did not come into my room or have any contact with me until I was washed, dressed, and down to breakfast. She stood there and recited all that to me as if she were reading an official proclamation.

Neither Mama nor Daddy had fastened their seat belts, which was the first important clue for Ian. He said that meant they were emotionally disturbed enough to be put into a panic and when people are in a panic, they forget to do things or do stupid things. Later, when we found out they had taken nothing with them, Ian was certain he was right. Mama had not even taken her pocketbook, much less any suitcase or overnight bag.

Ian thought Grandmother Emma's phone call had come, Daddy had hung up, and they had charged out of the cabin. Mr. Pitts said they had left some lights on and the door unlocked. Ian thought that they had been in the middle of their discussions, which he thought were still more like arguments, and whatever Grandmother Emma had told Daddy, Daddy had blamed on Mama and then Mama had blamed on him. He said they must have been in the middle of a horrible argument.

The police report noted that Daddy had been drinking and a blood test revealed he was above the limit. Mama must have been quite upset to let him drive, Ian concluded.

Those were the pieces of the puzzle the way he saw them.

That morning he was at breakfast before me. Nancy accompanied me out of my bedroom and down the stairs. She made me feel like a prisoner, but I could see she was terrified of being accused of not following Grandmother Emma's orders. Whatever Grandmother Emma said to her must have been threatening and Nancy didn't want to lose her position. She was paid well and had been here many years. Eventually, we would find out she was sending money to a sick brother, and it was the only money he had.

"What do you know about the accident?" Ian asked her as soon as we entered the dining room.

"I don't know anything about it," Nancy said. She quickly started for the kitchen.

"What time did it happen?" Ian shouted after her.

"I don't know," she said, and went into the kitchen.

"Are they all right?" I asked Ian.

"I don't know any more than you do," he said. He quickly drank his juice. He was already very suspicious. "I certainly don't know why they would leave to come home at night. Everything had been arranged. If they didn't want to stay together, they wouldn't have left together anyway. Mother still had our car and Father had to have his rental yet."

Nancy brought us oatmeal with raisins. There was a plate of buttered toast as well. She put everything on the table the exact way she always did. I even saw her glance at Grandmother Emma's chair as if Grandmother Emma was sitting there observing and making sure she was doing everything correctly. I could understand that. I often felt the same way when she wasn't where I expected her to be.

"What time did my grandmother leave the house?" Ian asked.

"I'm not sure," Nancy replied.

"What time did she wake you up?" Ian pursued.

"Between four-thirty and five o'clock. I'm sure she will call here soon," she added, and again made a quick exit to the kitchen.

"I can't imagine why they would be on the road at that hour," Ian muttered, and started to eat.

After we finished our breakfast, we remained downstairs in the living room. Ian got the idea to call the highway department to see if he could learn about any accidents in the vicinity of the route Daddy and Mama would have taken. He returned to the living room to tell me there was an accident discovered about ten-thirty that could very well have been theirs. His mind was already whirling with the possibilities and he looked at me angrily.

"I bet Grandmother called them after she found me in your room. I bet that's why they left to come home," he said.

It took my breath away. I was trembling as it was, just waiting to learn something. Had Mama been angry at me? Daddy? Was this somehow my fault?

We heard a car approach the house and Ian jumped up to look through the window. "It's Felix," he said. "He's alone."

We waited until he came to the door and rang the bell. Ian and I rushed out to greet him.

"Your grandmother would like you both to come with me to the hospital," he said.

Nancy stood waiting behind us. He and she exchanged a very serious look.

"You don't need anything. You can come as you are," he added, and turned away.

Ian started after him, stopped, and reached back for my hand. "Come on,

Jordan," he said.

Felix opened the rear door for us and we got in. As soon as he did, too, Ian started to ask questions.

"I don't know everything," Felix said, almost sullenly. "I was just sent to get you. I'll get you there as fast as I can."

Ian sat back. Frustration clouded his eyes. He seemed to shrink into a tight ball, fuming, while I could barely keep from crying.

I should have gone to the bathroom first, too, but I was afraid to mention it. Ian, however, looked at me squirming and told Felix he had to find a place where I could go.

"She should have gone before we left," Felix said, not hiding his annoyance. Perhaps Grandmother Emma would blame him for this short delay.

"The world is full of 'should haves,' " Ian told him.

He said nothing after that. We pulled into the parking lot of a diner and Ian walked me into it to go to the bathroom. Felix came in and bought some gum and a cup of coffee to go, and then we were off again.

No matter what Grandmother Emma believed, I thought, my brother always looks after me.

She was waiting for us in the lobby. It

wasn't until I saw her standing there speaking with a doctor that I came to understand and appreciate how much in control she could be even under great pressure. No matter what you thought of her, if you needed someone upon whom to rely and depend, she was that person.

She saw us enter, but continued her conversation with the doctor. When she was finished, she turned to us. "Come with me," she said, and led us to an elevator.

"How are they?" Ian asked as soon as we were alone with her.

"Your father has seriously injured his spine. He will be paralyzed from the waist down," she said.

I started to cry.

"There's no time for that, Jordan. The damage is done and we have to deal with it," she said. "He also has a broken shoulder and a broken leg, a concussion, a broken nose, and a fractured cheekbone. He had a ruptured spleen and the spleen has been removed."

"Removed?" I asked.

"You can live without a spleen," Ian said. He looked dazed and a bit pale because of what she had said about Daddy. "You just have some added risk of infections."

"Ian is right," Grandmother Emma said.

The door opened and we stepped onto the floor that had the intensive care unit or ICU.

"What about Mama?" I asked her.

"Your mother miraculously did not suffer any broken bones, but she wasn't wearing her seat belt. Neither was your father for that matter, and she apparently struck her head either against the windshield or even on the metal roof. She is in a coma. The doctors are not sure yet what it means and they are continuing to evaluate her condition."

"What's a coma?" I asked.

"It's like being asleep," she said.

"Only you can't wake up," Ian added. "You could be in a coma for years and years. She probably has swelling and pressure and that's why she's in a coma."

"Yes," Grandmother Emma said. "At the moment they are not sure how serious the damage is."

We entered the ICU. Patients were on both sides with a nursing station in the center. Monitors of all sorts were going and two nurses were behind the counters while two others were attending to patients. Some of the patients were in the open, but many were in areas walled off by curtains the nurses pulled back. Both Mama and Daddy were behind these, side by side.

"Your father's as good as in a coma as well at the moment," Grandmother Emma said. "He's been sedated because of the pain. You can try to talk to him. You can talk to your mother also, but she won't respond to anything. Even if you touch her," she added, looking at me.

I glanced at Ian. His eyes were small and narrow and he was looking around the ICU. I was doing all I could not to cry since she had reprimanded me, but it was hard smothering my tears. We approached Daddy first and looked at him. His right arm was in a cast that went right over his shoulder. His left leg was in a cast. His face had all sorts of black and blue marks, red marks, and some bandages over his eyes and around his ears. There was a tube inserted in his left forearm and there were wires on his chest. He moaned.

"Does he know he won't be able to walk again?" Ian asked Grandmother Emma.

"No," she said. Grandmother Emma looked at him more with a mother's disgust and annoyance than sadness, I thought.

She looked at me and nodded at him, giving me permission to speak to him.

"Don't tell him," Ian warned.

I couldn't imagine doing that.

"Daddy?" I said. "It's Jordan and Ian. How are you? Daddy?"

He moaned again. His eyelids fluttered, but he didn't speak.

"He's too out of it," Ian said, sounding grateful. "Let's look in on Mother."

We stepped over to her bed. She had monitors wired to her as well, but her face was remarkably clear, not a scratch on it. She looked like she was only taking a nap. Her good appearance encouraged me. I reached for her hand quickly.

"Mama, it's me. Mama, wake up. Please," I said, shaking her hand. It was so limp in mine. Her fingers didn't bend or move.

"What are they doing for her?" Ian asked Grandmother Emma.

"Evaluation. I told you. We might move her to a bigger, more complex hospital where there are specialists in this sort of thing. We'll know soon," she said.

"Mama," I cried, and drew closer. I put my hand on her arm and then her shoulder. "Mama, it's me. Can't you wake up? Please, Mama." I shook her a little.

"When people are in a coma," Ian said, "they don't respond to voices or light, smells, or touch. It's like their brains have shut down, Jordan."

"No," I said. I didn't care how smart he

was or what he knew. I wouldn't hear it. "Mama, we're here. Please wake up."

"Don't raise your voice, Jordan," Grandmother Emma said. "There are other very sick people in here."

"Mama," I cried, and put my forehead against her arm. She felt as warm as ever, but she didn't move. I finally started to cry, sobbing loudly.

"We'll have to take her out," Grandmother Emma said. "Come along, Jordan. You're not helping by doing that now. Come along," she insisted, and reached for me.

I pulled my arm out of her hand and clung to Mama's arm. "NO!" I shouted at her.

One of the nurses came to Grandmother Emma's side. "What is it?"

"It's her daughter. I made a mistake bringing her in. I'm sorry."

"Oh, that's all right," the nurse said in a sweet, soft voice. "Let me take care of it."

"Ian," Grandmother Emma said, "we'll leave now."

He looked at me and then turned and walked away with Grandmother Emma.

The nurse stepped up beside me and put her hand on my head, softly petting me the way Mama often did.

"It's all right," she said. "You shouldn't feel bad about crying. And you know, sometimes, even though they don't seem to respond, people in comas hear you. She knows you're here, sweetie, and she's trying to get better for you. You want to help her do that, right?"

I nodded.

"Well, you let us do what we have to do and take care of her for you and she'll get better. You know, there's a candy machine out in the hallway. Why don't we get you something nice? Later, you can return. Okay?"

I looked at Mama. She hadn't moved. Her eyes didn't open. Was the nurse right? Did she hear me? Did she know I was here?

"Come on," the nurse urged me. "Lean over and kiss her cheek. Go ahead."

I did and then I held my face close to Mama's and watched her eyes hopefully, but they didn't open.

"It's all right," the nurse said. "She knows. Come on, sweetie."

She took my hand and we walked out of the ICU. As she promised, she brought me right to the candy machine and asked me what I wanted. I chose a box of chocolate-covered peanuts because I knew they were Mama's favorite. I thought when I went back in to see her, I would tell her I had them and she would open her eyes and

320

smile at me. The nurse bought it for me and then brought me down the hallway to the small waiting room where Grandmother Emma was on the phone and Ian was reading a magazine.

I thanked the nurse. Grandmother Emma nodded and smiled at her and I sat next to Ian.

"Mother's doctor just had Grandmother Emma paged," he whispered. "She's on the phone with him now."

I knew that meant something very important was to be told or happening.

"Yes, I understand. You're absolutely correct. Please do make those arrangements," Grandmother Emma said. "Thank you."

She hung up and looked thoughtful for a moment. "It will be some time before we learn the full extent of your mother's brain injuries," she began. "When she emerges from her coma, we will see what we will see and know what has to be done.

"Until then, I'm having her moved to a hospital that specializes in this sort of thing and where there are well-known specialists in the field. A good friend of mine, Dr. Samuel Blakely, has made arrangements for your mother to be transferred to the Albert Einstein Medical Center in Philadelphia."

"When?" Ian asked quickly.

"As soon as it can be arranged. Your father will remain here until he is stabilized and then he, too, will be moved to a hospital that specializes in his condition. He will be involved in a long recuperation that will involve therapy. There is much to be done and little time to waste now," she added.

"When will we see Mama again?" I asked.

"There is little point to seeing her until she emerges from the coma."

She looked at her watch. "I'll let you go in again, Jordan, if you promise, swear, and cross your heart that you won't cry and act like a child when you're asked to leave. Well?"

"I promise," I said quickly.

"Ian?"

He looked at me. "I'm not going in again," he said. "It doesn't make a difference right now. Grandmother Emma is right."

"No, she's not," I said, firmly disagreeing with him for the first time in a long time. "She can hear us. The nurse told me she could."

He just shrugged.

I got up quickly.

"I'll speak with the nurse first," Grandmother Emma said.

I followed her down the corridor to the door of the ICU. She told me to wait outside and she went in. I looked back and saw Ian standing with his hands in his pockets and gazing out the window. He turned as if he felt my eyes on him and looked at me. Then he looked out the window again.

Grandmother Emma stepped out. "You have five minutes, Jordan, and then you must leave with me. Do you understand?"

I nodded.

She opened the door and I walked in again. The nice nurse smiled at me and I smiled back. I looked in at Daddy. He was still moaning and moving his head softly, but his eyes were closed. I felt so sorry for him, especially since he didn't know how terrible things were for him. He looked like he had won a place forever in my worst nightmares.

I took Mama's hand in mine as soon as I stepped up to her bed. "Mama, I'm back, but I can't stay here long. They're taking you to another hospital where they'll make you better faster. Grandmother Emma says I won't see you until you wake up. Please, try to wake up soon. I need to talk to you, okay?

"I won't forget to take my medicine. I promise, but I need you to help me with other things as soon as you can. Okay?"

I waited, hoping and praying she would open her eyes and smile at me and all would be better. Daddy would get better quickly, too, and everyone would forgive everyone else. I stroked her arm softly and kissed her hand and pressed my head against her upper arm and shoulder, and then I stroked her hair and whispered in her ear.

"Please wake up, Mama. Please."

Out of the corner of my eye, I saw the nice nurse starting toward me so I kissed Mama on the cheek. I thought a moment and kissed her again. "That's for Ian," I said, and squeezed her hand softly before I let go.

I stood there staring at her face, but her lips didn't even tremble. Then, without being asked, I turned and started out and stopped when I remembered something.

I hurried back, opened Mama's hand, and put the box of her favorite candy in it, closing her fingers around it.

When I stepped out of the ICU, Ian was there in the hallway waiting by himself. Grandmother Emma was on the phone again in the waiting room.

"Well?" he said. "I was right, right? She didn't wake up and she didn't know you were there."

"Maybe not, but I left her a box of her

favorite candy."

"She doesn't know she has it," he said.

"Yes, she does."

He shook his head at me with a look of pity on his face.

"And then, I kissed her for you," I said.

His arrogant, confident expression faded.

And for a moment, he looked more like a little boy than my older brother.

18
Too Old for a Nanny

Neither Ian nor I had any idea how much Grandmother Emma had already done and decided about us before we even had arrived at the hospital. Ian said she could easily have been a Nazi U-boat commander because she was so decisive and unemotional when she made a decision.

"She must have been thinking about all this even while she was rushing to the hospital and especially when she learned about Father's and Mother's injuries," he told me afterward.

Strangely enough, he didn't sound angry or critical about it. To me, he even seemed a little in awe of Grandmother Emma. Even though in his mind she was the cause of it all, his respect for her grew. She was all business and no nonsense, he told me, as if he were speaking about a superhero.

I had already been thinking about her in a similar way. I knew she didn't care that much for Mama, but why wasn't she at least sadder about all that had happened to Daddy? Did she ever cry? Or did she do all her crying in secret, behind locked doors? Was it shameful or unladylike to shed tears in public about your own son's pain and trouble?

On the other hand, Ian hadn't cried either, I thought. He was thinking and acting like another doctor and not like a son. Would he, too, cry in secret?

Apparently, while we were on our way to the hospital, at the hospital, and returning back to the house, Nancy had been very busy following Grandmother Emma's new orders. She moved everything of mine from my room to the room that had been Daddy's, the room right across from Grandmother Emma's bedroom. All my clothes, shoes, underwear, toiletries, toys, books, and games were transferred, as well as my school desk. Until we arrived at the house and walked in with her, Grandmother Emma didn't tell me and Ian what she had ordered Nancy to do.

Nancy greeted us in the hallway.

"Is everything done?" Grandmother Emma said before Nancy could ask about my parents.

"Yes, Mrs. March."

"Good." She turned to me. "Jordan," she said, "you will be living and sleeping in your father's old bedroom for now. Ian, you are to remain where you are and not come to that side of the house unless I specifically ask you to do so."

Of course, I was totally surprised, as was Ian. I couldn't help feeling frightened and nervous about being uprooted like this, but I was also intrigued about being in Daddy's room and on Grandmother Emma's side of the house.

Both Ian and I hurried up the stairs and looked in at my room. Even the bedding had been stripped and taken to Daddy's old bed. Apparently Nancy had turned the mattress because there in plain sight were the stains from my first period. The sight of the emptied room as well as that gave me a chilling feeling.

"Holy schmoly," Ian said. This was also when he called her a U-boat commander.

"This way," Grandmother Emma called to me. She was standing at the head of the stairs, about midway down the hall, beckoning. "Don't dillydally. All of your things have been moved. Don't worry. We have much to do. You can go to your room, Ian."

I looked at Ian. He lowered his head and

walked to his own bedroom and shut the door.

"Come along," Grandmother Emma said.

I followed her down the corridor to her side of the mansion and paused at the open doorway to Daddy's old room. I looked in at my bedding, my desk, my toy chest, pictures on the walls, and other things.

"Where are Daddy's things?" I asked.

"Never mind about that. Go on," she said, urging me into the bedroom.

Daddy's old bed was as big as mine, but it was made of a darker wood as were all the furnishings. The room itself was larger, but the windows looked out in the same direction as mine did. I knew Nancy cleaned the room periodically, but it smelled like she had just polished all the furniture, vacuumed, and washed the windows.

The tub in the bathroom was larger and, Grandmother Emma explained, had a whirlpool as well. She showed me where all my things had been placed in the cabinets, including my medicine. As she explained it all to me, a thought came.

"What if Mama doesn't want me to move into this bedroom?" I asked.

She tilted her head a bit and looked at me. "While your parents are recuperating, I am in charge of both of you," she said. "I am responsible for your well-being. When your mother comes back, if she wants you to return to that bedroom, we'll discuss it then.

"In the meantime, you will be just across the hallway from me and I will feel much better about it. Is that all right with you?" she asked. She didn't ask it in a tone of voice that said she really cared about my opinion. It was more like, *It had better be.*

I nodded.

"Well, I'm happy we have that issue resolved," she said. "Get used to the room, pick out something to wear to dinner, and get yourself ready. We'll go down to dinner in exactly an hour," she added, glancing at her watch.

"What about Ian?"

"Don't worry about Ian. I'll make sure he's aware of everything," she said.

"Are we going back to the hospital to see Daddy?"

"Yes, of course, but not for a few days. It's better to let him rest and recover enough so he can enjoy your visit."

"He'll be very, very sad when he learns he can't walk."

"Yes, I'm sure," she said.

"When will I see Mama?"

"As soon as I have completed all the arrangements and we have her settled. Anything else you want to know?" she asked petulantly.

I looked around the room. Even though my things were in it now, it still looked cold and unfriendly to me.

"I don't like it here," I said. Without any of Daddy's things, it didn't hold the magic I had hoped it would. The guest room downstairs was nicer, I thought.

"Yes, well, as you will discover about most things in your life, Jordan, it's a matter of growing accustomed to it. And you will," she said. Again, it sounded more like, *You had better.*

She turned and walked out, closing the door behind her. I stood there feeling alone and afraid, as if I was standing on an icy mountain and would start sliding down any moment. I couldn't help it. I just stood there crying. In a matter of mere hours, our lives had been turned entirely upside down and there wasn't anything either Ian or I could do about it. With both our parents out of the house, Grandmother Emma's hold over us was truly ironclad.

Because of what she had seen Ian doing with me, her view of him, the way she spoke to him, was even firmer and colder than it had been. He didn't speak back to her or disagree in any way with anything she told him to do. He had always been able to shut himself off from everyone else anyway. Now, even the tiny windows he had permitted to be open to his world were closed. For a long moment at dinner that first night, I looked at him in the same way he had gotten me to see the caterpillar. He looked like he had curled up, only this wasn't with hope. It was with total withdrawal. I had the sense he would never straighten out again. He would be gone forever.

I think this pleased Grandmother Emma. She didn't mind Ian's silence and with-drawal. She was happy to act as if he wasn't really there and turn all her attention to me. None of the things she directed at me was directed at Ian. It was as though my parents' accident had paved the way for her to shape me in her image, finally and forever. Mama had been a buffer between us, a shield, and that was gone. I was now clay in her hands.

She began that night by instructing me about how to sit at the dinner table.

"I'm not asking you to sit stiffly, Jordan, but you should work on that slouch. I've told you before that when you're not eating, you should put your hands in your lap. That way you won't fuss with your implements or do anything to distract others. Children your age are always fidgeting.

"The daughters and granddaughters of some of my friends have been incorrectly told never to put their elbows on the table. It's far more graceful for a woman to have her elbows on the table when she is conversing and leaning toward someone.

"But don't tip your chair or rock it. Your mother often reaches across you or Ian to get something. That's not proper. You can reach for something as long as you don't go across someone else's plate."

She lectured throughout the dinner. I listened but I didn't say anything. I was happy when we were finished eating because I was so nervous I didn't enjoy anything or even remember tasting anything.

"Are you calling the hospital?" Ian asked her, finally lifting his gaze from his food or just down at the table.

"I have already," she said. "Nothing's changed except arrangements to move your mother have been completed. She'll be going in the morning.

"You've both had a very hard and emotional day," she added quickly, turning mainly to me. "I want you to go right up to your rooms, read or watch television until nine p.m., and then go to sleep.

"Jordan, I will come to your room early to

be sure you've taken your medication. Tomorrow, I will call Dr. Dell'Acqua and arrange for another visit. I'd like to have a better understanding of your condition and treatment. I'm not sure all the right questions have been addressed."

"What would you have done if we were still up at the cabin?" Ian asked her.

For a moment she looked like she wouldn't answer. She didn't even turn to him. Then she did so, very slowly.

"You're not at the cabin any longer, Ian. You're here. She's here and all of the responsibility for both of you, especially Jordan, has fallen on my shoulders. Parents today don't have the same sense of obligation and concern that people of my generation had and have," she continued.

"Are we excused?" Ian asked her, making her feel as though everything she had just said had gone in one ear and out the other.

"Not just yet," she said.

She folded her hands and sat there a moment as if she had to gather her thoughts and say everything perfectly.

"Tomorrow, someone is coming to this house. Her name is Miss Harper. She will serve as your nanny until your parents are capable of taking charge of you again."

"Nanny? We're too old for a nanny," Ian

said, curling his lips in at the corners.

"Perhaps that is not the right term in this particular case. In my time such a person was also known as a minder. Whatever, her name is Miss Harper and you two are to afford her the same respect and obedience you would to me or your own parents.

"You are not to leave the property without her. You are not to go anywhere together on the property without her. There are times I will not be here for meals. She will take them all with you, tell you when to appear. Jordan, she will assist you in what to wear. She will assist you when you bathe and dress. If you have any problems of any kind, you are to bring them to her attention. She has vast experience with young people of all ages and it is apparent to me that you two need someone of her caliber and background to address your problems."

She paused and turned her eyes slowly toward Ian as though she were resetting a cannon. "Especially your problems, Ian."

"How did you find her so quickly?" he asked, without skipping a beat.

"When you've reached my age and have had my experience, Ian, you will, I hope, be someone of some resource, too, and you will understand how things can be done efficiently and correctly."

Despite what she had suggested about him, Ian looked like he appreciated her answer because she had included him.

"How old is she?" I asked.

Grandmother Emma's whole face tightened as she raised her eyes toward the ceiling. "I'm not accustomed to being cross-examined by children, Jordan. You will be told what you need to be told about Miss Harper and you shouldn't ask people personal questions. It's not polite."

"Knowing her age isn't all that personal," Ian muttered.

"You're both excused," Grandmother Emma said sharply. She could have just as easily brought down a gavel to end the discussion.

Ian and I rose from the table, pushed our chairs in properly, and started out of the dining room. She followed us into the hallway and watched us walk up the stairs. When we reached the top, Ian turned to go left. I stood there, feeling frightened and alone. I had the urge to just run after him and go into my old bedroom and refuse to come out.

"Jordan," I heard Grandmother Emma say. "Go on to your new room and prepare for bed. I'll stop by in a while," she added.

She sounded friendly and caring. When I

looked at her, she nodded. I started toward her side of the mansion and then paused to look down the hallway at Ian. He was standing there watching me. Then, acting sillier than I had ever seen him act, he put his thumbs in his ears, turned toward the stairway, and waved his fingers while he stuck out his tongue. Of course, she couldn't see him from below.

I smiled and he waved and went into his room. I waited a moment and then walked slowly into my new bedroom. Having my things there gave me some comfort, but it still felt cold and lonely. I sniffled back my tears and went to the bathroom to prepare for bed. Afterward, I put on my pajamas and crawled into what had been Daddy's bed. Of course, I had never slept in it. I had never really had a chance to look at it. The larger room made me feel so much smaller, too.

I glanced at the clock and saw I had at least an hour before I had to turn off the television so I started to watch something. I flipped the channels until I found a channel that was showing a documentary about, of all things, butterflies. Even though it was fascinating, it reminded me of Flora and what she had done to me. My mind started to spin around all the questions that had sprouted from the experience. I wanted to think more about them, but I couldn't keep my eyes open. I actually fell asleep with the television on and vaguely woke up when I saw Grandmother Emma clicking off the set, fixing my blanket, and then turning off the night lamp.

She stood in the doorway a moment. Silhouetted by the hallway light, with her hand on her hips and her elbows out, she looked like a giant moth.

Seconds later, she closed the door and left me in darkness with only the vague light of a quarter moon threading its way through gauzelike evening clouds.

I thought about Mama and wondered if she felt the box of candy in her hand, woke up, and smiled to herself knowing that I had been there.

And that I would be back. That gave me a sense of relief and I closed my eyes, but suddenly, I heard a great deal of noise in the hallway. I listened hard. Grandmother Emma was telling Nancy and Felix, her driver, to move quieter. Why?

I slipped out of bed and peered out my slightly opened door. I saw Nancy carrying what looked like an armful of clothing. Whose clothing was it? Where was she taking it? Grandmother Emma was standing and watching her go down the stairway with Felix, carrying clothing, too, right behind her. I watched until Grandmother Emma started to turn and then I closed the door quickly and hurried back into the bed.

It all seemed like a dream. Maybe I was already asleep, I thought. Maybe I didn't even get up and look out that door. I closed my eyes. I was so tired, so tired. That thought opened the doorway to sleep and sent my tears for Mama back to the well of sadness from which they had been drawn.

The sunlight hadn't even begun to open the curtain of darkness when Grandmother Emma was back in my room, switching on the lights and telling me it was time to take my medication. She watched as I did it and then put it back in the medicine cabinet. She went directly to my closet, studied my clothing for a moment, and chose a dress for me to wear.

"I'd like you to look very nice this morning," she said. "Miss Harper will be arriving shortly and will take breakfast with us, in fact."

"When am I going to see Mama?" I asked.

"I told you, Jordan. After she is settled in at the new hospital, we'll see when it's appropriate to visit her. It's not polite to ask adults the same question repeatedly. The answer won't change because you do that either.

"Let me give you a bit of wisdom," she said, approaching the bed. "It's difficult enough as it is to hold the attention of other people meaningfully. Don't waste it on nonsense or whining or repetitious questions. When I was your age, I wasn't permitted to speak at dinner unless I had been spoken to first, for example. Parents today permit their children to quack after them with 'why this?' and 'why that?' like ducks.

"Besides," she said, "you will soon learn that it's more to your advantage to listen. It will help you make wiser decisions. Do you understand?"

I shook my head. I didn't feel that I did understand. Why wasn't she permitted to talk at dinner?

"You will," she insisted. "Eventually. Now, get yourself up, washed, and dressed. Fix your hair so you look your best. First impressions are more often final than not and I'd like Miss Harper to have a good impression of you." She flashed a smile.

"I have cramps," I blurted. They had started just minutes before she had arrived and were now a bit more intense.

"Pardon me?"

"My stomach. I have cramps and I might

need that" — I had forgotten the name — "thing that looks like a white cigar."

It was the first time I had ever seen my grandmother blush. Her left hand seemed to flutter up to the base of her throat.

"Did your mother show you how to use it?"

I nodded.

"This is extraordinary," she said. "Go into the bathroom and do what must be done. And don't mention this or talk about it in your brother's presence."

"He knows about it," I said before thinking.

"Knows? You mean you told him?" I hesitated. "Well?"

"Yes."

"Did your mother know this?"

"I don't know."

"Did he . . . did he watch you insert it or in any way participate?"

I shook my head. How could he participate?

She looked relieved.

"We will be going to see Dr. Dell'Acqua today," she said firmly. "From today on, however, Miss Harper will be the only one besides me with whom you will ever discuss any of this. Never, never talk about yourself with Ian again, Jordan. Do you understand me?"

I nodded, but she didn't look satisfied.

"This won't do," she said as though there were someone else in the room besides us. "Where is that book he gave you?"

"I left it at the cabin," I said.

"Good. Miss Harper will answer your questions from now on."

"Is she a doctor, too?" I asked.

"Never mind what she is or isn't," she snapped. "Direct all questions to her and never to your brother or anyone else, for that matter."

"I can tell Mama," I said.

"Yes. You can tell her, but will she ever hear you? That's the bigger question," she muttered, and started out of the bedroom. "Don't mess the bed," she added when she turned back. "Go do what you have to do. Extraordinary," she repeated, and left as though she was afraid to stay much longer.

I hurried to the bathroom and found what I needed in the lower cabinet. Mama had given me a whole box before we had gone to the cabin and Nancy had placed it there. After that, I washed and dressed and brushed my hair. I took longer than I thought and Grandmother Emma sent

Nancy up to tell me to come down immediately.

"Is Ian downstairs?" I asked her.

She didn't answer. I checked myself in the mirror and hurried after her.

Ian was already there, sitting quietly and waiting. Across the table from him was a tall, pretty woman with reddish blond hair neatly styled about her ears. Her lips were so orange, she didn't need lipstick. There were ribbons of faint freckles over the crests of her cheeks, just touching the bridge of her small nose. I liked the way she brought her lips back gently when she smiled, but her turquoise eyes were almost independent from the rest of her face because they were cold and penetrating like a doctor's eyes, full of questions as she turned her gaze fully on me.

Even though it was summer, she wore a high-buttoned gray blouse closed at the base of her neck and a darker gray ankle-length skirt. She wore no earrings, no necklace, and no rings, just a watch with a big square face, more like a man's watch, I thought. When she stood up, I saw she was quite tall, but part of the reason for that was that she wore four-inch square-heeled black shoes. She would surely tower beside Grandmother Emma, I thought.

343

One interesting thing I noticed about Grandmother Emma was when people were that much taller than she was, she didn't tilt her head back when she spoke to them or they spoke to her. She looked forward and usually they had to tilt their heads or even slouch.

"Jordan, this is Miss Harper," Grandmother Emma said. "She is here to help me with you and Ian," she added, as if we were the invalids and not Daddy and Mama.

"Hello," I said, so softly I wasn't sure I had actually uttered it and not just thought it.

Her smile widened, but her eyes remained as they had been. "Hello, Jordan. I'm very pleased to meet you. I have heard so much about you that I feel we've known each other for some time," she said.

I looked at Grandmother Emma. What would she have told her already? Ian still had his head lowered, his eyes down. From the way his lips were tucked in, I knew something was bothering him a lot. Had Grandmother Emma told Miss Harper something nasty about him before I had arrived or even before she had met him?

"Take your seat, please, Jordan," Grandmother Emma told me. She watched me closely until I set my napkin correctly on my lap and pulled my chair closer to the table. Miss Harper watched as well and smiled and nodded at her.

Nancy began to serve our breakfast, which I knew was to be special because she brought out the assorted Danish Grandmother Emma usually reserved for Sundays. Miss Harper asked Grandmother Emma about the dining room chandelier and while she explained it and its history, I looked at Ian. He raised his eyes and leaned toward me to whisper.

"She put her in Mother and Father's room," he said. "She had all the things removed last night."

And I realized what I had seen in the hallway was no dream.

19
A MOUTH FULL OF SOAP

After breakfast, Grandmother Emma decided to give Miss Harper a tour of the mansion. Ian and I were ordered to go along, but not to speak unless we were spoken to. Lecturing about the house was still one of Grandmother Emma's most enjoyable activities, and even our present tragedy didn't distract her or depress her enough to lessen the joy. We could hear the pride in her voice as she spoke. Miss Harper was properly impressed, nodding and commenting about the beauty and the value of everything in the March Mansion.

Ian smirked and shook his head. He leaned over to whisper, "She's an apple polisher just like Nancy."

"It's not proper to whisper behind anyone's back," Grandmother Emma said, without turning to us or skipping a beat in her tour.

It was always wrong to underestimate

Grandmother Emma's hearing or sight.

We did listen attentively, however. It was during the walk-through that we learned Miss Harper was the daughter of one of Grandmother Emma's oldest friends from Philadelphia and that she had been a third-grade elementary school teacher in a private school, but had lost her job because of a budget cutback. She had been living with her mother and had even lived at home when she attended college.

Grandmother Emma primarily wanted us along to reinforce her rules about the house in front of Miss Harper. This included what door to use when we went out to the pool, where to wipe our feet, and what areas were still restricted as far as we were concerned. She never wanted us to go into what had been Grandfather March's office, now her office, for example. It was clear Miss Harper would enforce all the rules as stringently as Grandmother Emma did.

Afterward, Ian was given permission to return to his room and I was told to go with Miss Harper and assist her moving into the house in any way she required. I couldn't imagine what I could do for her. Grandmother Emma had still not explained why she had moved her into Mama and Daddy's bedroom. At the foot of the stairs, she finally did.

"For the time being, Miss Harper will be taking what was your parents' bedroom," Grandmother Emma told us. "When your father returns, he will not be able to navigate the stairway. He will be in a wheelchair and I don't intend to mar the beauty of this extraordinary staircase by installing one of those lifts on a mahogany balustrade, so I am having the downstairs guest room set up as their room."

"What if Mama doesn't like that?" I asked.

For a long moment, we could hear a pin drop. Even Ian looked surprised at how sharply I had asked the question, but I couldn't help feeling I should speak up for Mama, who was unable to speak up for herself. Grandmother Emma glared at me a moment and then continued as if I hadn't spoken.

"Under the circumstances, it is better for Miss Harper to be where she can attend to you children easier. It will be some time before either of your parents is able to do much parenting, and I have a great many new responsibilities, thanks to this unnecessary event. For one thing, I'll have to take a more active role in the supermarket. I will be reviewing the books, the procedures, and interviewing for a new full-time general manager. Maybe it will start to become profitable," she added for Miss Harper, who immediately smiled.

"It is most unfortunate that you have so much to do at this time in your life, Mrs. March," she said.

Ian nearly groaned. I saw how his lips contorted with visible disgust.

"Frankly, Millicent, I can't recall a time in my life when I didn't have major responsibilities. I wouldn't know how to handle so-called retirement."

They laughed.

"Ian, you can go to your room. You can go out, but stay on the property and do not go swimming until we return," Grandmother Emma added, and turned to me. "In about an hour or so, you will go to the doctor with Miss Harper and me.

"Welcome to our house, Millicent," she said to Miss Harper, and extended her hand to her. They shook gently.

"Thank you."

Ian quickly started up the stairs and didn't look back. Sullenly, I followed Miss Harper to what had been my parents' bedroom. Grandmother Emma had even had the bedding and the curtains completely changed, using the bedding and curtains I had seen in the downstairs guest room. Nancy had already put away Miss Harper's things, hung up her clothing in the closet, and put her shoes where they belonged. None of Mama or Daddy's clothing had been left. Even the pictures of us and of them had been removed.

I saw that Miss Harper had very little on the vanity table and nothing of Mama's remained. She checked the bathroom and then stepped out and smiled.

"Well, it looks like there's not much for us to do. I feel as if I have lived here for years," she told me. "Why don't we have our first heart-to-heart chat. You can sit on the settee and I'll sit here," she said, taking the cushioned chair that I knew to be Daddy's.

I gazed about suspiciously. Grandmother Emma surely knew everything had been done for Miss Harper. I was positive she just wanted me to be alone with her to have this first conversation. She wanted to be sure Ian wouldn't be present. Miss Harper held her smile, but those eyes were still so cold, it was as if her face was a mask and the real Miss Harper was somewhere behind it, watching me, studying me. I sat as perfectly as I could so there would be no slouching for her to report.

"Well now, let's get to know each other

better. You were just seven, right?"

I nodded.

"It's better if you say yes or no when people ask you a question, Jordan. Just nodding or shaking your head makes it seem like you don't want to talk," she said. To me it sounded exactly like something Grandmother Emma might say. "You were just seven?" she repeated.

"Yes," I said.

"For many years, I taught little girls and boys who were about your age. You're going into the third grade this coming September. I'm going to help you be so prepared, your teacher will recommend promoting you into the fourth grade. How would you like that? Would you like that?"

"I don't know," I said. "I don't do schoolwork over the summer."

"This summer you will. At the end of the summer you will know just as much as any fourth grader."

"You're going to be here all summer?" I asked.

She stared coolly. "It appears that way, Jordan. It's important you don't get too optimistic about your mother's recovery."

"What's optimistic?"

"See? My students would know that word. It means essentially too hopeful. You have to be realistic about how long it will take for your mother to fully recuperate. You can't rush something like that. It wouldn't be good for her and you want what's good for her, don't you?"

"Yes," I said. Of course, I thought. Why did she even have to ask?

"Good. Now, back to what I was saying. Imagine getting ahead of all the other students in your class this year," she continued. "Wouldn't you feel your summer wasn't so terrible after all?"

"It will be terrible until Mama comes home," I said. Nothing she could do and nothing wonderful for me could change that.

She sucked in her breath through her nose and pulled up her shoulders. I could see she didn't like my answers, but why should I pretend I was happy she was here?

"Try to concentrate on what I'm telling you. I'm telling you a good thing could come out of all this. I'm a qualified elementary school teacher and you will be my only student for the whole summer. I'll be able to devote all my time to just you — and Ian, of course," she added, but not with any enthusiasm.

I smiled at that and said, "Ian could be ahead of everyone in his school. Some of his teachers think he should already be in college."

"Is that so? Well, for now, then I won't be so concerned about Ian. I'm really concerned only about you. You have a great many new problems, more than a girl your age is supposed to have, and I want to help you with all that, too. In order for me to do that, you know what I need from you?"

I shook my head and then quickly said, "No."

"I need you to be very, very honest with me all the time. I need you to trust me and I need to be able to trust you. Will you try to be honest all the time?"

"Yes. I don't lie," I added. "Ian says I'm not a good liar anyway. He says anyone could take one look at my face and know I was lying."

"That's not a good reason not to lie to people, Jordan," she said quickly. "That makes it sound like you would if you could do it better. You shouldn't want to lie because it's wrong and if people think you lie about one thing, they won't believe you about another. A person is as good as his or her word. Do you understand?"

"Yes," I said. "I don't lie," I added.

"Good. Let's begin slowly. Making close friends, as close as you and I are going to be, takes time. It's like easing yourself into a hot bath, getting used to the water. Do you know what I mean?"

"I don't make the water that hot," I said.

She didn't smile. She looked like she was chewing the inside of her mouth for a moment, chewing on her words or thoughts, but instead of swallowing them, blowing them out toward me.

"Sometimes people don't mean exactly what they say. You must learn not to take every word exactly as it seems."

"If they don't mean what they say, they might be lying," I said.

Again, she didn't smile. She stared at me, nothing in her face moving this time.

"I think your grandmother might be underestimating you," she said, but it seemed to me she was saying it to herself and not to me. "Okay," she continued. "I know about your little problem. I know why we're all going to see the doctor in a little while. I had some students who had the same problem you have," she said. "I can help you with all that."

I lifted my eyebrows. Why did she call it a little problem when everyone else made it sound big? Was it only a little problem? If she had students with the same problem, she would know things to tell me. Would she tell me the same sort of things Flora had told me? Without my book, without Ian and Mama talking to me, I felt as though all the questions hovered above me like persistent tiny flies people called no-see-ums. Answers were the only way to move those annoying flies away.

"Grandmother Emma said you would answer all my questions from now on and I should ask only you."

"That's right. I know you've already been told a great deal and I'll have to be sure you were told everything correctly, so I might go over things you supposedly know."

"It's important to know what's happening in your own body," I said, parroting Ian and getting more enthusiastic. Perhaps my conversations with her wouldn't be so boring after all and wouldn't be anything like being in a classroom. Grandmother Emma might just have done a very good thing bringing her to the house, I thought.

"Yes, that's true about your own body, as long as you learn things about it from mature and responsible people. I know you will have many more questions about yourself than girls without your problems have at your age."

I thought a moment and then decided to test her.

"I still don't understand what an orgasm is," I said, and she bristled like someone who had just had a dozen ice cubes dropped down her back.

She shot up.

"That's disgusting coming out of the mouth of a girl who was just seven. That's entirely inappropriate and we're going to deal with such filth immediately. Get up!" she ordered.

I stood up slowly. Why did she want me to get up?

She approached me, reached out, and seized my wrist, pulling me across the room to my parents' bathroom. She pulled so hard, I nearly tripped, but I sensed she would drag me over the floor if I fell anyway. I protested, but she didn't stop.

At the sink she ran the water and then put a cake of soap under it. I watched her, confused, until she slapped it against my mouth and held the back of my head so I couldn't retreat as she scrubbed against my clenched teeth, the taste of soap seeping through and making me gag.

"This will clean out your filthy mouth," she said.

Then she released me.

I spit into the sink and as soon as I could, screamed at the top of my voice. She slapped my face and clutched my hair, pulling so hard, I felt tears burn my eyes. I kept screaming.

"Stop that screaming immediately. Stop it!" she ordered.

I sucked in and heaved as I held my breath.

"That's better. I'm sorry, but I had to teach you a lesson quickly. We don't have all that much time to waste and your grandmother is very, very concerned about what has been done to you and what has happened to you and what could happen to you. I'm sure you learned that word from Ian.

"When you calm down, I'll tell you more and you'll understand, but for now, this is the best way. I know. I've been a teacher of children your age for many, many years. Now wash your face and dry it and we'll continue talking until your grandmother calls for us."

Tears were streaming down my cheeks. I dried my face slowly and then spit and spit into the sink, but the taste of the soap wouldn't go away. Impatient with how long I was taking, she grasped my shoulders and forcefully turned me from the sink. She held onto me to direct me to leave the bathroom. When we stepped out, I saw Ian standing in the bedroom doorway.

"Why was she screaming?" he demanded, his hands on his hips. I was never so happy to see him.

"You need to learn some manners, I see," Miss Harper replied. "When you enter a room, especially a lady's room, you knock and wait to be admitted. You don't come barging in like this. Now turn around, close the door, and knock," she said.

Ian looked at her and then at me. "What did she do to you?" he asked, ignoring her.

"If I have to call for your grandmother, this will become a major incident. Is that what you want?"

"Jordan?"

She had no idea how well Ian could ignore someone. It made me smile, but Miss Harper's fingers squeezed harder on my shoulders.

"You are supposed to be a very smart young man," she said. "You're not acting very intelligently. With your parents both seriously injured, this is not the time to be a troublemaker in your grandmother's house."

"Are you all right, Jordan?" he asked me.

I kept my eyes directed to the floor. If I told him what she had done, I knew he would get very angry, shout, and tell her to let go of me. He might even go after her the

358

way he had gone after Flora and Addison. Grandmother Emma would come rushing here to see what was happening. He would get into more trouble, I thought.

"Yes," I said, but I didn't look at him. Ian would know the truth in a second if I did.

"If you hurt her, you'll be sorry," he said, turned, and walked out.

"You did the right thing, Jordan," she said immediately. "I'm beginning to wonder if you're not the more intelligent child here."

She turned me around and I looked up at her. She smiled, but I didn't like her smile. Those eyes never warmed, even when she softened her lips.

"You know your grandmother is very concerned about what has been going on between you and Ian. You know that's one of the reasons she has me here now. Whatever his reasons for his actions with you, they were inappropriate, Jordan. Your mother was on her way home to make that clear, too," she said, and I raised my eyes to look at her again. "I have to take her place now. That's why your grandmother wanted me here."

How did she know that Mama had been coming home for that reason? Did Grandmother Emma tell her that and tell her Mama was angry at Ian? Was Daddy?

"It's unfortunate that she and your father were in the accident, but your grandmother is a very wise person. You know she is, right?"

"Yes," I said. I was still very hurt and didn't want to be with her or talk to her and I hated agreeing with her now.

"Well, as I said, I'm here now to carry out what your parents were surely going to do. They would make sure you were protected, that you weren't abused by anyone, and that your problem was handled in a professional and successful manner. It is not the subject for discussion among children. Curiosity can be a good thing if it is done properly, but you remember that curiosity killed the cat," she said, with that smile mask back on her face.

I knew that expression.

"Satisfaction brought him back," I muttered. Ian always said that whenever anyone talked about the cat. He believed curiosity was healthy and important and that the only people who feared it were people who had something to hide or something about which they would be embarrassed.

She glared at me now, even her weak smile disappearing. "Sit," she said, nodding at the settee again.

I moved obediently to it.

"Now then, there are words you may use and words you may not as regards your problem. If you should have the womanly problem that occurs monthly, for example, I want you to refer to it as your monthlies. Understand? You tell me you think you're having your monthlies. Do not use any other word for it. Even so, never say it aloud, even to me. Whisper it. What we'll do is make sure you have a sanitary napkin."

"It's not a napkin," I said. "It's a cigar."

Her eyes widened. "I will give you the benefit of the doubt because of your age, Jordan, but that, I want you to know, is also disgusting. Think before you say such things to me or anyone else. If you must," she said, "ask it as a question. Ask if it's all right to say this or that. But only ask me and only whisper it to me, even when there is no one in the room with us."

I scrunched my eyebrows together. Even when there was no one in the room with us? Why would I have to whisper to her then?

"Someone could be listening in. Snooping," she muttered, and glanced at the door as if she believed Ian was just outside it with his ear to it. "Besides, a real lady never says things like that aloud. She hates to even have such words cross her lips. She hates even thinking about it.

"Now, where was I?" she asked. She look very flustered. "Oh, yes. You are unfortunately now at a point where being underdressed or in any way undressed is not permitted in the company of others, not even other girls. It's unhealthy. You are not to parade around your room without your body being covered properly, even when you are alone. I will want to see your bathing suits to be sure they are adequate in that regard."

"Mama just bought new ones for me," I said quickly.

"Well, I'm sure she picked out the right sort of bathing suit, but it will still be good for me to see it. I'm only trying to do what is necessary to protect you," she added. "Your mother would want that. She would do the same things I'm doing if she could."

"Mama never put soap in my mouth."

"Mothers are important people, but they are often too busy to study how to educate their own children. That's why they depend on people like me, professionals."

"Do you have any children?" I asked.

"I'm not a married woman, Jordan. How can I have children?"

"Then how do you know about mothers?"

She was silent again, and again took a

362

deep breath before answering me.

"I can see why you and your brother are difficult for your grandmother. We are going to spend a lot of time together so you can learn what is proper to ask and what is not. You just don't say everything that comes into your little head. I know about mothers because most of my professional life, I have had to deal with mothers, talk to them about their children, and help guide them in bringing up their children. I am an expert when it comes to that. Are you satisfied?"

"I want my mama back," I said as an answer.

"Yes, well, we all want things we can't have when we want them and things we can never have."

"What do you want that you can't have?" I asked quickly.

It snapped her head up so fast I thought I was going to be marched back into the bathroom for another bout with soap.

"You are not to ask me another question about myself. Is that clear?" she said firmly. "It's inappropriate for you to question your elders. It's quite disrespectful, in fact. I won't tolerate it."

I knew the answer. I thought it or did I say it? I thought it so fast and so confidently, I might have said it. Her eyes widened.

"What did you say?"

I bit down on my lower lip and shook my head. "Nothing."

She stared at me, but I knew the answer to my question, the question I wasn't permitted to ask.

Children.

She wanted children and she would never have them.

20
MISS HARPER IN CHARGE

If there was any doubt that Miss Harper would have a major role to play in my life now, it was put to rest when we went to see Dr. Dell'Acqua again. Grandmother Emma introduced her to the doctor as my minder and guardian and she was permitted to sit in on all the discussion about me. Dr. Dell'Acqua was very upset about what had happened to Mama and Daddy and was eager to do whatever she could for me. With Miss Harper present, she reviewed her initial findings. I watched Miss Harper's face as she talked, especially when she repeated that my vagina was estrogenized. She looked like she was going to be sick.

Grandmother Emma wanted to be sure I was getting the best possible medication and treatment and Dr. Dell'Acqua reassured her about that, citing some recent medical studies. I thought Ian would have liked to hear about that. I thought he might even know about it already.

Then Grandmother asked her if she thought Mama had waited too long to bring me to see her.

She shook her head and said, "I don't think so, Emma. Her condition is not irreversible. We'll help her. However," she continued, "there is another consideration here, Emma, the psychological. I'm sure," she said, looking at me and smiling, "that Jordan has many, many questions about herself and what is going on in her body. It's important you don't feel you're in any way freaky, Jordan. It's just a medical condition we'll correct. You should not be afraid to ask anything," she added, and my eyes shifted toward Miss Harper. Her gaze drifted toward the ceiling. She looked like she wasn't enjoying being in here with me and Grandmother Emma.

Dr. Dell'Acqua turned back to Grandmother Emma. "I did tell Carol that she might need some professional therapy with this."

"That's why I have brought in Miss Harper," Grandmother said. "She has years and years of experience with children her age."

"Hmm," Dr. Dell'Acqua muttered. I could see it wasn't exactly what she meant, but she didn't want to contradict my grand-mother. "Okay, but if you need any additional assistance, please call and I'll point you in the right direction."

"I feel we're in the right direction now, Rene. Thank you."

She nodded, but when she glanced at me, I could see she wasn't as happy about it as she could be.

"From now on," Grandmother Emma told me in the limousine on our way home, "Miss Harper will be in charge of your medicine. She will determine what you should wear every morning and what you should do with your day."

"I'll make up a schedule for us," Miss Harper said, "just the way I would if you were in my schoolroom. We'll spend time on lessons, but you will have time to yourself, to play, to swim, and do things you like. It will be the most productive summer of your life," she assured me.

"Are you going to make up a schedule for Ian, too?" I asked. It would be like home-schooling and Ian was always saying he could do better if he had homeschooling, but I think he meant without a teacher, just teaching himself.

"We'll see," she said.

"Ian has a way of amusing himself all day

anyway," Grandmother Emma said. "So, tell me, now that we finally have a quiet moment, how or why did he get into a fight at the lake? It's not in his nature to be physical."

"I don't know," I said quickly, too quickly, because she pursed her lips and narrowed her eyes with disappointment.

"Perhaps you'll talk about it with Miss Harper," she told me.

"Of course she will," Miss Harper said. "When she and I have gotten to know each other better, she won't keep any secrets from me. We already agreed she would be honest and truthful all the time, didn't we, Jordan?"

I started to nod and then quickly said, "Yes."

Grandmother Emma smiled at her. "I am grateful you could come to my assistance, Millicent. You can see how much work has to be done on these children, and with my son and daughter-in-law in the condition they are now in, I needed professional assistance. It's fortunate for all of us that you were available and agreed to come here."

"After all you've done for me and my mother, I'm grateful to repay you in any way I can."

"Thank you. Your mother and I were once

inseparable. I do miss her."

"I'll see about having her visit," Miss Harper said.

"Yes, that would be nice. Well, I'll have Felix drop me at the supermarket first since it's on the way and then he'll take you back to the house. After I'm finished there, I'll make a trip to the hospital and see about Christopher."

"Can I go, too?" I asked quickly.

"No, you can't. You will have too much to do at home and your father is not ready for visitors. I'll tell you when it's the right time for you and Ian to visit him."

"I don't have anything to do," I said. "If it's not time for visitors, why are you visiting?"

"I hardly think it's necessary to explain why to you, Jordan. I have much more to do there than just chat with your father, who I do not believe is even up to that, and you do have much to do. You just heard Miss Harper. You're going to set up a schedule with her. Please don't waste my energy on such questions," she added.

As soon as Grandmother Emma stepped out of the limousine at the supermarket, Miss Harper turned on me.

"I thought you and I had discussed why you shouldn't do that with your elders,

Jordan. You never, ever cross-examine your elders like that. Not only is it impolite, but it's a sign of very poor upbringing and reflects badly on your parents. I'm not surprised, however. Most children your age have not been properly schooled in their manners and decorum. Parents today are too involved in themselves. They are not willing to make the sacrifices in time and energy. Hereafter, before you question anyone, you'd better look to me to see if you should. I'll nod or shake my head and that will help you to know."

"What if you're not there?" I asked.

Once again, she gave me that cold, ice blue stare first. "I'll always be there now," she replied.

Always? Will she follow me around everywhere? What about after Mama returns? I wondered, but decided not to ask. Instead, I curled up in the corner of the seat and became an Ian caterpillar until we arrived at the house. Ian was outside with his big magnifying glass looking at something in the grass. I practically leaped out of the limousine and started to run to him.

"JORDAN!" Miss Harper shouted. It had the effect of a lasso thrown around my neck.

I stopped short and turned.

"You're to go directly to your room. We're

going to begin there," she said.

"I want to talk to Ian," I said.

"Go directly to your room, please." She took a step toward me.

Ian stood up and looked at us. He knew where we had gone, of course. "Jordan," he said. "Did the doctor say anything new?"

"JORDAN!" Miss Harper cried. "You have been told not to discuss your problem with anyone, especially your brother. Now go directly to your room. I will not tell you again. If I do, I'll count it as a serious demerit."

"Demerit?" Ian asked, smiling. He walked toward us. "What's that mean? Are you going to take away her dolls or something if she gets too many demerits or are you going to assign her to detention?"

"That's enough from you, young man. You can be sure I'm keeping track of your misbehavior, too. Jordan, do as I say."

She reached out toward me. I looked at Ian. He shook his head and returned to whatever he was studying. I wanted to stay with him, but I was really afraid of what she might tell Grandmother Emma and what Grandmother Emma might do to both of us, so I took her hand. She clasped mine with surprising firmness, practically crushing my fingers.

"I am not accustomed to having to raise my voice like that," she muttered as she tugged me toward the front door. I looked back at Ian. He was staring at us and even from this distance, I could see his eyes were narrow and full of darts.

As soon as we entered, she ordered me to my room. "Go on. I have something to tell the maid and then I'll be there," she said.

All I could think of was Mama. I prayed for her to wake up and come home. Head down, I walked up the stairway and into my bedroom. I was surprised to see my bed was not made and the clothes I had worn the day before were not hung up or taken to be washed. The towel I had used in the bathroom was where I had left it crumpled up, too.

"Good," I heard, and turned to see Miss Harper march into my room. "I was afraid she might have forgotten her new orders. We'll begin with straightening and cleaning your room. From now on, this will be your first chore of the day."

"But Nancy always does that," I said.

"Nancy will not be doing it either for you or for Ian anymore. It is only when we take care of our own things that we learn the value of them," she said.

"But what will Nancy do?"

"That is not your concern, Jordan. Honestly, I have never met a child your age who is so cantankerous."

"What's that mean?"

She raised her eyes to the ceiling and then slammed her hand, palm open, against the wall. The action was so unexpected and so hard, I winced with sympathetic pain. It had to hurt, but she didn't act like it did.

"Question after question after question. Vocabulary lessons will take place later," she said, suddenly very calmly and sweetly. "Now, have you ever made your own bed?"

"I did it with Mama at the cabin," I said.

"How fortunate. Let me see you do it now," she said, and folded her arms under her small bosom as she stepped back to watch.

I began slowly. The bed in the cabin wasn't as big as this one, Daddy's old bed, but I began as I remembered Mama had taught me. Miss Harper watched and didn't step forward to help when I struggled with the blanket. When I was finished, she stepped up to the bed and tore it apart again.

"Too messy," she said. "You don't leave the top sheet that wrinkled and you don't leave your pillows looking as if you were just lying on them. Do it again."

"It's the way Nancy makes it," I said.

"I doubt that. Do it again. Do it!"

I did it again, and again, she was dissatisfied. This time I hadn't tucked in the sheets neatly enough.

"Why does it have to be so perfect?" I asked, which was another mistake.

"Sit," she told me, pointing to my desk chair. I did. She stood in front of my desk as if we were really back in her classroom. "Why is it important to do things as perfectly as we can? Who knows the answer?" she asked.

I know my mouth fell open a little. Who knows the answer? Who else was in the room? Ian wasn't here.

"Well?" She glared down at me. "Why?"

"So they'll look nice," I said.

"Before you speak in my classroom, raise your hand and be recognized," she said.

"This isn't a classroom. It's my father's old bedroom."

"Wherever I am, that is a classroom!" she said, with her hands on my desk and her face close to mine. "Go on. Raise your hand."

I felt very silly doing it, but I did.

"Jordan. Yes? Tell us why it's important to do things as perfectly as possible."

"So they'll look nice."

"Yes, but that's not the main reason. If we try to do everything we have to do perfectly, we'll always do well and it doesn't matter if anyone else sees it or not. We have to have standards for ourselves. It has to be important to us to do things well. Otherwise, we will become lazy and sloppy and we'll do poorly when we have to do things for others. What will happen to us then? Jordan?"

"We won't be liked?"

"Not just liked. We won't get jobs. We won't get appreciated. So what do we want to do always? Jordan?"

"Do everything perfectly."

"Very good. Now get up and do the bed again," she said.

I did it as best I could, making sure every little thing was as perfect as I could make it. She stood hovering over me.

"Well," she said when I was finished. "It's not absolutely perfect, but it's much better than it was the first time you did it, isn't it?"

I nodded.

"Isn't it?" she repeated. I had forgotten. Don't nod, speak.

"Yes."

"I think it's time you said, 'Yes, Miss Harper, no, Miss Harper.' That, too, is polite."

"Yes, Miss Harper."

"Good. We will get along after all," she said. "Now to your clothes."

I picked up my dress from the chair and she watched me fit it on the hanger. I did that well enough because she didn't ask me to do it again. In the bathroom, I folded the wet towel and put it with my undergarments into the hamper.

"There," she said. "Your first chores of the day are finished. Now, every day we'll then go to your medicine and you will take it after the chores are done."

"Mama wanted me to take it right away, as soon as I woke up, so I wouldn't forget."

"Well, you won't have to worry about forgetting anymore, will you? I'll be right here to remind you."

I shook my head. "Mama said to take it right away, as soon as I wake up."

Her eyes widened for a second and then she smiled. "You are a precious little piece of work," she said. "You remind me of a wild horse that has to be trained or a puppy that has to be housebroken."

She went to the cabinet where my medicine was kept and took it out. "What I'll do for you is keep it and bring it in when I come in to inspect your room in the morning," she said.

I shook my head, but she pretended not to see it.

"What we will do now is work on your school material. I'll be right back. I have books and workbooks for you," she said, smiled, and left my room with my medicine in her hands.

I heard Ian coming up the stairs and hurried to my doorway to call to him. He paused and looked my way. I had forgotten Grandmother Emma had forbidden him from entering this side of the upstairs. I hurried down the hallway toward him.

"What's going on?" he asked.

"She made me make my bed, hang up my clothes, and clean my bathroom. I have to do it every morning before I can have my medicine," I told him. "She's going to tell you to do it, too."

He thought a moment and nodded. "Good," he said. "I prefer that to having Nancy, as you know."

"I don't. I want Nancy to do it."

"Don't act spoiled. That's just what she'll tell Grandmother Emma. Where is she?" he asked, looking past me.

"She went to get my schoolwork. She's going to make me do fourth-grade schoolwork so I'll be ahead."

"Well, that's good, too," he said, which

infuriated me.

"I don't want to do schoolwork, Ian. It's summer. I want to go out to the pool."

"Look," he said, "we didn't ask for all this to happen. Grandmother Emma hired her, so let her work. Take advantage of the situation and improve."

"She'll make you work, too," I warned.

He smiled. "I hardly think she has anything valuable to teach me," he said, and started for his room just as Miss Harper came out of Daddy and Mama's bedroom carrying books and workbooks in her arms.

"What did you say to her?" she asked him immediately.

He paused, looked at Miss Harper, and then continued to his room.

"I'll be in to speak with you shortly, young man," she called after him.

He closed his door and turned the lock. She stood there a moment looking toward his room and then she continued toward me.

"What did he say to you? Did he ask you again about the doctor?"

"No," I said. "He said he didn't care about taking care of his own room. He likes that."

"He does, does he? We'll see what he likes and doesn't like. Back to your room," she ordered.

I turned and walked, but not fast enough for her. I could feel her practically breathing on my head, her feet right behind mine. As soon as we entered the bedroom, she told me to sit at my desk and then she put the books on it, explaining each one, the math book, the English book, the science book, and the social studies book. She had a fifth book I had never seen called *Becoming a Lady*. She said it was all about manners and proper behavior and was just as important as, if not more important than, the other subjects.

She opened each book to show me where she had marked off the pages for me to begin reading. Each book, except the one called *Becoming a Lady,* had a workbook to go along with it, which was something I had in school. She then showed me the pages in the workbook that I had to complete after I had done a section of reading in each book.

"I'm going to let you start on your own," she said. She looked at her watch. "You'll have enough time to do the math assignment and the English assignment before lunch. After lunch, you will do the rest and then we'll go over all the work together to see what you learned yourself and what I need to explain further."

I glanced at the window. It was practically a cloudless day and very warm, too.

"But I want to go swimming today. Grandmother Emma said she had the pool started for Ian and me. She said we could go swimming and I want to call one of my friends to come over, Missy Littleton."

"We will discuss that after you've completed all your work," she said. "But I can tell you that I frown upon any guests arriving on weekdays. You can begin now."

"I don't want to," I said. "I don't want to do schoolwork today. I want to go swimming. It's not weekdays in the summer. Every day is like a weekend."

"Not to me and not to you any longer. Work."

I couldn't help the tears.

She glared at me and then she looked at her watch. "I will return in an hour and a half. If you haven't completed the first two assignments by then, you won't have lunch."

She turned and walked out of the room, closing the door.

"I won't do it!" I screamed. My heart was pounding in anticipation of her returning, but she didn't. I listened and then I rose and peeked out the door to see her marching toward Ian's bedroom.

I watched her try the door and then knock

hard, demanding he open the door. He didn't. I could see her arms down, extended, her hands clenched into fists.

"You will regret this, young man," she warned, turned, and headed for the stairway.

I retreated quickly and returned to my desk, where I sat sulking, but I couldn't help but be curious about the schoolwork. Maybe Ian was right. Maybe I should get ahead. I started to read the math book and then look at the workbook. Some of it was easy, but some of it was confusing and I was impatient. I returned to sulking until that bored me, too. I got up and looked out the window.

Grandmother Emma's grounds workers were cutting grass and trimming bushes. The pool man was there cleaning. It was truly a beautiful day and I longed just to be outside to smell the flowers blooming, the grass being cut, and hear the birds. I even wished we were back at the lake and all that had happened was just a nightmare. I'd even risk meeting up with the black bear again.

Really bored now and frustrated, I went to the bed and just sprawled out. I closed my eyes and turned on my back and before I knew it, I fell asleep. A sharp slap across my left cheek woke me and I looked up at an enraged Miss Harper.

"How dare you? How dare you defy my instructions and ignore your assignments?"

I was too stunned to cry. No one ever slapped me like that, not Mama, not Daddy, and not Grandmother Emma. I touched my burning cheek and held my breath.

"Not only won't you go out today, you will have no lunch and will remain in this room now until all the work I assigned you is completed. And if you don't finish it by dinnertime, you'll miss dinner as well."

"No, I won't," I said defiantly.

"Oh, yes, you will," she said with a cold smile, and held up the skeleton key to the bedroom door. "I know how to housebreak puppies. I'll return in three hours," she said.

She turned before I could get off the bed and she walked out, closing the door behind her. I heard her turn the key in the lock and then I heard her walk away.

I slipped off the bed and ran to the door, smashing it with my little fists and screaming at the top of my voice. "Open the door! Let me out! Let me out! I want my mother!"

I waited, but heard only silence. My hands were red and hurt where I struck the door with them. I shuddered and sank to the floor, crying. I was sobbing so loudly, I didn't hear the tinkling sounds in the door lock when they first began, but when I heard them, I sucked in my tears and held my breath. After a few more moments, the lock snapped open. I rose and stood back quickly, terrified of what she would do next.

The door opened.

Ian was standing there with a screwdriver in his hands.

And I was never so happy to see him.

"Why did she lock you in?" he asked me.

"Because I didn't do the schoolwork she wanted me to do. She said I wouldn't get any lunch until I did it and if I didn't, I might not get dinner either. I want to go outside. I want to go see Mama."

"Calm down, Jordan," he said, and stood there thinking. "You should have tried to do the work, but she shouldn't have locked you in here. It's dangerous. What if there had been a fire?"

I nodded, suddenly very frightened, too.

"IAN!" we heard her scream. "How dare you do such a thing? You have disobeyed your grandmother, too. You were told not to come here."

Ian turned slowly and looked at Miss Harper. He held his screwdriver pointed at her.

"You shouldn't have locked her in the room. If there had been a fire, she could have died," he said. "My grandmother will not like that. Our parents will be infuriated as well."

"You are truly an insubordinate young man. Your grandmother has placed you both in my hands for the time being and your parents can only be grateful for what I'm trying to do here."

Ian blew air through his lips and she stiffened, seeming to grow taller.

"Go to your room this instant. There will be no lunch for you either. Go on!" she said, pointing toward his room.

Ian looked at me and then at her and walked slowly down the hall. When he reached the stairway, he started down.

Miss Harper shook her head.

"I told you to go to your room!" she shouted, waited, but he didn't reappear. "That boy is incorrigible," she said. "His misbehavior is much more serious than your grandmother assumed. Something very drastic has to be done immediately."

She looked at me. "Have you gone back to your desk and your work?"

I started to shake my head and stopped. I didn't want her to lock the door again.

"Yes," I said.

"Very well. I'll trust you this time. You can come down to lunch and then we'll work afterward together. If we make good

progress, we'll go outside, too," she promised. "Come along."

I hesitated.

Somehow, being nice to her seemed like a
terrible betrayal of Ian.

I had no idea just how right I was.

21
MISS HARPER'S PUPPET

Grandmother Emma didn't return from the hospital until shortly before our dinner was to be served. As it turned out, the work Miss Harper had given me took most of the afternoon and by the time I was finished and she looked at it, it was too late to go swimming. She reviewed the workbooks with a red pencil and marked all my mistakes. I really did feel as if I were back in school.

"Tomorrow, we will begin with your errors," she said, "and we will get you to understand everything and get everything right. Every two days I will give you a test on what you've learned and we'll decide if you will go ahead or go back. With this sort of concentrated effort, Jordan, I'll have you on a fourth-grade level well before the end of the summer. You'll see. You'll be very happy with yourself."

I gazed out the window. The beautiful blue

sky was now covered with a thick layer of dark clouds. We were going to have a thunderstorm. I had missed a wonderful day. I wondered if Ian had missed it, too. I hadn't heard him or seen him. He wasn't at lunch as I had expected either. I could see Miss Harper didn't know where he was. Afterward, I heard her ask Nancy, who told her Ian was like a ghost around here. She never knew when to expect him or where he was.

"That will come to an abrupt end," Miss Harper vowed.

I don't think Nancy cared one way or another, although when I saw Miss Harper talk to her, I noticed that Nancy seemed just as frightened of her as she was of Grandmother Emma.

We heard Grandmother Emma come up the stairs and down the hallway. She paused at my father's bedroom doorway and looked in on us.

"How are we doing, Millicent?" she asked.

Miss Harper glanced at me and then walked out, closing the door so I wouldn't hear them talk. I strained to listen. Their voices were quite muffled, but Grandmother Emma's was full of disappointment and anger.

"I'm sorry," I heard her say. "I'll see about him as soon as possible."

The door was opened again and Miss Harper told me to run my bath. "I'll pick out what you should wear to dinner," she said. "Go on. Get started."

"I want to see Grandmother Emma first," I said.

I think Miss Harper assumed I was going to complain about her, about how she had washed my mouth with soap and slapped my face and made me work on schoolwork all day. She smiled and without hesitation turned and called to Grandmother Emma.

"Emma, your granddaughter would like a word with you."

Grandmother Emma returned to my doorway. She had removed her light coat and had begun to unpin her hair. "What is it, Jordan? I have much to do before I get ready for dinner."

"How was Daddy?" I asked. "Is he coming home? Is he in a wheelchair already? Does he know he won't walk again?"

"It isn't polite to ask so many questions before you get the answer to one, Jordan," Miss Harper said, but in a much softer voice than she usually spoke to me.

"Your father has learned the full extent of his injuries and he is in a deep depression about it," Grandmother Emma began. "That will pass in time and that's when I will bring you to see him. As to his therapy, it will begin as soon as possible, but I'm afraid it will take most of the summer before I can have him brought back to the house and he becomes accustomed to his wheel-chair.

"Before you ask," she added, "there is no change in your mother's condition. She could be like she is for weeks, months, even years. It's not unheard of for people with her sort of injuries to be in prolonged co-mas.

"As you can see, this is why it is so important for you and your brother to behave and listen obediently to Miss Harper. We have to make the best of this situation and misbehavior cannot be toler-ated. No one has time for it. You can help your brother by advising him about all that and telling him to behave, not that he'll listen to anyone, I'm afraid.

"I'll deal with him in a little while," she added. "Anything else before I take my bath?"

This was my chance, I thought. I glanced at Miss Harper. She stood there with her smile mask on her face, waiting. Something in her eyes and in my grandmother's tired eyes told me that it would be a waste of time to complain and might even get me into deeper trouble.

"No," I said.

"Then do as you're told," Grandmother Emma said, and left me.

"Your bath," Miss Harper reminded me.

I went to the bathroom and ran the water. At least Nancy had brought my bath oil to this bedroom, I thought. Just smelling it when I poured it into the water reminded me of Mama and helped me feel she was nearby, watching over me.

After I got into the water and soaked in the soft, scented bubbles, Miss Harper came into the bathroom, but I noticed she took great pains to avoid looking directly at me.

"I want you to wash your hair as well," she said. She laid out my clothing. "I'll be back in a while to see that you've done so."

She started out again and out of curiosity, I pushed the whirlpool button. The air churned the water around me, making the bubbles bigger and bigger so fast, they nearly covered my face. It made me laugh. Finally, something was fun. However, Miss Harper was back in the doorway because she heard the noise. When she saw what I had done, she screamed at me.

"Shut that off! We take baths to get clean and not to play in the water. You're too old for that sort of thing. Shut it off!"

I did quickly. The bubbles had gone to the very edge of the tub.

"Look at what you've done. You could have soaked the floor here. Never do that again."

"But why is it in the tub if I can't do it?"

"It's . . . stupid," she said, flustered by my question. "Just don't do it. It's time you got out, dried yourself, and got dressed."

"I didn't wash my hair yet," I said.

"Then don't dillydally anymore. Wash it."

When I rose out of the bubbles, her eyes went to my buds. For a moment she looked intrigued, curious, and then she realized she was staring at my chest and pivoted like a soldier in a parade and was gone.

After I had dried and dressed myself, she returned to inspect me and finally gave me a compliment. "Very good," she said. "You know how to dress and brush your hair well. Now let's go to dinner. I understand from your grandmother that she has already begun to educate you on dining etiquette. I'll help with that at every meal."

I followed her out and down the stairs to the dining room. Grandmother Emma was already at the table. She looked very tired and very upset to me. Something new had happened. I was sure it involved Ian. He wasn't at the table.

"Where's Ian?" I asked.

"Your brother will not be taking any meals with us for the next three days."

"Why not?"

"He is confined to his room," she said. "He left our property today, which is a direct violation of my order. He went walking on the road where there is a great deal of traffic, too. All we need now is another injury in this family and I'll go out of my mind. He is not permitted to do any of the things he likes to do outside until he learns how to behave and how to listen to Miss Harper.

"If he disobeys me this time, I might have to send him off to a military school camp. I've told him that, warned him. I will do it," she said.

I had no doubt she would.

Miss Harper looked at me, her face soaked in self-satisfaction.

Nancy didn't care about us. Grandmother Emma was totally on Miss Harper's side. Ian was locked up and I was alone.

Mama, I cried inside myself. Please, oh please, wake up.

I sank to my seat and my dinner etiquette instruction began in earnest.

I was beginning to feel as if I had been a victim of some evil magician who had caused my parents' accident and turned me into Miss Harper's puppet. She held my strings tightly in her long, thin fingers and tugged especially at the one tied to my heart.

I didn't have much of an appetite, but I had to eat as much as I could while under Miss Harper's eyes and instructions. She did say it wasn't proper for a young lady to eat a great deal and look like she hadn't had a meal for weeks. She made me eat slower, too. I could see that Grandmother Emma not only approved of Miss Harper's comments and instructions, but truly appreciated them.

"Miss Harper's mother and I went to the same finishing school," she told me.

"That was fortunate for me," Miss Harper said. "My mother became my finishing school teacher after my father had passed away. Money wasn't as available. He never prepared for that eventuality enough," she continued.

Despite how much I disliked her, I couldn't help but be fascinated by what she would reveal about herself.

"Isn't that like most men?" Grandmother Emma said. "They think they'll live forever and need not worry that much about who will be left behind. I made sure my husband had plenty of life insurance. Every time I added to his policy or added a policy, he would rant and rave that it was money wasted. What it really did was remind him of his own mortality and no man wants that."

"No, they don't," Miss Harper said. She said it with such bitterness I wondered if she liked her father at all. I could see that he might not have liked her.

"Whatever, your mother did a fine job with you, Millicent."

"Thank you."

"How will Ian eat?" I asked when there was a lull in their conversation.

"He won't eat until tomorrow and then Nancy will bring him something to eat, but no sweets, no desserts," Grandmother Emma said. She turned to Miss Harper. "They say you can win a man's heart through his stomach. You can win his devotion and his obedience that way as well."

Miss Harper laughed.

It was the first time I had heard her laugh like that and I didn't like it because she was laughing at being mean to Ian. Her eyes shifted toward me and she saw the distaste I had for her in mine. I knew she did because she stopped laughing, cleared her throat, and then forced a smile at Grandmother Emma before glancing back at me, her eyes cold, angry, and even more hateful. It made me shudder inside and it took my breath away. I couldn't even swallow and was grateful when I was excused from the table and could hurry back upstairs.

I felt very sorry for Ian. I imagined he was very hungry, but I knew he would never complain or cry about it, even to me. I hesitated at the top of the stairway. I could hear Grandmother Emma and Miss Harper still talking at the dinner table. They would have their coffee and dessert for sure, I thought, and decided to risk seeing Ian.

He had his door locked. I didn't want to make a lot of noise, so I knocked softly and then I called to him in just over a whisper.

"Ian, it's me."

I waited and then he opened the door. "What?" he asked.

"Are you hungry?"

"No, I had an energy bar."

"Grandmother Emma said you can't come out for three days."

"We'll see. You'd better go before you get into trouble, too."

He started to close the door and then stopped. "Did she tell you anything about Father and Mother?"

I told him as best I could all that she had said.

"I know where Mother is," he said. "I'll be visiting her myself." He started to close the door.

"Ian."

"What?"

"I want to go, too," I said.

He thought a moment. "We'll see," he said. "Maybe," he added, and then closed the door.

I thought I heard Miss Harper on the stairs so I turned and walked quickly to my room to turn on the television set so she wouldn't know I had spoken with Ian. I had just gotten it on and sat when she stepped into my room. She looked at the books on my desk and picked up the one entitled *Becoming a Lady.* She brought it to me.

"Rather than watch something silly on television, you should read some of this, Jordan. We can talk about it tomorrow. Why don't you read up to here," she said, pointing to the beginning of chapter three.

"I'm tired of reading," I said.

"You should never be tired of reading. You should be tired of watching the idiot box first."

"What's the idiot box?"

"That," she said, nodding at the television set and then flicking it off with the remote. She tapped the book she had placed beside me. "Read."

"You said my schoolwork was over," I whined.

"This isn't schoolwork, Jordan. It's more like learning how to live correctly. You won't be tested on it like you're tested on math and science and English. We'll just talk about it and practice what there is to practice. When you're older, you'll thank me," she said. "Be sure to brush your teeth," she added, and left the bedroom. She didn't close the door behind her, however. I was sure she would come back soon to see if I were reading or if I had turned the television on again.

I opened the book and began to read how important it was to make a good impression on people and how that is done through your behavior. I didn't understand some of the words and it was very boring to me. Before I had read two pages, I felt tired and closed my eyes.

"Well," I heard a little while later, and opened my eyes to see Miss Harper standing there again. "I can see I'll have to read this with you. We'll have to put it in our daily schedule after we do your other work."

I rubbed my eyes.

"Go brush your teeth and go to sleep," she said, taking the book and putting it back on my desk with the other books. "Don't forget now. As soon as you wake up, begin your chores."

After she left, I walked to the bathroom to wash my face and brush my teeth. I was moving in a daze, but I did everything I had to do, changed into my pajamas, and crawled under the blanket on my big bed. The house was very quiet. I had gotten used to some of the creaks and groans I used to hear on the other side, in my room. They made me feel secure somehow. The stillness on this side made me nervous and fidgety. I imagined that because Grandmother Emma slept on this side of the house, the house didn't dare make a sound.

Before I fell asleep again, I thought about all the things Grandmother Emma had said about Daddy. I knew *depressed* meant feeling sad. He didn't have us and he didn't have Mama with him in the hospital and he had learned he wouldn't walk and had to be in a wheelchair. I felt terrible for him and thought about the clip-clop of his cowboy boots when he walked down the hallway. He wouldn't want to wear them anymore, or any shoes for that matter. Why wear them if he couldn't stand up?

Mama will surely feel sorry for him, too,

when she wakes up from her coma, I thought. She'll forgive him and she'll help him. That was why it was so important now, so much more important, that she did awaken. As soon as she did, she was sure to go to him.

I thought about her silence, too. Wherever she was, we weren't there. No one was talking to her. I was afraid she would feel we deserted her, forgot about her already. It was very important for Ian and me to go see her. I hoped he had a way to do it, but I couldn't imagine how. He couldn't drive and Felix wouldn't drive us.

Ian will think of something, I told myself. He's sitting in his room right now planning it out like one of his projects.

That thought and imagining Mama waking up and seeing us and smiling was what helped me feel secure enough to close my eyes and fall asleep in a room that had become more like a prison cell than anything else. I had to stay here and do schoolwork. I had to do my chores. I could be locked up in it, and most of all, no one I loved could come to me in it.

Maybe tomorrow, I thought. Maybe tomorrow will be better.

It wasn't.

I didn't wake up early enough for Miss

Harper, who was beside my bed, shaking me and yelling at me.

"You should have been up, washed, and dressed, all your chores completed by now. If it were a school day, you'd be in your classroom. We want to keep the same hours."

I blinked rapidly and then scrubbed my cheeks with my palms.

Impatient, she reached down, seized my right arm at the elbow, and nearly pulled it out of my shoulder tugging me into a sitting position.

"Out of bed!" she screamed. "I'll give you exactly ten minutes to complete your morning chores."

She walked out of the room and closed the door behind her. When I looked at the clock, I saw it was not quite seven a.m. Even Grandmother Emma wasn't usually up and dressed and down to breakfast as early as this, I thought. Did Miss Harper wake her, too?

Miss Harper returned to my bedroom and looked at my bed. She shook her head.

"Not much improvement over yesterday," she said. "When I was your age, I was helping my mother clean the house. Of course, I wasn't as spoiled. We had to watch our pennies. We couldn't afford a maid every day, and after my father died, we didn't have a maid any day."

"Where is my medicine?" I asked her. She didn't have it in her hands.

She stared at me with that same cold expression. My lips began trembling.

"Where is my medicine, please, Miss Harper," she replied.

"Where is my medicine, please, Miss Harper?" I parroted.

She looked at me as if she was still deciding on whether I deserved it or not. "You'll get it after you clean up the bathroom."

"It's clean," I said.

She went in and looked at everything. I had folded up my towel neatly.

"Wash out the sink," she ordered. "You spit your toothpaste in it and it looks disgusting."

I did it quickly.

"Follow me," she said after that. "You'll come to my room for your medicine every morning."

"Why?" I asked, and she spun on me.

"You didn't just ask me why, did you? You didn't start that questioning of your elders again, did you?"

I shook my head, and then I quickly said, "No."

"Good. For a moment I thought you

would have to be locked in your room without breakfast."

I followed her to what had been my parents' room. She went into the bathroom and brought out my medicine. Then she stood by as I inhaled it. She practically grabbed it out of my hand when I was finished and put it back in her bathroom.

"We'll go down to breakfast now," she said.

Again, I followed her out. I hesitated at Ian's door, but I heard nothing.

To my surprise I discovered that Grandmother Emma had risen even earlier so she could get herself over to the supermarket.

I was afraid to ask why, but Miss Harper answered my question by telling me my grandmother wanted to make unexpected and unannounced visits to see how well it was being run under the managers.

"It's the only way to deal with common laboring people like that," she muttered. "Surprise them."

She watched me begin to eat my breakfast and then started to complain about every move I made. I was too far from the table. I didn't bring my spoon to my mouth correctly. I didn't wipe my lips with the napkin when I should have. I made too much noise chewing. Before it was over, my stomach felt like I had swallowed stones.

"You can go upstairs and begin reading your textbooks," she said when I was finished. "I'll be up as soon as I finish my breakfast and make some phone calls. I have to see how my mother is doing. We'll start on all that you got wrong yesterday."

It was another beautiful day. Would I spend it all inside again? I was afraid to ask.

I started up the stairs, but stopped when I heard Ian whisper my name. I turned and saw Ian standing in the living room doorway. I knew he wasn't supposed to come out of his room, so I quickly looked back to see if Miss Harper had heard him. He beckoned for me to come closer. I practically tiptoed down the steps.

"Did you do your medicine?" he asked.

"Yes. She keeps it in Daddy and Mama's room, where she sleeps. I had to go in there," I told him.

"Where is Grandmother Emma?"

I told him.

"And where is Miss Harper?"

"She's still eating breakfast and then she's going to call her mother, she said."

"Good. Follow me," he said. He started for the front door.

"Where are you going?"

"To see Mother," he said. "Do you want

to go or not?"

I nodded quickly.

"Then come on. I have money. Be quiet," he added.

I joined him at the door. He opened it softly and we slipped out.

My heart was pounding.

"Just walk like nothing's wrong," he said. "People never know anything if you don't show it."

He started, stopped, took my hand, and then led me down the driveway. We picked up our pace when we reached the road.

"We're taking a taxi to the bus station," he said. "There's a taxi stand at the strip mall down on the four corners. It's not that far."

I looked back at the mansion disappearing behind us as we turned a corner. Ian felt my fear. He tightened his grip on my hand. "Don't worry," he said. "No one will hurt you."

I nodded. Ian doesn't lie, I thought, and he's almost always right.

And besides, we'll see Mama and we'll get her to wake up and then all this will be over.

I stopped looking back.

22
TALKING TO MAMA

Whenever adults spoke to Ian or he spoke to them, they always treated him as they would another adult and never as they would treat or speak to a child. I think that was because he was always so clear and so firm when he spoke or answered a question.

The taxi driver looked at us askance when we approached him. He was leaning against his car and talking to another man. I could see him watching us out of the corner of his eye as he talked. He was surely thinking, What do we have here?

"We would like to go to the bus station in Bethlehem," Ian told him. Then he looked at his pad. "We need to make the ten o'clock to Philadelphia."

The driver didn't answer. He looked past us for a moment to see, I think, if there was an adult accompanying us.

"We would like to go now," Ian said. "Please."

"It will be twenty-four bucks," the driver said.

Ian smiled. "Fine." He showed him he had money and the driver suddenly came to life, moving quickly to get into his cab.

Ian opened the door for me and we got in. It was the first time I was ever in a taxicab, but I tried not to act like it was. I sat back and looked out the window, swallowing down all my fear. The driver glanced at us in his rearview mirror and then started his cab and drove away.

"Why are you going to Philly?" he asked.

"We're visiting relatives," Ian said. And then, although it was clearly a lie, he added, "We've been there at least a dozen times."

"No kidding. Where in Philadelphia?"

Without blinking an eye, Ian rattled off an address. The driver was very quiet after that. When we arrived at the bus station, Ian gave him twenty-five dollars.

"Keep the change," he told him as if it was something he often said and did.

The driver nodded and watched us go into the station. Ian bought our tickets and we sat on a bench near an elderly black lady who had a large bag stuffed with clothing. She looked at us and smiled. I saw she was missing teeth, but she had a very warm, sweet smile that made me feel better.

"Ain't you a doll," she told me. "How old are you, honey?"

I looked at Ian to see if I should answer. His eyes told me it was all right.

"Seven," I said.

"And you're a big girl, going on a bus with your brother, is it?"

"Yes. Ian is my brother."

"I wasn't much older when I first went on a bus with my granny Pauline. Matter of fact, I think I was seven, too. Yes, I was. We went from Memphis, Tennessee, to New Orleans and we had to make a few changes in those days. Took us two days to get there. We slept in a station one night. She had a lap as soft as a downy pillow. My granny Pauline . . ." She stopped in the middle of her sentence and looked out the window. I thought her eyes filled with tears.

Ian poked me gently. "When we get to the hospital, you let me do all the talking, Jordan. Even if someone asks you a question, you wait for me to answer, okay?"

I nodded. "Grandmother Emma is going to be very angry at us."

"She'll get over it," he said. "We have a right to see our mother." He studied a bus schedule and then told me we would return on a bus that left Philadelphia at six forty-five.

"Where will we have our lunch?" I asked.

"Don't worry about lunch. Hospitals have cafeterias for visitors and staff."

"Can we go see Daddy, too?"

"Not today, but we will if we want," he said with determination.

"Will Mama wake up and talk to us when we get there, Ian?"

"Maybe. Maybe she's already awake and talking and Grandmother Emma didn't tell us," he said.

"Why not?" I asked, wide-eyed.

He shook his head. "Why does she do anything?" he replied, which made no sense to me. "We'll see. Just relax," he told me.

"Aren't you afraid, Ian?" I asked him.

He turned slowly. "We sat in the woods just a few yards from a black bear, didn't we?"

"Yes."

"Well, there's no one out there as big or as strong as a black bear."

That made me feel better, but my heart was still thumping when the bus we were to take pulled up in front of the station. Ian rose and nodded for me to do the same. We started out and I looked back at the elderly black lady. She was still sitting with her hands on her bag of clothes.

She smiled at me and said, "Have a nice

trip, honey."

Ian tugged my hand and we went out, but I could see her through the window, even when we got on the bus. She was still sitting there.

"Where is she going, Ian?" I asked him. "Why didn't she get on the bus, too?"

He looked back and shrugged. "Maybe she's not going anywhere. Maybe she just hangs out there because it's a warm place to be. She looks like a bag lady."

"What's a bag lady?"

"People who have no home," he said. "They wander around and carry their entire belongings like that in a bag. Some push carts."

"Why don't they have homes?"

"Lots of reasons, Jordan."

"Are we going to become bag people?"

He looked at me. "Hardly," he said. And then I saw his eyebrows rise and his eyes narrow. "Maybe, in a way, if Mother and Father don't return," he added.

As the bus pulled away, I looked back and saw the elderly lady step out of the station and start walking down the sidewalk. Ian was right. She wasn't waiting for a bus after all, I thought. What was she waiting for?

Suddenly, being out in the world like this was as frightening to me as seeing a black bear only yards away in the forest. What else would we find? What else awaited us at the end of this trip? Cities always made me nervous as it was, even with our parents beside us. There were so many people and cars and buildings. It looked easy to get lost and Mama always warned me about staying close and never listening to any stranger. There were traps everywhere. Could Ian get us through it all safely? Had I made a mistake going with him?

"How do you know where to go, Ian?" I asked him.

"I retrieved all the information we need through my computer," he said. "I have directions." He took some folded papers out of his pocket. "Once we get to the hospital, it will be easy to find Mother. I'm hoping the doctor will be there or someone with information for us. We have a right to know about her condition," he added. He put the papers back into his pocket.

"Miss Harper will lock me in my room again," I told him.

"We'll see about that."

"Grandmother Emma said she would send you to a military camp."

He looked at me as if he thought I had made it up.

"She did," I said.

"We'll see about that, too," he told me. "Remember how I told you to act when we left," he said as the bus picked up speed. "Walk as if there is nothing wrong, as if you know exactly where you are going and what you are doing. That way no one will question or bother us."

I nodded, but I wasn't sure I could do it as well as he could. I watched him constantly and tried to imitate the way he sat, how he looked forward, even his facial expression. When the bus arrived at the station in Philadelphia, he took my hand.

"We'll take another taxi," he said, seeing all the cabs parked nearby.

As soon as we stepped off the bus, we approached another driver. "Moss Rehabilitation Center," Ian told him, as though he had been taking taxicabs there for years.

This time the driver didn't question us to see if we had money or even give us a quizzical look. He opened the door for us and we got in. He asked us no questions while he was driving either. He just drove off, weaving his way quickly through the traffic as if we were actually on an emergency. He was driving so fast I thought we were going to be in an accident, which would surely make Grandmother Emma very angry, but Ian sat calmly staring out the window at the

411

people on the sidewalks, the stores, the traffic. I was quite interested in it all, as well.

After we pulled up to the entrance, Ian paid the driver and we walked into the center. I couldn't help looking at everything, even though Ian wanted me to be like him and keep my eyes forward and not look so confused and frightened. No one took much notice of us anyway, even though any other children we saw were with adults. Ian found the information desk and asked for Caroline March. The lady behind the counter was very pleasant and gave him a paper that showed how to get to where Mama was being treated. The woman didn't say anything else about her, but she did smile at me.

When we arrived on the floor, a tall, thin, redheaded nurse came out of a room and greeted us immediately. Ian explained who we were. She stood there staring at him and me for a moment and then asked who had brought us.

"Our grandmother arranged for us to come by limousine," he said without hesitation. "Is my mother's doctor on the floor?" he continued.

"No, not at the moment," she replied. She looked like she didn't quite believe him, but I could see she wasn't perfectly confident about it.

"Are you her case manager then?" he asked.

That raised her eyebrows. "No, Mrs. Feinberg is," she said. "One moment."

She went to the main desk and another nurse, much older, stouter, and shorter, looked up from some paperwork at us. She shrugged at the redheaded nurse and then came around the desk to us.

"Hello," she said, smiling. "I'm Mrs. Feinberg. I understand you are Mrs. March's children."

"Yes, ma'am," Ian said. "We're here to see how she is and visit, please."

"What do you know about your mother's condition?" she asked him.

"We know she had a brain trauma from the car accident and she's been in a coma. Has she moved into a vegetative state?" Ian continued, without showing any signs of crying or fear.

"You understand what that means?"

"Yes, ma'am. I am well aware that if she remains in that state too long, she would be less likely to regain full consciousness."

"Who explained all that to you?"

"I read about it myself," he said. "I intend to pursue a career in medicine."

"Oh, really. How old are you?"

"I'm sixteen," Ian said, which was another bold lie.

She looked at me and held her smile. "And this is your sister?"

"Jordan, yes. She knows she has to behave and we promise not to disturb anyone or anything you're doing. Is our mother in a vegetative state or is she still comatose?"

"Are you sure your sister understands all this?" she asked, showing her concern for me.

"She'll understand," Ian promised.

Mrs. Feinberg turned to me. "Your mother's eyes are open, honey, but she doesn't see yet. Don't be frightened or surprised about that, okay?"

"She won't be," Ian insisted. "She's seen her before, soon after the accident."

"It's always difficult to understand how someone can open and close his or her eyes, even move and make noises, but show no sign of awareness."

"We understand," he said. "I explained all that to her on the way here."

He hadn't, but I was afraid to say a word, even utter a sound.

She thought a moment and then she told us to follow her. We entered a room where Mama lay on the bed staring up at the ceiling. I saw her left hand open and close, open and close. She's moving, I thought. How wonderful. I wanted to shout for her, cry out immediately. I hurried to her side and put my hand into hers. She closed on it and then opened, closed and opened.

"Talk to her, honey," Mrs. Feinberg said.

"Hi, Mama. It's me. Jordan. Ian is here, too."

We watched her head, but she didn't turn toward me. Her eyes closed and then opened.

"How long does it take to evaluate her?" Ian asked.

"It could be a while. She's in our Responsiveness Program so we can work on her response to stimuli. Just keep talking to her, honey. You never know when a patient will start to respond, but it's good they hear familiar voices."

"If they hear," Ian muttered.

"I'll be back in a little while," Mrs. Feinberg said.

"Mama, please talk to us," I pleaded. I pressed my face against her shoulder and then I kissed her cheek. "We need you to come home."

She didn't respond. Her mouth didn't move. Her eyes didn't turn to me and her hand kept opening and closing on mine.

"When will she hear me, Ian? When? Why

can't she hear me?"

"It's difficult to know, Jordan. She might hear you — the nurse is right. But she might not be able to respond yet. Don't cry," he warned me in a loud whisper. "They might get nervous about us being in here."

"I can't help it," I wailed.

"You've got to help it, Jordan. See. That's why I wasn't sure I should bring you with me."

"Okay, okay," I said, sucking hard on my breath and squeezing myself to smother my sobs. "I won't cry."

"Just talk to her. Tell her whatever you want. Go on," he said, and then he wandered about the room, looking at all the medical equipment as though he really knew what everything was.

I started to tell Mama about Grandmother Emma bringing Miss Harper into the house to take care of us, to teach me during the summer. Then I thought if I told her the terrible things Miss Harper had done to me, Mama might make herself wake up. I saw even Ian considered that possibility because he watched Mama's face closely as I described Miss Harper washing out my mouth with soap, locking me in my room, slapping my face, and making me work on school stuff all day.

"She slapped you?" Ian asked. I hadn't told him about that.

"Yes."

"Tell me if she as much as threatens to do it again," he said with visible anger. Sometimes, when he got that angry, his whole body seemed to tremble like a mountain during an earthquake or something.

I continued to talk to Mama, describing the schoolwork, and then I remembered to tell her about Grandmother Emma moving me to Daddy's old bedroom and moving Miss Harper into her and Daddy's bedroom. I thought that would surely get her upset enough to come back to us quicker.

However, nothing worked. Mama continued to blink, to open and close her hand, but she didn't turn her head or smile. She did make what sounded like a small cry and that perked Ian's interest for a moment, but the sound stopped. I shook her hand and began to plead with her to wake up.

"That won't help, Jordan," Ian said. "We're just going to have to wait."

He hadn't yet touched Mama or kissed her, but now he approached the bed and did take her hand into his, looking down at it. That hand wasn't moving. He moved her fingers and then he brought her hand to his lips and kissed it. I watched him closely, awed by his emotional expression. He brushed back Mama's hair and then took a deep breath.

"We're just going to have to wait," he said, this time more to himself than to me.

Suddenly, Mrs. Feinberg returned. Her steps and speed turned us both to look at her.

"Well now, young man. I just happened to get off the phone with your grandmother," she said, and I knew we were in very bad trouble.

I also knew that no one could move as quickly and as decisively as my grandmother Emma. Apparently, the moment she ended her conversation with the nurse, she had a talk with the hospital's security. Two uniformed men were outside in the hallway even before we learned what Grandmother Emma had told Mrs. Feinberg.

"You ran away from home this morning," Mrs. Feinberg said, and turned to Ian. "You took your seven-year-old sister to the city without permission, and you lied to me, young man. You said your grandmother sent you two in a limousine."

"She should have," Ian responded, undaunted.

"You're not sixteen, either. You're just thirteen."

"Chronological age isn't what's important," he said dryly. "It's mental age."

"Whatever, it's not right to lie and to
sneak around, especially with a child this
young."

"She's with me. She's fine," Ian said. The
nurse couldn't get him to be repentant or
even be slightly afraid.

"That's a great deal of responsibility to
take at your age, especially without permission and especially with your family having
so many troubles," Mrs. Feinberg insisted.
"I have grandchildren not much older than
you are and it would be troublesome to me."

"I don't believe it's any of your business,"
Ian said, finally showing some emotion. I
knew how much he hated being thought of
as a little boy or in any way irresponsible.

Mrs. Feinberg reacted instantly. He could
have just as well stuck a pin in her. She drew
to attention like a military officer, dropped
any softness out of her face and eyes, and
stepped up to him with her hands on her
hips, her bosom out like the front of a
bumper car in the amusement park. I
thought she was actually going to knock him
back with her breasts. Ian didn't flinch or
retreat an inch.

"You will be escorted out of here by the
hospital's security and taken to a room

where you will sit and wait for your grandmother or her representative to fetch you
two, and you will not go anywhere else or
tell anyone else any more lies, is that clear?"

She glanced at Mama.

"You should be ashamed of yourself,
absolutely ashamed, coming here like this."

"Before you spoke with my grandmother,"
Ian said, his voice still firm, "you thought it
was a very good idea for us to be here and
talk to our mother. You know the value in
that. I am not ashamed that we did this."

She turned a bit red. "I . . . yes, that is a
good idea but only if it's done properly and
everyone knows where you are, young man.
You don't go off with your little sister like
this. Now march yourselves out of here,"
she said when the two security men stepped
up in the doorway.

I looked at Mama and then I squeezed
her hand firmly. "Mama!" I cried. "Please
wake up!"

Mrs. Feinberg put her arm around my
shoulders and turned to me.

"Don't touch her," Ian said. He had
Grandmother Emma's snap in his voice.

Mrs. Feinberg glared at him.

"Get your hands off my sister," he said in
an even sharper tone. She looked at the

security guards, who now stepped into the room.

Ian reached for my hand and I took his quickly and pulled out of Mrs. Feinberg's grip. Then he looked back at Mama.

"We'll be back, Mother," he said, and led me out of the room with the security guards right behind us and the other nurses and personnel in the corridor all stopping whatever they were doing to look our way.

The guards directed us down the corridor to a room that was usually reserved as a lounge for the nurses. They told us to sit and wait and not make any more trouble. They shut the door. I had to go to the bathroom and whispered it to Ian, who then rose, knocked on the door, and told the security guard. He made me wait until a nurse came back to the room to escort me.

"What about you?" the security guard asked Ian.

"Not at the moment," Ian told him.

"Fine," the security guard said, and closed the door.

The nurse stood by the bathroom door and waited for me like a security guard herself. Why was it that everywhere we were since Mama and Daddy's accident we seemed to be easily locked away?

Afterward, while Ian fidgeted and read

every magazine in the room, I fell asleep on the sofa waiting. I woke when the door was opened again. Miss Harper stood there looking in at us. She glared at Ian, her eyes blazing, and then looked at me before entering and closing the door softly behind her.

"Have you any idea, any idea at all, what you two have put your grandmother and me through? Do you have any idea of the panic, the embarrassment?"

"I have an idea of the embarrassment, maybe," Ian said, "but not the panic."

"Don't you be smart with me, young man," she said, moving toward him. "Don't you dare show your disrespect and insolence."

Ian shrugged. "Then don't ask me any questions that require truthful responses," he said.

Her cheeks reddened as though they had been slapped. "Get up, both of you. You'll walk out of here and go with me immediately to the limousine."

"My grandmother didn't come?" Ian asked. I was wondering the same thing.

"She had to go to the hospital to see about your father. In the middle of this terrible family crisis, you do this sort of stupid thing."

"It wasn't stupid," Ian said.

"A number of people," she began, "have done favors for your grandmother to get your mother into this wonderful treatment center under the care of the finest specialists. Because of your grandmother, the head of the Responsiveness Program himself has taken a personal interest in your mother. You can't imagine how embarrassed your grandmother was by what you've done and how badly this reflects on your family."

I glanced at Ian, who just stared at the wall.

"I will not blame your sister, Ian. She's too young to know what she's doing, but you are far too intelligent and mature not to have known and understood."

"Of course, I know and understand," he said, turning back to her. "We were doing a good thing, a thing we should have been brought to do immediately."

"I don't care to discuss it any further with you. Now march," she said, pointing at the door. "Go on!" she added sternly when Ian didn't move.

He rose like an old man and nodded to me. We started out. We walked out ahead of her. The nurses watched us leaving and the hospital security guard followed right behind Miss Harper.

Outside, Felix leaned against the limousine with his arms folded watching us approach. He looked a little amused by what we had done. Then his eyes went to Miss Harper and he moved instantly to open the door for us and step back. Ian and I got in and she followed, sitting across from us. She just stared at the two of us as if she had to convince herself we were really there and that it was all true.

What, I wondered, would life be like for us at the March Mansion now?

23
JUVENILE CRIMINALS

It didn't take long to find out. Almost as soon as we started back to the March Mansion, Miss Harper began.

"When we get home, Ian, you are to go directly to your room and remain there until further notice." She smiled coolly. "You will discover that your room has been emptied somewhat."

"What does that mean?" Ian asked immediately.

"All of your scientific equipment, your microscope, your telescope, the ant farm, books, magazines have been removed."

"Removed? Where are they?"

She didn't reply.

"You can't do that," Ian said. "That stuff belongs to me, not you."

She smiled. "Nothing belongs to you, Ian. Everything you have was bought for you using your grandmother's money, even the clothing on your back you now wear. I know a lot more about your family than you think, and your grandmother approves of everything I have done and decided. She is so distraught, in fact, she doesn't even want to know about it. When she found out what you did, she was nearly in tears."

"I don't believe you," Ian said.

"Whether you believe me or not isn't important to me, Ian. However, I wouldn't bother appealing to her, if I were you. She is in no mood to hear either of you whine, especially you."

"I don't whine," Ian said.

"It won't do you any good if you do," she said. Then she turned to me. "While it's true you're too young to be fully at fault, Jordan, you still bear some responsibility here. You should not have gone with your brother. You should have come right to me to tell me what he wanted you to do."

"She would never go to you to rat on me," Ian said.

"Perhaps so. She has misplaced loyalties and responsibilities. However," she said, looking at me, "you, too, shall remain in your room until told otherwise.

"And as for you, young man," she said, turning back to Ian, "if you disobey me this time, even in the slightest way, I'll see to it that your grandmother sends you not to a military school, but a behavioral school at which you will have no rights, not be able to communicate with anyone, and certainly not have any of your things ever. Just so you know, she already asked me for some recommendations and I have given them to her to consider."

She sat back.

Ian stared out the window. I had no idea why I wasn't crying. I think I was just too much in shock, my tears stuck under my lids.

"In time," she said in a slightly softer tone, "I will reconsider everything if you're good, and we'll see if we can rescue any of this summer for either of you."

Ian stared at her with his eyes so firm and fixed, she finally had to look away.

"I know you slapped her, you know," he said.

"Pardon?"

"I know you slapped Jordan and you washed her mouth out with soap."

"Really? Did you tell him what you said, Jordan, to deserve that?"

I pressed my lips together.

"That's good. I don't want to hear it. I just wanted to see if you would repeat it. Obviously," she said, turning to Ian, "she's learned her lesson. You can thank me for that."

Ian shook his head. "You couldn't do any of this if my mother was well," he told her.

"Yes, well, your behavior and your sister's behavior aren't going to help that situation at all. The more time your grandmother has to spend worrying about the misbehavior you two commit, the less time she can spend on seeing that your mother gets the best treatment possible.

"That," she added, "is why she needs me to be with you and with her. She has complete faith in me. I hope you won't force me to be any more severe than I have to be. Because," she concluded, "you should make no mistake about it — I can be."

We rode in silence the rest of the trip home. As soon as we arrived, Ian shot out of the limousine and into the house to see if she had indeed done what she had said she had done. By the time we had walked in and up the stairway, he had made his discoveries and stepped into the hallway.

"Where are my things?" he demanded.

"Get back into your room," she replied. She pointed to his door.

"I want to know where my things are!" he shouted. I had never seen him this angry with his face this flushed.

"You're not starting out on a good foot," she said. "I'm warning you. I'm moments away from calling your grandmother, who is dealing with another crisis at the moment and has no time for tantrums."

"What other crisis?"

She was quiet. I looked up at her and she glanced at me.

"Your father," she said, "tried to kill himself once he was told the full extent of his injuries."

"I don't believe you," Ian said, but his voice quivered. I could see he wasn't confident.

"It doesn't matter what you do or do not believe."

"How could he do that? He's paralyzed from the waist down."

"He used a knife with a serrated edge to cut his wrists and bled considerably before anyone discovered it," she said bluntly.

Ian looked at me. He knew I understood how that could happen. He had once told me how close I had come to doing something like that to myself accidentally.

"Your grandmother is busy arranging for psychotherapy and getting him moved to where he will have twenty-four-hour observation. Now, are you satisfied you made me tell you all that in front of your little sister?"

"You enjoyed telling us," Ian said, but he was deflated. He turned and with his head lowered, walked back to his room.

She followed him to close his door and I followed her. I had a chance to glance in before she closed it. Everything in his room but his bed was gone, even his desk, where he sat to write his notes and create his studies. I had a glimpse of his bookshelves, too. They were bare.

She slammed the door and spun on me. "Get to your room. You're never to come down here. Go on!" she said, pointing, and I hurried away. She trailed behind me. I expected she was going to shut my door again, and probably lock it, too, because she could, but she didn't. She followed me into my room instead.

"Sit," she said, pointing to the settee.

I did so quickly and she approached, folded her arms under her small bosom, and peered down at me. "Did he touch you?" she demanded.

"What?"

"When he took you out of here, did he touch you?"

What did she mean? He had held my hand, guided me by putting his hand on my shoulder. Should I say yes? I didn't know what to say.

She brought a chair to the settee and sat in front of me. "Let me explain this to you, Jordan. Your grandmother hired me after she discovered what Ian was doing to you in your room. She was and is very concerned about that. It's not normal for a brother to do such things with a sister. It's not normal for him to do it with any girl, for that matter. You're too young to understand all this. It's all happening to you much too quickly," she said.

She did sound very calm, very concerned. There was no anger in her face, and Mama had said the same thing about all this happening to me too quickly.

"He made me hold his hand," I admitted.

She nodded. "Yes, yes, go on. What else?"

"He put his hand on my shoulder."

"I see. Go ahead."

I shrugged. "That's all. He didn't want me to get lost."

She sat back, smirking. "He never put his hand between your legs? Don't lie," she followed quickly.

I shook my head.

"If you lie to me and I find out later that you didn't tell me everything, I'll tell your grandmother she has to send you away, too. You'll never see your mother again. How would you like that?"

I started to cry.

"Think carefully before you answer me, Jordan. Be sure you tell me the truth or else," she said, and then leaned toward me. "Did he touch your chest? Did he make you take off your clothes? Did he touch you when you were undressed? Did he show you his thing?"

She fired her questions at me so quickly, I could barely understand and envision one before another came flowing over it. There I was again, trying to be a good liar and knowing I couldn't do it well. Would I get sent away? I had made a pact with Ian, taken an oath. I couldn't tell her anything, but I didn't have to. She was nodding.

"He did, didn't he? He did all those things, didn't he?"

I started to shake my head, but she smiled and then she reached into her pocketbook and took out what I knew to be Ian's small notepad.

"It's all here," she said. "All of the disgusting things he did to you and thought about you. I didn't want him to know I had it yet, that I had found it in his desk, until I had spoken to you and confirmed it all to reassure your grandmother this," she said, shaking the notebook, "wasn't just imaginary.

"I knew it wasn't," she said, slapping the

432

notepad down on her leg. "If I ever saw one boy like that, I've seen a dozen. I knew it the first time I set eyes on him."

Again, I tried shaking my head, but she wouldn't even look at me now. She was looking up at the ceiling and rubbing the outside of the notebook as if she were washing it.

"That's good," she said. "That's good that you were honest. Your grandmother will be happy to know we've bonded and you trust me. That's good."

She stood up so quickly, I flinched and sat back.

"Don't come out of this room, understand. If he comes to the door," she added, more in a loud whisper, "then you can come out screaming for me. Yes, then you can come out. Otherwise, don't."

She put the chair back and went to the door. "It's going to be all right, Jordan. Soon, it will all be fine and you and I will have a wonderful summer together, okay? Just rest now, sweetheart. Go on, lie down for a while. You've been dragged through a horrible experience. You should rest and then we'll see about your dinner. You'll even get a nice dessert because you've been good."

She smiled at me and then walked out,

closing the door. I sat there staring at it until I realized tears were streaming down my face and dripping off my chin. Poor Ian, I thought, confined to his room with nothing in it, none of his precious and important things.

But more terrible than anything for him would be learning she had taken his notebook, his secret thoughts, his Sister Project. And then she would go and tell him I said it was all true and he would think I had broken my oath. I couldn't let her do that, but what could I do to stop her?

I cried harder and then I threw myself on my bed and buried my face in the pillow. All of it weighed so heavily on me, it felt like a dozen comforters had been cast over my body. I caught my breath and turned slightly, listening. The house was deadly quiet. What was Ian doing? What would I do?

My mind was in a turmoil, each thought sitting on a horse on a merry-go-round, spinning and spinning and spinning until I felt myself sink deeper and deeper into the two palms of warm exhaustion that eventually closed around me and locked me into sleep.

It was dark outside when I woke up. The lamp on the side table was lit and I heard some low murmuring voices. I turned and saw Grandmother Emma and Miss Harper speaking softly just inside the doorway of the bedroom. Slowly, I sat up and ground the sleep out of my eyes. Miss Harper saw and touched Grandmother Emma's arm. They both looked at me and then Grandmother Emma walked slowly to the bed.

"Are you hungry now?" she asked me.

I wasn't, so I shook my head.

"You should eat something. Under the circumstances, now that I've learned the totality of all this, we have agreed to permit you to leave your room and resume your normal activities in the house. I want you to wash your face and then come down to the dining room, where Nancy will serve you some roast chicken, sweet potato, and vegetables. I have a nice piece of chocolate cream pie for you as well. Go on," she said, nodding at the bathroom.

"Is Ian coming to dinner, too?"

"No," she said sharply. "Don't concern yourself about Ian for now. Go on," she repeated with more firmness.

I slipped off the bed and went to the bathroom. When I came out, only Miss Harper was there waiting.

"Your grandmother will join us downstairs," she said. "Come along."

She smiled and held out her hand for me. I didn't want to take it, but she stood there, waiting, and I could see she wouldn't move from the door until I had taken her hand. As soon as I did, she tightened her fingers around my palm and we walked out of the room. I looked down the hallway toward Ian's room. The hallway was dark and there was no sign of him. She turned me abruptly at the top of the stairway and we went down to the dining room.

I saw there was no place setting where Ian sat. Nancy began bringing in platters and then Grandmother Emma came in from her office and sat at the head of the table. She glanced at me and then turned to Miss Harper.

"You were right. He was very helpful and he's getting right on it for us."

"Yes, he's been a tremendous help to me whenever I had to make a similar recommendation to a parent."

"It's amazing how widespread the problem is in this country, so widespread there's a career for a man like that, an agent to place these children in the proper facilities. It's good, of course, but still, very sad as well."

"It is, but when you've gone through all the tried and true techniques and the parents themselves are so overwhelmed, there is often little choice. Of course, most people can't afford this sort of solution and that's why the streets are rampant with juvenile criminals."

"Yes, well, no March will be roaming the streets or committing such acts while I'm alive. Thank you. I don't know what I would have done if you hadn't diagnosed the situation so quickly and gotten to the heart of the matter like a surgeon targeting a cancer."

"You're quite welcome, but I do feel sorry for the young man. Such brilliance misdirected."

"It doesn't surprise me when you consider the way he was raised. As ye sow, so shall ye reap. I am sorry to say my son bears a great deal of the blame. He closed his eyes to too many things while he pursued his own selfish satisfactions. Men," she added, and my eyes widened.

"Men," Miss Harper agreed, smiling.

They both turned to me.

"You'll be all right now, Jordan," Grandmother Emma said. "You'll have Miss Harper all to yourself for the rest of the summer. I hope you'll come to appreciate what this means for you."

I gazed at Ian's empty place. "Isn't Ian ever going to be permitted to come out of his room?" I asked.

"Oh, he'll come out," Grandmother Emma said. "Soon enough, he'll come out. Now, let's eat before it all gets too cold."

"Is Daddy all right?" I asked.

"Your father will never be all right," Grandmother Emma said, "but he will be the best he can be. I'll see to that," she said. "Now eat."

I had even less of an appetite than I had before, but under her and Miss Harper's critical gazing, I did the best I could. The food churned away in my stomach almost as soon as I swallowed any of it. At different moments during the dinner, I thought I would just start to heave, but I kept swallowing and drinking and finally finished enough for Grandmother Emma to permit Nancy to take my plate.

She brought out the dessert. It looked good, but I didn't want it either.

"What's Ian getting to eat?" I asked.

"Ian's already had his dinner. Nancy brought him tuna fish and a salad."

"But he hates tuna fish," I said. I was sure she knew that.

"When you have nothing else to eat, you suddenly learn to love it," she replied.

"He won't eat it."

"That's enough about Ian. Finish your dessert and go up to take your bath and get

438

ready for bed. You've had a terrible day and the faster you get it behind you, the better off you'll be," Grandmother Emma said.

"It wasn't terrible. I saw Mama," I told her.

She pressed her lower lip over her upper and tapped her fingers on the tabletop.

"She'll be fine," Miss Harper said. "Just give it some time."

"Yes. You're probably right, dear. Thank you," Grandmother Emma said, and dabbed her lips with her napkin. "I have things to do in my office."

"I'll see to her," Miss Harper said.

"Thank you." Grandmother Emma rose. "Do exactly as you're told, Jordan," she said firmly. Then she walked out of the dining room.

As soon as she did, Miss Harper stood up, reached over to take the remaining piece of pie away from me, and then nodded. "Time to go up and do as you were told," she said. "Go on."

I rose, pushed in my chair, and hurried to the stairway. Maybe Ian would be outside in the hallway, I thought, but when I got upstairs, he was not and it was still dark and quiet on his side. I heard Miss Harper coming up behind me so I went to my room and started to run the bath.

She came in behind me and stood in the doorway of the bathroom watching. I started to pour in some of Mama's bubble bath and she stepped forward and seized it out of my hand.

"You don't need that to wash."

"But I like it in my bath."

"You don't play in a bathtub anymore, Jordan. You're too old now."

"Mama uses it and she's older than I am."

"Don't contradict me. Get undressed and into the water. You are to wash your hair, too. Who knows what filth your brother dragged you through today?"

"We didn't go through any filth. We just went in taxicabs and on a bus to the hospital."

She stared at me a moment and then nodded. "Your grandmother is absolutely right about you and your brother. You were simply brought up in too permissive an environment. It never fails. That's the world of children when they have selfish parents."

"My parents aren't selfish."

"No, they're the paragon of altruism," she said.

I grimaced. What was that? I'd have to ask Ian later, I thought.

"Get in the water. It's high enough," she ordered, and I went ahead and did so.

She looked at me more closely than ever and shook her head. "Nature can do some very freaky things," she muttered.

"I'm not a freak!" I screamed.

"Stop that shouting."

"I'm not." I started to cry.

"Just get washed up, do your hair, and get yourself dried and dressed in your pajamas," she said. "I'm actually exhausted from you two myself and need to get to sleep."

She left me and I did my bath quicker than ever because it wasn't at all enjoyable without Mama's bath oils. After I dried myself and blew dry my hair, I dressed in my pajamas and got into bed. The bedroom door was open and remained that way. She appeared minutes after I had gotten into bed.

"Good," she said. "Finally, this day is coming to an end."

She turned off my night-light. I wanted to tell her I always wanted it on, but I didn't say anything. I thought I would turn it on after she closed my door, but she didn't close the door. She left it open.

I heard her walk down the hallway to her room and then I tried to stay awake as long as I could, hoping that Ian would sneak out of his room and come to me so I could tell him all the terrible things she had said and

Grandmother Emma had said.

I wasn't sure if it was a dream or if he really did come to me, but suddenly, late at night, when even the house felt as if it had fallen asleep, he was at my bedside. He nudged me and I opened my eyes and looked at him.

"Ian," I said, sitting up quickly. "I didn't break our oath," I said before he could say anything. "She said she would say I did, but I didn't."

"I know. Don't worry about her."

"Aren't you afraid she'll know you left your room?"

"No," he said. "I just came here to tell you that everything will be all right."

"Mama will come home?"

"Someday, yes."

"And Daddy, will he walk again?"

"Maybe not, but he'll be all right," he said.

"And you and I?"

"We'll always be together. No matter what. Remember," he said, smiling. "You're my Sister Project."

And then he did something he had never done.

He leaned over like Mama would and he kissed me on my cheek.

He told me to lie down again and he fixed my blanket.

When I woke up in the morning I knew it wasn't a dream because my night-light was on.

And Ian would remember that I needed it to be.

24
MISS HARPER
DOESN'T ANSWER

Of course, I knew I had better complete my
morning chores or Miss Harper wouldn't
permit me to take my medicine. I was very
sleepy, but I rose and made my bed as best
I could and then, after I washed and
dressed, I cleaned up the bathroom. As I
worked I continually anticipated her arriving to pass judgment on my efforts and
maybe make me do over the bed, but she
didn't come to my room at all.

Instead, Grandmother Emma stepped into
the room. She looked at the bed and at me.
All dressed and anxious, I was sitting on the
small settee.

"Very good, Jordan," she said. "Did Miss
Harper see this?"

"No, Grandmother."

"She wasn't here yet this morning?" she
asked with surprise.

"No," I said. "And I have to have my
medicine."

"Yes. Where is it?"

"It's in her room. She said she would keep it there and I would have to go there to get it."

"Fine. That way she can be sure you always do it right. Go to her room then, but knock first," she warned as I started out.

She followed me to the stairway, nodded in the direction of my parents' and Ian's bedrooms, and then went down for breakfast. I walked slowly past Ian's door, which was shut. I wanted to knock on it first to see how he was, but I was afraid Miss Harper would leap out at me the moment I approached his door and pile some other punishment on top of the ones she had already placed on our heads, so I continued past and then knocked on hers.

I waited.

She didn't come to the door so I knocked again, a little harder and a little longer. Again, I waited, and again, there was just silence, so I called for her.

"Miss Harper. It's Jordan. I need my medicine now. Miss Harper?"

I waited and listened and still there was silence. Maybe she had already gone down to breakfast, I thought, but I knocked one more time. When there was still no response, I turned and hurried back to the stairway.

My grandmother was in the kitchen giving Nancy orders and Miss Harper was nowhere in sight.

"Miss Harper isn't answering when I knock," I said.

Grandmother Emma turned and Nancy stopped working and looked my way, too.

"Did you knock hard enough?" Grandmother asked.

"Yes. And I even called to her, but she didn't come. I need to have my medicine. Mama said I have to have it first thing every day."

Grandmother Emma looked at Nancy. "Have you seen Millicent this morning?" she asked Nancy.

"No, ma'am," she replied.

Grandmother Emma thought a moment, and while she thought, neither I nor Nancy moved.

"Maybe she was in the bathroom. Go back up and knock again and wait. If she doesn't answer come back," she told me, and returned to what she was telling Nancy.

I hurried upstairs. I was disappointed that Ian's door was still shut. I was hoping all the noise I was making would get him to wonder and come out, but he didn't and I stood there alone again and knocked as hard as I could.

There was still silence.

I called for her and then, after I heard nothing, I turned and nearly tripped running down the stairs. Grandmother Emma had gone into the dining room and was sipping a glass of orange juice. She looked up with confusion at my heavy breathing.

"What is it now, Jordan?"

"Miss Harper won't open the door," I said. "She won't answer me."

"Ridiculous," Grandmother Emma said, and rose. "I hope you didn't tap so softly no one could have heard."

I held out my hand. My knuckles were red.

"I hit the door very hard, so hard I hurt myself," I said. "I need my medicine."

"I know you need your medicine. You don't have to continually remind me," she said, and scowled.

I didn't care how angry she got. I wasn't afraid of showing my anger now, too. Mama had made nothing clearer to me than the importance of my having my medicine every morning. Grandmother Emma should be just as concerned as I was, I thought, and I didn't for a moment regret having her walk back to the stairway and go up to Miss Harper's room. She glanced at Ian's closed door, too, and smirked as she walked past it to Miss Harper's door. I followed closely and waited when she knocked.

"Millicent, it's Emma. Are you all right?" she asked, directing herself to the closed door.

There was no answer.

"Millicent?"

I stood there with my arms folded over my chest, satisfied she could see I was right. I could see how annoyed Grandmother Emma was getting. She looked at me and then she opened the door. I started after her, but she turned on me in the doorway.

"Just a moment," she said. "You wait out here."

I stepped back.

She entered, closing the door almost completely. A few moments later, I heard her cry out, "Oh, my God. Millicent! Millicent!"

I pushed the door fully open and peered in. Grandmother Emma was standing beside the bed, her right hand pressed flat over her mouth as if she was trying to keep in the orange juice she had just drunk, and her left hand on her head. I walked in and looked at Miss Harper, who was lying crouched over to her right as if she was going to vomit. Her eyes were wide open as was her mouth, and she looked like she had been screaming. In fact, she still looked like she was screaming, but it was a scream that no one else could hear.

Grandmother Emma stepped back. She shook her head and then she turned to me. "Get out!" she cried. "Go downstairs immediately. Go on. Get out!"

"What about my medicine?" I asked.

"Get out!" she shouted, much louder.

I had never seen her so wild and angry. It truly made my heart stop and start. I turned and ran out of the room, down the hallway and to the stairway, but at the top, I stopped and looked back because I heard Ian's door open.

Ian should know what was happening, I thought, and took a few steps toward him when he stepped into the hallway. He looked up at me.

"Something's wrong with Miss Harper," I said.

He glanced at her bedroom and at me and then, without saying a word, he turned and went back into his room and closed the door. A moment later, Grandmother Emma came out of Miss Harper's room. She closed her door and started walking toward the stairway. She didn't shout at me again. She looked like she was in a daze and didn't even see me. I waited for her until she realized I was standing there.

"Go on down, Jordan," she said. "I'll get you your medicine. Don't worry. Go on," she said in a low tone of voice that was only a shade or two above a whisper. I started down. "Tell Nancy to come upstairs immediately," she called to me.

I looked back and nodded. She turned and started toward her room and then turned and headed back to Miss Harper's room. I shook my head. She looked like she was confused and didn't know in which direction to go.

But of course I hoped she was going back to get my medicine for me. I practically leaped down the remaining steps and ran to the kitchen. Nancy looked up from the platter of toast and scrambled eggs.

"Grandmother Emma wants you upstairs right away," I said.

She brought her head back. "Now?"

"Yes, right away," I said.

"Everything's going to get cold," she said with regret. "Why would she want me up there now?"

"Something's wrong with Miss Harper," I said, and she widened her eyes.

"What do you mean?"

"She looks frozen," I told her.

"Frozen?"

"Uh-huh. Her mouth's open and so are

her eyes, but she doesn't talk."

Nancy's mouth opened and closed and then she hurried out of the kitchen.

I looked at the platter. Suddenly, I was very hungry, so I brought it into the dining room and placed it all on the table. Then I took my seat, fixed my napkin, and began to serve myself. After I began eating, I heard footsteps on the stairway and a moment later Grandmother Emma went by, hurrying to her office. A short while after that, I heard Nancy open the door so Felix could come in and follow her down to the office, too.

Grandmother Emma should have brought down my medicine, I thought. I buttered my toast and then I felt sorry for Ian. He was probably hungry, too, but no one was going to pay attention because of Miss Harper, so I carefully fixed a plate of eggs, toast, and jam and included a napkin. Then I went upstairs with it and knocked on his door.

"What?" he asked as soon as he opened it.

"I thought you might be hungry. Everyone's busy with Miss Harper."

He glanced at the food. "Thanks," he said, and took it.

"I'm still waiting for my medicine," I said.

"That's wrong," Ian said. "They should

worry about you more than about Miss Harper. If you don't get it in an hour, come back to me and I'll make sure you get it," he said. "You'd better go before Grandmother raises hell," he said, and closed the door.

I started downstairs again. Felix, Nancy, and Grandmother Emma were all starting up the stairway.

"What are you doing up there?" Grandmother Emma asked as soon as she saw me.

"I gave Ian something to eat," I said.

"Get back down here and stay here," she ordered.

"I need my medicine," I said.

"Oh, that damn medicine. Nancy will bring it to you. Now move," she said, and I walked past them as they all started quickly up the stairway.

I returned to the dining room and nibbled on a piece of cold toast and drank some more orange juice. Nancy finally brought me my medicine and I took it. She didn't wait to see if I did it right. She went back upstairs. I was happy she hadn't taken it back. Now I wouldn't have to wait for anyone before I could take it in the morning, I thought. Mama would be pleased.

I brought my dishes and glasses to the kitchen and then I wandered out to the stairway to listen. Felix came down and without even looking at me, went out. I went to the living room window that looked out on the driveway because I thought I heard the sound of a siren. Sure enough, an ambulance was turning into our driveway and right behind it was a police car. Another car, a black sedan, turned in after those two vehicles and all of them sped up to the front of the mansion.

Moments later Felix led two paramedics into the house. They carried bags and followed him up the stairway. Two policemen came in after them and then two men in suits followed, closing the door behind them. They all hurried up the stairway. I waited below, listening. The patrolmen came back down the stairway first. They saw me, but they didn't even smile or nod their heads. I watched them leave the house.

I wondered if I should go up to tell Ian I had gotten my medicine so he wouldn't worry about me, but I was afraid Grandmother Emma would really yell at us both. It didn't matter that all these strangers were in the house. If she was angry, she was angry.

What, I wondered, had happened to Miss Harper to cause all this commotion?

Finally, Nancy came slowly down the

stairway, her eyes down, shaking her head as she walked. She looked at me. "You know she's dead, don't you?" she asked.

I shrugged. How was I supposed to know anything?

"Do you know anything about it?" she asked me.

"About what?"

"About how she died?"

I shook my head and then remembered to speak instead of just shaking my head.

"No. I had to go to her room to get my medicine," I told her, and showed it to her. "She kept it there and I have to have it in the morning every day. She should have left it in my bathroom and there wouldn't have been all this trouble."

"Believe me," Nancy said, "that's the least of her problems now."

She walked to the kitchen and I waited at the bottom of the stairway. The front door opened again and Mac, the man in charge of the mansion's grounds, came in with the two patrolmen. They told him to wait in the living room and one of the patrolmen went back upstairs.

No one seemed to notice or pay any attention to me.

Moments later, the patrolman and both of the men in suits came down the stairway and joined Mac and the other patrolman in the living room. I could hear everything they said because I stood just across from the living room door.

"This is Lieutenant Risso and I'm Detective Ryan," one of the men in suits said to Mac. "You look after the property?"

"Yes, sir," Mac said. "And any odd job around the house itself, plumbing, electrical, whatnot." He glanced through the doorway at me and I thought he smiled.

"Have you been using any rodent poisons of any kind lately?" Lieutenant Risso asked him.

"Oh, yes, sir," Mac said. "We have a little problem in that regard. I use GoRodent Getter."

"What's the active ingredient?" Detective Ryan asked.

"Strychnine. May I ask why you ask?"

"We have a possible incident that might involve that poison. Are you missing any?"

"Don't know. Hafta check the storage shed," Mac said.

"Let's go check," Detective Ryan said.

Mac shrugged and all of them left the house together. Mac winked at me, but no one else looked my way.

The paramedics came down the stairs next, but much more casually. They turned and went into the kitchen. I followed and saw that Nancy was giving them cups of coffee.

"What happened to her?" Nancy asked them.

"It sure looks like she was poisoned," one of the paramedics said.

"She suffered severe convulsions and we're pretty sure it was strychnine. Usually, with strychnine, the victim remains in a convulsed position like the one she's in, eyes wide open and the face in a look of agony, just like hers," the other said, and then added, "The victim goes into rigor mortis almost immediately after death."

"Billy is studying to become a medical examiner," the first paramedic said, smiling.

"Sweet Mary and Joseph," Nancy said.

"It's strychnine," Billy said. "Stake my reputation on it."

"What reputation?" the other paramedic said, and they both laughed.

If Miss Harper were dead, how could they be funny about it? I wondered.

Nancy smiled at them and offered them some of her homemade corn muffins. They both said yes and she sat them at the kitchen table and brought them muffins and jam.

"I always wondered what this place looked

like inside," Billy said. "Don't know how many times I've gone by here. It's a wonderful mansion all right," he said, nodding at the ceiling and the walls.

"Isn't so wonderful if you're the one cleaning it," Nancy said, and they all laughed again.

I guess it was all right to be funny, I thought. They all finally saw me standing in the doorway.

"Oh, Jordan. Do you want something to eat now?"

"I already ate, Nancy. I brought Ian food, too, remember?"

She shook her head. "I don't know if I remember my name this morning."

The paramedics smiled.

I turned when Mac and the two detectives returned. Mac came toward us, but the detectives hurried up the stairway again.

"Helluva thing," Mac said, stepping into the kitchen.

The paramedics looked up at him. Nancy offered him some coffee.

"What?" she said when he took the cup.

"Someone was in my shed. I got a can of GoRodent Getter missing."

"I'll be damned," Billy said. "Told you, strychnine."

Nancy gasped and brought her hand to

the base of her throat.

Suddenly, they were all looking at me, but before anyone could say anything, Lieutenant Risso was in the hallway by the bottom of the stairway calling to me. I turned and looked his way.

"You're Jordan?" he asked. I nodded. "Come with me," he said, and led me into the living room. "Go ahead and sit on the sofa, Jordan," he said, nodding at the Victorian parlor settee.

"It's a settee," I told him.

"Huh? Oh, yeah, sure."

I sat, clutching my medicine against my stomach.

"What'cha got there?" he asked.

"My medicine. I have to take it every morning. Where's Grandmother Emma?" I asked him.

"She'll be right down," he said. "Now, tell me about Miss Harper," he said. He smiled at me but it didn't make me feel better.

I looked toward the doorway. What was I supposed to tell him about her?

"She's helping Grandmother Emma with us this summer," I said. "She used to be a school teacher, but she lost her job."

"Is that right? Do you like her?"

I shook my head. I was afraid to lie and I really didn't see why I had to lie anyway.

"Why not?"

"She washed out my mouth with soap. She slapped me. She locked me in my room. She took my medicine and kept it in her room. She took all of Ian's things out of his room because we went to see my mother in the hospital."

"Is that so?"

"Uh-huh," I said, nodding.

"So I guess Ian's mad at her, too?"

I was going to just nod, but again I remembered Miss Harper's warning about saying yes and saying no.

"Yes. She shouldn't have taken his things. He was upset, too, when she didn't give me my medicine. He said if I didn't get my medicine in an hour, he would get it for me."

"I see. So, did Ian say you guys should do something to Miss Harper because of all she had done to you two?"

"No," I said.

"Never?"

"No."

"Didn't you and Ian go to the shed to get something?"

"No."

"Do you know if he did yesterday?"

"No. He couldn't. He had to stay in his room. Miss Harper said so. She said if he disebeyed her, she would have Grandmother Emma send him away and he wouldn't get to see Mama or Daddy."

"I see. All right. You wait here," he said, and started out of the living room.

I was uncomfortable sitting on the Victorian parlor settee. Grandmother Emma was never happy about either me or Ian lounging about on this furniture, especially without anyone else in the room.

Suddenly, I heard Grandmother Emma's voice coming from the stairway. "What do you think you're doing?" I heard her demand. "Where is my granddaughter?"

I rose and went to the doorway. The detective was at the bottom of the stairs waiting as Grandmother Emma came down.

"It's pretty clear that someone put that rodent poison in her water glass, Mrs. March," he said.

"Nevertheless, you know you don't speak to children, especially my grandchildren, without an adult present and certainly not without counsel."

"But Mrs. March . . ."

"I'll thank you to wait for the arrival of my attorney. He should be here momentarily," Grandmother Emma said.

She looked past him toward me. "Jordan, I'd like you to go directly up to your room immediately," she said. "Go on."

I hurried to the stairway and past the detective. When I got upstairs, I looked down the hallway and saw the policemen standing outside Miss Harper's bedroom doorway. Ian's door was still shut. I couldn't help but wonder what he was doing in his room without any of his things, the things he loved, and with all this commotion in the hallway. Ian hated not knowing things.

When I went into my room, I stood there for a moment deciding what to do. I put my medicine in the bathroom cabinet and then I went to my desk and despite how much I had not wanted to do it before, started to thumb through the schoolbooks Miss Harper had given me. I even found myself doing some of the workbook pages as if I thought she would be in at any moment to check on me.

Of course, she didn't come, but Grandmother Emma did, accompanied by her lawyer, Mr. Ganz. He was a short man, not much taller than she was, with curly black hair that looked like a mass of tiny springs. Some were lined with gray. His eyebrows were so thick they reminded me of caterpillars and I immediately thought about curling up on my bed. If there was ever a time to hope for hope, this was it, I thought.

"Jordan, you know Mr. Ganz. He has been here for dinner with his wife. He wants to talk to you and I want you to tell him the truth, understand?"

"Yes, Grandmother."

"So," Mr. Ganz said, pulling up a chair. "Tell me what happened here between you, Ian, and Miss Harper."

I looked at Grandmother Emma and then I began. I told him everything I could remember. I told how angry Ian was when he found out she had taken his things.

"Were you with Ian after Miss Harper brought you two back home last night?" Grandmother Emma asked, looking impatient. "Well?"

"I thought it was a dream," I said.

"What was? Tell us everything, Jordan. This is very, very serious now," she said.

"I thought it was a dream. He came to see me when I was asleep."

"And? What did he do?" she asked, stepping toward me. "Tell us immediately."

"Easy," Mr. Ganz said. "Don't frighten her, Emma."

"Oh, these children will be the death of me. Well, Jordan?"

"He didn't do anything. He told me not to worry. He said everything would be all right."

"And that's all he said?" Mr. Ganz asked.

"He said Mama and Daddy would be home and maybe Daddy would walk again."

Mr. Ganz looked up at Grandmother Emma. "It's the scene of a murder, Emma. They can go through this house."

"Okay," she said. "It's time we had a talk with my grandson and brought this all to a quick resolution."

"Oh, I don't think we'll have a quick resolution," Mr. Ganz said.

"Yes, we will," she told him.

It was as if she had put a stamp on everything, a seal like a queen would put on her papers.

"You stay here," she told me, and they left me.

It was getting nice outside again. Maybe today we would be permitted to go swimming, I thought. After everyone leaves, I'll ask Grandmother Emma. Maybe she would even let me invite Missy Littleton. Ian liked her, too.

He would put on his underwater mask and we would toss pennies into the water for him to find. We did that one summer day for hours and he always found them. Daddy came out that afternoon to swim, too, and he could find them without a mask. Ian wouldn't open his eyes in the water without the mask because he said the chlorine irritated them. Daddy said that was nonsense.

He pounded his chest like Tarzan and said, "Real men don't need underwater masks."

Missy Littleton laughed, but Ian glared at him with such anger, I got a chill and had to wrap my towel around myself.

Later, at dinner, Daddy's eyes were red and Ian told him so.

Even Grandmother Emma said it was true and he was stupid to get them so irritated.

Daddy ignored her, but Ian looked happy.

I wondered if he ever would look happy again.

25
DADDY COMES HOME

I didn't go swimming. I would go later, but not very often that summer because Grandmother Emma didn't hire anyone else to look after me.

I was very lonely.

I really didn't understand everything that happened until much later, but Mr. Ganz was right about what the police could do and couldn't do. They brought in two forensic detectives who went into Ian's room and found traces of the rodent poison. Later, he admitted to putting it into Miss Harper's glass of water, which she kept by her bed when she slept.

While she was taking a bath, he snuck into her room and did it. He was very upset about her reading his journal, he said. He told the police that it was more than a violation of someone's privacy; it was a violation of their very soul.

He went into great detail about some of

the other things in his journal, his notations about people, animals, and plants. Everyone agreed he was one of the most intelligent young boys they had ever questioned. I don't know why Grandmother Emma told me that, but she did. It was almost as if she was trying to save some face, to brag about one of her grandchildren, despite it all.

She couldn't keep the scandal out of the newspapers or off television either. It seemed Mama was right, opening closets and drawers would release the brown moths and disgrace would generate so much gossip, the moths would circle the mansion for a long time.

It had a very bad effect on Grandmother Emma's social life. Her friends started to avoid her, decline her invitations, and not invite her to their affairs, dinners, and teas. I began to realize that she was drifting into a world cloaked in as much loneliness as mine.

Daddy was still in the physical therapy hospital and Mama was still in a vegetative state. Finally, Grandmother took me to visit them both. Daddy was almost as quiet as Mama was. He had learned how to use his wheelchair and was being taught how to do more and more things for himself, but Grandmother Emma said he was a reluctant learner and so it was taking longer and longer to get him released to go home.

When he learned about Ian and what had happened, he said he wasn't surprised. "I always knew that kid was weird," he said, as if he were talking about a neighbor's child and not his own. He didn't seem sorry or sad for Ian at all. He was too involved in his own misery and went right to complaint after complaint until Grandmother Emma threw up her hands and told him if he didn't snap out of it, she would stop visiting him.

All the while she was overseeing the supermarket, and then I learned one afternoon that she had managed to sell it to a supermarket chain, and in her words, "Get that albatross off my back."

Daddy had no business at all now, I thought. I even said it, and Grandmother Emma said, "Why would he need one? He couldn't run it properly when he was healthy."

Anticipating that he would come home soon, she had the bedroom and bathroom that he would use redone to accommodate a person in a wheelchair. She had a special bed put in as well. Before the summer ended, she hired a full-time nurse and made arrangements for a therapist to work with

Daddy at our home. She said neither she nor Nancy was equipped to deal with such a situation and they would need all the help they could muster.

"It's difficult enough when a normal person suffers such a catastrophe, but a spoiled person such as your father makes it nearly impossible," she told me.

I wondered if she ever felt sorry for him at all. I still never saw her cry about him or speak about him with a tone of pity. If she spoke about him at all, it was usually to complain about his attitude.

I found that she talked to me a great deal more. I was permitted to be with her more often in the living room or she would linger at dinner and she would sit outside and watch me either swim or just play croquet. She took me to Dr. Dell'Acqua for a checkup and we were both very happy to hear that the medicine was working. I had not had another period and she thought my growth spurt was in check. Grandmother took me shopping twice for more clothing, new shoes, and even, to my surprise, to buy a computer game I could hook into the television set.

There was just one thing she was adamant about not doing with me, and that was visiting Ian. She was quite clear and firm about

468

it, so that I was afraid to ask.

"Isn't he afraid?" I did ask.

"Hardly," she said. "The truth is, I'm sure the caretakers are more afraid of him than he is of them."

I was never quite clear about those caretakers or where Ian was. However, I began to pick up bits and pieces from conversations I overheard Grandmother Emma have with Mr. Ganz and other people, some very important people. Despite the fact that she had lost and was losing the friendship of many of her rich and once powerful friends, she was still Emma March and we were still one of the most prominent families in Bethlehem.

Because of Ian's age, he was considered a juvenile offender, but Grandmother Emma was able to get the court, the district attorney, and everyone else involved to agree that Ian need psychological help more than any form of punishment. He was sent to an institution for the juvenile mentally ill and it was unclear to me if he would be there for a long time and then go to a real prison or be released to come home someday. Grandmother Emma never wanted to discuss it with me. She wanted to shoo it all off as she would the moths.

I never knew what Miss Harper had done

with Ian's things. Grandmother Emma had everything left taken out as well, all his clothes and shoes especially. His room was closed up the way Daddy's used to be, with Nancy cleaning it occasionally. I hoped she was doing so for his eventual return.

Grandmother Emma asked me if I wanted to return to my room now or remain where I was. I decided I would be quite lonely on that side of the mansion all by myself, so I told her I would stay in Daddy's old bedroom. She seemed very pleased by my decision. She told me my old room would be the nurse's room when she arrived.

Everything that had belonged to Miss Harper was returned to her mother, of course, and for the time being, Daddy and Mama's old bedroom was closed down as well.

"The house is in retreat," Grandmother Emma muttered one afternoon when she thought about all this. She became very quiet and very sad about it.

I was actually finding myself feeling sorry for her almost as much as I was for Mama and Daddy, Ian, and myself. She wasn't moving as quickly as she used to. Her steps were softer in the hallway. She spent less time in her office and rarely left the mansion. Her business manager and her attorney came more often to her than she went to them, and there were many nights when I took dinner alone and learned she was having hers in her room. The loneliness was beginning to slow me down, too. I lost interest in all my toys and games and I didn't even watch television that much.

Ironically, I spent more time reading the textbooks Miss Harper had left than reading or doing anything else. Ian had thought it was a good idea for me to do it and I felt closer to him by doing what he approved. I looked forward to the day we would see each other again and I could tell him how much I had learned. He could ask me questions and I would answer them so well he would be impressed.

When I did go with Grandmother Emma to see Mama, I sat and told her about the books, too. Mrs. Feinberg remembered me, of course. She and Grandmother Emma went off to talk. I was sure it was all about Ian. Later, Mrs. Feinberg was even nicer to me. She told me to keep talking to Mama.

I didn't tell Mama about Ian. I imagined she was wondering where he was, but when he had visited her, he didn't really talk to her much anyway. I thought if she knew about him and what had happened, she would become so sad, she would never wake up. Grandmother Emma thought I was right.

"That was very smart of you, Jordan. You are growing wiser. I am sure you will be a fine young woman," she said.

Hearing such compliments from her surprised and delighted me. I couldn't wait to tell Ian about it. He might not care or think as highly of it as I did, but I had to tell someone. I did tell Daddy and he looked at me strangely, as if he thought it was odd I should care what his mother thought of me.

"You know," he said, leaning toward me while he sat in his wheelchair, "I can't watch you when you go swimming anymore. If something happened to you, I couldn't do a damn thing about it."

He just blurted that out and I hadn't even talked about my going swimming at all.

"I'm not sure they'll even let you ride with me in a car, once I get one of those specially made cars for cripples like me," he added.

"She has no idea what you're talking about, Christopher. What point is there in your unloading your self-pity on a child anyway?" Grandmother Emma told him.

"Right, thanks for straightening me out, Mother," he said, and turned his chair around to stare out the window.

"Don't let your father depress you,"

Grandmother Emma told me afterward. "All that has happened to him is his fault. He has no one to blame but himself."

"Mama, too?" I asked.

She looked like she wasn't going to answer, and then she said, "The two of them can blame only themselves."

Why was that? I wondered. Mama hadn't been driving. Why would she be at fault at all? I didn't ask Grandmother to explain.

Days continued to tick by so slowly for all of us that even Nancy remarked it seemed as if there were thirty hours in these days and not twenty-four. Finally, at the end of the first week in August, Daddy came home. Grandmother Emma purchased a special van for Felix to use to drive Daddy around. It had a lift that Daddy could wheel onto and when it was raised, wheel into the van. He didn't even have to leave his wheelchair if he didn't want to. She then had Mac and some of his workers build a special ramp for Daddy to use to get in and out of the house. That was as far as she would go to accommodate him and spoil what she called the classic look of the March Mansion.

I was playing outside, really imitating Ian and pretending to look for unique bugs and weeds, when Daddy was driven up in the van. I hurried to the front to watch the door open and the lift lower him in his wheel-chair.

It was a beautiful August day, not too humid, and there was a very nice breeze. The sky seemed to be flowing from one horizon to the other in a constant light, almost Wedgwood blue with puffs of clouds dabbed randomly about it, some looking like they weren't moving at all. I imagined the whole world, birds included, was hold-ing its breath as Daddy's wheels rolled off the lift and onto our driveway.

He was dressed in one of his bright blue short-sleeve shirts and a pair of dark blue pants with his favorite boat shoes. He looked like he had just had his hair styled, too, and wore one of his pairs of designer sunglasses. Despite his unhappiness, I could see his pleasure in his homecoming. Felix came around and took the handles of his wheelchair to push him toward the ramp. Mac and his workers were there to greet him.

Daddy's new nurse, Mrs. Clancy, had just arrived at the house that morning and, as Grandmother had told me, taken my origi-nal bedroom. She had short dull brown hair, brown eyes, and very thin lips. Al-though she was slim, I saw she had real small but ropelike muscles in her forearms.

I didn't think Daddy would like her because she wasn't pretty, and I wondered if Grandmother Emma had hired her knowing he wouldn't.

Nancy came to the front entrance, too, and stood beside Grandmother Emma. They watched Mrs. Clancy quickly go down to greet Daddy. She had been introduced to him in the hospital and had met with his nurses and doctor there to get information about his condition.

He nodded at everyone, but he didn't say anything. I went to him and he started to reach for me and then stopped and shook his head.

"Just get me inside," he told Felix. He gestured at him and cried, "Meet CPS, Crippled Person Service."

No one laughed. Grandmother Emma shook her head and Nancy backed into the house.

"I'll take it," Mrs. Clancy told Felix, and practically pushed his hands off the wheelchair. "You want to start doing this yourself, Mr. March," she told Daddy as she brought the chair to the ramp. "It will be hard at first, but it gets easier as your upper body develops even more."

"Whoop-de-do," Daddy said. "I have something to look forward to after all."

I followed them up the ramp and into the house. I didn't think Daddy knew until that moment that he would be sleeping in the downstairs guest bedroom. He complained about that immediately because it had no view and was far smaller than either bedroom he had used upstairs.

"I've already had everything done to it to accommodate you, Christopher," Grandmother Emma told him, "and how would you manage the stairway?"

"You could have had a lift built, Mother."

"And ruin that classic balustrade?"

"Well, Mrs. Clancy," Daddy said, looking back at her, "you don't have to wonder what my mother's priorities are here. House first, son second, maybe third or fourth. Don't mess anything up," he warned.

"We'll do just fine," Mrs. Clancy said, and continued to push him along.

"Are you hungry, Mr. March?" Nancy asked, stepping out of the kitchen. "I've got your favorite meat loaf sandwich ready."

"Just serve the crow my mother prepared," Daddy said, and Mrs. Clancy pushed him forward to his new sleeping quarters.

I looked at Grandmother Emma to see if she thought I should follow or what. She just shook her head.

"You can go back outside, Jordan," she

told me. "It's too nice a day to waste in here under these clouds of self-pity."

I lowered my head and walked out, disappointed. I knew Nancy had prepared Daddy's favorite cake, a flourless chocolate cake, for his dinner and I was hoping we would have a real "welcome home" celebration. I had fantasized every night for the last week about his being so happy to be home and to see me, he would let me wheel him about the grounds and we would talk about everything, especially Mama. He would fill me with confidence about her homecoming, too, and then we would talk about how we could bring Ian back so we would all be a family again.

Instead, Daddy was in his room, the room he hated, and I was outside, alone, sitting on one of the lawn benches, just staring at the house. I looked up at a flock of sparrows and recalled my conversation with Ian about the birds. Soon, their instinct would tell them to go south, I thought. Ian and I once saw a flock of geese going south.

The birds are luckier than we are, I decided. They know when to come and go.

I just sat there, not knowing whether I should go in or out of my house, even if I should try to talk to my own father. Why couldn't something just click inside me and take me through my whole life, helping me make all the right decisions and never any mistakes?

Ian would think that was silly. I was sure. Maybe, I would write him a letter, I thought. Yes, that would be wonderful. I could write him and he would write back to me. I would ask Grandmother Emma to send the letters to him. She shouldn't be upset about that. I could tell him all that was going on here and all about Mama. Otherwise, how would he ever know any of it? I couldn't wait to tell him about all I had already learned from Miss Harper's schoolbooks. That's it, I thought. I'll put a math problem at the end of each letter and show him how I solved it.

The idea gave me new energy and I went back inside and up to my room to begin.

That evening we had our first dinner with Daddy at the dining room table. The wheelchair fit well and he almost looked like his old self sitting at his place. He seemed a bit happier and enjoyed the way Nancy fawned over and around him, especially when she brought out the cake. He started to ask questions about everything, the supermarket, Mama, and finally Ian.

Grandmother Emma wouldn't discuss Ian in front of me. She made that clear. He didn't seem to care. He didn't care when she told him about the sale of the supermarket either. All he cared about now was watching sports on television. Mrs. Clancy let me push him in his wheelchair back to his room after dinner. He had his own television set there and didn't care to go to the living room.

"I wouldn't want to roll over one of my mother's precious Persian rugs," he said.

The chair and Daddy felt heavier than I had anticipated, but I kept it straight and didn't bang into any walls on the way to his room. When we got there, he told me where to place him and then I turned on the television set for him. He watched me as I moved about the room and then, he finally reached out to touch my hand and hold me for a moment.

"Thanks, Jordan," he said. "I know this isn't going to be any picnic for you either with your mother the way she is and your brother gone. I'm the child here now." He turned angry again and then he pulled me closer. I thought he wanted to kiss me, but he wanted to whisper something to me that neither Mrs. Clancy nor Grandmother Emma could hear. "You don't need this," he said. "Be smart. Stop taking your medicine and grow up fast and get the hell out."

His words were so shocking, I couldn't

speak or move. I thought he would smile and laugh and say he was just kidding as he often did when he said something Mama thought was silly or bad, but he didn't smile. He stared hard at me and then he let go of my hand and flipped the channel selector until he found something he wanted to watch.

After that I could be there with him or not. It didn't make any difference.

I hurried out and up to my room, my heart thumping. Stop my medicine? Grow up fast? Where would I go? What did he mean? Mama is going to be angry he said all that, I thought. I probably should never tell her nor ever tell Grandmother Emma.

But I would tell Ian. I'd put it in my letter because, as always, he would know exactly what Daddy meant and what I should do and think about it. I sat at my desk and began.

Dear Ian,

I don't know where you are or when you are coming home. When?

I am writing you a letter to tell you Daddy came home today. He is in a wheelchair and Grandmother Emma has a nurse to help him. She is sleeping in my old bedroom. Her name is Mrs.

Clancy. She is not pretty and I noticed she had little hairs over her upper lip like a mustache.

I have gone to see Mama twice. She is not any different because she did not say anything. She still moves her hand the way she did. I talked to her for a long time. I did not tell her that you were away.

I wish you were here to talk to me about the birds and everything. I wanted to tell you that Daddy just said a strange thing to me and I need you to tell me why.

He said I should stop taking my medicine. He said I should grow up fast and get out.

What did he mean? Where would I go?

Can you tell me when you are coming home? I have been looking for your things, but I haven't found them yet. I will keep looking.

Jordan

I folded the letter and put it in an envelope. Then I wrote *Ian March* on the front of it and sealed it. I didn't have any stamps, but I knew Grandmother Emma had them in her office and she would have to write the address on the letter anyway.

She was downstairs in her office, in fact, when I was finished. I knocked on her door even though it was open because she told me to always do that. She wasn't at her desk. She was in the big leather chair and had her head back. I realized she had fallen asleep so I tiptoed to her desk and put the envelope on it, but as I started out, she opened her eyes.

"Oh, Jordan. What is it?" she asked me.

"I wrote a letter to Ian and I wanted to ask you to mail it to him for me, please."

"I see. Yes. That's probably a good idea," she said, which surprised me.

She sat up farther. "Is your father rolling around the house?"

"No."

"He was a handful when he was a child; he'll be armsful now," she muttered, and started to stand.

Suddenly, she was dizzy. I knew because she moaned and reached out for the back of the chair. She swayed, too. I didn't know what to do. I never had seen her almost fall, but I reached out and took her hand. She had her eyes closed and gradually grew steady again. Then she opened them and realized I had taken her hand into mine to help her.

She smiled at me. It was the warmest, most loving smile I had ever seen her give me.

"Thank you, Jordan. I must have risen too quickly. That can happen to you, sometimes, even when you're young. I'm tired, though. I think I'm going up to bed. How about you?"

"Yes," I said.

"I'll see to it that Ian gets your letter," she promised, nodding toward her desk.

I let go of her hand.

She turned and started out. "Coming?" she asked me, holding out her hand.

I was surprised again. I moved quickly to take her hand and we walked out together, down the hallway and to the stairway. I had never held hands with her before. She let go at the stairway and leaned on the balustrade more as she ascended. I followed closely behind. At the top of the stairway, she paused and took a deep breath.

"Maybe I should have installed that lift," she said. "For myself." She glanced at me and then she took my hand again and we walked together down to our bedrooms. "Are you all right?" she asked me.

"Yes."

"Good. Don't let your father depress you," she warned me again. "Sometimes," she said as she stood by her bedroom doorway, "the people we love don't love us as much and sometimes they become lead weights around our ankles, pulling us down if we let them. The trick is not to let them," she said.

She was back to tossing tidbits of wisdom at me.

"Can you remember that, Jordan?"

"Yes, Grandmother."

"Good. Good. Let's go to sleep. Now that your father's here, we're both going to need our full strength." She opened her door and went into her bedroom.

I wished I hadn't finished Ian's letter and put it in the envelope. Now I had much more to tell him and to ask him.

26
A KALEIDOSCOPE OF EMOTIONS

Daddy was so demanding and so nasty to Mrs. Clancy that she threatened to quit twice the first week. Grandmother Emma had to raise her salary to keep her working for us. He had temper tantrums and threw things, including his food. He refused to cooperate with the therapist and for two whole days, he refused to leave his bedroom. I heard Mrs. Clancy say he messed himself deliberately. She told Grandmother Emma she had worked with disabled people enough to know when someone needed more psychotherapy and Daddy was someone who definitely did. She suggested he had been released too soon.

"He's not ready to face his life as it now is," she told Grandmother Emma.

"Few people are," Grandmother Emma responded. "Let's do the best we can and hope he improves."

Mrs. Clancy stayed on, but she was very

unhappy. Grandmother Emma started to search for her replacement, anticipating that even the added money wouldn't hold her much longer.

I tried to help. I brought Daddy food. I offered to wheel him around and talk to him as much as I could. He resisted bathing and often looked very disheveled and dirty to me. All the time I was with him or saw him with his nurse or Grandmother, I never heard him once ask to be taken to see Mama. I finally asked him myself if he would like to do that.

"What for? Two cripples looking at each other? From what I hear, she's the one better off," he said. "At least she's in her own world."

"But don't you want her to come home, Daddy? Maybe if she heard your voice, she would wake up more."

"If she heard my voice, she would retreat more," he replied. "I was driving that night, remember? I was rushing." He paused and looked at me. "What did your brother do with you?" he asked. He looked like he had just remembered everything.

"Nothing bad," I said quickly. "He made me his Sister Project and he was trying to help me get better and he wanted to write everything down so doctors and scientists would learn from him. It's in his journal, but I don't know where that is. Miss Harper took it."

"Miss Harper," he said, nodding. "There was a piece of work."

I hadn't known that he had known her, but I should have because her mother and Grandmother Emma were close friends. Or had been. I couldn't imagine them being friends now, because her daughter died in Grandmother Emma's house.

"Weird kid, your brother, weird kid. I tried to make him normal. Don't ask me whose side of the family he takes after. My side has some real winners in it, too." He looked at me closely. "Is the medicine working on you?"

"Yes, Daddy."

"I suppose that's good," he said.

I wanted to remind him about what he had told me the first night he had returned and I wanted to know what he meant, but I didn't. I was confident Ian would have the answers anyway when he wrote back to me.

It was very difficult for everyone in the house. Food Nancy had made for him so many times before he suddenly hated or said wasn't made well. The therapist resigned because Daddy was so uncooperative and unpleasant, and Grandmother

Emma had to find a new one. Mrs. Clancy complained about the nasty things he was saying, too. I overheard her tell Grandmother Emma that he had made obscene requests. She continually pressured Grandmother Emma to get him to psychotherapy.

And then one day things changed. I wouldn't say they changed for the better in the long run, but for the time being, they were good changes for Daddy.

He had a visitor. She was a visitor Grandmother Emma did not want him to have, but he had gone on the telephone and he had asked her to come see him. When Grandmother Emma heard about her impending arrival, she complained, of course, but Daddy said, "What difference does it make now? Why does it matter now?"

She couldn't prevent it, so she ignored it.

Daddy, on the other hand, cleaned himself up. He even asked me to bring him some of his clothing and help him decide what looked nicest on him. He had a hairdresser come to the house and a manicurist. And later that day, he wanted to be taken outside and to the pool, where he could work on his tan. I went swimming that afternoon. Mrs. Clancy was with us, sitting in the shade and reading. She was happy about his change of attitude and didn't care if he had made a deal with the devil or what as long as he was turning into a human being. At least, that was what she told Grandmother Emma, who replied, "You're not so far off. He did make a deal with the devil."

I had no real idea what all this meant until days later when the woman arrived and I realized that she had been Daddy's old girlfriend, the one he had hired for the supermarket, the one who had upset Mama, and the one Grandmother Emma had sent away.

Her name was Kimberly Douglas and I was forced to admit to myself that she was very pretty. She had a dark, almost caramel complexion with lime green eyes shaped like almonds, a small nose, and a mouth with full lips. There was a slight cleft in her chin. Her dark brown hair was tossed in a style Grandmother Emma thought was simply messy, but I heard Mama once call it the "bedroom look" that was popular.

When Kimberly stepped into the mansion that day, she was wearing a tight yellow tank top and a light green skirt with thongs that showed her orange toenails and ankle bracelet. She wore a gold watch that had tiny diamonds around the face. I found out later that it had been a present from Daddy.

Despite my desire to hate her as much as

I could hate anyone, she burst into the mansion with a smile that seemed to me to drag sunshine in behind it. Her eyes were twinkling with infectious excitement hard to resist. I think part of the reason for my reaction was we had been living under such dark clouds and moving through so many thick shadows since Daddy's return. Everyone tiptoed about. Voices were kept low. The sound of laugher was so rare, it came as a surprise whenever it was heard, no matter what the reason.

"You must be Jordan. Hi," she cried, and before I could back away or put up any resistance, she hugged me. She smelled good, too, and delicious flowery and fruity aromas were as rare as laughter. Instead, we had the smell of cleaning fluids and alcohols for Daddy's rubdowns. I thought the mansion reeked of it, because it could find its way upstairs, around corners, and even into closets. It just stuck to the inside of my nose, I guess.

I didn't say hi. I stared at her.

Daddy, who had anticipated her arrival, wheeled himself out of his room and called to her from the hallway. It was Mrs. Clancy's day off and she had gone to visit a sister, so he was in charge of taking care of himself. I saw that he had dressed in the shirt and pants outfit I said looked the nicest. He did look like his old self.

"Chris," she cried, and hurried down to him. I watched her kneel to hug him and saw his hands around her waist. He held onto her for quite a long time, I thought.

When she straightened up, I couldn't hear what they were saying, but a moment later, she helped Daddy turn around and wheel back into his room. I started toward it, too, but they closed the door so I stopped.

I didn't think Grandmother Emma had been paying any attention and therefore didn't know Kimberly was here, but she stepped into the doorway of her office and looked my way. "Your father can't live without his toys," she muttered. "Go amuse yourself and forget them, Jordan," she instructed, and waved toward the front of the house.

One of the changes that had occurred since Ian's departure was Grandmother Emma's giving me more freedom. I could go outside by myself as long as I stayed away from the pool and didn't leave the grounds. There wasn't very much to do by myself, however. I enjoyed playing croquet, but most everything else required another person. Nevertheless, I went out and walked the grounds to watch Mac and his staff trimming bushes, fertilizing plants, or whitewashing fences and storage sheds. Once, he let me help paint. I got messy, but Grandmother Emma didn't complain or bawl him out for permitting me to do it.

As I walked around the house, I thought about Daddy's friend and about Mama and tried to remember when she looked as pretty and as vibrant. If she got better and really woke up, would she come home and look as wonderful and alive again or would that take a long time, too? Was Daddy just tired of waiting? Was that why he wanted his friend to visit? She sounded so happy to see him. Would Mama be as happy or would she be as Daddy thought, still angry at him?

All these questions fell into that pool of mystery Mama used to call adult talk so I would stop asking about them. Was I still too young to know the answers?

I didn't deliberately do it, but I rounded the house and found myself walking toward the windows of Daddy's room. When I realized it, I stopped as if I were approaching some forbidden area, an area as off limits as the pool without supervision, but then my curiosity took over and like a puppet master pulled the right strings to get me to draw closer and closer to those windows until I could actually look into the room.

At first I saw no one and thought they had gone out and were somewhere else in the house, but then I saw Kimberly walk out of the bathroom and I felt the blood drain from my face as a ripple of electricity flowed down and through my body.

She was naked.

And smiling.

I had to shift to the right to see where she was going. She was walking toward Daddy, who was naked as well on his bed. She stood beside the bed looking down at him. He reached up for her hand and then she lowered herself over his face. I saw her left hand go to his knee, but before I could see anything else, I heard a lawn trimmer right behind me and spun around to see Mac doing the edges of the grass near the patio stone.

He looked my way and I shuddered with embarrassment because I knew he could see I was peeping through Daddy's window. I turned and quickly ran toward the front of the house, my heart pounding with each step until I reached the portico and Daddy's ramp.

A kaleidoscope of emotions went swirling through me. I was excited, frightened, and angered by what I had seen. I didn't know which emotion was most comfortable and welcome. All that I had learned about making babies came rushing back, too. Daddy could put tadpoles into that woman. What would happen then? Why was he doing that with her? Mama would be so upset, I thought. So would Ian and so would Grandmother Emma. I wondered if I should tell her so she could stop it.

Daddy would hate me for sure, I thought as I walked up the ramp and into the house. I stood there in the entryway trying to decide what I should do. I heard Grandmother Emma come out of her office, close the door behind her, and walk toward the stairway. She saw me standing there and stopped.

"What's wrong, Jordan? Why are you just standing there like that?" she asked.

I shook my head. I couldn't say it or tell. Instead, I ran past her and up the stairs as quickly as I could.

"Jordan!" she called after me. "Jordan March!"

I didn't stop. I ran to my bedroom and I closed the door. There was really only one person I could tell and that was Ian, I thought. I went immediately to my desk and started to write another letter. I told him what Daddy's friend looked like. I told him how she had hugged him and how he had held onto her, and I told him what I had seen through the window. I asked him what he thought I should do and then I folded the letter twice and sealed it in an envelope.

Grandmother Emma took a long while to come upstairs, but when she did, she came to my room. "Did something happen outside, Jordan?" she asked me.

I shook my head and said, "No."

"Well, why are you so upset?" She waited and then added, "Is it because of your father's female friend?"

I looked at her and then I nodded without saying yes.

She nodded, too. "You have a right to be upset," she said, "but unfortunately or fortunately depending on the way you view it all, your father still has manly needs. There are names for women like that, but there is no reason to talk about it with you. Just think of it as nothing important, nothing more than his going to the bathroom," she said, and smirked. "It's the way I thought of it when it came to your grandfather," she added, which raised my eyebrows.

She shook her head. "I'm tired," she said. She had never said that to me in the middle of the day before. She's just very upset about Daddy, I thought.

She turned and went into her room and

closed the door.

I went to my textbooks and read and did some workbook pages. Then I fell asleep for a while. When I woke up, I remembered the letter I had written to Ian and I took it and went downstairs to Grandmother Emma's office. I went in and put it on her desk so she would send it off as she did with my first letter. Every day I had been anticipating a letter back from Ian, so when the mailman came, I was right there waiting, but none had come yet. I was sure it was because he was thinking hard and long about what he wanted to say so it would be perfect. Ian always wanted everything he did to be perfect.

Just as I stepped out of the office, I heard laughter and saw Kimberly wheeling Daddy out of his room. They both saw me standing in the doorway.

"What are you doing, Jordan, having a business meeting with your grandmother?" Daddy asked.

"No," I said. "I left her my letter to Ian. She mails them to him for me," I told him.

He stopped smiling. Kimberly held hers, though, and continued to look at me.

"Is that so?" he asked, but he didn't wait for an answer. He pushed his own wheels so they would continue down the hallway. I was surprised to see them go into the living room, where I heard Daddy tell Kimberly to make him a vodka cocktail. Later, I found out he had asked her to stay for dinner and had told Nancy to prepare another setting.

I was positive Grandmother Emma would be upset about it. I wondered if she knew yet. It was drawing close to dinner so I went up to wash, fix my hair, and change my clothes. Grandmother Emma still liked me to look dressed up for our dinners. When I was finished, I started out and saw that her bedroom door was still closed. It made me hesitate. She was usually downstairs by now, giving Nancy orders. I went to her door and put my ear to it to listen for sounds that would tell me she was still in her room. If she was, I was going to warn her about Kimberly staying for dinner.

At first, I heard nothing and then I heard what sounded like water running. I listened hard. It was water running and running and running. It didn't sound like her shower or her bath either. I decided to knock on her door when the running water continued. She didn't answer so I knocked harder and then I called for her and waited. Still, she didn't answer. I tried the door knob and it opened.

"Grandmother?" I called, and waited with

the door slightly opened.

Now I was sure the water was running in the sink, so I pushed the door completely open and I walked into her bedroom. She was nowhere in sight, but the bathroom door was open. I walked slowly to it, calling for her as I did so. She didn't answer.

When I reached the door, I stopped and stared as if I was in a dream.

The bathroom sink was overflowing. Grandmother Emma was lying on the floor, wearing a full slip, and reaching up toward me, her mouth twisted in the funniest way. She looked like she had messed herself, too. All I could do for a few moments was continue to stare, then I turned and ran out. At the top of the stairway with all the power of my lungs, I screamed for Nancy.

But the music from the living room was very loud so I had to go down the stairs and scream from there. Finally, Nancy heard me and came out of the kitchen.

"Something's wrong with Grandmother Emma!" I cried.

"What?"

"She's lying on the floor in her bathroom and the water is running out of the sink."

Nancy wiped her hands on her apron and hurried to the stairway. I started up and she hurried past me, rushing down the hallway to the room. I followed as quickly as I could and stood in the bedroom, looking through the doorway as Nancy knelt down to talk to Grandmother Emma. Then she shot up, turned off the faucet, and went to the telephone. She punched 911 and screamed for an ambulance.

"I think she had a stroke!" she told the operator. After that she returned to Grandmother Emma and began to make her comfortable. She brought her a pillow and began to prepare a cool washcloth. I waited and watched, unsure of what I could or should do.

"Go down and tell your father what's happening," Nancy instructed as she dabbed towels into the water on the floor.

I hurried out and down the stairs. The music was still loud. When I entered the living room, Kimberly was swaying to the music in front of Daddy, who was holding his cocktail and laughing. Kimberly saw me and stopped. Daddy didn't realize why for a moment and then she turned down the music and nodded in my direction.

"Jordan needs you," she said.

"Needs me? How could anyone need me?" Daddy asked, still smiling. He turned his chair so he could see me. "What's up?"

"Grandmother Emma's on the floor in her

499

bathroom. Nancy called for an ambulance."

"Huh?"

"Your mother . . ." Kimberly said, as if she had to explain to him who Grandmother Emma was. "What happened to her, Jordan?"

"Nancy said she thinks it's a stroke, whatever that is," I said.

"Stroke? My mother?" Daddy blinked his eyes. I could see the news was sobering him up quickly. He put down his drink and looked at Kimberly. "You'd better go up there and see what's going on," he told her.

She nodded and started out. "Show me the way, Jordan," she said. After all, she had never been in the mansion.

I didn't care to do it. I didn't want her seeing Grandmother Emma like that, but I led her out and up the stairs to her bedroom. Nancy had put a blanket over Grandmother Emma, who had her eyes closed now and was turned away from us.

Kimberly looked at Nancy. "How is she?"

"She ain't good. I think it was a stroke. I called for an ambulance."

"Is she still breathing?" Kimberly asked, squinting and smirking as she looked down at Grandmother Emma.

"Best I can tell she is. You know anything about this sort of thing?"

"Not a clue," Kimberly said. She backed away. The sight of Grandmother Emma on the floor was frightening to her. "I'll go tell Christopher." She turned and hurried away.

"You stay with her," Nancy told me. "I'll go look for Felix."

I nodded and looked down at Grandmother Emma. She made a small groan and her eyelids fluttered, but they didn't open. I sat beside her on the floor and waited. It came to me to take her hand in mine and that caused her to turn her head and open her eyes.

I thought she shook her head before she closed her eyes again. She didn't say or do anything else before the ambulance arrived, and the paramedics, who just happened to be the same two who had come for Miss Harper, came up the stairs with a stretcher. I got up quickly as they rushed into the bedroom and to Grandmother Emma. Then I stood back and watched them take her blood pressure and try to get her to be alert. They carefully placed her on the stretcher after they called in her condition and then started to carry her out.

Felix came rushing up the stairs and offered to help them, but they had everything under control. He followed them down to open the door. I walked slowly behind them.

Daddy was outside the living room watching everything and Kimberly stood beside him, neither of them speaking. I went to the front of the house with Nancy and watched them place Grandmother Emma in the ambulance. Nancy put her hand on my shoulder. Felix came back into the house and asked Daddy if he wanted him to bring the van around.

"Yeah, I guess so," Daddy said. "Although I don't know what the hell I can do for her." He looked up at Kimberly. "I'll call you later."

"You want me to do anything with Jordan? Stay with her, take her to dinner?"

Daddy looked at me. "Naw. She's a big girl. She'll be fine here by herself, right, Jordan?"

I nodded. I didn't want to do anything with Kimberly anyway. She took out a piece of paper and wrote her telephone number on it for Nancy.

"Just in case you need some help," she said. "Don't hesitate to call me."

Nancy looked at it and then stuffed it into her apron with a look that told me she would never even glance at it again.

Daddy wheeled himself out and he and Kimberly went down the ramp. I watched Felix get him into the van and then I watched them drive off after the ambulance, Kimberly following in her own car. She turned in the opposite direction at the base of the driveway and drove away.

A great pall of silence suddenly fell over the house and the grounds. Everything had happened so quickly, I felt like all the air around me had been sucked up to the sky. I couldn't breathe. My heart, which had been pounding, was now so still, I wasn't sure that it hadn't evaporated in my chest.

"There's nothing more we can do," Nancy said. "I'll put out some dinner for you, Jordan, and wait for your daddy's return, okay?"

"Yes," I said.

"We'll be just fine," she told me, but I thought if I ever needed Ian, I needed him now. Why couldn't I call whoever was keeping him and beg them to bring him home? Wasn't it more important for him to be here with me?

When I thought about him, I remembered I had left my last letter for him on Grandmother Emma's desk. Now she wouldn't be able to send it to him until she got better. That saddened me as much as anything else.

I went to her office to get the envelope. I didn't want Daddy or Nancy or anyone to find it and read it. I would keep it in my room until Grandmother Emma came home, I thought.

It was right where I had left it. I picked it up and then I thought maybe I could find stamps in her desk drawer and maybe Ian's address, too.

I searched the top drawer and got excited when I found a roll of stamps. I quickly put one on the envelope. Then I opened the side drawer and started to look through the papers, hoping to see something with Ian's name on it. I stopped when an envelope fell out.

It was my first letter to Ian.

She had never sent it.

But she had opened and read it.

I couldn't help myself. I sat on her desk chair and just started to cry.

Nancy heard and came running to the office door. She saw me sitting behind the desk, sobbing with my head down on my arms.

"Oh, Jordan," she said, approaching, "don't worry, honey. Your grandmother will be all right. You'll see. She'll be home in no time."

I looked up at her. "I don't care," I said, flicking off the tears.

"What did you say?"

"I don't care if she ever gets better. I don't

care if she ever comes home either!"

Nancy gasped. I clutched the two letters I had written and rose from Grandmother Emma's desk chair.

"Jordan!" she cried, and shook her head. "What a terrible thing to say."

I held up my letters. "No, it's not. She never mailed my first letter to Ian," I moaned. "She said she would and she didn't. She lied. Mama told me people tell you what you want to hear. She said people do it all the time. She said . . ." I gasped. "She said, 'Welcome to the adult world.'"

"Well, I don't want to be in the adult world," I said, and ran out and up to my room.

No, I didn't want to grow up at all. I'd never forget to take my medicine. I'd take it forever if it would keep me from lies and liars.

I was about to find out just how impossible that was going to be, because the biggest lie of all was waiting to show me its ugly face.

27
Daddy in Charge

Daddy didn't return for dinner. Felix phoned Nancy to tell her that Daddy had called Kimberly from the hospital and she and he had gone out to eat at a restaurant. He never called to tell Nancy beforehand so she was upset because she had prepared enough food for all of us and another of his favorite desserts, which took some time, a fresh fruit tart. After Felix phoned to let her know, she went into the kitchen and dumped out food, slammed the stove and refrigerator doors, and swore aloud that she would look for new employment.

I sat alone in the dining room listening to her. When she came in to see how I was doing, she told me everything and also said Grandmother Emma had suffered a stroke and was being evaluated in the hospital, but it was clear she was very, very ill.

"Whenever you go see her, you'd better not be mean to her, Jordan, because she forgot to send out your letter," Nancy added. "For your information, young lady, elderly people who suffer strokes have trouble with their memory and she might have been having that just recently. I know because my mother had a stroke."

I knew she was telling me all this to make me feel bad, but I was still angry about my letter to Ian.

"The truth is she hasn't been herself since your father's return," Nancy continued, clearing things off the table. "Look at all that woman's had to carry on her shoulders, with your mother and all and then this horrible, terrible thing your brother did. It's enough to give a twenty-year-old a stroke, much less a woman of her age."

I suddenly realized that although Grandmother Emma was always quite firm and seemed even angry at times when she spoke to Nancy, Nancy really admired and respected her. I wouldn't go so far as to say love, but she certainly held Grandmother Emma in high regard and excused any of her abruptness and sharpness as being simply the way a woman who was a leader and an important member of the community had to be.

I did feel bad about what I had said. I hoped Nancy wouldn't tell Grandmother

Emma. Much later, after I had gone to bed and was falling asleep, I heard loud voices and laughter coming from downstairs. I rose and went out in my pajamas to the top of the stairway so I could listen. Had Grandmother Emma gotten better already and been brought home? I wondered.

I soon realized it was Daddy and Kimberly and they were carrying on just as they had before Grandmother Emma had gotten ill. I went down a few steps and saw Kimberly wheeling him toward his bedroom. From what I overheard, I understood she was staying the night. Nancy was nowhere to be seen. I imagined she had gone home, and Mrs. Clancy was still away.

I sat on the step and listened until I couldn't hear their voices anymore. For a few moments I debated whether or not I should go down, knock on Daddy's door, and ask him what had happened to Grandmother Emma, but I didn't want to see him with Kimberly. I was afraid I would see them doing what I had seen them doing when I peered through the window. I rose and returned to my bedroom, but now falling asleep wasn't as easy as I thought it was going to be.

I missed everyone, Mama, Ian, and even Grandmother Emma, despite her not mailing my letter. It had been comforting to know she was just across the hall from me. She was still as powerful as a queen in my mind and she could keep the demons from our doors. What would keep them away now? I wondered. I was sure I would have nightmares. Would I be able to do what Ian prescribed, blink my eyes and pop them out of my head?

Trembling, I descended into the darkness of sleep.

Nothing woke me until morning, however. First, it was the sunshine pouring through the windows because I had forgotten to close the curtains, and then it was Nancy coming to see how I was.

"I'll make you a good breakfast," she said.

I nodded, rose, washed and dressed, and took my medicine. I expected to see Daddy and Kimberly in the dining room, too, but they weren't there. Nancy told me they hadn't woken yet. She heard nothing coming from that side of the house. Then Mrs. Clancy came in and Nancy intercepted her in the hallway to give her all the news.

"I'm not surprised, not a bit," she muttered, "considering all that poor woman has to contend with."

She came into the dining room to have some breakfast and coffee.

"Someone's here with Daddy," I said.

"I heard," she said, her face grimacing like the face of someone who had just bitten into a very tart lemon.

As if on cue in a play, Daddy and Kimberly came out of his bedroom. Kimberly wheeled him to the dining room. She was wearing one of his bathrobes and his slippers. Daddy had a pajama top and a pair of sweat pants on with no shoes. The first thing I thought when I saw them was Grandmother Emma would never permit them to come to the dining room table dressed like that.

"Well, everyone's eating breakfast without us, Kimberly," Daddy said. "This is Mrs. Clancy," he added.

Kimberly smiled at her but didn't say anything and Mrs. Clancy only glared back. Then she put down her coffee cup.

"I don't imagine you took your medications this morning," she said.

"Oh, sure I did. Didn't I, Kimberly?"

"He did," she said. "Maybe not the exact same medicine, however," she added, and they both laughed. "Oh, look at those corn muffins." She sat beside him and poured herself and then Daddy a cup of coffee.

"You have a therapy session at one today," Mrs. Clancy told Daddy.

"I think I've already had enough therapy for a while," he quipped, and both he and Kimberly laughed again. They were acting like two teenagers. "Besides, we're taking a ride over to Kimberly's apartment today to get some things together. She's moving in to take over most of your duties, Mrs. Clancy. There is no more reason for you to stay. I'll see to it that you're given a month's salary."

Mrs. Clancy's mouth dropped open, but then she quickly closed it and smiled. "Why, it seems that Christmas has come early this year," she said.

Kimberly thought that was hysterical and broke into laughter again. Daddy laughed, too.

"Touché, Mrs. Clancy. I'll miss your sweet and warm smile every day, and those loving hands of yours."

Mrs. Clancy rose so quickly, she nearly tipped over her chair. "I'll pack up immediately," she said. "Give my best wishes to your mother."

"Will do," Daddy said.

Nancy stood in the doorway listening to everything and not moving. Mrs. Clancy glanced at her and then left the dining room. I had been holding my breath the whole time.

"Oh, look at little Jordan," Kimberly said. "Don't be frightened, honey. I'll take very good care of your daddy."

"That's for sure," Daddy said. "Nancy, I'm starving. How about some cheese omelets."

"Very good, Mr. March," Nancy said, and returned to the kitchen.

"Now that Kimberly will be here full time, Jordan," Daddy said, "you can invite some of your friends over to go swimming. She can supervise. Okay?"

I nodded, but thought Grandmother Emma was going to be very, very angry about all this. And what would happen when Mama woke up and found out, too?

"In fact," Daddy continued, "things are going to change radically around here now. We're going to bring some fun back into this place. Just think of it as a constant party."

Kimberly giggled.

"What about Grandmother Emma?" I asked.

"What about her?" Daddy said. "She wasted most of her life being so serious and never enjoying all that she had and look what it's gotten her. Now it's too late for her to enjoy it, but I'll make up for it for her," he added, and Kimberly smiled and nudged him. "I mean, Kimberly and I will."

"She'll be angry if we have parties here all the time, Daddy."

"She won't know anything anymore, Jordan." He leaned on the table. "Your grandmother has had what is called a stroke."

"I know."

"It's severe. She won't recuperate. She'll never be what and who she was. In fact, I'll be arranging for her to be in a facility."

"She's not coming home?"

"I doubt that very much. We don't have a lift on the stairway, remember?" he said with a cold smile. "And we'd have to rip apart some more of the mansion to accommodate her and you heard what she said about that. She wouldn't disturb this house any more than she had to for me and that was done begrudgingly. No, this is no place for a woman in that condition. Maybe Mrs. Clancy can get a job in the facility and care for her.

"Don't look so worried. You'll be happier, believe me."

"What about Ian?" I asked.

"There's not much to do about Ian at the moment. We have enough to deal with anyway."

"And Mama?"

"Whatever she needs, she'll have, but it doesn't look like she's going to need much, Jordan. I'm sorry about it all, about your father being in this damn chair, about your brother and your mother, but we'll either roll over and die or ring some bells and blow some whistles," he added, and smiled at Kimberly.

She smiled and then leaned over to kiss his cheek. I couldn't help how I looked, but whatever the expression was on my face, it brought them both back to that teenage laughter.

Nancy served them their omelets and when they began to eat, I wiped my mouth, excused myself, and went upstairs to brush my teeth. I heard Mrs. Clancy coming out of her room, carrying her two suitcases. She saw me in the hallway.

"Try to ignore them, Jordan," she said. "That's the best advice I can offer." She descended the stairs and walked out of the mansion.

Not long afterward, I heard Daddy and Kimberly leaving to go to her apartment. He had Felix drive them in the van. He would also help them with anything. Daddy was giving the orders now, not Grandmother Emma, I thought.

Just before lunch they returned with all of

Kimberly's clothing, toiletries, shoes, and other personal things. I watched Felix carry it all to Daddy's bedroom. Nancy was told to help hang things up in the closets and then Daddy and Kimberly decided they would take lunch on the patio facing the pool. Kimberly got into a very abbreviated two-piece bathing suit and Daddy surprised me by putting on his bathing suit as well. He told me to put on mine and go swimming with them.

It was a very warm, sunny day. I was pulled in two different directions. I wanted to be angry about everything, but I did want to go swimming, too, and I always wanted to call Missy and some of the other girls to invite them to the house. For now, I saw no reason to pout in my bedroom so I did put on my bathing suit and joined them at the pool.

Nancy brought out some sandwiches. Daddy sent her back for champagne. He had music piped out and it did seem to be the beginning of endless parties.

"You can call some of your friends tomorrow," Daddy said.

I ate a sandwich, listened to them giggle and talk, and watched Kimberly parade around like a swimsuit model for Daddy. She was on his lap or constantly throwing her arms around his neck and kissing him. It all made me feel very nauseated.

"When are we going to visit Grandmother Emma?" I asked him, and they both suddenly stopped laughing. They had drunk almost two bottles of champagne.

"Your grandmother would not like to have anyone see her in the condition she is in," Daddy said. "Believe me, I know. I'll be speaking with her doctor about it and we'll see when to visit and when to arrange for her transfer to a care facility. Don't dwell on sad things, Jordan. This is the best time of your life. I wasn't permitted to enjoy it like you will, believe me. Now I have to make up for it," he added, and reached for Kimberly.

She put her arm around his neck and they both looked at me.

"I'm tired," I said. "I got too much sun."

Daddy shook his head. "There's a lot of Emma March in that girl. We have our work cut out for us, Kimberly."

"We'll change her. Don't worry," she said.

They returned to their champagne and I hurried back to the house. When I looked back at them, I saw Kimberly was helping Daddy onto a lounge and then lying next to him. They were kissing again.

Ian would absolutely vomit, I thought. I

almost did.

When I entered the house, I discovered Nancy looking out the dining room window at them. She looked at me, shook her head, and then returned to her work. Later she stopped in my room to tell me Grandmother Emma's lawyer, Mr. Ganz, had called to tell her to tell me that Grandmother Emma wanted to see me at the hospital tomorrow in the morning.

"She does?"

"Yes."

"But I thought she was very, very sick."

"She is," Nancy said.

"Is Daddy going, too?"

"I don't believe so. My understanding is Felix will be taking only you. It's the way your grandmother wants it."

Even from a hospital and in a hospital bed, Grandmother Emma, stroke or no stroke, was still in charge, I thought. That made me feel good.

"Okay," I said.

"Your grandmother is an extraordinary woman," Nancy said, turning away. "Oh," she added, turning back. "You'll be having dinner alone again, I'm afraid. I was just informed that the prince and princess will be dining out." She smiled. "I made one of your favorites, Chinese chicken salad. It's too hot to eat heavy anyway. But I did make you a chocolate cream pie," she added.

"Thank you, Nancy."

"You're welcome," she said. She glanced at Grandmother Emma's closed bedroom door and lowered her head before walking away.

Later, when I saw Daddy just before he was leaving for dinner with Kimberly, I anticipated him saying something to me about my visiting Grandmother Emma at the hospital the next morning, but he didn't mention it and I had the feeling he didn't know anything about it. I decided not to tell him.

He and Kimberly slept so late the next morning that I was finished with my breakfast, dressed, and ready to go with Felix before they appeared. Nancy told me they could get their own breakfast and went about her daily cleaning routine. I stepped outside just as Felix came around with the limousine.

"Ready?" he asked, opening the door for me.

"Yes, Felix."

I got inside and felt ten times smaller alone in the big black car. Funny, I thought, how Grandmother Emma never looked small in here, even when she was driven off or back from somewhere and I saw she was alone.

"Never thought something like this would happen to your grandmother," Felix said as he drove. "Thought everyone else would fall apart around her first, including yours truly."

I could see his face in the rearview mirror. He shook his head and his eyes looked glassy, tearful. Everyone who I thought was afraid of Grandmother Emma and really worried she would yell at them or fire them seemed to really like her now.

"If anyone looked like she was made of steel, it was Emma March," Felix continued. "Holding up your grandfather, helping your parents, especially now with all that's happened, your brother and all, and doing battles with anyone or anything that crossed her path. They don't make them like that anymore, believe me. I hope you inherited some of her grit," he added.

After he parked at the hospital, he took my hand and we went in and up to Grandmother Emma's room. Dr. Dell'Acqua was in the hallway speaking with a nurse and saw us walking toward her. She turned to us and smiled at me.

"How are you, Jordan?"

"I'm fine. I'm here to visit Grandmother Emma."

"Good. That will cheer her up," she said. "She's doing a little better, but she's still a sick lady and she won't be the same to you." She looked at Felix. "She has paralysis on her right side and it's affected her speech," she told him. "Her attorney is in there with her," she added.

Felix nodded. "How's it look?"

"Too soon to tell how much of a recuperation there'll be," Dr. Dell'Acqua said. "You taking your medicine every day?" she asked me.

"Yes," I said.

"Good." She patted me on the top of the head and walked off with the nurse.

We entered Grandmother Emma's room. Mr. Ganz was seated on her left, a long yellow pad in his lap. Grandmother Emma's bed had been raised so she was in more of a sitting position. I couldn't remember ever seeing Grandmother Emma in her bed. She had a bed as big as the one I slept in, so I imagined she looked small in hers as well, but in the hospital, without her elegant clothing, her hair neatly brushed and pinned, she looked aged and tiny. She looked like she was shriveling right before my eyes.

"Morning, Mrs. March," Felix said. "I brought Jordan as you asked," he told her.

Grandmother Emma nodded and looked at me and then at a chair. Felix understood immediately and brought the chair up to the bed so I could sit beside Mr. Ganz to talk with her. Then he stepped back and left the room.

"You know that expression, no moss gathers on a rolling stone?" Mr. Ganz asked me, smiling.

"No, sir."

"It means as long as you're busy and you keep moving, nothing will slow you down and cause you to fail. That's your grandmother here," he said, nodding at Grandmother Emma. Her mouth was twisted so I couldn't tell if she was smiling or smirking, happy or angry about what he said. "Another woman her age would be thinking about herself and getting better, but she's thinking about all her business needs and about you," he added.

I looked at Grandmother Emma. Me?

"She's worried that now you have no one to look after you. The truth is," Mr. Ganz continued, "your grandmother never gets surprised because she anticipates the good and the bad. She's been doing that for as long as I've known her and that's a long time, Jordan."

Grandmother Emma made a guttural sound and moved her left hand.

"All right, all right. She wants me to get right to it," he said.

Right to what? I wondered.

"Your grandmother has always been a realistic person, Jordan. She never sugar-coats anything. I tell her that's because she's a Sagittarius and she has to tell the truth come hell or high water."

Grandmother Emma grunted and tried to say something. She slapped the bed with her left hand in frustration.

"All right, all right, Emma. I'm getting to it. Your grandmother realizes that she is seri-ously incapacitated and her recovery, any recovery, will take a long time and may not be a full recovery."

Again, Grandmother Emma grunted and made a guttural sound.

"Won't be a full recovery," Mr. Ganz corrected. "Consequently, she is aware that she will not be able to do the things for you she had intended to do and she is concerned about that.

"She is also well aware of the fact that your father won't be able to do these things as well."

"His friend Kimberly is still there helping

him," I interjected.

Grandmother Emma made a sound that resembled a long "Noooo."

"Your grandmother is aware of that. She actually found out all that last night," Mr. Ganz said. "That's part of what I meant by a rolling stone gathers no moss. No moss grows under her feet, or bed in this case," he added. "This has reaffirmed her belief that you won't get the attention and care you deserve.

"Of course, you know your mother can't do much for you right now either. Soooo," he said, leaning back in his chair, "your grandmother would like you to live with her sister, Francis, for now."

I knew I looked stupefied, shocked, and even somewhat foolish with my jaw dropped.

"Your great-aunt Francis lives alone on a nice property. I've been there from time to time for legal matters. You'll go to school and back on a bus and I'll see to it that you have all you need, medically and otherwise."

"But . . . Daddy wants me to live at the mansion with him and Kimberly," I said.

Grandmother Emma grunted.

"Your grandmother has arranged for this alternative," Mr. Ganz said. "I'll be meeting with your father today, too, and he will be in agreement about it. Believe me," he added, and exchanged a knowing look between himself and Grandmother Emma.

"I never saw my great-aunt Francis," I said.

"Nevertheless, she knows all about you and Ian and always has," Mr. Ganz said.

"Will Ian come live with her, too?"

"Someday, maybe. Maybe," he emphasized.

"Mama might be upset about it."

I was sure Grandmother Emma was trying to laugh. Mr. Ganz smiled, too.

"No, we're pretty confident your mother would prefer this arrangement to the one your father was suggesting, Jordan."

"Daddy will be very upset," I insisted.

Grandmother Emma reached for Mr. Ganz with her left hand. He seemed to understand every look she gave him and every move she made, even her distorted words.

"Why don't we say this then, Jordan? If after I meet with your father, he is opposed to the arrangement, we'll forget about it. Okay?"

I looked at Grandmother Emma. Even as sick as she was, she had that same light of confidence in her eyes. She was still the queen.

I nodded.

"Good," Mr. Ganz said. He smiled and brushed my hair with his left hand. "You'll be fine, Jordan. Everything will be good for you from now on."

I looked at Grandmother Emma. Her eyes shifted and she lay back.

"Your grandmother's tired now, Jordan. The doctor didn't want us to have too long a meeting. Say good-bye to her for now," he told me.

I nodded and stood up. Grandmother Emma turned toward me. Then she lifted her left hand, her good hand, and I reached out to take it. Her eyes looked teary, and in fact, I saw the first drop sneak out the corner of her right eye. She held my hand tightly. I glanced at Mr. Ganz, whose eyes looked full of amazement.

And then I leaned forward and I kissed her on the cheek.

Her tears flowed freely then.

And I couldn't hate her for not mailing out my letter.

I couldn't hate her for anything.

28
She Will Never Hate You

I suppose there are so many reasons, even after I listened to Ian and wrote my story, that I still think of my life as being a dream. Smiles and laughter, grimaces and tears swirl about in my memory like ingredients tossed into a blender. It's hard sometimes to separate the happy times from the sad. So often after I had left the March Mansion, I would start to laugh about something Ian and I did or Mama and I did, or Daddy and I and Mama and Ian had done together, and then I would stop suddenly, and for reasons I couldn't explain, begin to sob.

I'd have a good cry and then I would stop, take a deep breath, and go on doing whatever it was I was doing, just as if I had closed the cover of a photo album, cried over a lost loved one, and put the pictures back in some desk drawer. That album is tied with four ribbons, each one representing a different good-bye.

Actually, that's what I remember most clearly, the good-byes. That's what haunts me now and will haunt me forever, because what I did learn, what I can tell Ian with that same certainty that characterizes all the things he told me and tells me, is that good-byes were times when I became most like Grandmother Emma, when I saw what was real and what was true and when I knew I could no longer be a child because I couldn't pretend or deny or ignore any of it.

"Nothing," Grandmother Emma once told me, "will make you grow up faster than facing reality, than walking right up to it and putting your nose against it. It's like going uphill and losing the grip on your mother's hand and your father's hand. You start to fall back, finding yourself all alone. You have no choice but to become a woman, to climb the rest of the way on your own. There will be no more medicine to slow it down, no more fairy tales to help you avoid what's hard or ugly or painful.

"But don't be afraid of it," she said. "Embrace it and give yourself a name. You had one name as a child. Now you have another."

I was too young to understand, but after my good-byes, I began the journey toward that understanding, the journey that has taken me here.

My first good-bye was good-bye to Daddy. When I left Grandmother Emma and Mr. Ganz at the hospital, I felt numb. Ian would tell me I had shut down and frozen just like some overloaded computer. Something or someone would have to unplug me and then plug me in to start me over.

I wasn't looking forward to arriving and facing Daddy and Kimberly so I was happy to learn that he had been summoned to Mr. Ganz's office. Nancy told me it was a meeting Daddy had asked for himself almost the moment Grandmother Emma had left in the ambulance. He had called Mr. Ganz from the hospital that day, apparently, and set everything in motion, only the direction it took was a surprise even to him, maybe especially to him.

I was upstairs in my room working on another letter to Ian when Daddy and Kimberly returned. I didn't hear them come in, but not long afterward, Kimberly came to my room to tell me my father wanted to see me in my grandmother's office. I followed her downstairs.

Daddy looked so awkward and out of place sitting behind Grandmother Emma's desk in his wheelchair that I almost smiled.

Because of the way the large desk wrapped around him, he looked like a child pretending to be an adult. He fumbled papers and documents as if he really didn't know where anything belonged or what anything meant. It was the first time I could remember him being so nervous, too. He was fidgeting while he waited for me to enter and take my seat. Kimberly stood awkwardly, too, not sure if she should sit on the settee, stand beside him, or just leave.

"Well, Jordan," Daddy began, sitting back and trying to look relaxed, "it seems you've already visited your grandmother and spoken with Mr. Ganz in the hospital."

I nodded and then in almost a whisper, said, "Yes."

Daddy glanced at Kimberly and then he leaned forward to put his arms on the desk. "Once again, even in her feeble condition, in fact, your grandmother has taken the reins of control here. I must admit she had to have done a good deal of preparation, anticipating the day when something serious might happen to her. I suppose I have to . . . we have to respect her for that.

"My mother," he said for Kimberly's benefit more than for mine, "is rarely, if ever, taken by surprise, even by her own body."

"Not much excitement and fun in that," Kimberly said.

Daddy grunted and looked down at the desk. "You know," he continued, "that your grandmother would like you to live with your great-aunt Francis. She's right to assume I have too much against me right now to be a good father. Between my therapy and all this paraphernalia I have to contend with and develop," he said, waving his arms as if there were wires and cranes everywhere, "I will be quite involved and not have as much time for you as I should."

When did he ever? I wondered, but dared not ask.

"The way your grandmother has constructed the finances kind of puts me in a box, too, Jordan. She's been a busy little bee, arranging all sorts of trusts and devices to funnel the funds we all need and there are preconditions for almost everything. My mind is still spinning after my session with her attorney, and I know something about business. I can't imagine what someone else would do," he added, looking again at Kimberly.

All Daddy knew about business was how to fail at it, I thought, but again, slipped those words under my tongue.

"The truth is, I've given her plan a great

deal of thought and I have to agree for now, at least, it makes sense. You'll attend a good school, have plenty of space at the farmhouse, be of some help to your great-aunt, who has no one but herself, and you'll have all the support you need financially. All of your medical needs are arranged as well, and your great-aunt has been filled in about all of that."

"Did Mr. Ganz say anything about Ian?" I asked quickly.

Daddy stared at me a moment and then shook his head. "Ian is in for a long haul. He did a very bad thing and people have to be certain that he would never do anything like that again. I know you admire your brother very much, but between what he was doing with you and what he did to Miss Harper, he falls somewhere between Dr. Jekyll and Mr. Hyde."

"Who are they?"

"You'll find out yourself. Maybe," he said. "Now, Kimberly and I have discussed all this already and we've decided we would come visit you regularly. You know exactly where Great-aunt Francis lives, right?"

"Not really."

"Well, she's on that farm my father found for her years ago. She has someone who maintains everything for her, a black guy slightly younger than her. He lives with his own family on the property, his daughter and her daughter, a girl five years or so older than you, I think. In short, you'll be well cared for there and have lots of company.

"Believe me," Daddy said, suddenly full of anger and pain, "if I weren't sitting here in this wheelchair, none of this would be happening. I'd challenge everything your grandmother's arranged and I'd take control of this family as I should have years ago," he declared, slapping the desk. His eyes did look full of frustration, and even, for a short moment, flooding with tears.

"Take it easy, Chris," Kimberly gently advised him.

He cleared his throat. "If you like, Kimberly will help you get what you want together for your move."

"I'm going now?"

"Soon," he said. "Grandmother Emma arranged for you to go see your mother tomorrow. Felix will be taking you. Day after that, he'll drive you to Great-aunt Francis. There's not much time now before a new school year starts for you, and you need to be settled in, adjusted, and comfortable. Those are your grandmother's exact words," he concluded.

He lowered his head for a moment. Then

he sighed deeply and sat up again. "You'll be all right," he continued, smiling. "We'll bring you back here for visits time to time as well, and next summer we'll all go to the cabin at the lake, maybe. You'll do fine, just fine."

"Sure you will," Kimberly said.

The eagerness with which she wanted to get rid of me didn't slip past me. I glared at her, putting on my Ian face and turning my eyes into Ian eyes. It worked. She looked away quickly.

"What about when Mama gets better?" I asked.

"When and if that happens, we'll see," he replied. "But for now, you've got to concentrate on yourself. You can't dwell on your mother and your brother or me."

"Your father's right, Jordan," Kimberly said.

"You don't know what's right," I said. "When my mother gets better, you'd better go away."

"Jordan!"

"It's all right, Christopher."

"It's never all right to be disrespectful. Kimberly's only been trying to help make things easier for you. The truth is she would have been a better companion than your great-aunt Francis, but there's nothing I can do about it and that's that," Daddy said, growing irritable.

"You're getting tired, Christopher," Kimberly said. "You should take a rest."

"Yeah, right. Anyway," Daddy said, looking at me, "that's the way it is and will be. When anything makes you upset or unhappy from now on, blame it on your grandmother," he told me, and started to wheel himself out from behind her desk.

Kimberly rushed to help him. "He needs a nap," she told me as she pushed him along.

He was staring down at the floor, his shoulders turned in, his head lowered.

She looked back just before the doorway. "This is why it's better for you to do what your grandmother wanted," she threw back at me, and pushed Daddy out of the office.

I sat there staring at Grandmother Emma's desk and I thought maybe she was right.

That night I began to arrange my things, the things I would take with me. Nancy came up after dinner to help me. I didn't want Kimberly doing it. Nancy knew everything by now and while she worked, she told me she would probably leave the March Mansion soon herself.

The following day, just as Grandmother

Emma had arranged from her hospital bed, Felix took me to Philadelphia to see my mother in the hospital. He told me Grandmother Emma had set things up so that he could take me there from time to time, even from Great-aunt Francis's home.

I wondered aloud if Ian would ever visit Mama again. Felix didn't say.

Although Mama's nurse, Mrs. Feinberg, was happy to see me, I could tell from the way she greeted me and looked at Felix that she already knew about Grandmother Emma. Considering all the bad news that had fallen around and over me, she was eager to tell me something good.

"Your mother has made a little progress with responses," she said. "It's too soon to tell what it will mean, but her doctor is very happy about it. Every little change looks big to us now. But don't get your hopes up too high too quickly, Jordan. People often take years to make significant progress."

Mama didn't look any different to me when I entered her room, but I immediately noticed that her hand wasn't opening and closing the way it had. It was still.

"Go on," Mrs. Feinberg urged. "Talk to her."

I sat beside the bed. Mrs. Feinberg and Felix stood in the doorway watching. I decided Mama had to know everything because that might get her angry and excited enough to force her to get well.

"Hi, Mama," I said. "I've come back to see you and I hope you're getting better and that you'll get better even faster because until you are, I have to go live with Great-aunt Francis. Grandmother Emma had a stroke and is in the hospital and Daddy, who is in a wheelchair, can't take care of me properly."

I hesitated, glanced back at Mrs. Feinberg and Felix, who both smiled at me and then left, and then I turned back to Mama and took her hand into mine.

"That old girlfriend of Daddy's, Kimberly, is in the house with him now. They told Mrs. Clancy, the nurse, to leave, and Nancy is going to leave soon, too. I don't like Kimberly being there. You've got to get better, Mama. You've got to, and you've got to come home. Please, Mama. Please get better."

I couldn't stop the tears from flowing freely down my cheeks now. They dropped off my chin and some fell on my hand and hers. I lowered my head against her arm and I sobbed for a while.

Suddenly, I felt Mama's hand tighten slightly around mine. I was sure of it. I raised my head quickly and looked at her. She wasn't turning her head toward me and her eyes were still fixed on nothing, like the eyes of a blind person, but I was still positive she had squeezed my hand. She wasn't doing it now, but she had. She had.

"Mama? Mama, can you hear me? Will you get better? Mama?"

I squeezed her hand gently and I rose and kissed her cheek.

"Mama, say something. Mama!"

"Easy, dear," I heard. Mrs. Feinberg returned to the room and put her hand on my shoulder.

"She squeezed my hand," I said. "Mama squeezed my hand."

"Did she?"

She smiled and we looked at Mama's hand in mind. It wasn't squeezing anymore, but I knew it had. I was so sure.

"Yes."

I could see Mrs. Feinberg wasn't convinced.

"Why don't you believe me? You said she was getting better."

"There were some small reactions to stimuli in her legs, honey. It's going to be a while yet before we can tell you anything, okay? You just be a good girl and do what you have to do."

"Her hand moved. It did," I said firmly.

"Okay. Don't cry." She wiped my cheeks with a tissue. "Sit and talk. Go ahead," she urged.

I sat again and stared at Mama and then, after I caught my breath, I did talk. I told her everything that had happened in as much detail as I could. I told her I had gone swimming. I told her about my work, and then I let slip the bad news about Ian. I just forgot.

"He didn't mean it," I said. "He was just so angry and he didn't like what she had done to me. So you see," I said, "you have to get better and come home now so we can go get Ian and bring him home, too. They'll listen to you and know Ian wouldn't hurt anyone again."

I sat there, staring at her.

Felix came to the door. "We've got to start back, Jordan," he said.

I nodded and stood up. I still held her hand. "Mama, I have to go. Tomorrow, I'm going to Great-aunt Francis, but I'll return to see you. Grandmother Emma promised I would. Don't worry about me. I take my medicine every day, and I'm okay, but I know Ian must be very unhappy. We need you, Mama."

I leaned over and kissed her cheek, and

then I felt it again.

I felt her hand tighten on mine.

And I knew that she would come home someday.

Someday, we would be together again, her, Ian, and me, at least.

I've got to tell Grandmother Emma, I thought, as we left the hospital. If she knew this, she wouldn't have me sent away to live with Great-aunt Francis. She would know all would soon be well.

"I want to see my grandmother, Felix," I said when we got into the car. "Please take me to that hospital. Please, Felix."

"I'm supposed to bring you directly home again," he said.

"We can stop there on the way, can't we? Please, Felix," I begged. "I have to see her one more time. I have something very important to tell her. Please."

"Okay, okay, we'll just stop for a few minutes. You're right. It's on the way anyhow," he said.

I sat back, full of hope.

Hours later, Felix drove into the hospital parking lot and opened the door for me. I saw people getting in and out of their cars look our way, probably wondering, Who is this little girl who has a uniformed chauffeur taking her around in a limousine? Is she a princess?

Hardly, I thought. I'm as far from being a princess now as anyone could be. Even if a handsome young prince fell in love with me, he'd find out about my family and he would hurry away. Who could blame him?

Felix took my hand and we walked into the hospital and went directly to Grandmother Emma's room. Her private nurse was standing outside her door talking to another nurse.

"Oh," she said when she saw me. "I didn't know you would be visiting your grandmother tonight. I would have brushed her hair and put her into one of her nicer nightgowns."

"That's not important," I said. Even I thought I sounded like Grandmother Emma. "I'm not here for a party."

She recoiled as if I had tried to slap her face, and then she grimaced at Felix, who shrugged.

"Well, excuse me. You're right. This isn't a party. For anyone," she added.

Slowly, I entered Grandmother Emma's bedroom. There was only a small lamp lit next to her bed and she had her eyes closed. I quickly stepped up to her and touched her left hand. Her eyes opened and she looked at me. I thought she was smiling even though it was hard to tell because of the way her lips remained slightly twisted.

"Grandmother Emma, I just came from visiting Mama. A wonderful thing happened while I was talking to her. She squeezed my hand. She really did. She's going to get better and sooner than everyone thinks. I just know it. When she does, she'll be very upset if I'm not home. She won't want me to be living with Great-aunt Francis. You've got to change everything and make Daddy take care of me now. He can do it. I'll put up with Kimberly until Mama comes home and then you'll come home soon, too, and everything will be the way it was. Please," I said, and I waited to see what she would do.

She shook her head.

"But why, Grandmother? Why do you want me to live with your sister? You never see her, or hardly ever, and she never visited us, not once. Maybe she doesn't want me to live with her. It's not good to force her, is it? She'll resent me. She'll hate me. It will be horrible. Please, Grandmother."

Again, she shook her head.

I couldn't help crying now. Why was she being so stubborn and mean?

"You didn't send my letter to Ian," I said sharply. "I found it in your desk. You lied to me. You always told me not to lie. You always said it was important to do and say what was true no matter what.

"I don't want to go to Great-aunt Francis's house. I don't. I don't need someone else to hate me," I said firmly.

She stopped shaking her head and just looked at me. Then she raised her hand and made a gesture with it I didn't understand. I shook my head and she did it again and suddenly, I understood.

She wanted to write something.

I jumped up and ran out to her nurse. "My grandmother wants a pen and paper. She wants to write something to me."

"Write something?" She grimaced and looked at Felix, who shook his head. Then she shrugged and went to the desk to get me a pen and a pad.

As soon as she handed it to me, I ran back to Grandmother Emma. She pointed to the bed so I put the pad there and then I put the pen in her hand. It was very hard for her to write anything. I was so intrigued now that I couldn't move a muscle or complain as she struggled to create squiggly lines that made sense.

I waited and then, after what seemed to exhaust her, she stopped and closed her eyes.

Slowly, I turned the pad and read. It took me a moment to understand the letters because of the way they ran into each other.

But I finally did.

She had written, "Take care of Francis. She needs you more than I do, more than I ever could. She will never hate you."

I read it and reread it to be sure I understood what she was telling me.

How could the great-aunt I didn't know, and who didn't know me, need me more? How could any grown-up need me? Shouldn't it be the other way around? Surely, Grandmother Emma was confused because of her illness, I thought.

She opened her eyes and gestured for the pen and paper again. Again, I waited as she scribbled, almost illegibly. I turned the paper around.

She had added, "Someday you'll know more about this family than your father does and you'll understand it all, even me."

Again, I was confused. How could I ever know more than my father knew about his own family? I wanted to ask her, but I could see she was exhausted, perhaps from the effort to write.

I folded that paper neatly and stuck it in my pocket. Somehow I knew it was the most important thing she had ever told me and maybe ever would.

She smiled.

Then she closed her eyes.

I hesitated, but after a moment, I leaned over to kiss her cheek.

Her lips relaxed into a bigger smile.

And that was the way I left her.

THE LAST GOOD-BYE

Before I left the mansion to go live with my great-aunt Francis Wilkins, I had to write one last letter to Ian. Daddy had made it sound like it would be a very long time, maybe years and years, before I would see Ian again, and if and when he returned here, I wouldn't be here.

I didn't realize until I was home that I had taken the pen Grandmother Emma had used. There seemed to be something magical about it.

I thought of her smile and then I decided I would use the same pen to write to Ian.

I would use it whenever I wrote to him.

And he would know. Somehow, some way, my brother Ian would know that magically we would be together again.